# THE ALPHA KING'S
# POSSESSION

BOOK I OF THE RUTHLESS KINGS TRILOGY

## MOONLIGHT MUSE

# THE ALPHA KING'S
# POSSESSION

# Contents

# PROLOGUE

MORGANA

"DID YOU HEAR THAT?" A sharp voice asks.

"No, what is it?"

"I thought I heard something."

I cover my mouth, calming my beating heart as I hide behind a thick oak tree. I'm almost out…

The guards walk past. As soon as they are out of sight, I continue running through the trees, a faint smile crossing my lips. *Finally!*

The wind rushes through my hair, the moon peeks through the trees, and the distant sounds of forest animals reach my ears. My heart beats with excitement as the sound of the gushing water and the scent of the lake reaches my senses.

I slow down, looking back over my shoulder to make sure none of the patrols had followed. I step to the river's edge, slipping my shoes off and removing my nightdress but staying in my lingerie, and get into the water. I giggle. The wine in my system from earlier is making me feel lightheaded and giddy.

I dip my head under the water, holding my breath for a few moments before breaking the surface and gasping for air as I burst out laughing in breathless excitement. I splash the water, and then I lay back, swimming around as I stare at the stars above, humming a song. I love coming out here in the middle of the night. My mother used to bring me here as a child...

I trail my fingers through the water of the lake when I suddenly feel as if I'm not alone. The alcohol slugging my system makes it hard for me to focus as I spin around, crossing my arms over my breasts, knowing my white lingerie is probably see-through as I scan the trees.

"Who's there?" I call out. My voice echoes off the rocky hills that surround the area. I scan the trees behind my back, the rushing waterfall drowning out any chance of picking up any other sounds.

I turn away, only for the intensity of something watching me to return once again. I swim to the edge of the lake and step out. Picking up my nightdress, I quickly slip it on and am suddenly yanked back into the lake. My scream is cut off by a hand clamping over my mouth, and I am pulled under for a second. I'm pulled above the surface and slammed against a hard wall of muscle. My heart thunders in my chest as I struggle.

"Calm down," a deep, husky voice orders, sending an odd sensation through me.

I still instantly, my heart pounding as I become hyper-aware of his touch and ironclad hold. One arm is wrapped around my waist, pinning my arms to my sides. Whoever he is, he's strong, but why do I have this strong feeling that he won't hurt me?

Sensing that I wouldn't scream, he removes his hand from my mouth, trailing it down my neck. His other hand grazes down my stomach, making me shiver with pleasure.

"Who are you?" I ask icily, trying to remain composed when my body is yielding to him.

"Hush..."

What is this? How is my body reacting to a stranger's touch? My dulled senses can't make out his scent properly, but it's rich, deep, and seductive. I can feel his chest heaving against my back and the bulge in his pants against my ass. The heat from his body tells me he's not one of my kind, but even then, no alarm bells of danger go off, and when his lips meet my neck, I gasp as pleasure courses through me before settling deep into my core. My eyes flutter shut, and I lean into him, a soft moan escaping my lips as I arch my neck, allowing him better access. His hand reaches for my right breast, squeezing hard. I can't seem to care that this is a stranger. Something deep within tells me to trust him.

"Nh..." I moan when his finger finds my hardened nipple through the thin fabric of my dress.

He sucks on my neck, making me whimper louder. My hand grips the wrist of the hand that is wandering lower and pulling my silk dress up. His hand slips down, cupping my pussy, and I gasp when he massages me over my soaking panties. My core clenches at the sensation of burning pleasure that consumes me. I didn't even realise he had torn my underwear off. His fingers run between my slit, finding my clit. A delicious moan leaves my lips, and I press my ass against his now-hard manhood. I bite my lip. All I want is him.

The moment his thick finger thrusts into me without warning, my eyes fly open as I stare up at the starry sky, resting my head on his broad shoulder. The pleasure from his touch destroys all sense of logic or thoughts.

"Oh, fuck," I mewl, my own voice unrecognisable to my ears.

His assault on my neck becomes rougher and hungrier. A second finger intrudes into me, stretching me out as he speeds up. I reach behind me, cupping his head, and my fingers tangle in the short, tight curls on top as my orgasm rips through me, making me cry out. The delicious spasms of pleasure that rock my body leave me feeling weak.

"Mine..." I thought I heard him snarl possessively, but I wasn't sure. He slips his fingers out, massaging my pussy, and I knew if we weren't in this lake, his hand would have been coated with my juices.

"W-who are you?" I whisper, trying to reach behind me for the hard shaft that is pressed against my ass, but he grips my wrist, stopping me, and pins my arm to the small of my back as I gasp.

I try turning my head, but he holds me in place, breathing hard. His nose is buried in my neck. I was about to ask him again when the sound of a distinct bell makes my eyes snap open and my heart thunder.

An alarm signalling danger, a threat, or death.

That bell was only used for extreme situations. My heart thrums against my chest like a drum, and I rip myself from his strong hold, rushing from the lake.

"I-I need to go!" I cry, my voice shaking as fear spreads through me like poison.

I pull my soaking dress down and turn back to the water only to see he is gone… but I have no time to ponder over it.

The bell… I had heard it once before… years ago. The night my mother was killed.

# SIBLING RIVALRY

TWO MONTHS LATER

MORGANA

THE HARSH COLD BITES into me, even though I don't feel the cold easily. My chiffon knee-length dress does nothing to help, but I wasn't really bothered.

I look down at the grand black marble tombstone of my father. The late King Araton.

That night, I wished I had been at the palace. I was one of our finest warriors, but I hadn't been. Instead, I had been frolicking in the lake with a mysterious man that I didn't even see. I feel bitter, broken, and empty.

The wind whips around me as I crouch down, placing my slender hand on the cold marble. *I'm sorry, Father. I should have been there.*

Two months have passed, but the ache in my chest at his loss is still present. I close my eyes, breathing deeply to control the hurricane of emotions that devour me.

"Lady Morgana, the king has called for you!" A breathless male servant calls.

I stand up gracefully, turning around and looking at the man who is bowing down to me. Not uttering a word, I make my way back to the palace to see why my brother, who usually doesn't even want to see my face, is summoning me.

When my father was murdered, the king's champion, his closest confidant, died trying to protect him. With the champion's death, the spell cast upon me by him to disguise my eyes had vanished, eyes that had made my brother hate me even more simply because they were darker than his. In our kind, the deeper and darker the eye colour, the stronger we are.

I don't bother knocking on the door to his office; after all, he had summoned me. Pushing it open, I step into the large room that is lavishly decorated in rich forest greens and gold shades. The room smells of sex and sweat. I wrinkle my nose in disgust.

I scoff when I see him on the sofa. One woman dressed in barely anything is massaging his shoulders as she kisses his neck, and another, who is completely naked, is on her knees before him as she gives him a blow job. I look away in revulsion and snap my fingers loudly.

"Out," I order coldly. I hear my brother's irritated groan as the women scurry to scatter.

"Really, Morgana? You could have waited outside," my brother's drawling voice complains.

I don't reply, waiting until I hear him zip his pants up before turning and shooting him a withering glare.

"Really, Azrael? You called for me when I was at my father's grave. If you had no patience to wait, then I have no patience with letting you entertain your whores," I snap, coldly staring up at my brother as he rises from the sofa and approaches me.

I'm tall, standing at five-feet-eleven, yet I feel small in comparison to his six-feet-seven. His long, straight hair that falls below his shoulders contains two small braids, leaving the rest open. His intricate gold crown sits upon his head.

"Remember that I am your king, Morgana."

"And remember that you have a child on the way, and a wife," I replied quietly.

It wasn't odd for a king to have many women, but those were women of the court who were classed as his mistresses. Messing around with the servants and any random woman was wrong. I feel sorry for his queen.

"You don't need to interfere in my life!" He snaps. "I called you here because I have heard rumours that you have been spreading your legs for one of the warriors." I scoff in disbelief. Is he really going to question me after he had his cock down a woman's throat just now?

"Oh, do forgive me, brother. I forgot that only you're allowed to be the whore around here."

"Morgana!" He shouts, his deep red eyes blazing bright as he grabs my neck tightly. "Remember who you are talking to! You need to learn your place, dear sister! Father is no longer around to entertain your crap. Remember that! One wrong move, and I'll end you," he hisses. I pull free, irritation burning within me.

"Don't touch me with those filthy hands! As for knowing my place, you are a king, Azrael, not a god! As for what or who I bring into my personal life, it has nothing to do with you! I am not a child!" I hissed.

No, I hadn't been fucking any men as of late, but I was not going to plead my innocence to him.

"Well, it clearly shows you are your mother's daughter. A whore." His words cut me like a dangerous knife. I glare back, clenching my jaw as I look at him resentfully.

"She was not a whore," I whisper, my voice trembling with rage.

Azrael's mother was the queen, whilst my mother was one of the women from court that my father had taken as his mistress. She had been the only one besides the queen who had borne a child.

"Oh, really? I highly doubt you were even my father's daughter!"

My eyes flash in anger, and I rush at him, my rage overtaking me. I grab him by his neck, only for him to grab me by mine and slap me hard across the face with his other hand. I gasp at the bruising pain that jars through my face and neck.

"Respect," he threatens, tangling his free hand into my hair painfully. "It's high time I made use of you and married you to one of the high-ranking members of the council. Many would be satisfied with you, and you will behave, Morgana." He looks me over with hatred, and I am equally disgusted, wrenching free from his hold.

"You can't control my life, Azrael!" My heart is beating fast. I know he would stay true to his words.

"You need not worry about anything but listening to me, dear sister. I have thought of a solution to the age-old argument between us and the werewolves as well. I will accomplish something father was never able to," he says, turning his back on me. I frowned.

"What do you mean?"

"I will extend the hand of friendship; I have already written to the Alpha King. Father had distorted beliefs -"

"You are willing to give in to their demands? Our father spent his life fighting for the betterment of our people and our land! You can't just throw that away! You know they are probably the ones who killed him!" His head snaps towards me, a flash of warning in his eyes.

"He's dead, Morgana. I'm the goddamn king now!"

"Azrael, Morgana, please calm down."

We both turn in the direction of the door. Our uncle, Malachi, our father's younger brother, stands there, frowning softly. Concern is etched on his forehead.

"Uncle! Azrael is trying to marry me off just because of a few baseless rumours!" I snap. "Not to mention, he wants to make peace with the werewolves!"

"They are growing in power, dear. Azrael isn't wrong."

"But to give up everything Father stood for?" I can't believe what I'm hearing.

"The humans are beginning to side with the werewolves, too, Morgana…"

"But we can't just give in! They are monsters!"

"They are cutting off supplies -" Uncle began.

"There has to be another way! How can we side with our father's killers!" I exclaim, looking at the two men in shock. Are they really willing to make peace with those… beasts?

"You have no say, Morgana! Just do as you're fucking told!" Azrael thunders.

A knock on the door disturbs us, and I glare at the two guards.

"My king, we have a visitor here to see you. He demands an audience with you," one of them explains, both bowing to Azrael.

"Oh, for fuck's sake! Who is it?" Azrael snaps.

"The Alpha King, Kian Araqiel of Clair De Lune"

# Alpha of Alphas

KIAN

*I* FROWN DEEPLY, TURNING AWAY from the window where I had been watching my men train. Running a hand through my tight curls, I sigh as the memory of the first time I saw her returns to me. She had been beautiful and alluring, her voice… I throb hard at the memory of my mate, the woman I had been searching for, for many years, yet when I found her, she was not suitable to be my Luna or Queen.

"Come here," I command, looking at the gorgeous woman I had called for, one of the unmated she-wolves of my pack. Her curvy body, with her ample tits and curvaceous hips clad in just lingerie, was appealing. Her long brunette locks were curled to perfection, and her sultry makeup was enticing. A beautiful she-wolf.

She comes toward me, sashaying her hips sensually, and I find my gaze dipping to the front of her lacy panties. The moment she reaches me, I tangle my hand in her hair, staring into her deep grey eyes. She wastes no time, running her hand over my crotch. I groan as I bury my head into her neck, kissing her hard and enjoying the feel of her hands on my body. One hand pushes my pants down, grabs my hardened cock, and strokes it expertly. I growl and pull away, spinning her around and pushing her up against the wall near the window. I tear her underwear off roughly, not caring that it would sting, as I slam into her with one hard thrust.

"Alpha! Oh, fuck!" She moaned.

My eyes blaze gold as I fuck her roughly, my mind stuck on an image of another woman. Imagining it is her before me. With every thrust, my anger grows. The screams and moans of the she-wolf before me don't matter.

My mate… fuck, I need to find her. Since I had laid eyes on her, she was ruining me. It isn't only my dreams; even when I am awake, she is all I can think of.

I barely register when the woman before me comes as I speed up, chasing my own release as I imagine another. Her dark black hair, her cool, pale skin… her full breasts… I groan huskily, pulling out and shooting my load over her ass.

A few days later, I pace my office while talking to my Beta, Luca.

"The conflict is only growing, and the humans are getting caught up in this, too, Kian. Someone needs to do something," Luca says quietly. I massage my jaw, nodding.

"I know, Luca, and I'm trying to think of a solution where all four species in power can somehow agree to a stalemate," I muttered coldly.

"You do know, Kian, if you put it forward, you will come off as weak."

"And I don't fucking care. Let them think what they want. Right now, our people matter more."

"And that is why Kian will become one of our finest kings in history."

I look up to see Sage walking in. Dressed in a pair of fitted pants and a plunging top, she smiles confidently. Her light brown hair is pulled back into a braid.

"Sorry if I'm interrupting," she says, her blue eyes locking with mine.

"Not at all." I look away, frowning deeply.

"Well, I'll leave you two to it," Luca says with a wink before he walks out, closing the door behind him.

"Kian, what's on your mind?" She asks, placing a hand on my arm. I frown, looking down at her. I can't really share my true issue with her, so instead, I just play with a strand of her silky hair.

"Just work," I mumble, pulling her into my arms.

Sage is the ideal Luna. At twenty-three, she is only one year younger than me and hasn't found her mate. Marking and mating her is something I knew many were hoping for. She is a strong female and the daughter of the previous pack's Beta.

"You know, I'm here if you ever need to de-stress," she replies quietly, sensually biting her lip.

"I know," I answer arrogantly. Leaning down, I claim her lips in a deep, hungry kiss. Once again, my mind flitters to another.

Fuck. No matter what I did, I couldn't stop her from filling my mind…

My decision was made. I would find her, and I would keep her. No, she could never be my Luna, but she is the only one who could satiate the carnal desire that she had awoken within me, one that no other she-wolf is able to.

*I will find you and you will be mine. No matter the cost.*

I have searched high and low for her for the last month or so, trying to hold onto her fleeting scent that lingered in my mind. I finally found remnants of it in the Sanguine Empire, more so around the king's palace. Yes, I knew she was a vampire… but to be so close to the royals wasn't what I had taken into account. Back then, she had been outside of any claimed land…

I walk through the luxurious halls of the Vampire King. It is clear from the architecture and the portraits on the walls that they had walked this earth for far longer than werewolves could even remember. Or perhaps it was just that they lived and aged so differently.

Four of my best men flank me, and ten of the vampires. Showing up at their doors, let alone the kingdom, without warning might have threatened them. Knowing I made it through their patrol and security without them even realising it must have bruised their egos, but I liked making a statement. I am not here for a fight but for my mate, something even my men didn't know.

Her scent clings to these halls, and my wolf rages inside of me.

**Mate.** That is all I can get from him.

The urge to claim her is growing, but I am not going to mark her. I just need her, to keep her close.

We had been told to wait until someone had gone to announce my arrival to the Vampire King. He agreed to see me, and now, here we are, being led through a pair of huge doors.

The man sits upon a golden throne on a raised dais, dressed fully in black, with a long-sleeved shirt and a crown upon his head. There are several people in the room, flanking the king. I can tell from their clothing that they are of high rank. Each one of them oozes wealth.

The room holds pillars all around, and above is a balcony that looks down onto the huge hall. In the centre is a huge chandelier made of hundreds of crystals.

"Well, to what do I owe the pleasure of the Alpha King to come knocking at my doors?" His drawling voice makes my eyes flash dangerously, not missing the mockery in his tone. Does he really think he is powerful here?

"I am willing to work on a treaty with you under one condition," I state coldly.

My aura swirls around me, and the power in my voice is clear to everyone in the room. I am no mere wolf; I am the Alpha of Alphas. I know we hold certain powers over them. Despite this kingdom being large, mine is growing. The vampire race is dying out in comparison to how ours increases with each passing decade. I see the surprise on his face, which he masks quickly.

"Oh?" He asks, resting his elbow on the arm of his throne and his chin on his knuckles.

"I have one condition," I repeat, getting to the point. Curiosity flits across his face, and he raises an eyebrow.

"I figured as much… and what might that be?" He asks, his fangs flashing as he gives a full, predatory smile.

"I want one woman from this kingdom as my slave," I say emotionlessly, my voice exuding power.

All eyes snap to me, and I can sense the surprise in them. My own men don't move, trained well to mask their emotions. After all, they are my warriors.

"That's all? You can have ten if you want," The king chuckled. "Who knew the Alpha King had a fetish for our kind?" My anger blazes around me, and I glare coldly at him.

"I may be here in your kingdom, but don't forget, the lives of your people are in the palm of my hand," I warn him. "One woman will do, but I will choose which one."

In fact, my anger rises when I realise the man before me smells of sex, and the smell of my mate lingers around him. He seems to realise my growing anger and simply nods.

"Then so be it. I will call the most beautiful women of my kingdom forward. You may choose whichever you want at tonight's banquet. What do you say, Alpha King Kian?"

Now we're talking.

"Perfect."

# MORGANA'S RESOLVE

MORGANA

"THIS IS COMPLETE RUBBISH."

I run a hand through my hair, my irritation only growing. How could Azrael agree to such a stupid request?

"How can he allow this to happen? He will send one of our women to a beast!" I snap, trying to free myself from my uncle's hold.

"Morgana, you really need to hold that tongue," Adelle, one of my brothers' mistresses, says, raising her nose in distaste. "You know you will be punished if you don't."

"I am the princess, Adelle. Remember that," I snap coldly, "Leave me be, Uncle!"

"Promise me you won't do anything stupid," he pleads, concern clear in his voice. I exhale sharply.

"I won't."

He sighs, relieved, and lets go of me. I shake my head, turning and storming out of the hall.

Word had gone around that the Alpha King was in these very halls. In fact, Azrael is actually going to display our women as if they are livestock. Oh, fuck him and the Alpha.

I enter my room, slamming the door shut behind me. How could he? When it was clear that father was killed by them... okay, maybe there was no proof, but he was killed weeks after this very Alpha threatened to kill him. Moreover, the Alpha King's showing up like this is enough proof that they could easily sneak in. Does no one see this?

I sit down on my bed, gripping the mattress as I glare at the floor. My chest heaves, my emotions a storm within me. Fine. If the Alpha King wants a present tonight, then I will give him one myself. When he feasts his eyes on our women, I will kill him. Even if it results in consequences, I will not let him out of here alive.

I stand up, walk over to one of the large cabinets against the wall that holds my collection of weapons, and select one of my daggers. Spinning it in my hand, I throw it up into the air, watching it spin as it comes spiralling down towards me.

*You came for a taste of passion, then I'll give you a taste of mine.*

I catch the knife, and, spinning around, I throw it across the room, piercing one of the large tapestries on the wall. My eyes blaze with hatred. *You will regret ever stepping on our land.*

"A no is a no, Morgana! I don't trust you!" Azrael hissed. He spins around, his eyes blazing as he glares at me.

"I just want to attend the banquet! Nothing more. Besides, Azrael, if he even thinks of trying to kill you… I can stop him, you know that," I plead.

"Oh, please, we both know you would let me die," Azrael snaps.

"Uncle, please. You know I just want to be there," I beg, turning to Malachi. Okay, now is the time to work my charms. I pout, batting my long, thick lashes pleadingly at my uncle. "I swear I'll behave."

"Azrael, you know Morgana is feisty and temperamental, but she means well. She's just very passionate," he offers, his blood-red eyes filled with sympathy for me. I smile faintly and heave a sigh.

"I just want to see him… I have heard a lot about him. Do you know that he is not the eldest brother? Despite being the middle one, he still fought for the title of Alpha King. Out of thirty men, including his brother, he came out victorious at the mere age of nineteen," I explain, hoping that they buy it. Azrael scoffs.

"That's nothing special. Nineteen is an adult for them," he mutters. "Fine! But I don't want a scene, or I swear, Morgana, I will throw you in the dungeons for a month!"

"Fine," I agree, my heart skipping a beat.

One month or ten years in the dungeons, I don't care as long as I get what I want. I leave the room with a small smile gracing my lips. Now it's time to lace a dagger in poison and wear something that can hide my weapon…

I am dressed in a fitted lace and sequin black dress that shows off some cleavage and most of my upper back. On top of the dress is a layered satin skirt that trails on the ground with enough room to hide a dagger or two. My hair is coiled up on my head in an elegant updo, and I'm wearing a thin tiara to show my rank. My flawless pale skin is left free of foundation, but my eye makeup is dark, my cherry red lips painted a darker shade of red, and a bit of blush was added to my otherwise snow-white cheeks.

I make my way into the lavish banquet hall soon after. Two rows of tables laden with gold dishes full of food run along the sides. Maybe we should have used silver. I would have loved to see the Alpha King try to eat with silver cutlery. I smile slightly at my own thoughts. Now that would have been some entertainment. As vampires, we eat for the sake of it, we don't really need food to survive.

I blend in, not wanting to join my brother at the table at the top of the hall that faces the rest of the room. I glance towards it, but it isn't my brother who catches my attention. For once, he doesn't hold the strongest aura in the room. My eyes find the source… and my heart skips a beat. The Alpha King…

He didn't need a name tag or a crown to tell me that the man before me was a king. He exudes power like it's nothing, and the arrogance and pride on his handsome face are clear from across the room. He is built and a lot more muscular than any vampire here, with a body that had been made to perfection, from his delicious chocolate-coloured skin to the small beard that defines his prominent jawline and the earring that glinted with every small movement of his head, captured my attention. My heart thuds when those piercing hazel eyes snap towards me.

Our eyes lock, and my breathing quickens. His eyes flash gold, a frown knitting on that handsome face of his. My heart races under the intensity of his gaze. For a moment, everything else zones out, and it is just the two of us... My breath comes out shakily as his eyes slowly run down my body. I don't miss the glint of desire that crosses those eyes, and although it somehow didn't repulse me, the cold reminder that he is here for a slave from our people makes reality hit me like a sharp slap in the face. I cast him a cold glare before moving out of his line of vision. I would lay low until I found my chance to kill him...

I make sure to stay out of the Alpha King's sight as much as possible. He hadn't touched the food presented before him, simply sitting in his seat with arrogance and importance. Once or twice, I feel his burning gaze upon me, but I don't entertain him.

"Well, now that we have feasted, allow me to show you the finest women of our kingdom," Azrael offers, and I do my best not to lash out at him, too. How can he even subject our women to this?

The doors open, and four guards enter, flanking ten women. All ten are dressed in skimpy dresses, with their hair and makeup done perfectly. They are indeed some of our finest women. My face pales when I see one of them is the younger sister of Azrael's wife. How can he do this? She is barely an adult! In human years, she would be classed as fifteen! Does Anastasia know her husband is auctioning her sister off? But then again, what power would she have to stop him? Azrael is a coward. How can a king do this to his own people? Isn't he meant to protect us?

I watch in disgust as all the nobles, some of whom are even related to the women presented, simply sip their glasses of wine as if watching a show. My eyes snap to the Alpha King. He is simply sitting back in his seat, massaging his jaw, his lips set in a pout, his eyes on the women before him.

"There are another forty. You can round down -"

"I've already chosen." His voice cuts through Azrael's, radiating his status and power. The room that had been silent seemed to still completely.

"Ah, really? Great! We can get to signing the treaty. Who is the lucky lady?" Azrael asks, clearly relieved that he doesn't have to entertain the werewolf king for much longer. I look at the women who, despite trying to keep their faces passive, are anxious. A few look downright terrified, including Annalise, Anastasia's sister. The Alpha King's gaze suddenly snaps towards me.

"The woman in black," he says.

I feel all the colour drain from my already pale skin as Azrael looks at me in shock. But the look changes quickly, and I realise he would agree.

"Of -"

"Over my dead body!" I hiss.

Without thinking, I pull the poisoned dagger from within my skirts. Spinning around, I throw it with all my force, my eyes blazing red as I focus my powers on the dagger and its destination. Everything seems to move in slow motion, my thudding heart racing in my chest as the dagger zooms towards the Alpha King's heart. The dagger is inches away from him when he suddenly raises his hand, catching it between two fingers. His eyes blaze gold with anger rolling off of him in waves.

Before anyone can react, he is before me, grabbing my body by the neck and slamming me against the marble pillar behind me. A menacing growl rips from his throat, and anyone who had been about to move stills. I grab his wrist, trying to free myself. My heart is pounding. His seductive scent and his presence are messing with my senses. My eyes blaze as I try to free myself, but he is stronger. I hold his gaze, trying to compel him to let me go, but it isn't working.

"Let go of me!" I choke out. Is no one going to intervene?

I glare at the Alpha before me, but he simply stays silent. What the hell is going on in that mind of his? He lets go of my throat, suddenly dropping me to the ground, and swallows hard as he looks away. I stand up, pulling out my second dagger, but before I can do anything, he grabs hold of my upper arm, knocking the dagger from my hand and turning towards Azrael, who is standing there glaring at me. Wow, great brother…

"I will take this one, and you have my word that I will not attack your kind. I will sign in blood." His words resonate off the walls, and I know the high lords are wondering if the king would agree.

"I am not a prize or a possession," I hiss, only for the Alpha King to clamp a hand over my mouth. For a second, I remember the man at the lake and shudder. This man is nothing like him.

"Very well. The woman in your hold is my sister, Morgana, the one and only princess of the kingdom. Our most prized possession…. Let the deal be done," Azrael says clearly.

"Your Majesty…" Uncle Malachi whispers, his face pale as he looks at me with worry in his eyes. I pull my face free from the Alpha's hold, glaring at Azrael.

"You can't do this to me, Azrael!"

"Please do reconsider, Your Majesty. Morgana was dear to my late brother. Please choose any other woman but her," Uncle pleads, looking at the Alpha King. But the beast holding me tightly, as if I was nothing, doesn't budge from his decision.

"It will be her or no one. Let's not forget she tried to attack me; I could use that alone to tear her body to shreds. Let's remember that," he says coldly.

I look at the vampires before me, my people… yet no one seems to care to defend me. Do they not realise that he was possibly the killer of the late king? If we all fought together, we could defeat him!

I struggle, but it's useless. His arm wraps around my waist, his other hand once again covering my mouth.

*No! Azrael, please!* I scream in my head as I stare at my brother, who simply motions for someone to bring a file forward. It is presented to the Alpha King, who lets go of my mouth. Biting his finger, he signs the form with his blood.

"Azrael! Don't do this!" I shout.

"You wished to come tonight… you must pay for your mistakes. You are now the Alpha King's possession."

I suddenly feel empty. Is this it? Am I really just someone's belonging?

I am dragged from the hall. No one moves; not my guards, not my father's friends… none of the men who wished to claim me as their wife… I am no longer the beloved daughter of a king but a slave of another. A king of beasts…

I had been bound and knocked unconscious the moment we left the palace. I wake when we go down a curved stone hall that leads downwards, and with it, the temperature gets colder. The Alpha King is carrying me over his shoulder, and although I struggle, he only delivers a sharp slap to my behind, leaving a stinging pain in his wake and silently warning me to stay quiet. Dim lights on the wall light the path. I don't understand why the king is handling me. Didn't he want me as a slave? Why go through so much hassle as to bring me down here himself?

"Do you manage your slaves yourself?" I spit, struggling to rip free from his hold, but it is futile.

He doesn't reply, walking towards the end of the row of metal cells. Some contain prisoners, others are empty, and my stomach begins to churn. This is reality... my reality.

"I swear, when I get out, I will kill you," I hiss when he unlocks the cell right at the end and throws me inside. I stumble, hitting the ground, my arms still painfully tied behind me.

"I'd like to see you try," he replies coldly before slamming the door shut, locking me in, and turning away. So he can hear me. I was beginning to think he was deaf.

"Hey! You cannot leave me down here!" I shout.

No reply. His footsteps fade away, and my heart begins thundering louder.

"Open this goddamn door!" I shriek.

I can see the two guards standing down the hall, but no one pays attention to my shouts and screams. I'm beginning to agitate the other prisoners, but I don't care. I want out. No, I demand out! I shake the bars, trying to use my abilities to bend them, but they stand fast. What are they made of?

I manage to break the cuffs on me, my bleeding, bruised wrists a mess as I slam my hands against the bars, shaking and rattling them, and screaming as loud as I could.

"Let me out!"

Nothing. It has at least been an hour or two... but I don't give up. Although my voice is hoarse, and I feel exhausted, I am not going to stop. I fall to my knees, slamming my bruised hands against the bars.

I hear the sound of steps, and the king's deep, seductive scent fills my senses. He walks towards my cell, and I stand up, breathing heavily as I glare at him through the bars. He is shirtless, and I can tell he had just done a workout; a thin layer of sweat coats his perfect body. It's hard to ignore his chiselled six-pack or his chest...

"If you don't shut up, you won't be fed," he growls murderously, his eyes flashing gold as he glares at me, snapping me from my thoughts. I glare back at him; his menacing aura doesn't scare me.

"Make me," I spit with hatred laced in my voice.

Suddenly, he unlocks the door and enters the cell. My heart skips a beat as I make a dash for the door, only for him to catch me by my arm and slam me up against the wall of the cell. I bite back a cry as the impact sends a searing pain through me, making my vision blacken for a moment. His hand closes around my neck, and I know if I make one move, he'll tear my head off.

"Behave and learn some respect," he hisses coldly.

"I will never submit to the likes of you." I glare into his blazing gold eyes, not missing his elongated canines or the way his chest is heaving with anger.

"I will make you submit, Princess. Continue disobeying me, and you will be punished."

"I'd rather die down here than spend a minute more in your presence," I snap. Raising my hands, I splay them on his chest, trying to push him away. I gasp when he steps closer, crushing our bodies together.

"Who said anything about dying?" He asks quietly, cocking a brow.

His gaze dips to my lips, and my heart thuds. What does he mean? The closeness of his body is distracting me. His scent consumes my senses as I try to focus on his now hazel eyes, noticing the dark ring around the deep green and the gold flecks....

"What do you want from me?" I ask quietly, very aware of his body heat, his body centimetres from mine.

"Everything," his cold reply answers, his eyes skimming downwards as he runs his gaze over my breasts and then back up to my eyes. What he is insinuating is obvious.

"Over my dead body," I spit with as much hatred as I can muster. His eyes flash, and he growls, letting go of me roughly as he steps back. I fall to the ground, massaging my throat. His aura rolls off him in waves, and it suffocates me.

"You will learn respect, or you will fucking die," he growls angrily before he storms from the cells, leaving me alone once again…

# Stolen Sleep

KIAN

*I* COULDN'T EVEN FUCKING SLEEP after last night. Knowing that she was down there in the goddamn cold, even if she was a vampire. At the same time, her anger and hatred towards me only pissed me off immensely. I clench my fist, my claws digging into my palm, drawing blood. Luca watches me, his arms crossed, waiting for me to stop my pacing.

"I'm kind of confused… I mean, I don't understand why you agreed to this. You do know those bloodsuckers have been stealing our people, especially the humans, to feed on them, right? I admit that woman is beyond beautiful, and I get why you probably wanted her, but agreeing to this over one sexy woman?"

My eyes flash, and I growl, slamming my hand down on my desk. It splinters down the middle.

"She is mine!" I hiss murderously. His calling her beautiful only fuelled the inferno that blazes inside of me. He looks completely confused and shocked.

"Whoa… okay…" Luca backs away, raising his hands in surrender. "She's yours… but is there more to it, Kian?"

I don't say anything, frowning deeply. I had fought against so many, including my own brother, for this position to show them that I was the strongest. If anyone finds out that my mate is a vampire… this is a position

I fought against everything for, and it is not one I would let go of, especially for a vampire. I frown in disgust; I dislike her kind… yet at the same time, she ignites a forbidden desire within me that I never wanted to feel, especially for one of them.

"There is nothing more to it. Don't butt into my personal business, Luca," I growl.

"Okay… I won't, but really, try not to let it get to you," he says, shoving his hands in his pockets. "Anyway, I'll make sure the security for the upcoming Alpha summit is in place. You know how these things go." He scrubs a hand down his face, sighing. Yeah, I fucking know. The strongest Alphas in the country in one room always cause some drama, and I have to sit through it and deal with it. The downside of being the Alpha of Alphas…

Luca takes his leave, leaving me in my office. There is a light knock on the door, and the scent of honeycomb and lavender fills my nose. I look at the closed door. Sage… I don't want to see her right now.

"Enter," I call, dropping into my seat. She steps inside, dressed in a tiny white dress that leaves little to the imagination, and walks over to me.

"Hey, you okay, Kian? You seem so stressed…" She walks around my chair, placing her hands on my shoulders as she begins massaging me.

I frown, my mind flitting back to the woman in the cell once again. Morgana… that was what her brother, the scum, had called her. It was a strong, sexy name…

"Kian…" The moment Sage's lips touch my neck, I tense, pulling away from her touch.

"Leave." I can sense her concern, but I don't care. I just need her gone.

"Is everything okay? There are rumours you brought a -"

"Mind your business, Sage," I growl, my eyes flashing as I turn towards her.

**Kill her,** Thanatos growls in my head. I block him off as I look at Sage, who is clearly concerned.

"I'm sorry... I didn't... if you need me, Kian, you know I'm here. Even if you just need someone to talk to," she offers, perching on the edge of the broken desk.

"Yeah, well, right now, I don't want to talk, Sage," I mutter.

She stands up, nodding before she walks out. Sage — she is considered my girlfriend in some ways by others, but I am not exclusive to her, and she knows it. She is the potential future queen, yet right now, all I can think of is the princess in the cells… one who was born with royalty and wealth. How had she spent her night? Fuck, I need to stop worrying about her.

I need to go for a run.

Night falls, but I can't bring myself to stay away from her any longer. I silently make my way through to the cells, masking my aura. I mind-link my men, telling them to leave.

I keep my distance, knowing that a vampire's hearing is very efficient. I find her standing in her cells; the top skirt of her dress was removed, and the fabric of her lace dress clings to her figure. Her bare back is towards me, showing off her jutting shoulder blades, and my eyes take in her plump behind. I feel myself throb hard.

She is perfect in more ways than one; tall and slender, yet at the same time, she has the curves of a woman, from her peachy ass to her bouncing breasts that aren't huge but on the larger side for her build. There is just one thing about her that is far from perfect. Her race. She is a vampire…

I look away, frowning. I need to get over her. Perhaps one night is what I need, and then I can be done and dusted. Yeah, maybe that is the best course of action because I can't keep this up. She consumes my mind day and night, and I need a taste of her. I have a plan… I will forward a deal to her, and I am sure she will accept it.

I glance back at her, seeing her sigh as she leans against the stone, sliding to the floor. Her gaze turns towards the moonlight that seeps through the tiny, barred window far above her. It illuminates her gorgeous face, her angled cheekbones, her jutting jaw, her pointed chin... plump, pouty lips, and those large eyes that hold fire and innocence all at the same time.

**Our mate,** Thanatos spits angrily at me.

Yeah, I know he's pissed, but this is about more than him and us. I can't forsake everything for one woman.

I return to my bedroom, shutting the door behind me and mind-linking Gerald, the head warrior, and Andrei, the head Omega in charge of the house staff.

**The vampire woman in the cells: have her collared and cuffed with the correct measures. Andrei will put her to work. Gerald, make sure**

she has someone watching her at all times. **I don't want her to attack anyone for blood. I will feed her when I deem fit,** I relay coldly.

**Yes, Alpha,** Gerald's curt reply follows.

**Of course, Alpha, I understand.** Andrei's reply comes next.

I pull my shirt off and drop onto my bed, staring at the ceiling. The lights from outside cast shadows on it. I'd like to see how long she stays arrogant. Soon enough, she'll realise she is nothing here. I'll break that spirit of hers.

I close my eyes, that night down by the lake replaying in my head. I frown deeply, my eyes snapping open. I glare at the ceiling. You have stolen my sleep, and you will pay for it, my little blood rose…

# Chapter 5 Resistance

MORGANA

"Get up!" someone shouts.

The screeching sound of the hinges of the cell door being opened makes me open my eyes. I'm leaning against the wall; I'm not sure when I fell asleep last night.

"I'm awake," I reply icily, glaring at the two men before me haughtily. "What do you want?" The taller of the two cocks his brow, scoffing as he looks at his partner.

"Did you hear that, Gale…? She's got an attitude even when she's locked up down here," he sneers.

"Lee… don't. You know Gerald's orders," Gale mutters, turning to me. He glares coldly. "Get up."

I raise an eyebrow. Am I getting out of here? My heart thuds as I slowly stand up, tossing my hair over my shoulder. My wrists are still bloody and a mess from the other night. I am weak, and due to the lack of food, I'm not healing well either. I need blood, but I am not going to ask these beasts for anything. The urge to sink my teeth into one of them is very tempting, but I would never drink from one of these mutts.

He makes to grab hold of my arm, and I jerk away, glaring up at him dangerously.

"Touch me, and you will lose your hands!" I hiss.

"Feisty… I thought vampires were regal, stoic creatures," Lee sneers. "Don't worry, none of us wants to touch you." His gaze rakes over my body, and I look away disgusted. I am still in the clingy gown that stuck to me like a second skin, one that was splattered with my blood.

"Keep walking. One wrong move and we will cuff you," Gale warns me.

I feel the sharp poke of a blade being held to my back, so I carry on walking out through the cell door and towards the stone steps that lead upwards. We emerge in a less dingy-looking corridor. Although the walls are made of stone, it is a lovely cream colour, with chandeliers above casting a warm yellow glow along the walls. The floor is a dark wood that shines pleasantly, and the walls are decorated with some artwork here and there. We continue ahead, and I keenly make sure to pay attention to the smallest of details as we climb up another flight of steps. It is then that I realise the lower floor doesn't have windows.

We reach the top, and my heart leaps when I see light shining through a large pair of doors up ahead.

"Don't get any ideas!" Gale growls.

*Well, I already have an idea…*

I spin around, kicking the knife from his hold. My other hand darts out and uses my telekinesis ability to throw him back. I catch the knife and throw it straight at Lee, who looks alarmed. He ducks, so I knock his legs out from under him. The sound of fabric ripping tells me I have ruined my dress, but that's the least of my worries. Gale is up, shifting into a huge wolf and running at me. His menacing growl echoes off the walls, and the saliva that drips from his mouth tells me he is angry.

"See you later! Oh, wait… more like never!" I shout, running for the doors. A small smile crosses my lips. Despite the circumstances, I love the exhilaration I get out of exciting situations.

I burst into the sunlight just as the wolf pounces. I duck, and he goes flying right over me. I speed up. The smooth paved stone beneath my feet is a welcome change from the snow back home.

"Grab her!" Lee shouts.

*"Can you fools not do anything?"* A third voice thunders.

I don't turn back, not wanting to waste precious seconds. Before I can get any further, I am lifted off my feet and thrown over a strong shoulder. I gasp, feeling the air knocked from me. The tingles at the touch tell me it's the Alpha King himself before his scent even registers.

"Don't move," he growls murderously.

I can feel his anger radiating off of him as he slaps my behind hard. I feel my cheeks burn, but I am glad that, due to my pale skin, it is barely noticeable.

"Let me go!" I shouted, pummelling his back and trying not to pay attention to the huge tattoo that covered most of it. Why is he shirtless?

"Sorry, Alpha!" The voice that I didn't recognise says as he stops before the king. I crane my neck to look, only for the Alpha to spank my behind again.

"Stop that!" I snapped, irritated. What is this? His favourite pass time?

"If I give you a job, Gerald, it was meant for you to do it yourself," the Alpha says coldly.

"Yes, Alpha... I'm sorry," Gerald replies quietly.

"Cuff her and give her some clothes." He grabs me and throws me to the ground.

"Ouch!" I yelp when my ass hits the hard floor, glaring up at the Alpha. I hate how I am distracted by his perfection. The sun shines down on him, his perfect-coloured skin glistening, his defined abs and Adonis belt very prominent.

"If you try to run again, I will fucking throw you in that cell for the rest of your life." His cold voice, which is laced with a threat, makes my eyes snap up to his face.

"I'm quivering with fear." The snarky reply leaves my lips before I even register it.

Standing up, I brush my dress off and massage my sore ass. Silence ensues, and a surge of power makes me look up innocently. Well, what did he expect? Me to beg and plead? Cry, 'Yes, Alpha, I'll be a good girl,' and behave like a scared, meek little prisoner? Yes, that's not happening.

"I warned you," he growls, turning his blazing golden eyes towards one of the men. "Take her, bind her, and put a fucking gag on her!"

"I never knew the baby Alpha got so angry..." I mutter in a cooing voice, pouting provocatively. The man named Gerald grips my arm painfully tight.

"What did you just say?" The Alpha asks dangerously.

"What? You are a baby in my eyes. How old are you? Thirty? Forty?" I taunt, knowing he was younger. He clenches his jaw, his fists shaking.

"Take. Her. Away."

I smirked, "Children and their tantrums…" I chirp just as Gerald clamps his hand over my mouth.

"Do you wish to die, bloodsucker?" He growls, dragging me away from the seething Alpha.

Oh, if I had my mouth free, I would have had a lot to say, but I settle for glaring at him. I would have to plan my escape carefully and not do something reckless like that again. I will get out of here, even if it takes me some time.

I was given fitted black pants and an oversized black top that falls to my mid-thigh. The fabric keeps slipping off my narrow shoulders annoyingly. I wasn't given any shoes, but I don't really care at this point.

My wrists, ankles, and neck were cuffed with iron that burned my skin, laced with nightshade and wolfsbane. I can feel them doing their job and weakening me. I find it ironic that they would use wolfsbane when it was harmful to them, too. We rarely have any of it back home. At this rate, I'll probably collapse before the day is over. I refuse to show them the effect it's having on me, though, keeping my chin up as Gerald gives the chain that is linked to my left ankle cuff to those two buffoons from earlier to hold.

"Make sure she is under your watch at all times," Gerald growls.

I roll my eyes. Well, giving me idiots to work with would make my escape easier… much easier. Gerald ties a cloth around my mouth, much to my irritation.

"Yes, sir!" Lee says, dragging me from the room.

Twenty minutes later, I am put to work peeling potatoes for dinner.

"I don't think you should let her touch our food," one of the women remarks. I can tell from their clothing and what they are doing that these are Omegas - the low-ranked werewolves who usually work for the rest of the wolves.

"No one asked your opinion, Cherise," Andrei, the head Omega, cuts in.

I had been handed over to him to order around, and he had been the one to assign this job to me. I wish I could tell him I had never cut a potato in my life… but giving me access to knives… I'd try to sneak one or two.

So, I was trying. The cuffs didn't help, the weight and the poison slowing me down.

"Well, did she wash her hands?" Cherise grates irritatingly.

I shoot her a glare, satisfied when she moves back nervously. *Good, stupid woman…*

I may be bound and weak, but I can take her any day.

"It isn't hard to peel a potato, girl," Andrei growls, watching me. I frown, looking at the potato that is half done. "Goddess! She will waste half the potato! Food doesn't come cheap!" He mutters, his green eyes full of annoyance. "Cherise! Go make her do the mopping in the food hall!"

There goes my chance to sneak a knife…

"This way, Vampire," she spits, making sure to stay closer to the guards as Lee yanks on the chain, leading me out.

I sigh. I would rather be stuck with Azrael for twenty-four hours straight than with these killers… and I still had a score to settle with him, too. How dare he allow me to be taken…

Three hours have passed. I finish with the main hall and am told to do the hallways. Werewolves spend a lot of time outside, and, unlike in the vampire kingdom, where the palace is for the royals alone, it seems like everyone is in and out of this huge place. The doors stay open, and many men and women enter and leave, sometimes leaving a lot of dirt in their wake. My irritation grows with each dirty beast that enters and ruins my just-cleaned floors.

I am hungry, and the sound of their pulsing hearts tempts me with the reality that there is fresh blood simmering through their veins…

I'm working on one corner of the hall again, my vision blurring at times. I can't even pretend to be okay anymore. I'm barely able to move, but I refuse to argue, not that I could with my mouth gagged!

The buffoons follow me around, but I can tell they're bored of having to watch me.

"Let's get some food. She's about to collapse anyway," Lee remarks.

"We can't leave her alone," Gale growls.

"Have you seen her? Besides, she won't step outside. The sun is bright today, it will only weaken her," Lee scoffed.

"Okay, fine. The kitchens are just down the hall. Let me tie her to something…"

They were right, I could barely move…

The moment they're gone, I stop. The cloth falls from my hand, and I lean my forehead against the wall, breathing heavily through my nose. I don't even turn to see where he tied the chain. I slump against the wall, shivering considerably. I need blood…

I close my eyes that sting with pain.

*Breathe…*

I count in my head, trying to regain control when the sounds of children laughing and giggling make my eyes fly open. My head snaps in the direction of the open door a few feet away. Three little children, all under seven years of werewolf age, giggle and laugh as they carry a muddy ball.

My stomach sinks when one of the girls turns to me, tilting her head.

"Oh, look, that lady is sad," she says, her innocent eyes sparkled with concern.

*No, don't come near me.* My heart thumps as she and the other girl walk towards me whilst the boy hesitates.

"Lorna… come back," he murmurs. Wise child…

"Why is she tied?" The other girl asks.

"I don't know, Jody," Lorna replies. Reaching over, she pulls the cloth off my face. They gasp.

"Her teeth are strange…" Jody whispers.

"Girls… Momma said she's not one of us…" he hisses.

"Go away," I whisper weakly. My eyes burn as my gaze flits to their necks.

"Why, Miss?" Jody asks innocently.

*Blood…*

My body fights against me, wanting to sink my teeth into their necks and drink them dry… but I would not do that to innocent children, even if they are the children of monsters.

"I said, move away! I will hurt you!" I warn.

"Miss, are you okay?" Jody asks, touching my forehead.

It's the final straw as my self-control snaps, and my gaze shoots to her neck…

# BATTLE OF WILLS

KIAN

*I* HAD SPENT THE MORNING attending to paperwork and am tempted to go see what she's up to. I'm not even halfway down the stairs when I hear her.

"I said, move away! I will hurt you!"

"Miss, are you okay?"

My heart skips a beat as I run down the stairs in a blur, only to see Morgana's fangs out as she backs away against the wall from Jody and Lorna, who are steadily approaching her.

"I said I'm dangerous. Go away!" She snaps, stumbling as she falls backwards.

I stop in my tracks; she isn't attacking them…

Where are those fucking fools? I will see to them… but…

My gaze snaps back to her as I watch her struggle. I would jump to protect the pups if need be, but seeing her do her best not to hurt them makes a strange emotion tighten in my chest. She looks beautiful, even though she is pale as death. Her cherry-red lips are dry, and the struggle in her eyes as she stares at the children before her is apparent. I step around the corner and her heart thuds.

"Get them away from me!" She hisses, glaring at me hatefully.

"Why? You need blood. Take it."

"Don't play fucking mind games!" She hisses.

"Lorna... go over to the lady," I command. She looks at me with a tilt of her head and bravely walks over to Morgana.

"You're fucking twisted!" She spits. "Isn't this child under your care?"

I cock a brow; her struggle is obvious. The black top she wears clings to her rapidly heaving breasts and hangs off one shoulder. Her creamy skin looks so appetising. Just thinking of feeling her against me once more makes me throb. I frown coldly, hating the effect she has on me.

I walk over to her, grab her by her hair, and push her closer to Lorna, who looks a little afraid now. Her scent is intoxicating to me, and with each moment in her presence, my self-control is fucking weakening.

"I'm giving you a chance. Drink." Her only reply is to glare at me with hatred burning in those deep red eyes of hers.

"Fuck you," she spits with so much venom that I wonder how it is even possible for someone so beautiful to hold so much hatred.

I scoff, about to say something, when her eyes flutter. She tries to force them open, but she fails, falling limp in my hold. I let go of her hair and glance at the chain that holds her, breaking it and ignoring the burns that cover my fingers.

"A-Alpha…" Lorna stutters, her eyes filled with worry and uncertainty. I frown. I hadn't even realised that I could have scared them…

"You should go play outside," I say quietly. "And stay away from this woman," I add coldly. Alec nods, grabbing the girl's hands and running off.

The moment they are gone, I scoop her up. She barely weighs anything…

**Throw Lee and Gale in the fucking cells for a few nights… I gave them a job that they fucking didn't do,** I mind-link Luca.

**Got it.**

I carry her upstairs, heading to the third floor, and take her straight to my bedroom. Kicking open the door roughly, it bounces off the wall before it slams shut behind us. I walk over to the bed and place her on it. Her heartbeat is alarmingly fast, and I clench my jaw. I want to leave her, but… I can't. My anger swirls around me as I break the cuffs from her and toss them aside. I stand over her, my own heart raging.

**Our mate, claim her now!** Thanatos growls in my head. There's no way I would ever claim her.

I reach down, brushing my knuckles down her cool skin. She's like an ice sculpture… cold, yet beautiful and carved to precision…

Fuck it.

My gaze dips to her plush lips, and I wonder how they'd feel against mine. I lean down, the necklaces I wear around my neck grazing her chest. I want to move back, but… her scent… I bury my nose in her neck, inhaling her intoxicating aura. Goddess… this woman is divine…

**Alpha, you have… guests.** Luca's strained voice comes through the link, and I move back.

**Oh yeah? Who?** I ask.

**Your brothers.**

My mind clears as if I had just been doused in ice water, and I step back from the bed. Right… what was I even thinking? I'm a king with an aim and reputation…

A vampire has no place in my life.

Thinking about Kai and Cain, I frown. Yeah, there is no place in my life for the likes of her. I glare at the woman on the bed with renewed hatred, trying to ignore the way her breathing is becoming increasingly laboured…

**I'm coming,** I answer coldly.

I turn away before exhaling sharply and turning back towards the bed angrily. Biting my thumb sharply, I draw my blood and place it on her lips. I don't want her, nor do I care for her… perhaps if she did die, I'd be free from this torment.

I try not to lose myself in how I feel. She latches on, her lips wrapping around my thumb. Fuck, it feels good… she sucks hungrily on the blood, still asleep, but I pull away the moment I feel the wound heal up fully, trying not to focus on my dick partially hardening.

I turn away, leaving the room. Why had they turned up unannounced? I clench my jaw, heading down the stairs that lead to my personal quarters. Despite many people living in the castle, I have a separate entrance and exit to my quarters, which I use often enough. Sometimes I just need to get away from it all. I push open the door and look at the two men that are seated on the sofa. My blood boils as I try to control the rage that I feel.

"Well, look what we have, the Alpha King," Cain says mockingly, standing up. The hatred in his eyes isn't even hidden, and I smirk coldly.

"Well, obviously, if you're going to come to my home, you're going to find the king," I remind him arrogantly. I don't miss the way his jaw clenches, his dark eyes glaring at me. *Yeah, I fucking thought so.*

"Kian," Kai greets, standing up. We meet with a hug, and I slap his back.

Kai is two years younger than me at twenty-two, and Cain is thirty. Growing up, I was closer to Kai. Although our father always pitted me against Cain, who is six years my senior, I would always win, and with time that rivalry became bitter, from his side anyway. He hated seeing me grow to be better, stronger, and more powerful than he was.

When the first rumours of war spread, our dad, the previous king, had told me that if anything was to happen to him, he wanted me to fight for the Alpha King title. The way to be chosen as Alpha King isn't through birthright; the strongest Alphas would enter the tournament, and we battle it out. Five years ago, I entered. Despite not being a firstborn, I was still stronger than the common Alpha. When the final round for the crown came, I had made it through the ranks, and it was then that I had been levelled up against my brother. For the first time in history, two brothers would fight for the crown… and I won, becoming the youngest Alpha King to ever take the throne. I had a reputation and the power, wit, and strength to keep my people safe. The only thing I didn't have was my mate.

At the age of eighteen, we are able to sniff our mates out as long as they are over sixteen. In Cain's case, he had found his mate at the age of twenty-one when she had been sixteen. She couldn't sense the bond until she turned eighteen, but he had made it known to her that she was his and, like many wolves, they would pursue their mates and build a relationship with them until they were of age. Yet here I am blessed - no, given a mate I don't want. She isn't a blessing but a curse. Vampires or Fae were behind my father's death, I just wasn't sure which one yet. When I find out… it is going to rain blood.

I sit down, making no effort to hold back my aura as I look at them.

"Why have you come here?" I ask coldly.

"Kian, you might be the King of Clair De Lune, but this pack, the Midnight Eclipse, is still my home. So… since you have… taken the title from me, I can at least reside as a member of this pack, can I not?" I don't trust him…

"It took you six years to decide you want to join my pack? What of the pack you formed with half my men?"

"You mean *my* men. Even if you became the king, I was still the Alpha of the pack," he growls.

"The Alpha is the fucking strongest, and you, brother, were clearly not…" I mock coldly. His eyes flash, and I can feel his anger before he slams his fist on his leg.

"It's not the same. Things are hard, the place we settled… it isn't that big, and with more and more wanting to join you…" I smirk victoriously.

"And there we have it." My voice is cold as I look him in the eyes. "You came back because your men were deserting you."

Our eyes meet, and the power that surges around us only grows like a storm ready to destroy its target, but it doesn't bother me. Power is my cup of tea and Cain… Cain is the target.

MORGANA

I wake up feeling a little better. A sweet taste lingers in my mouth, and I clutch my throat. The last thing I remember is the Alpha yanking my hair as he pushed me towards that child… *Oh, how dare he!*

But why am I more energised? Probably the lack of poisoned cuffs… I glare at the broken shackles that lie on the ground near the bed.

His scent lingers in this room. I look around; I'm lying on a huge bed with white bedding. It smells like him; deep, seductive, and irritatingly enticing. The room is minimal, with just a matching wooden chest of drawers, one entire wall lined with floor-to-ceiling shelves that hold many books, along with a large set of wardrobes, and a second door that is ajar, showing me the bathroom.

I get off the bed, stumbling. My legs feel shaky, but… I'm alone. Why would they leave me alone? And without the cuffs? My heart skips a beat. This is my chance…

I walk to the bedroom door and press my ear against it, but I can't hear anything. I frowned. Is it a trap? I stagger to the window, yanking at the handle - locked. I focus on it, moving my hand as I use my powers to break the handle away. I flinch at the loud crunching sound it makes, pausing to hear if anyone comes running. When nothing happens, I push the window open slowly and peep out.

Damn… I'm pretty high up. My waist-length hair blows in my face, and I push it away. I am an utter mess.

I glance at the sun. It isn't as bright now. If I manage to stick to the shade, I should be okay. Looking down, I press my lips together. I could easily use my powers to break my fall. I just hope I have enough strength…

Climbing onto the window ledge, I keep a sharp eye out for anyone passing by, but, given the silence, this has to be at the back of the castle. I look down and see there is a window directly below this one that has a balcony. I appear to be on the third floor. If I jump, what are the chances someone might be in that room? Well, there's no harm in trying. I have nothing to lose.

Taking a deep breath, I jump, ready to land lithely on my feet and use my powers to slow me down. Big mistake; I'm not able to handle it, too weak to even break my fall. I land with a sharp thud, my head hitting the stone railing of the balcony before I tumble to the ground. Pain flares through me, and my body screams in agony…

KIAN

"Either way… we are back for good. I am ready to reside here," Cain says coldly.

Forced to break eye contact first, he looks at Luca, who is standing to the side with his arms crossed. He gives him a cold glare before he looks back at me.

**I don't trust him, Kian.** Luca's voice comes through the link.

**Neither do I, but I have no choice right now but to agree. If he's fucking planning something, I'd prefer him close. You know what they say: keep your friends close and your enemies closer.** I look at Cain emotionlessly.

"Welcome home then, brother." That threw him off. He narrows his eyes at me.

"You're okay with it?"

"Why wouldn't I be?" I ask, raising an eyebrow. My eyes hold his challengingly, and he clenches his jaw.

"Of course, I shouldn't have doubted you… I just thought since you took the Alpha King title from me… you wouldn't want me here."

"You being here doesn't threaten me. I think you forget that I won that damn title, fair and fucking square. Now, if we're done -"

I am cut off when I hear a sickening thud from outside and a yelp.

Fuck. I know what that was, and I do not want Cain to see her. If he gets an inkling of how she makes me feel or any kind of suspicion on the topic...

**Get her and fuckin-** Before I can even finish my command to Luca, Cain interrupts,

"What is that...? Or more like, who?" Cain stands up. Before I can even react, he is at the door, pulling it open and stepping out onto the balcony. Fuck it.

"None of your business," I growl. It was too fucking late. He yanks Morgana up by her arm and the urge to rip him to pieces for touching her fills me, but she simply groans, half out of it and clearly in pain. She's injured. The smell of her blood fills the air.

"Well, well, well... a vampire. So, the rumours were true. You brought a vampire home." Cain turns and looks at me, a keen look in his eyes.

"Not that it's any of your concern," I remark emotionlessly.

The last thing I am going to do is give him any kind of leverage on me. I smirk coldly and walk over to him, pulling Morgana from his clutches. She stumbles deliriously, her head hitting my chest, and if I hadn't caught her around her waist, she would have fallen flat on her behind.

"But yes, I did. She's rather appealing, isn't she?" I comment casually.

Morgana looks up at me, seeming to realise she is in my hold. She begins to struggle, not realising she is only tempting me further. Her breasts rub against my chest, and the fabric between us irritates me.

"Oh... I never knew you were interested in their kind..." Cain remarks, his eyes trailing over her. My anger flares, and I try to contain myself.

"Oh, I fucking hate them," I growl. I fuel the anger I feel at him into my words, hoping he fucking bought it. "But you've got to admit she's a pretty thing."

"That she is... well if you ever get bored and you haven't killed her in the process... I wouldn't mind a taste," he remarks. I clench my jaw. He's fucking disgusting. He has his mate... I am no better, though, when I'm degrading my fated mate like this...

"Sure," I mutter, the words leaving a bitter taste in my mouth. There is no fucking way, whether I hate her or not, that I'd let anyone else have a taste of her.

"Let go of me," she mutters weakly. She is already weak, and that fall didn't do her any favours.

**Take her to my room. I will deal with her very soon,** I order Luca before glancing at Kai, who is staring at Morgana, looking slightly pale.

"What's your problem?" I ask him coldly. He shakes his head, his dreadlocks moving as he speaks.

"I just… hate or not, she's a person… Dad wouldn't have liked this," he mutters. I frown. Is he actually trying to teach me fucking manners?

"Yeah? Well, he isn't fucking here. Get her the fuck out of here."

A short while later, I had told Andrei, the head Omega, to make sure the other wing was cleared for Cain and his family, who would be arriving in the coming days, and also to situate them on the complete opposite side of the castle. Kai would take a singular room at the packhouse, which was for unmated wolves.

Luca himself lives at the castle with his family. The place is fucking big and always lively, but I like my own quarters where I can walk away at times and just be alone. I head to my room, my anger bubbling with each step. She had messed this up. Catching Cain's cunning attention was not a wise move…

I open my bedroom door to see her bound tightly with rope, her mouth gagged, and her legs tied as well. She glares at me, but it lacks the force that was there yesterday. I lock the door, my eyes darkening as I walk to the bed and pull off the gag.

"Fuck you!" She spits before I can even say anything. Seriously, where does she get the energy from? I grab her jaw tightly, glaring into her stunning face.

"Keep up with the attitude, and I will fuck you," I growl. "What the fuck did you think you were doing? I hope you learned your lesson."

"I am done with you." She tries to free herself from my hold on her face, but it's a losing battle. She is currently far too weak.

"The thing is, you're mine. You no longer have a choice. Unless you want me to keep you as my whore, you better shut this pretty little mouth of yours from spewing poison, and obey, or I will put it to good use," I growl.

She scoffs, "You don't know me then, Alpha." The way she said 'Alpha' is anything but respectful, as if it was the most disgusting word on the planet.

"I don't need to know you to get what I want, but if you want to live, fix your attitude!"

She frowns and seems about to say something when she closes her eyes and takes a deep breath. What is wrong with her?

"I need blood," she admits, gritting her teeth. I cock a brow.

"I was offering you that pup before, but you lost your chance."

I let go of her and push her back onto the bed, trying not to pay attention to the way the ropes tighten around her waist and shoulders, or the way they squeeze her breasts, emphasising them even more and making desire rage up with me.

"I am not going to harm innocent children or play your sick games," she shoots back.

"Even if you die?"

"I'd rather die than spend another minute around you!" She hisses.

"Then maybe you'd rather have mine? I'm far from innocent, right?"

"I'd rather die!" She spits venomously. Her words make Thanatos growl. My eyes flash gold as he struggles to take over, but he is a beast, and I can't allow that. He'd either take her right here or mark her out of rage.

"Don't wish for something that I might give you sooner than you want," I hiss back.

"You're sick." I looked down at her coldly.

"Where exactly do you expect to get blood from?" I ask, now grabbing her by her throat and leaning over her with my knee on the bed.

"I don't know, nor do I care…" She glares at me, but she is weakening.

"So the precious vampire princess has now fallen to such an extent that she is willing to settle for any blood? That's rather funny, don't you think?" I taunt, squeezing her throat slightly. Her breathing is ragged, and I know I'm cutting her oxygen off at times, but I don't really care.

"I would drink the blood of a dog if I had to. Even that would be better than yours." Her voice trembles with unbridled anger, and my eyes flash dangerously, trying to ignore those plush lips of hers. I squeeze her throat, and she gasps. I lean closer, my nose brushing her ear.

"Then let me make one thing perfectly clear to you, Princess: the only blood you'll ever taste again will be mine," I hiss.

"Never." I let go of her. We will fucking see because when it comes to the game of wills, I always win.

"You will because it will be your only choice," I promise her dangerously, casting one final glance at the bound woman on my bed. Her chest is heaving with rage, but she is far too weak to argue anymore.

I don't wait for a reply. Walking out of the room, I slam the door shut behind me.

# CAUGHT UP IN THE MOMENT

KIAN

ANOTHER DAY PASSES, AND she still refuses to drink when I offer her. Her colour is ashy, I can see the pale blue veins along her skin, and her fangs are longer. I know she needs to drink, or she will die.

On the other fucking hand, Thanatos's anger is raging; angry at her for her disobedience and angry at me for my stubbornness. He has to remember that I am not going to bend to his will. I am in charge.

I left her in my room and posted guards outside my window just in case she tries something stupid again, although she literally has no energy to do anything. She isn't even able to talk anymore, but even then, her stubbornness still prevails. When I dragged her to my neck, she refused.

It angers me that she dares to defy my will. I hate that she does not yield to me as she should. I know there is something there because she had allowed me to get close to her back at that lake. Although she had been slightly drunk, she was still in her senses... but now? She resents me, and that fucking pushes me to a dangerous place. I want to break her into submission, but I wonder if she'll die before I am able to.

I'm seated in my office; my Beta, Luca, and my four Deltas are all present. As the king, I broke away from the norm of having one Delta and selected four. It makes things a whole lot easier. We are discussing the upcoming summit and arrangements.

"Their quarters have been set up, and with those who have issues, we've put them apart," my Delta, Ajax, explains, frowning. His chin-length black hair covers one of his eyes.

"Good, we don't need them ripping each other's throats out," Luca adds.

"What are we doing with Alpha Cain here?" Corbin, another of my Deltas, asks, looking up.

"He isn't part of the summit, so he's not in the fucking equation," I say darkly.

"Unspoken, but he is one of the strongest... if he wants in, he will be voted in," Luca hesitantly adds. My eyes flicker for a moment as I look at him, tilting my head slightly.

"Are you questioning who has more power? The Alphas at the summit... or me?" I ask. My voice is calm, yet I feel fear and tension in each one of them. I don't need to exude my aura to show them who's the Alpha in the room.

"Of course it is you."

"Good answer... Cain will have to prove he has a pack that's one of the strongest in the country to take a seat at that summit. He doesn't have one." The room is silent. I look at the map spread across the large table, gripping the edge. Cain never would. Not as long as I was king.

"We need to make sure that no one is sneaking in from the Oblivion Pass, as there have been some mysterious attacks down that side as well. I'd rather it be dealt with before it becomes a real fucking problem," I state coldly and look up sharply at Reuban. "Take a small team down there, scour the area, and find out what exactly is going on with those attacks. The Alpha of the Ruby Moon Pack has tried to downplay it. I don't know what he might be hiding, but I want you on it."

I glance at my last Delta. Unlike the other three, he isn't as skilled when it comes to battle and fighting, but he is smart.

"Oliver, I want you to keep an eye on Cain and Kai discreetly. They may be back, but I don't trust them."

"But Kai, he isn't like Cain, Alpha," Luca says, clearly surprised by my order.

"I know, but Cain may be using him. I can't fucking afford to take risks, Luca," I reply chillingly.

"Yes, Alpha, understood," Oliver replies with a nod.

"Dismissed." I turn my back on them and lean against the table, crossing my ankles as I glare at the wall behind me. They leave the room until only Luca and I remain.

Morgana… she's fucking consuming my mind, way too fucking much.

"Alpha… is it wise to have the vampire here?" Luca asks as if he knows what's on my mind.

"Yeah. End of discussion," I hiss, snapping my head towards him as my eyes locked with his blue ones.

"Kian… why are you so hung over her? You've even kept her in your room… you don't allow anyone there but Sage. If she knew -"

"I'm the fucking Alpha, Luca. Remember that. Who and what I do is my fucking business. Who cares if Sage knows or not?"

"I'm your friend, and I know you are the Alpha. I'm just saying don't hurt Sage over a woman that means -"

The moment my eyes burned gold, he stops, paling considerably before looking away and lowering his head.

**Kill him now,** Thanatos spits in my head. He's fighting for control, and it's pissing me off. I slam him behind my barrier, blocking him off and glaring at him.

"Because I consider you a friend, I'm warning you to stay out of my fucking business when it comes to her. Understood?" He frowns but nods.

"As you wish, Alpha," he says, his voice clipped.

I don't bother replying and walk out, my anger only rising as I head towards my quarters of the castle. I hate being fucking disobeyed. Walking swiftly through the dark halls, I reach my bedroom and unlock the door. I enter, shutting it behind me.

She hasn't moved… not even an inch. Her scent fills the room, intoxicating me as I walks over to the bed. Her eyes are half-closed, and I'm not sure if she's even conscious…

Reaching behind her, I rip the ropes that bind her right from her. My mind flitters back to her brother, who had willingly given her to me. What kind of life did she even have before I brought her here?

Who cares? I push her onto her back, my gaze flitting over her; the ropes had chaffed her skin, leaving angry red marks that had drawn blood in areas. I frown - it was her own fucking fault.

I sit down on the bed, scooping her into my arms. She is shivering ever so slightly and she doesn't even fight me. *If only you had been a good little rose to start with, you wouldn't have been in this position...* I take hold of her chin, rubbing my finger over her dry lips. She is beautiful...

I remove my thumb from her lips. Holding the back of her, I bring my thumb to my lips and bite into it, letting the blood pour out before I slip it into her mouth. For a few moments she doesn't respond, until her eyelids flutter and she looks up into me through those thick lashes of hers. Her breathing becomes stronger, and she begins sucking on my thumb hungrily. Her eyes that had dulled now deepen. Her teeth pierce my thumb, but I don't allow her to drink more, pulling my thumb from her mouth. If she wants my blood, then she's going to have to beg for it. I smile coldly down at her, seeing that familiar spark of defiance return, but it's coated with hunger.

"If you want to drink, you're going to have to ask."

She look at me, a small frown creasing those perfect brows of hers. Her delicate fingers clutch my shirt as she tries to pull herself into a sitting position. I push her into a sitting position with the arm that had been supporting her neck before I lift her into my lap, and she instantly locks her arms weakly around my neck. I tense at our position. My urge for her only grows... I need her...

"Ask you?" She whispers, her voice barely clear enough to understand.

"Yeah, obviously." She gives me a weak smirk.

"In your dreams, Alpha," she whispers before she shifts her position with a spurt of energy, straddling me instead.

A flash of surprise rushes through me, my hand instantly going to her waist... but before I can say anything, I feel a sharp sting as she sinks her teeth into my neck. My hand reaches up, ready to rip her from my neck, anger blazing inside of me... but...

Burning sparks trail through my body and if I had once thought being fed from was fucking degrading and disgusting, I was wrong. The pleasure I feel right now, it is more than anything I had ever felt before.

I can sense her emotions; the hunger, the desperation, her pain...

Her lips brush my skin, and I swear, "Fuck..."

I throb hard as she moans against my neck, drinking hungrily. Her fingers grazing the back of my head, she arches her back, moulding herself against me completely. My hand runs up her back, my fingers raking down her spine, making her moan louder. She gyrates her hips, rubbing her core against my hardening dick. The scent of her arousal fills my nose, pleasure rushing south. Drinking my blood is turning her on...

The possessive feeling that she had probably fed off many men and felt like this only angered me further, but I'd deal with that later. One hand twists into her silky locks tightly, biting back a groan as I run my hand over her peachy ass, squeezing it hard. Her nails digging into the back of my neck feel just as good, but it's the way she wriggles her ass in anticipation that makes my eyes blaze. I grab her ass, pulling her harder against me. Fuck… she is…

She whimpers in pleasure, grinding herself against my dick. I don't let go, carnal desire consuming every inch of me. All logic is gone as I grab her hips painfully tight, grinding her against me. She gasps.

"Fuck…" she whispers, her lips brushing the wound she had created. She seems to click on to what was happening, her breathless moan ending in a sharp suck, but all I can focus on is the faint blush on her pale cheeks that now look as radiant as the first time I fucking saw her. The scent of her arousal is fucking with my head. I need her...

Before she can react, I place my lips on her neck. Those cherry-red lips part as she lets out a wanton moan and relaxes. I move back, guiding her by her hips. My gaze skims down, watching her boobs bounce I tighten my hold, making her hiss in pain, but I don't care. She deserves it for disobeying me. I hate being disobeyed.

Fuck. I can't focus on anything but the temptress before me, and the pleasure she is inflicting me with, without even having to undress. I hear her gasp as her entire body tenses. I reach over, kissing her smooth, creamy neck. I want to mark her, but that is not a fucking option. I suck hard on it instead and she cries out as her orgasm tears through her.

I don't stop, chasing my own release that is so fucking close. Seconds later, my own orgasm shoots through me, and all I want is to ram into that tight little pussy of hers and fuck her senseless. As her hands gripped my shoulders and she tries to recover from her orgasm, my own arms wrap around her as I breathe heavily into her soft tits.

The reality of what she had done hit me like a fucking lightning bolt. I tense, my eyes flashing before I stand up, letting go of her as if she was the fucking plague. She wasn't expecting it, and she fell to the ground, her head hitting the floor behind her. Her eyes flashed in anger, and, is that confusion? I don't know, and I don't fucking care.

I walk past her, heading to the bathroom, not caring that a tiny part inside of me felt a tinge of pain for doing that to her, but this is what I wanted. I would use her... and when I had my fill, I would get rid of her.

# Pushing His Limits

No... THE MAN AT the lake was nicer... but was he? We didn't speak, it had just been an intimate moment that I had somehow fallen into. Even now, I have never gotten so aroused in such a way whilst drinking blood. Usually, I drink from a glass, but when I have drank directly from a human, I have never gotten turned on. Yes, I've felt exhilarated and even high, but nothing like this…

My chest tightens painfully when I remember the anger in his eyes as he threw me to the floor. For the first time in my life, I feel lost. I'm angry at myself for allowing that to happen, angry at him for his treatment of me, angry at Azrael for allowing him to take me… I had tried to escape twice, and both times I had failed. I really need to play smart from here on out.

The bathroom door slams open, and my breath hitches, my heart skipping a beat at the bang. I look up, my heart thudding as I stare at the god before me, his entire muscular physique on perfect display. I can see he has a tattoo wrapping around his right lower leg that looks like a forest. My gaze travels upwards, taking in the navy towel wrapped around his waist, water trickling down his six-pack and into his towel, making my core clench. I slowly force my gaze up to his face, my heart thudding when his cold hazel eyes meets mine.

"You didn't run. You had your chance. Why didn't you take it?" He asks coldly, approaching me. I squeeze the edge of the dresser, holding his gaze.

"We both know that I wouldn't have gotten far," I reply, equally coldly. He reaches over, gripping my chin tightly in his fingers and forcing me to tilt my head upwards.

"True. I'm a hunter and I love a game of chase," he whispers. I glare back defiantly, feeling stronger now that I have fed, but I do not want to be bound in a painful position again and left in it for two days, or maybe even more so this time…

"Clearly," I spit resentfully. I hate him. He smirks coldly.

"Looks like the she-devil is finally beginning to break…" he taunts.

I am going to kill him, but I'll do it on his terms… I'll make him lower his guard at some point, and when he does… I'll kill him. He raises one of those perfect brows, almost as if he knows what is going through my mind.

"Now… how about you go get cleaned up, and then I'll decide what to do with you," he suggests coldly, turning away from me and walking over to the large wardrobes that cover the entire wall near the bathroom door. Opening the first one, he begins to take some clothes out for himself.

My gaze falls to the large tattoo on his back. It is a huge dragon that spreads across his entire back… an interesting choice for a werewolf. My gaze shifts to his right calf to see that the back of his leg tattoo contains a wolf, too, blending in with the trees.

"You have nine minutes left to get cleaned up," he says darkly, and my heart skips a beat.

I'm not going to refuse the offer. I walk to the bathroom as fast as possible, despite my legs feeling weak. Upon entering, I quickly lock the door, closing my eyes for a moment. Taking a deep breath, I open them, looking around the bathroom. Mosaic tiles in cream, brown, black, and gold cover the entire walls. The ceiling is dark wood with fitted lights. A counter runs along one wall with a shelf of towels, toiletries, and two basins. On the opposite wall there is a toilet and shower, and to my left is a huge tub, large enough to fit five of me. The floor is glossy dark brown tiles that sparkle perfectly. Splashes of water left by the Alpha are clear on them and I frown, quickly making my way to the shower and stripping off my dirty clothes.

Turning on the water, I step in, relishing in the cool water that runs down my skin. I quickly grab the body wash and scrub myself before I pick up the shampoo bottle. From the packaging, I can tell it was an expensive brand and not one I had heard of, but, then again, we usually used our own brands rather than take anything from the werewolves. I squirt a large dollop of what smells like shea butter shampoo onto my hand and apply it to my wet locks.

I close my eyes, rinsing off, and feel so glad he had allowed me to bathe. It's probably his only decent act since he had brought me here. I apply some conditioner, enjoying the way my fingers slide through my locks before I turn the shower off, not wanting to take longer than he gave me. I step out, grabbing a towel and wrapping it around myself before taking another of the towels and drying my long locks. My eyes fall on the shelf of hair products; serums, oils, hair treatment products... *So, the Alpha takes good care of his hair...* That's not something I'd have expected.

With nothing to wear but the towel, I silently open the door, hoping he's gone. However with my luck as of late, he is still here, seated at the edge of the bed, completely dressed. His elbows rest on his knees, head in his hands. The moment he hears the door, his head snaps up. The arrogance and power he usually exudes surrounds him once again.

I stand there, now realising how small the towel is. With my five-foot-eleven frame, it just about covers the main bits. I watch as his eyes run over me, filled with a primal hunger that made my core knot. What is this? How can he hate me and yet look at me like that?

"I need something to wear," I say icily. I may not run, but I 'm not going to just listen to him and act like a meek, useless woman either.

"There's the fucking drawer." Standing up, he walks out of the room, slamming the door behind him. Does he not know how to do anything but slam doors?

I frown, glancing at his wardrobe. Does he expect me to wear one of his items? Just the thought disgusts me, but right now I don't really have a choice...

*Well, Morgana, you literally humped him and drank his blood - I'm sure his clothes aren't so bad.* I scoff at my thoughts and pull the drawer open, taking out a blood-red shirt that I'm surprised the moody Alpha even possesses. I mean, all I had seen him in are bland colours.

I pull it on, relieved that it doesn't hang off my shoulder. I still need something to wear underneath... I rummage around, finding his under-wear drawers before I wrinkle my nose, I am not going to wear anything so intimate of his! I decide to settle for some shorts. I pull them on, tightening the drawstring around my waist and turning to one of the large mirrors that hangs on the inside of the wardrobe. I look ridiculous. His shirt falls to my mid-thigh and his black shorts fall to just above my knees. Wow… I don't think I've ever looked more stupid in my entire life.

Deciding to make the most of it, I begin prowling around for a brush. I find a wide-tooth comb and smile victoriously. Brushing my hair out, I sigh in relief. It feels good to feel so clean. I replace the comb, braiding my hair in a fish plait. I sigh, knowing it wouldn't stay. My hair is very silky, and it always comes out unless pinned or tied.

I se some moisturiser and take a little drop, applying it to my face before looking at myself; my skin is glowing, well, as much as my pale skin can. My dark lashes stand out like spider legs, and my plump red lips look as soft and appealing as always. I apply the cream gently to my face, pondering over what happened earlier.

He had tried to make me beg but I refused to… but then how did drinking blood end up with me orgasming like that? I sigh deeply. Even back home, I wasn't the type to have many men or engage in casual sex often enough. So why did I do that?

The door opens and I jump, startled. I turn to see a pretty woman with light brown hair and blue eyes that are staring at me accusingly. She's curvy with large breasts that are on display from the plunging neckline of her fitted blue dress.

"What are you doing in here?" She asks, pursing her plump lips. I raise my eyebrow, irritation flashing through me. I hate being spoken to like that.

"You should ask your Alpha," I answer coldly.

She frowns deeply, her eyes scanning the bed. Her eyes fall on the discarded towel that the Alpha had left, plus the two that I had put aside. Her eyes flash as she stares at the bed that was quite rumpled. She glares at me.

"Kian is mine…" she spits. I raise an eyebrow.

"Oh? Then, please, do tell your precious Kian to keep his hands off of me," I hiss.

If he had a woman, then why was he messing around with me? Another Azrael… I'm disgusted, but then a sudden thought comes to me - the Alpha doesn't have the mark of a mated wolf. Is this woman lying?

"We all know you're probably trying to seduce him," she whispers coldly, glancing at the open door next to her. Is she scared of being heard?

"Funny, who would have thought I would be able to seduce the Alpha King? I wonder if that is a compliment or an insult?" I scoff, dropping onto the bed. I brace my hands behind me, leaning back as I cross my legs gracefully.

"I'm warning you, bloodsucker… stay away from the king or I will stop you," she spits. I raise an eyebrow mockingly before smirking tauntingly and tilting my head.

"Oh, yeah? You and which army?"

Her eyes flash, and she is momentarily rendered speechless. I smirk, playing with a strand of my hair that had already escaped my plait, and watch her with amusement. She is about to speak, when she turns sharply. I can hear approaching footsteps. She spins around, but before she can leave, he's back. I see his frown deepen as he looks at me sitting on the bed and then at the woman before him.

"Kian… I thought I'd come to see if you're okay." Her tone is shockingly soft now. I briefly wonder if it was the same woman from seconds ago. Aww, how sweet. Is she madly in love with her precious little Alpha king? So cute. I roll my eyes when she places her hands on his hard chest.

"Sage, I would call you if I needed you. Don't show up unless I say," he says coldly.

"I'm sorry, Kian. I just knew you had a lot going on and wondered if I could ease that tension," she whispers seductively, lacing her arms around his neck.

Should I look away? I don't know what to think. As a child, my mother told me that werewolves were different from us, how they loved one and only one and would stay true to them. Unlike the majority, she didn't think they were as bad… but seeing the man before me, I wonder how many more women he had behind him.

Sage, as he called her, tugs him down. As she presses herself against him, I frown. Is he really going to kiss her after messing around with me? His cold gaze flickers at me, and I think I see a hint of a cold smirk before he claims her lips in a deep kiss. His hands grip her hips, and I look away in disgust, but there's more. I feel a stinging pain inside, and I don't know if it's from the fact that he had used me only a short while ago, clearly displaying I am nothing more than something he wants to use and toss aside. It disgusts me. Although I hate him… if he'd had even a little decency…

Her soft moan as he presses her against the door makes my stomach coil. I stand up, walking over to them before I slip out from behind him. My arm brushes his back lightly. The moment I am out the door, he pulls away from her, grabbing me by my arm suddenly.

"Where the fuck do you think you're going?" He growls. I raise an eyebrow, looking between them.

"I thought I'd give you two some privacy… I won't run," I answer, frowning as I glare at him. Ripping free from his hold, my eyes flash with irritation.

*She's not even affected.* I flinch slightly at the shrill sound that accompanies his thoughts that flitter into my head. I look up at him, seeing his anger. Why would I be affected?

"Do carry on," I said mockingly before turning and walking off down the hall with no destination in mind.

I massage my temple. This is the one ability that even Azrael doesn't know I possess, one that Father had told me never to mention, saying it could be my end or my saviour…

I look around the halls. They're so much darker than the lighter interior of the lower floors. Are these his private quarters? Seems so. The walls have a few artworks, but they're just paintings of sceneries. Unlike the wall art downstairs, there are no people in any of these pictures. I continue down the hall, hearing the couple talking quietly. I can't make out anything, and there are often large gaps when I assume they're kissing or mind-linking.

I stop at the end of the hall, tilting my head and looking at one particular portrait. It is a dark forest with a wolf's silhouette, his golden eyes glowing as he stares right back at me. It is made of oil paint, but the detail is impressive. I stare into his golden eyes. I can almost feel the anger and rage in him. My heart skips a beat. He looks almost… real.

I gasp when a hand clamps onto my shoulder. I spin around, my heart pounding. I hadn't even heard him approach. I look up into the Alpha's eyes, trying to calm my raging heart.

"What the fuck do you think you're doing?" I frowned.

"Looking at this monstrosity of a picture," I state, tossing my hair that had already come half undone. His frown only deepens.

"Sage will put you to work, and any mistakes you make, I will personally see to your punishment," he says coldly. I cock a brow, crossing my arms.

"I will never take her orders. If you want me to cooperate, then I have a few conditions." I had acted recklessly enough. It's high time I think wisely. I was one of the best strategists in my father's court, so it's time I put that to use.

"You're in no place to make conditions, sunshine," he spits coldly. I hate that word, especially when he knows the sun only weakens me and I am far from a sweet, sunny person. I glare at him.

"Aww, did the baby Alpha forget that I can make life hard for him? I'm sure if I cause a scene, it wouldn't look good on the Alpha King," I coo. He slams his hand against the wall near my head, but I don't even flinch.

"Watch that mouth of yours," he hisses. I raise an eyebrow,

"You might think I'm your possession, but I'm not, and unless you want to see me lose my shit and become a psycho, you better not push me too far," I say dangerously. "Now, are we going to talk conditions, pup, or not?" His eyes flash gold, and I can feel his struggle.

"What are they?" He finally growls through gritted teeth. I smile faintly.

"Now, that's better. First of all, I shall only take orders from the man in the kitchens who put me to cutting potatoes and cleaning the floors. Sadly, you have a lot of nincompoops around and I don't want to spend time with them. As for that woman, I will not tolerate her. If she dares speak to me disrespectfully again, I will attack." My eyes burn with anger as I remember the way she had spoken to me. The image of them kissing flashes through my mind, irritating me to no end. He frowns, looking down at me, and is about to reach for my face when I knock his hand away. "Don't touch me with those filthy hands that have just been all over another," I say disdainfully.

"Watch it, little she-devil," he hisses. His eyes flash, his aura settling around us like a blanket weighing down upon me. "Fine. I'll see if Andrei can put you to work." I nod.

"Secondly, I want one glass of blood a day, at the very least." I don't know how much I had drunk of his… but it tasted so good…

"You will get blood every night. Next," he says, through gritted teeth.

"I need clothes. I'm not going to go around like this," I say coldly. "Besides, unlike your kind, we are more proper and prefer to wear shoes."

"Yet your king willingly gave his sister up without even a fight. What a loving family." His words sting, but I would not let him see that.

"Azrael and I are half-siblings, and he never liked me. But what about you and your brother? I can tell how much you two care for each other," I mock. His eyes flash before his hand wraps around my throat.

"Don't you dare try to fucking act like you know anything about me and Cain. Stay out of my fucking business or you will regret it," he hisses, his hold tight, yet I don't mind it.

My stomach knots as our eyes meet. I am aware of his proximity, his chest grazing mine. My core throbs, and I hate that I feel my nipples stiffen. I hate the effect he has on me… my heart is racing. Even though I know I was pissing him off, I wasn't able to stop myself.

"I'm so scared," I say, emphasising my words with my large eyes.

The growl that resonates from him echoes through the halls, and at the same time as he slams me against the wall, I kick out, hitting him straight in the chest with all my might and knocking him backwards. His blazing eyes fly open in shock as I drop to the floor, landing gracefully. I run at him, raising my hand, summoning my powers, and blasting him back. He reaches out, digging his elongated claws into the walls, fighting against the force I had used to throw him off as he keeps his stance. His alpha aura rolls off him in waves. The sheer weight of it suffocates me.

"You've fucking done it." His voice is more animalistic than human, and it is at that moment that I realised I was no longer looking at the Alpha King… but the beast he truly is in his wolf form…

His raging eyes are ready for the kill as another growl rips through the halls, and the moment he shifts into a huge wolf with dark fur, I turn and run. My heart pounds in my chest as the beast closes in on me. I reach the stairs, running down them faster than the wind. Raising my hand, I send another blast at him, but, to my horror, it doesn't affect him at all. He'll reach me within seconds…

*I shouldn't have looked back… shit!* It cost me, and I trip, falling to the ground just as the huge beast lands with a ground-shaking thud. His four paws trap me beneath him, and I look straight up into the eyes of a true beast. His eyes hold rage, hunger, and the urge to kill. His dangerous aura suffocates me, yet I simply stare back into those eyes...

I'm not afraid of anyone. No one.

# Thanatos

KIAN

**W**HEN SAGE KISSED ME, she didn't even fucking care, and it only made me kiss Sage harder. The fucking problem is that I didn't enjoy it, not one bit. I wanted to feel her lips on mine, not Sage's. No matter how much I hate her kind… I still want her, but she clearly doesn't feel the same. For the most part anyway.

She pushed me too far, and Thanatos took control. His rage and anger are so strong that I can't even regain control.

**Don't hurt her,** I growl.

**I think I'll be the one to deal with our little mate,** he throws back at me. I see him gaze down at her...

*Run.*

But she just slowly sits up, glaring back at Thanatos. He growls venomously at her, and she glares back.

"Don't growl at me. I'm not scared of you," she snaps to my complete surprise.

**Why she!** Thanatos growls, his anger raging.

For the first time in my life, I feel an ounce of amusement. I stop fighting him, curious to see what she would do next. I watch her stand up, the clingy fabric of my red shirt draped over her perfect breasts as she brushes her hair that is coming out of her plait onto her face and stares Thanatos in the eye.

"Listen to me. By having a temper tantrum, you won't get what you want. I placed my demands forward, now it's your job to listen to them. Otherwise, I assure you I am really good at creating hell," she says, completely unafraid of the Alpha wolf before her. What is she made out of? How can she look him in the eye and not cower in fear? I feel something stir inside as she pouts, placing her hands on her narrow waist as she waits for a reply.

**She's… brave,** Thanatos grunted. **She isn't afraid of me. She truly is our mate.** The moment I feel him soften, I know I have to take back control. Pushing him to the backseat, I regain control and shift back.

Her eyes fly open, snapping straight downwards. I raise an eyebrow, seeing her large eyes grow even rounder and, to my fucking surprise, a very faint blush covers her cheeks before she looks away, crossing her arms. Despite her now racing heart ,she acts casual. Does she like what she saw?

"Well, for a kid, you sure are well endowed," she states with a flick of her hair. It's my turn to look at her, surprised and annoyed. Did she just say that…? I frown when the first part of her statement registers.

"I'm not a fucking kid," I growl. I am a fucking Alpha, and what does she mean 'for' a fucking kid? She rolls her eyes, completely unaffected.

"So, do we have a deal?" She asks, turning back to me, although her eyes stayed firmly on my face. I step closer, and she steps back. I raise an eyebrow. So, she's backing away from a naked man, but is okay to face off against a wolf that is her fucking height?

"Why so scared, little she-devil?" I ask coldly. She glares back.

"Don't change the topic, and stop calling me those stupid names! Can you not invade my personal space?" She huffs.

"You weren't scared of an Alpha wolf ready to tear you apart, but you're scared of a naked man?" I ask, smirking coldly as I back her against the wall.

"Oh, please, that thing down there is more of a monster than that wolf!"

"Still thinking about it?"

"You wish." I almost smirk at the glare she gives me. Is that another faint blush on those porcelain cheeks of hers? She pushes me away and turns her back on me, crossing her arms.

"I have a few conditions, too," I remark. She turns her head slightly, a small frown on her gorgeous face.

"What are they?"

"You will be put to work in the kitchen as you requested. You are to stay there and not come in front of any of my men. Secondly, you will sleep in my room, so I will know if you try to run away and third…" I continue, not letting her speak as I close the gap between us and snake an arm around her, placing my hand on her stomach. Her heart is racing as I press her against me. It takes my all not to focus on her behind pressing again my dick.

"Third?" She asks in a clipped tone.

"You will be given blood every night… but it will be mine," I whisper in her ear. Her scent tingling my senses and the sensation of her body pressing against mine makes me throb.

"No to that last one," she says, grabbing hold of my wrist as she tries to push my hand off her stomach to no avail.

"Come on, we can both agree on one thing, that it was pretty good…" I don't know why I said it, but it was the truth. I hear her suck in a breath. I caress her stomach, feeling the softness of her flat stomach, and the jutting hardness of her hip bone.

"Fine," she whispers. Did I hear a faint sigh? She pulls out my hold.

"Then we have an agreement."

She turns and looks me square in the eye, those dark red orbs of hers glinting mysteriously. No, I don't trust her, and although I'd be keeping her in my bedroom, I know she'd try something… sooner or later… when she thinks my guard is down… but by then I'll have taken what I want. Neither of us look away, and I know she doesn't trust me either, knowing that I don't trust her, but that was perfect. After all, this is a game of passion and hate and only one of us will make it to the finish line…

I had told Liana, Luca's mate, to get Morgana some clothes and then take her to the kitchen. I commanded Ajax, Corbin, and Oliver to alternate between watching her. I am not going to trust anyone other than the Deltas to watch her. I had chosen the idiots Gale and Lee because, despite being idiots, they were trustworthy, but they needed a fucking beating to get through those thick skulls of theirs.

I stand with my arms crossed, watching Liana measure Morgana. The woman looks nervous. I know she's Sage's good friend, so for her to do something for Morgana is not going to be her cup of tea. I watch them sharply, not trusting the vampire, but, surprisingly, the she-devil was not fighting. A bored pout sits on her gorgeous face. From this angle, I can pay attention to her jutting cheekbones, angled jaw, and the way her slender nose is so perfect. She has her hair tied back, but I prefer it open…

She turns towards me and instantly gives me a dirty look, her dark red eyes full of contempt before she turns her nose up and looks away. I frown deeply. I know I don't fucking deserve anything else, but it irritates me that others don't get this same fucked up treatment.

"Okay, for now I've brought these for you, and by evening we will have your new items ready… Alpha Kian, how many sets of clothing do you want us to get?" She asks. I raise an eyebrow.

**However much a woman needs, there's no need to cut corners. She was the princess of the Sanguine Empire, and we will show her we are no less when it comes to wealth,** I reply coldly through the link.

**Is that really the reason?** Thanatos comments snidely.

**Fuck off,** I growl back. Ever since she hadn't cowered away from him, he kept putting explicit images of her in my fucking head.

**Our mate will taste good.** An image of actually tasting her fills my head, and I exhale sharply, blocking him off. Dick head.

Morgana takes the clothes and enters the bathroom whilst Liana looks at me.

"Alpha…"

"Don't butt into my fucking business., I cut her off.

"I… yes, Alpha Kian."

A tense silence follows, remaining in place until the bathroom door opens to reveal the she-devil herself. She really is the devil with her sinful temptations. She's everything I don't fucking want in my life. I frown deeply, my eyes skimming over her. The black top with long sleeves and a boat neck hugs her figure tightly and makes her breasts bulge. I can tell the bra she wears s a size or two too small. The pants she has on hug her figure so snugly I could see the tiny triangle between her thighs. I glare at Liana.

"Aren't they too fucking tight?" She looked surprised, turning her head towards Morgana.

"I thought you said she was slim, so I got a small size…" Yeah, slim with fucking tits that are not small.

"Get her to the kitchen. Andrei knows what he needs to do," I growl. Morgana slips the pair of shoes on, brushing her hair that she had tied back over her shoulder.

"I'm ready to go," she states with an air of eloquence. Liana nods and both women walk out.

I give them a head start before jumping out of my window, climbing down onto the ground floor, and walking around to the kitchens. The doors and windows are open; the hustle and bustle of people busy attending to their chores can be heard, as well as the pleasant chatter of the staff, and the mix of several smells filled the air. I mask my aura, staying out of sight as I peer inside.

"So, I've been given this job…" Andrei says, rubbing his head.

I raise an eyebrow. He didn't seem to have the balls to say that to me. Morgana smiles suspiciously sweetly, showing off her fangs. She looks more like a she-devil than a vampire as she looks at Andrei who is slightly shorter than her. Andrei steps back, chuckling nervously.

"Please, don't… I would appreciate it… umm, what is your name, miss?"

Miss?

"Morgana…" she answers softly. I glance at her, not missing the flicker of pain in her eyes before the familiar devilish smirk crossed her lips.

"Nice name… so…"

"What's your name?" She asks, leaning closer to him. Andrei jumps back. I can hear his heart racing from here. She suppresses a giggle. "I told you I won't eat you… I promise," she says with a sly little evil smile on her face. Liana hides a smile as Andrei clears his throat.

"I'm not scared of you… I, uh… I just got alarmed is all. I am Andrei, Omega Andrei, and I am the head of all the functioning of this castle. From dinner to breakfast to the heating to making sure all of our never-ending guests are attended to… the castle is cleaned…"

"So, you're a very important part of this place," she says, now serious. Her words make me glance up at her sharply. For a moment, that arrogant she-devil is gone as she smiles faintly at Andrei. The older man's chest swells with pride at her genuine compliment.

"Ah, of course!"

I frown. I don't get it… the hatred she holds towards our kind… no, more like me… I feel my anger growing and, just as her eyes snap upwards as if she had sensed she is being watched, I quickly move out of sight.

**Alpha, there's some bad news,** Luca's strained voice comes. **There's been another attack on the Black Dawn Pack at the border.** I frown.

Fuck. This is not good.

## MORGANA

The funny little male housekeeper is rather strange. He's really pale for a werewolf, with a head full of ginger curls and pale green eyes. He is slightly on the tubby side, and he isn't so tall. But the best part is he's scared of me. This will be fun…

"Okay, ma'am, Liana, I will take care of Morgana…" he says, gulping visibly. It seems yesterday he was braver, but for some reason, he seems more worried today. Did someone tell him something about me? Oh, well…

"Don't worry. Corbin will be keeping an eye on her," Liana assures him, casting me a look. I just look back at her; she is at least five inches shorter than me. I'm not sure what to make of her yet. I know she doesn't like me, but no werewolf is going to like a vampire just as I don't like them.

"Okay, so, Morgana… what are you good at?" Andrei asks when Liana turns and leaves.

"In the kitchen… not much. Back home, I wasn't allowed to be in the kitchen. It wasn't fitting," I explain quietly. I'm not really anyone anymore…

"Ahh… okay, what were your hobbies back home?" I cast him a faint smile. Although I would love to say weaponry, training, and strategy, I'm not about to tell anyone anything more than what I have already displayed.

"I was just the spoiled daughter of my father," I say simply. I was his favourite child, although being the daughter of a mistress wasn't something the queen or her family had appreciated. I'd had several attempts on my life growing up.

"Okay… well, I will put you to work cutting the vegetables…" he decides after a moment. "You can start with this bucket of onions. Peel them like this…."

He begins demonstrating how to peel an onion. I'm not that clueless… but I guess after the potato fiasco, I can't really blame him.

"Then cut it in half and put it here…" he continues, placing it on a chopping board and dicing it. This would be easy. I'm good with a knife.

"Okay."

He nods and puts the knife down before stepping away. He glances at someone behind me, and I figure it's probably the man sent to watch me. I hope he isn't as stupid as the previous ones.

I pick up the knife and look around the kitchen. Several people are working in the huge kitchen. It was extremely large. There are five cookers along the far wall, each with six rings and all with an oven underneath. Then, there are four large sinks underneath the windows. The worktops around the room are all in use, and there are four islands in the centre where utensils, pots, and pans hang from hooks above them. The drawers and shelves are full of spices and sauces. I can see the large cupboards behind me contain dishes, and two doors lead off to the back, where some young women are bringing frozen goods and fresh produce. Clearly, a storeroom and a cold room. To the left, near the sinks, is a large double door that leads to the garden, one I had felt like I had been watched from earlier.

These wolves don't have muscles or any scars, a clear sign they are just ordinary people. They aren't monsters like the rest… right? I guess, like the children, they are innocent until proven otherwise. As for that woman… Sage… well, I don't like her. I wonder if she is a warrior. I'm sure I can land her on her big behind with one strike!

I frown, peeling the onions swiftly. Is that the Alpha's preference? Curvy women with big butts and boobs? Then, why did he even bring me here? Stupid man. I slam the onion down on the board. *This is his head…* I slice it in half, smiling at it. Now I shall chop him to bits… I giggle as I begin chopping it quickly. Now the next one…

I look up, feeling watched, and see that all eyes are on me. They look a little disturbed and scared. I smiled faintly, making sure to keep my mouth shut so my fangs don't scare them off.

"Are they not correct?" I ask, looking at the two onions I had already cut.

"Ah… no, they are perfect… you are fast with a knife. I thought you had never been in a kitchen before."

"Oh, I haven't… but I'm good with a knife. I was just imagining that these onions were someone I really want to dice up," I reply sweetly. He visibly gulps, his hands trembling on the pile of colanders he's holding. "Don't worry. It isn't you."

He jumps, dropping the pile; I tilt my head. I didn't even say anything scary… oh well. Back to cutting baby Alpha's head…

Much later, I finish the onions and am given three times the amount of peeled potatoes, which are to be cut into chunky fries for dinner. My mouth is actually watering. I wonder if they'd give me any. Back home, we would usually have more posh food here and there as it wasn't really necessary to eat, but the pleasant aroma that now fills the kitchen has my stomach rumbling and, with it, the reminder that I need more blood.

The staff that had been working in fear and silence to begin with are now back to what I assume is their usual hustle and bustle, chatting and working once they realised I'd mind my own business and do what I was given. I mean, if I wanted, with the weapon in hand, I probably could have killed them. I'm sure the Alpha knew that, but he still let me work here. Are the lives of the low-rank wolves not important to him? Well, it was probably the case! I mean, he had been pushing an innocent child in my face to feed off of!

"Morgana…" Andrei starts, walking over to me with a glass of what smells like carrot juice. "Here… I know you must be hungry, but we can't give you blood. I mean, we don't have blood…" He places one hand on his neck, and I smile, amused.

"Don't worry, this will do," I said, taking the juice. "Thank you." He looks surprised at that. I sip the juice; it's nice and cold and, to my surprise, very tasty. "Oh, this is delicious," I exclaim.

"You haven't had carrot juice?" He asks curiously.

"We don't really get access to much. As vampires, our produce is kept for the humans who reside in our kingdom and those species who need it," I explain, sipping the juice. Andrei frowns and nods.

"I see… you need to keep the humans fed to have blood, I presume."

"Yeah, I guess so… but they are still our people, even if we do need them. We usually have a system where humans are asked to give blood. It's in place of what one would call taxes. Once you come to an age, you pay by blood and only the elderly, pregnant women, and children are exempt."

"You don't kill your people?" He asks, confused. I raise an eyebrow.

"Why would we kill them? Don't listen to all the rumours your kind spread," I state, frowning.

"Ah, of course, sorry…"

"No need… I mean, apart from your Alpha being a ruthless beast, you don't seem too bad." I hear a growl and turn to look at the man who has been standing there watching me. "Oh, don't growl at me! He is ruthless,"

I snap, my anger flaring. He tenses as the staff around us start shaking. "If you have a complaint, then you can tell your Alpha. I'm not afraid of him."

I turn back to my work, frowning deeply as everything stills once more. I see Andrei looking at him and know he's probably using their mind link. It's a strange thing, knowing that you can enter anyone's mind... but I'm sure it's also very efficient, especially for coordinating an attack.

Time passes, and I'm given more onions to peel for tomorrow. The rest rush to serve dinner, and, by now, my hands are aching, and my fingertips are raw red. Despite being good with weapons, this is something different.

"Morgana, you have done a lot. Here, you can stop and eat now," he says, holding up a large plate full of chunky hot fries, scrambled eggs, and mushy peas. I take it slowly, feeling confused. After the rough treatment by their Alpha, I am surprised that they're being so kind. I give him a small smile.

"Thank you."

"Not at all, you have worked well," he says, giving me his first relaxed smile. "You are not a bad person." I roll my eyes.

"I think my being a vampire is enough to be hated," I say softly, going over to the sink. I wash my hands with some soap before I pick up the plate again. I am rather excited.

He looks towards the large table that stands towards the doors that lead to the hall, where most of the other Omegas are eating and chatting, hesitating. I smile gently, knowing he doesn't want to say anything, but I also know those Omegas wouldn't want me there.

"Is it okay to eat on the step that leads outside?" I ask. He looks surprised and relieved as he nods.

"Of course!"

I take my plate and walk away, hearing a whispered 'Thank God' from one of the women. I know they had been talking about me throughout the day, but through their mind link, not that it bothers me. I was often the subject of talks back home, so there is nothing new there. For a vampire, I am too energetic and, as Azrael would put it, 'unruly.'

I sit down on the stone step, placing the plate in my lap and gazing up at the starry sky. The worst thing about being away from home is missing my friends, although I only had a rare few, my uncle and the graves of my parents.

From the corner of my eye, I see the man, Corbin, take a seat at the table. His eyes are fixed on me, although he is eating. I turn back to the stars; he can do what he wants. I'm not going to run until I have a foolproof plan. I would need supplies, including a map of the place...

# PROTECTING THE WEAK

MORGANA

THE STARS TWINKLE, AND I smile sadly, suddenly feeling rather alone. One day… I will return home…

I pick up my fork and begin eating slowly, only glancing up when Andrei places a hot mug of something chocolatey next to me. Oh, it smells divine, and it looks almost as good as baby Alpha's skin. I frown. Stupid man…

My cheeks burn when I remember what I had seen earlier. He really is extremely well-endowed… lucky women, I guess, or it could be painful. I shake my head, pushing the thoughts out. Urgh, I cannot believe that I had gotten turned on by drinking his blood…

I pick up the mug, taking a sip. It's chocolatey and milky; I hadn't ever had something so tasty before! I wrap my hands around the warm mug and drink it down, not bothered that it is still rather hot. I finish half of it, placing it down, when I hear some whispered scuffles coming from somewhere nearby. I frown, drowning out the people behind me and honing in on the sounds.

"…it. You need to behave and comply, bitch!" A male voice hisses in a low growl.

I stand up silently, placing my plate down. I glance at the guard over my shoulder, who seems to have relaxed. *Oh, how easily they get distracted.*

I slip outside and follow the sounds until I come to a small cove near the back, where a pile of bins sit along one side, only to see a man pinning one of the kitchen girls I saw earlier up against the wall, his large hand groping her breast. Her eyes are wide and tear-filled. Her heart thumps as the man makes quick work of unbuttoning her pants. My anger flares inside of me. No matter if she's an Omega, no one should have sex with anyone unless they're willing.

She spots me first, her eyes widening in fear. In a flash, I am behind the man, who is too busy unbuckling his own pants to notice, and rip him off her, throwing him to the ground.

"No one touches a woman without her consent," I hiss.

Leaning down, I punch him across the face. He knocks my hand aside, growling lowly and jumping to his feet, but I blast him back. He hits the bins, causing a loud crash, and crumbles to the ground.

"Y-you shouldn't have! He's a warrior… I'm just- I'll get into trouble."

She's trembling. I pity her as I look at her with a frown. She didn't want him to touch her, yet she still fears for her life for the trouble caused.

"Leave. I'll handle it," I promise. She is about to protest, but the man is up again, his claws out. She turns and runs off just as he lunges at me.

"You deserve to die," I say coldly.

I hated men like him. I duck before twisting out of his way and jumping on his back. I grab his head just as his claws dig into my arms. Before he can do more damage, I snap his head, and he crumples to the floor.

"Stop!" The man who had been meant to be guarding me growls. He yanks me off the man roughly, although I know he is still very much alive.

"He's alive," I snap, ripping free from his hold.

"Delta Corbin…" Andrei looks at the man on the floor and then at me in fear.

"You tried to run…" Corbin growls.

"I didn't, actually," I shoot back.

"Why else would you attack him then?" He thunders. I roll my eyes,

"Because his ugly face annoyed me," I retort, folding my arms.

"The king can deal with you himself," he mutters, yanking me roughly past Andrei. He looks at me with concern clear in his eyes, but I simply give him a small smile.

"Thank you for the delicious drink, whatever it was."

"Hot chocolate," he says just before I was yanked around the corner.

"You were given a chance, and you blew it," Corbin hisses as he pulls me painfully around half the house and to another entrance to the mansion. This one is around the side, and the garden is empty. I frown. Isn't this the area where I tried jumping from? Two guards let us in, and I am pulled inside roughly.

"Do you beasts have a habit of man-handling women?" I snap. He ignores me, pulling me along.

"Alpha!" He calls, and I realise we are in the hall that I had been in earlier. *And here we go…*

KIAN

The moment Luca had mind-linked, I made my way to my office to see what was happening. Reuban had already left this morning, and I was sure by nightfall, they would be around that area and would hear what's going on. But to make sure he knew, I had sent someone else to catch up with them with the latest development.

Corbin had also kept me updated with the little blood rose's antics, from her strange amusement in cutting vegetables to her not trying anything funny. I hate how even though I was trying to keep busy, even when I was busy heading a training session and had a short discussion with Kai, she was still on my mind… consuming my thoughts like a sweet poison.

Everything had been going well. I just finished off a pile of paperwork, and I thought the day would go without a fucking hitch. That was until Corbin linked me that she had tried to escape and attacked Alistair, a guard. I just reach the bottom of the stairs when he enters, pulling her in. Her arms are covered in blood, and I know it's hers.

"Let go of her," I growl, hating the way he was dragging her. He obliges, and I look at him coldly. "Leave."

"Yes, Alpha." He bows his head to me before I mind-link the guards to allow no one else in. Morgana glares at his back as she touches her arm gingerly.

I cross my arms, looking at her coldly. Even with the smell of cooking and blood surrounding her, her scent still seeps through. Rage festers in me, but I'm not sure if it's because she tried to run away or because someone else had touched what's mine. No one had permission to hurt her but me. She now glares at me.

"I wasn't running away," she states.

Something tells me she isn't lying. I frown as I walk over to her. Grabbing her shirt from the middle, I tear it open, making her gasp. She crosses her arms over her boobs that are spilling out of her tight bra, making my dick twitch. Fuck, she's tempting. I grab her arm, looking at the claw marks that run up her forearms, anger surging inside of me.

**Throw Alistair in the fucking cells… I will deal with him tomorrow,** I hiss through the link to Gerald. How many fucking idiots do I need to deal with? How dare he hurt her…

"You are all the same!" She struggles to free herself, but I refuse to let her go.

"Will it heal?" I ask her. She has her other bloody arm covering herself, but I don't think she realises her slender arm is doing nothing to keep her lush curves from me.

"Yes," she snaps, yanking away from my hold and covering herself. "How dare you rip my clothes!"

"You had the audacity to attack one of my men," I remind her. Grabbing her elbow, I pull her up the stairs. "Why did you do it?"

She doesn't reply, but her heartbeat quickens. I kick open my bedroom door and pull her in, tossing her on the bed. I hate being disobeyed. Her breasts bounce, and my gaze falls to them, the outline of her nipple clear through the lace. She grabs a pillow, hugging it to her chest as she glares up at me.

"Don't look at me!"

"You're mine, and I can if I want to," I growl.

"What can I say about your men when you yourself are just as bad!" She spits.

I frown. What did she even mean by that? If she wasn't already injured, I would have taught her a fucking lesson.

I walk to my wardrobe, open the drawer that is now full of clothes and other items for her, and grab a top before taking the first aid box from my side. I walk to the bed, and she snatches the top, pulling it on and giving me a fleeting glimpse of her gorgeous milky white breasts and her smooth, taught stomach. She grabs the box from me and gives me a dirty look.

"I hope I don't get some sort of disease from being clawed by an animal." She's glaring again.

I raise an eyebrow, crouching down before her and looking her square in the eye. Tangling my hand in her hair, I yank her towards me.

"What have I told you about disrespect?" I ask icily.

"Well, I'm afraid I have not learned manners," she shoots back.

Fucking lie. I know how she is with Andrei... but what confuses me is why she hasn't been difficult with him. In fact, when I asked how she was, he said she was doing very well.

Our eyes meet, and I realise that her eyes had changed colour. After drinking blood, they were a lot darker, but now they are lighter. She blinks, her thick lashes caressing her cheeks lightly before she looks back into my eyes. I really had never seen a more beautiful woman in my life, and I had seen many.

"So... care to share why you attacked him?" I ask again, letting go of her hair that I had half pulled out of her plait.

She frowns. I give her a moment, taking the box from her and flipping it open. She sure heals slower than us. I pull my shirt off, wiping the blood away from her arms. She's staring at me intensely, but I ignore her, using a wipe to cleanse her arms before taking some gauze and lifting one of her delicate wrists. It's tiny... the opposite of mine in every way. Like the rest of her, her skin is pale and smooth, like a china doll. But I know she isn't as fragile as she looked. I wrap her other arm in gauze, frowning. What am I even doing? I don't attend to people's injuries.

**Taking care of our beautiful mate,** Thanatos adds very unhelpfully.

**I don't care for her,** I shoot back. He's worse than a fucking pet. One meeting with Morgana, and he wants to mate and mark her right there.

"I won't keep repeating myself," I say dangerously, tying the end of the bandage and looking into her eyes. She frowns but still refuses to speak. "Fine. If you won't fucking speak, then you won't get blood for the night."

She closes her eyes and simply nods. I yank her up from the bed roughly, and she hits my chest. My hand sneaks around her waist, but she simply pulls away.

"You will be punished for disobeying me."

Reaching beneath the bed, I pull out the chain that had been attached to the cuffs and walk over to her. I yank her arms above her head, wrapping the chains around her. I pull her to the window and, reaching up, wrap the chain around the curtain pole. She could probably pull free with ease, but I don't care if she does. I only want a fucking answer.

It's strange... she doesn't even argue. She simply frowns, her chest heaving in anger. But even then, she refuses to submit. My eyes flicker to her wrists that I had tied above her head, twisted uncomfortably, and although she looked rather sexy all tied up... my stomach churns as I force myself to look away. Thanatos's growl fills my head, but I refuse to listen to him.

**Don't hurt mate!** He growls. Whenever his emotions get intense, his sentences seem to lack intellect.

"You will remain like that until dawn."

She presses her lips together but doesn't reply, looking away. Fine. If she wants to be fucking stubborn, then she will pay for it. I turn the light off and get into bed. She's silent, and so am I. The only sound in the room is our beating hearts. I can't sleep, not when she's tied in a standing position, but I refuse to let her down. Each passing moment in her presence is blurring the lines of limits within me. I steady my breathing, pretending to sleep, but I can't. I hear her sigh softly, and I wonder how much time has passed. Would she try anything?

She begins humming a song ever so quietly, and that night at the lake returns to me...

*The scent had drawn me here, and I cross into the Sanguine Empire, but I can't stop myself... not when it is so intoxicating. I know it isn't a werewolf's scent, but still, I follow it until I finally find it. A woman's laughter and the sounds of a song being sung make my heart race.*

*That's when I see her, the woman in the lake. Her long black hair is splayed in the water behind her, and she's swimming around, her laughter like a tinkle in the wind. My heart is pounding as my eyes drink her up. She's ethereal... a goddess gracing the earth.*

*I can't stop myself from approaching her, like a sea siren luring me to her...*

What if I didn't follow the scent that night? Could I have protected myself from all of this? I doubt it... that scent would have consumed my mind still.

Her breathing becomes heavy, and I open my eyes. She seems to have fallen asleep, leaning against the wall behind her. My stomach twists as I watch her. She had been working all day, and, once again, I didn't give her any blood...

I get out of bed silently and walk over to her. I wrap my arm around her waist gently, my fingers brushing her stomach through the thin fabric of her top, and she gasps, her eyes fluttering open.

"Don't say a word, or I might change my mind," I whisper dangerously.

She looks back at me, confusion in those gorgeous eyes of hers, and with my other hand, I reach up and untie her. The chain falls to the floor with a clang, and I pull her towards the bed. Through her sleepy eyes, I know she wants to ask, but I have no answers, praying she didn't speak. I push her gently onto the bed.

"Sleep," I command coldly before walking around to the other side and lying down on the bed once again. Her heart hammers as she looks at me, but she doesn't speak, curling up and wrapping her arms around herself, closing her eyes once more.

I watch her fall asleep again. Reaching over, I caress her cool cheek. Why does she have to be a vampire? If she had been one of my own…

**Would you have accepted her with that sassy personality?** Thanatos asks.

I don't reply, turning my back on her. I know the answer, but I wouldn't admit it. Not now. Not ever.

# AN APOLOGY

KIAN

THE FOLLOWING DAY, I leave before she even wakes up. Posting one of the Omega girls in the room, I tell her to tell Oliver, who is standing right outside the door, to take her to the kitchens to work if she wakes up. She can spend the day without blood. She deserves the punishment. I don't know why I am avoiding her, but last night I wasn't able to sleep. Turning towards her, I had just watched her.

She moves a lot in her sleep, not something one would expect from a vampire. The stories are that they are stoic things who sleep as if they are dead. But this one turns from her side to her back, then onto her stomach, then onto her side, which gave me the perfect view of her breasts. The moonlight had shone through a crack in the curtains, illuminating her. She really is the daughter of the night, and it is at night that she looks even more breathtaking. She had turned onto her stomach only to roll onto her back again. The cycle never stopped. She talks in her sleep, too, although it made no sense. I guess she really had too much energy during her slumber…

But I hadn't been able to sort myself out. It was weird; I had sacrificed my sleep to simply watch her. I forgot everything until morning came, and reality settled in once again. She is my slave, nothing more. I will reject her and cut this stupid bond, and if she refuses to accept my rejection, then I will kill her.

**You won't,** Thanatos says quietly.

**I will,** I reply coldly, shutting him out.

**Keep shutting me off, Kian, and there may come a day I'll cut you off,** he growls before I put my wall up. That ruined my mood for the entire fucking morning.

Way after lunch, I am doing some paperwork in my office. I had asked Andrei to get someone to bring me my lunch upstairs. I had heard from him that Morgana had gotten to work without a word. I hate that she doesn't answer when I ask her to. A light knock on the door makes me growl.

"What is it?" I snap.

"A-Alpha… lunch," a young woman's voice answers. I clench my jaw, trying to reign in my irritation.

"Enter," I growl.

I frown when I realise she barely looks seventeen at most… if she had been older, maybe I could have gotten some pent-up emotion taken care of. Women don't really say no when it comes to me, but just in case they agree out of fear, I usually get Luca to arrange someone for me. Morgana flashes in my head, and I exhale sharply. Since she arrived, my sex life was fucking suffering.

The girl before me places the tray down, shaking. I'm sure I had seen her before several times, and I'm sure she hadn't been shaking then.

"Stop it," I snap, making her flinch.

"A-Alpha…" she whispers, brushing a strand of her brown hair off her face. "C-can I have a moment of your time?" I frown. What does she want? Doesn't Liana handle this sort of thing or Sage?

"You can talk to Sage or Liana."

"It-it's to do with M-Morgana," she whimpers. The fear is rolling off her, and I look at her coldly.

"Then stop shaking with fucking fear. What is it?"

"Last night, she only attacked the-the guard because of… me," she ends in a hushed whisper, her heart racing disturbingly fast. My anger dissipates, and I sit back.

"Meaning?" I asked.

"That g-guard… he… he tried to force himself onto me… and I didn't want to," she whispers in fear. My stomach twists, trying to comprehend what she's saying. Did Morgana really do that? I doubt it… why would she protect a she-wolf?

**Because our mate is a Luna.**

"You don't need to try to defend her just because she pretended to be your friend. She's a sly one," I growl, ignoring Thanatos.

**We both know this Omega can't even speak because of fear. I doubt she'd try to protect our mate,** Thanatos grumbles.

"Did she scare you to talk to me?" I ask sharply. She looks confused.

"No, Alpha… last night I told her not to tell anyone, and she told me to leave before anyone appeared," she explains hesitantly. My heart races as I realise my mate had protected one of my pack members from someone who should be protecting them… and I had instead punished her…

"Why did you decide to tell me?" I ask coldly. She pales, looking down at her hands.

"I… she looks ill… she's hungry, and she almost fainted earlier… I don't want her to be starved be-because of me," she says, fear clear in her voice.

"Leave," I order coldly.

She looks up, and I can see from the corner of my eyes that she is near tears. She struggles to speak, and, finally giving up, she lowers her head before she flees. I look at the plate of food before me and push it back. How could I fucking eat if I had starved her for no reason? If only she hadn't been so fucking stupid.

Alistair… I think I have a visit to make.

"Leave him there. If he makes it, he makes it. If he doesn't, shame," I say coldly, stepping out of the cell. Not only did he try to hurt one of the women in our care, but he also hurt my mate.

**A mate you don't accept,** Thanatos adds moodily.

**Fuck off.**

**I live here!** He growls. **You hurt our mate, too!**

I know I did. The guilt is still there, making a noticeable place inside of me. Fuck this.

A while later, I had just showered. I don't bother eating, knowing that she didn't get blood... but I refuse to admit that I was in the wrong. If she had just told me the truth...

"Kian..."

I turn to see Kai walking towards me. Of the three of us, he was most like our mother in terms of personality and looks. Dad had actually paid little attention to him once Mom died, as he reminded him of her a lot. I had taken it upon myself to be there for him, although I had been only ten when Mom passed away, and he had been eight.

"Kai."

He falls in step with me as we both walk towards the training fields. Even yesterday, he found me, making small talk and saying he was glad to be back. I know he wants to ask me something but hasn't been able to muster the courage. Back then, he wanted to go with Cain, and I had told him the choice was his... even if he had only been seventeen.

"I was wondering if there's anything I could do... like, in the pack. Can I join the warriors or..." I look at him. His hazel eyes, that are a shade darker than mine, are full of hesitance.

"Kai. You are a part of this pack. You never denounced the pack, nor did the pack ever officially split. It was one pack that settled in two places. This is still your home. If you want something, speak like a fucking man - ask for it. Even then, if you aren't given it, then fight for it and take it willingly. I am your brother, regardless of the fact that we have not spent the last five years together," I reply coldly. He looks away. I won't lie, it had fucking hurt when he had turned his back on me, too. He was the only family I had left that I cared about...

"I'm sorry," he whispered. Guilt laced his words.

"Don't be, I'm not."

It's unspoken, but we know what's running through the other's mind. He takes a deep breath and looks at me with confidence and determination.

"I want to join the warriors. I want to be part of the king's pack. I want to make up for the wrong decision I made years ago," he says firmly, determination blazing in his eyes. I smirk slightly.

"Spoken like a true Araqiel," I say arrogantly. The tension between us lightens slightly.

"I want to be man enough that I can at least apologise for my mistake," he says with a small chuckle as we glance out at the fields where two sets of groups are training.

I frown, looking up at the blazing sun. Man enough to admit my mistake…. I clench my jaw. I guess it's time to fucking do the same.

"Well, I'll tell Gerald to fit you in. He'll assess you and set you accordingly. The rest who came with you will also need to do their initial inspection before they can be assigned anywhere. I will let him know. You can go join in for now."

"Now?" He asks, surprised.

"Yeah, why put off things you can do fucking right away?"

He smirks, "True!" He jogs off, and I fill Gerald in quickly before turning and heading back inside. Man enough to admit my fucking mistake…

**Yeah, you hurt our mate.**

**Fuck off.** Didn't we already have this conversation?

I head to the kitchens, masking my aura and scent as I peer through one of the open windows. There she is, dicing away at some carrots, dressed in a white cotton top that shows off the outline of her bra, paired with flared mint pants. Her hair is open and cascades over her shoulder. She looks as gorgeous as ever, but her heaving chest and her pale skin tell me she needs blood. I was depriving her… for what? For doing the right fucking thing?

**Andrei, send Morgana out through the back, but don't mention me,** I order, moving away from the window.

**Yes, Alpha!**

"Morgana…"

"Hmm?" Comes her soft reply. A flare of jealousy rushes through me. I only hear her voice full of hate and anger…

"Can you go place these baskets outside?"

"Where about?" She asks.

"Just outside near the steps. The sun is out, and they will dry."

"Okay…" She sounds hesitant, and it's then I realise the sun is dazzling brightly today. Fuck, I didn't think of that. She would feel even weaker out in the sun.

I hear her footsteps until she steps out, holding four large plastic buckets. She looks up at the sky before separating the boxes and placing them upside down in a line. I watch her, trying not to stare at her ass as she bends down to place the final one down. Damn…

Her hair shines, and I realise her black locks have a hint of blue in them. She stands up, placing a hand on her head as she makes to go back up the stone steps into the kitchens when I step forward, grabbing hold of her wrist.

"Morgana."

Her head turns sharply towards me, those gorgeous eyes widening as she stares down at me in complete surprise. Fuck, I just called her name... and it sounded so fucking perfect.

MORGANA

My heart thuds as I stare down at him.

Morgana.

The way my name sounds on his tongue... my stomach knots, and my core throbs just at that. How can someone I hate so much have this effect on me? I'm already weak, and being in the blazing sun is only making matters worse. Maybe the heat and light are getting to me.

"I know you want to torture me, but, really, unless you want me to collapse due to the sun, then let me go," I say coldly. A frown creases those gorgeous thick brows of his. He doesn't say anything, simply turning and pulling me down the steps. "Can you stop pulling me? What do you want?" I glare at his back, trying not to notice the way his sky-blue top stretches over his muscles...

He stops suddenly, and I almost stumble before he pulls me into an alcove. The shade instantly takes away the weight of the sun that was pushing down upon me. I feel relieved, taking a deep breath as I lean against the cool stone. His entire frame is blocking the sun out, and he finally lets go of my wrist, instead placing his hand on the wall beside my head.

"Why didn't you tell me the truth last night?" His question takes me by surprise. I just cross my arms, trying to put some distance between us, my gaze flickering to his plump lips. I look away, refusing to answer. "That Omega told me what happened today. Why did you cover for her?" He asks coldly. I look up at him sharply. Had she told him, or is this a trick?

"I have no idea what you mean. I am a cruel bloodsucker. I don't have compassion," I counter, glaring at him. For once, he doesn't seem phased.

"Oh, yeah? Then why did that girl lie? Shall I punish her for that?" My heart thuds, but still, I worry. "Alistair also admitted to it," he adds quietly.

Oh…

"She was scared, so I told her to leave," I say icily.

"Why care for her? She's just a beast, correct?" He leans closer, and I wonder, does he not know what personal space is? His deep, alluring scent always messes with me, and the urge to taste his blood is filling my head.

"She isn't one. Unlike you and your warriors, she is just a simple young woman living her life," I say, placing my hands on his chest and trying to push him back, only for him to step closer.

"Who knew the Vampire Princess had a heart?" He asks coldly.

I am no longer a princess. A familiar sting tugs at my chest, but I ignore it.

"You don't know a lot about me, Alpha, but I do have a heart, one that influences my every decision. I care with passion, I love with passion, and I hate with that same passion. I won't let an innocent person suffer, regardless of who they are. I am not a monster like you."

His eyes are unreadable, but I don't feel any anger from him. His other hand reaches up, but rather than clamping around my throat as he seems to love to do, he runs his fingers through my hair, surprising me. My heart thuds as I tense, but despite that, my stomach is a mess of butterflies. He steps even closer, his feet now on either side of mine. I press my back against the wall behind me, my hands squeezed between our chests. I try not to pay attention to his hard, firm body beneath my fingertips.

"So much hate doesn't suit you, my little she-devil," he says quietly. My cheeks flush. What is he doing? His voice confuses me. Why is he being so… so…

My eyes flutter shut when his knuckles brush my neck, leaving a trail of sparks in his wake. His hot, minty breath fans my face, and I know if I open my eyes, I'll be lost in those hazel orbs of his.

"This time… I was wrong… and for that, I admit it. Drink," he murmurs sexily.

My eyes snap open, my heart thudding as his fingers lace into my hair. Tugging me closer, his nose brushes mine, and for a moment, I wonder how he'd taste, and I don't mean his blood…

*Focus, Morgana.*

A hint of a smirk curls the corner of his mouth before he arches his neck to me. To my kind, that is an act of submission. Does he not realise that? He is willingly allowing me to drink from him. I could even try to rip him to pieces. Maybe when I am stronger.

I reach up, wrapping my hand around the nape of his neck and ignoring the sun's heat on my fingers. His body presses against mine as I reach up, extracting my fangs. I bite into his neck, feeling him tense. I close my eyes, a soft moan escaping my lips as I let the deep, rich liquid trickle down my throat. With each suck, my energy returns, so I suck harder, drinking faster, my fangs still sunk into his neck. My breath hitches when I feel him throb against me, his arms wrapping around me tightly, crushing me into him. Fuck...

My core clenches, and I wish I was a little taller so his manhood could press against the ache that only he could ignite within me. The very realisation makes my heart rate increase. I don't get it, this hatred, this attraction... I can't deny either. His hand runs over my back, and I remove my hand from his chest, settling it on his arm, not wanting anything between us.

Is it really just an infatuation? Why does his body seem to react so well to me? Even when he was kissing Sage, his body was not crushed against hers like this.

Sage.

Alpha Kian Araqiel.

Reality hits me in the face, and I realise I've had enough. I move back, licking up the blood, not missing the way his breath hitches. *Let go of me.*

He takes a moment, seeming to come out of the haze. I know drinking one's blood is pleasurable for both parties, but I had never felt so turned on before, and never had I been in such compromising positions. If I did drink blood from the body, it would usually be from behind. His strong arms are still wrapped around me, looking down at me, our faces inches apart. His gaze flickers to my lips before he looks sharply into my eyes.

"I apologise for last night," he whispers, making my eyes fly open in shock. A small smile crosses my lips after a moment, and I raise an eyebrow.

"Is the Alpha actually admitting he made a mistake?" I can't help but comment. His eyes narrow, and I'm ready for him to lash out, but he only exhales and clenches his jaw.

"I'm still a person. I can make mistakes just like anyone else," he says coldly. "Or do you think you're perfect and have never made any?"

Are we actually having a conversation? I'm very aware of our bodies pressed together, moulded together, as if we were created to be one, something that is not even possible.

"Perfect? Far from it, but in your eyes, I'm not a person but a devil, right?" I raise an eyebrow; it's taking me my all not to run my hand over the plains and curves of every muscle in his arm.

"She-devil. There's a difference,"

"Oh? Will the baby Alpha care to explain what the difference is?" I ask airily.

A small smirk crosses his lips and, for the first time since I saw him, I see a flicker of amusement on his handsome face. He looks a thousand times hotter if that's even possible. My stomach flutters as he tilts his head slightly.

"Since you're ever the smart one, I'll let you figure it out, sunshine," he mocks.

"Well, you always act like the smart one. Why don't you fill me in?" I shoot back lightly.

"All in good time…" His smirk fades as our eyes meet, dark red against dreamy hazel…

"Who says you have time, Alpha?"

"You're mine. I assure you, we have time."

Neither of us breaks eye contact. His gaze dips to my lips, and I lick them, swallowing hard. My mind is a storm. What are we doing? He leans down, closing the gap between us, but before those plump lips of his can touch mine, I turn my head away. His lips graze my jaw, leaving a tingle in its wake and my heart beating louder than a thousand drums.

I feel him tense. Reality hits us both, and he lets go of me, stepping back. I look up at him, the sun shining down on him. He really does look like a perfect god…

But one moment doesn't fix anything. I don't know why he distracts me, but at the end of the day, he is still the man who was probably behind my father's death, the same man who had brought me here as a slave, the same man who kept me tied and thrown into a cell.

No words are spoken as we simply stare into each other's eyes for a moment before he turns away and walks off without uttering a word. I close my eyes, leaning back against the wall. I stay there for a few minutes, trying to regain my senses.

"What are you to him?"

I look up sharply to see the man from the other day. From what I had gathered that day in my pained state, he is the king's elder brother, Cain. My heart thunders. I hadn't even sensed him approaching.

"Just a slave," I say smoothly. I don't like this man... there's something off with him.

"One he treats incredibly well..." he says, his eyes trailing over my body, so much so that I almost recoiled in disgust.

"Well, it's a shame you can't learn from him," I shoot back, turning to walk off.

"Kian isn't one to keep slaves. There must be something about you that makes him want to keep you."

"Well, I hate him," I state coldly, relieved when I see the kitchen stairs. To my relief, he stops before he comes into view.

"I know you're here against your will, and I can help you, Morgana Araton, Princess of the Sanguine Empire. Let's join hands, and I give you my word that I can help you get home." His words are low, yet I can hear the power in them. I glance back at him, and he simply smiles. "Think about it."

I don't say anything, hurrying towards the kitchen entrance. His words echo in my head. A chance at freedom... but what would the cost be?

# A Decision

KIAN

*I* RUN MY HAND THROUGH my hair, knowing I'm only fucking it up, but I have no idea what overcame me earlier. The urge to kiss her... I pace my main office, although I had meant to be planning for the upcoming summit.

Morgana... fuck, I hate it.

**Did you hate it? Or are you just being a dick because she refused you because you have an ego that's way too big?** Thanatos's snide fuck of a voice asks.

**Have I ever told you that I fucking can't stand you at times?** I shoot back.

**Yeah, plenty of times, but too bad for you because I'm just a part of you, so just the way you can't stand me - I'm sure many people can't stand you,** he tosses back at me smugly. Fucking asshole... **I think our mate is - besides being smart, beautiful and sexy - very intelligent and compassionate,** he adds.

**Intelligent? She fucking jumped from a window without even thinking of the fucking consequences. There's nothing smart about that. She fucking stood up to you when you know the chances are high that she could have been killed.**

**Well, maybe she is a little... brash and reckless, but she is smart and compassionate,** he persists. I snort. Yeah, fucking smart at being a sassy little she-devil... an incredibly sexy one...

The plan was one night… but would it be enough?

No.

I drop onto my chair, sighing. There is so much crap with these attacks, the upcoming summit, Cain… the guards who had kept an eye on him said he had slipped away today for a short while. I can't really post more guards to keep an eye on him, as I can't have him knowing. Besides, if he is up to something, I want them to catch him out. It might be ideal to put my Deltas to watch him… but that would mean leaving Morgana unguarded…

**Are you worried she'll run or that something might happen to her?** Thanatos remarks.

*Both.* I don't even need to reply. He fucking knows that. I take a deep breath; I think I need a fucking run.

An hour later, I'm on my way back. My body is covered in a layer of sweat, and my pants sit low on my hips. Someone passes me a cold bottle of water, and I gulp it down before tossing it back. I'm almost at the castle when I get stopped.

"Kian," Sage's voice calls, making me look up.

I look at her. The sun is shining down on her. Despite the fact that I had always thought she was beautiful, I mean, she still is, but there's none of that interest in looking her over or wanting to be around her that I had once had…

"What is it?" I ask coldly.

"The summit… are we making that announcement?" She asks, closing the gap between us. Her hand touches my abs as her face tilts up to mine with a pout on her face that just isn't fucking natural… I prefer Morgana's height. It's ideal not to have to bend down to kiss her.

**Not that you ever had a problem with the height difference before,** Thanatos remarks.

I block him off, thinking of what she had just said. The announcement… the unspoken discussion that everyone wanted to see a fucking queen by my side. I look into Sage's blue eyes.

"Let's discuss this later."

I'm about to walk off when she grabs my arm. My eyes flash, and I turn my gold glare at her. She lets go instantly.

"Sorry… but, Kian, we can't keep putting it off," she says, her hand now going to my shoulder and her breasts brushing against my arm. I head inside, not wanting anyone to hear us.

"They just want to see a Luna by your side. I'm already doing that job, it's just a formality. Nothing will change between us. We're friends, too," she says the moment the door to my quarter of the castle shuts behind us. Her arms snake around my neck, and I frown, looking down at her.

It's true… she was already doing the job of a Luna. Announcing her as my official fiancée would get a lot of people off my back, not to mention satiate Cain's curiosity towards Morgana. Walls have ears, and he's been asking around about her… I tilt my head, looking down at her.

"You're correct." I frown. She looks surprised before smiling in relief.

"Perfect. It's the best thing to do," she says softly, placing a kiss on my chest. Morgana flashes through my head, and I pull out of her hold. "There's something else that's worrying me, Kian… what the vampire did to one of our men… maybe you need to lower the dose of blood you are giving her. It's clear she's strong. God knows who else she may hurt," Sage says. Anger flares inside of me, and I growl menacingly.

"What I give to her or don't is none of your fucking concern, Sage."

"Baby… I get that, relax. I love you, Kian… and it hurts to see that you have an interest in this woman…"

"So it wasn't fucking concern about our people, but jealousy?" I ask coldly. She looks hurt but simply sighs softly, kissing my shoulder.

"It's been days, and you haven't even come to me…" she whispers, locking her arms around me tightly. I frown deeply.

"Don't give her too much importance. She's nothing," I say, despite how bitter those fucking words are on my lips.

"Is she? No other woman has gone to your room, Kian… I know you have other women, but none in your room. It's been so long, and you haven't even called me here," she complains, running her hands up my waist.

"She is nothing to me," I repeat firmly.

**Who are you convincing, her or yourself?** Thanatos's quiet voice asks before I slam the walls back up. If they want fucking proof…

"She really is no one to me, Sage. You will be my Luna. Worry more about the well-being of our people. As for the guard… he tried to fucking assault an Omega. Morgana only protected her. I've fucking killed him... but I wish I had asked him a few questions before I let my anger take over... it's been at the back of my fucking mind. I wonder if he hurt others..."

She looks shocked at that, but I'm too lost in thought. I need to do a thorough sweep and let every fucking man under my reign know that I will not tolerate anything of the sort...

"Are you sure? I don't think vampires -"

My eyes flash, and I turn back towards her, reaching out. I grip her chin tightly, my anger seeping through me like poison, ready to take over completely.

"Are you saying I'm lying? Or that I fucking don't know what happened?" I hiss.

"No, Kian, never. I'm just worried that she's brainwashing -" she begins breathlessly.

"Get out," I hiss.

"Kian, please," she whimpers.

*"Out!"* I thunder. She flinches at my tone. My alpha command is absolute, and she lowers her head in submission, placing her hand tenderly on my chest for a second before she turns and leaves.

I hate people telling me what to do or acting like I don't fucking know shit. I do what the fuck I want to do. I turn around, slamming my fist into the table that stands near me, splintering it into pieces.

**She never used to piss you off... why so defensive, Kian?** Thanatos asks quietly.

I don't want to answer that. The control of my emotions is slipping, and I hate losing in anything. One vampire woman is not going to step into my life and destroy the person I am. I am the ultimate fucking Alpha, one who had to always be in control. No matter what.

Night falls, and I tell everyone I don't want to be disturbed, deciding to do some work in the privacy and silence of my own place. I keep glancing at the time, and I know I'm waiting for Morgana to return home. After what happened earlier, I don't even want to face her... yet at the same time, I want to see her.

When my Delta signals they are coming and that her day had gone fine and she had behaved, I feel satisfied. At least she isn't causing me trouble... women...

**Yeah, it's just women who are so fucking annoying. I mean, you're not high maintenance at all...** Thanatos adds sarcastically. What the fuck did I ever do to get a fucking dipshit with a mouth on him as a wolf? **Karma, you get what you are. Now stop fucking being a grump, grab our mate, and let's put Mini-Kian to use,** he orders.

I hate it when he refers to my dick as that. Do he and Morgana have nothing else to refer to me as? Baby Alpha, pup, little... fucking idiots... and no, I am not going to do that, although it's the primal instinct that courses through me every time I see her. All I want is to fuck her. I also have to remember she's not a fucking plaything. More than that, she doesn't want me. Not yet, anyway, but that's going to fucking change soon...

I stand up and walk out of my office and down the hall. I stand at the top of the stairs, arms crossed, watching as she enters before Oliver leaves, shutting the door behind him. She looks as fucking radiant as ever. Undoing her hair from its tie, she shakes it out, letting her long black hair cascade down her back. From her round breasts to her tiny waistline that I could wrap my hands around completely, she's fucking gorgeous. If there's one thing the moon Goddess did right, she at least gave me a mate that's fucking ravishing...

Years back, when I thought I'd find my mate, I had this image in my head of how my mate would look like... but Morgana is so much more than that. I doubt there is another woman on the entire fucking planet that can even hold a candle to her beauty. Her plump, pouty lips and those high cheekbones... she had been chiseled to perfection.

She stops running her fingers through her hair as if sensing me watching her. Our eyes meet, and suddenly the silence feels deafening. I don't need to read minds to know that the same fucking memory is in both of our minds. What happened earlier between us...

Suddenly, the tension between us is too fucking much.

# A Dangerous Game

MORGANA

THE DAY GOES BY in a haze. No matter how much I try, I can't forget what almost happened earlier.

I sigh in frustration, watching two of the four head cooks argue over salt. All day these two have been at it. I realised yesterday that only Griselda is usually here, and from what I gathered, the two never seemed to get on. Usually, the work schedule is set up in such a way that they wouldn't have to be together, but one of the chefs is ill, so Griselda is replacing her.

I'm sick of it; it's complete nonsense, and their Alpha is already consuming my mind like a plague you can't get rid of. I'm no longer sure if the potato in front of me is baby Alpha or the two chefs before me.

"No, I assure you, I didn't put anything in your pot!" Griselda barks. She is a large, boisterous woman with a very sturdy build, standing at around five feet five. Markus, on the other hand, is the exact opposite, being a very tall and thin man. He now glares coldly at the robust woman.

"Shut that pie hole, Griselda. I know what happened. Your memory is worse than a damn goldfish!" He growls back.

"Oh, zip it! We all know you have a stick shoved too far up your ass!"

"What did you just say? You fat -"

"Oh, you did not just fat shame me! You are fucking going to get it! I'm going to tear you a new one!"

"Oh, dear…" Andrei hurries over. I sigh. They really are giving me a headache.

"Please calm down, the both of you!" Andrei commands.

"Andrei, we know she has an issue with my dishes! She always acts very carelessly! How can you simply not know what dish is yours or not?" Markus hisses.

"Okay, okay, you both listen to me. Next time I want you both-"

"Just add some fucking vegetables!" Griselda shouted. "The salt won't be so strong then!"

"Don't tell me what to do before I dunk the entire fucking pot on your head, woman!"

"I'm warning you, Markus!"

I slam my knife down, making everyone turn towards me. I glare at the two chefs.

"Can you both zip it? I don't want to come over there and have to chop you both to pieces and make broth out of you!" I snap. "Honestly… a woman can't even think in silence…"

I pick up the knife and a new potato. I really am sick of cutting vegetables… I need a new job, one that doesn't involve the kitchen. I sigh. Maybe I can talk to the arrogant jerk of an Alpha.

Luckily, after my small outburst, no one speaks, and the two simply get back to their jobs. Now, this silence is so much better…

Later on, I'm just about to have a mug of hot chocolate when I see Sage enter the kitchen. Her eyes find me, and instantly they flash. I raise an eyebrow. She's nothing in comparison to me, and I'm ready to show her that if the need arises. I cock a brow, taking a sip of my hot chocolate, not blinking, satisfied when she breaks eye contact first, her jaw clenched.

"Andrei, a word. With the upcoming summit and the evening dinners, I just want to make sure that you have everything necessary for the menu that I gave you."

"Yes, ma'am, we do, down to the desserts… just the way you wanted. All the supplies are ready, and the food will be plenty. The seating and everything else will be taken care of, too…" Andrei says politely.

"Good. I don't want Alpha Kian to be disappointed," she says, making me roll my eyes. I turn away, sipping my hot chocolate. "And why is she drinking out of a cup that we use?" I turn back, smirking. "Her kind are filth," she adds.

"Bitch, control that tongue of yours, or I swear I'll rip it out of your mouth," I state coldly.

"How dare you!" She hisses.

"Sage… Alpha does not want you around her," Oliver, who is on watch duty, reminds her.

"Still, for her to be putting her lips on that cup -"

"Are you for fucking real? Your man wanted to kiss these lips, so instead of complaining over a damn cup, go get him in line," I remark, my eyes flaring dangerously into hers. Her face burns with rage, and gasps flitter through the kitchen at my words. I don't care if I'm a fucking slave here. I won't tolerate disrespect, especially from her. My anger seems to rear its ugly head a lot faster when she's around.

"Sage, leave, or I'm going to have to call the Alpha," Oliver says seriously.

She doesn't say anything, her lips trembling before she slams the notepad she had been carrying onto the counter and storms out. I roll my eyes.

"Children and their tantrums…" I hum, sipping my hot chocolate.

No one says anything, and I am sure baby Alpha will hear about this when his precious woman goes crying to him. I don't really care. I won't bow to anyone. Once the kitchen is almost clean, I'm told to go, and with relief, I follow Oliver out.

"So, does the Alpha know what happened?" I ask. He frowns, concerned.

"No. Sage said there was no need to mention it," he adds tersely.

"Oh?"

Hmm, does she want to save her own ass? Then again, I'm probably the one who'd get punished. With every step towards the king's quarters, I just get angrier and angrier, remembering how that bitch had come and tried to act with me. I told Kian I do not want her anywhere near me, nor does she have any right to speak to me.

My chest is heaving, and even when Oliver lets me inside, I hope the Alpha says nothing to me… I'll flip. The door shuts with a thud behind me, but in the empty hall, even that is loud.

I pull my hair tie out, letting my hair down, trying to calm myself down when I feel an intense feeling of being watched, and I know exactly who it is. I look up to see him standing at the top of the stairs. His scent fills the air, and I try to simply inhale it. Despite its owner, it is tempting.

"Wash and get to bed," he says coldly.

I don't reply. Giving him my best icy glare, I'm up the stairs in a flash, brushing past him and ignoring the sparks that coursed through me. I'm about to walk through when he grabs my arm.

"Why the fuck are you pissed off?"

"I really don't want to argue with you, so let go of me," I say, glaring up into those hazel eyes of his. They narrow, his anger flaring up, and as predicted, he doesn't let go.

"I won't tolerate disrespect from anyone," he says coldly.

"And I won't tolerate anyone manhandling me!" I exclaim angrily.

"I'm going to only ask you once more, what the fuck happened?" He questions dangerously. His hand pins my wrists to the wall behind me, his body leaning against mine. Our hearts race as one. I look into those intense hazel orbs of his. Should I tell him?

"Why do you care?" I ask coldly.

He doesn't reply, but he doesn't let go of me either. His body brushes against me, and the front of his jeans presses against my pubic bone. My heart is pounding, and his closeness is getting to me.

"Tell me, Alpha, when your entire kind is disgusted at the thought of me... then why do you want me so much?"

"What do you mean?" I scoff, looking away from him.

"Really. I do believe that we are speaking the same language, are we not?" I mock.

"I don't have time for games, sunshine. I won't ask again, but I do have ways to force the answer out of you."

Should I tell him? I don't know if it's going to do any good, but I am really fed up. Although it's nothing big, her words anger me beyond anything else. There is just something about her that really grates on my nerves.

"Well, if you really want to know, I have a question for you, Alpha."

"What is it?"

"Why are you so interested in me?" He frowns, not seeming to have expected me to say that. Narrowing his eyes, he glares at me coldly.

"What has that even got to do with anything?"

"Well... your precious girlfriend seems to have an issue with me using the same dishes as your kind because, apparently, I am too filthy. But I don't get it. I wonder what she would think if she knew her Alpha seemed to crave these very lips," I say softly, my voice holding a touch of mockery to it.

"Did she say that?" He asks, his eyes narrowed.

"Why? Does me saying anything to her upset you, Alpha?"

"No..."

"That's good because that bitch deserved it. I told you I don't want her anywhere near me, let alone to speak to me, yet she dared to."

"How come no one told me about this? I thought everything went well without a hitch," he questions, but I can see the irritation on his face. I'm surprised he isn't lashing out in anger at me.

"Well, your precious Sage told your Delta not to say anything. That it was no big deal," I inform him with a roll of my eyes. "How about you let me go because, seriously, I've had enough of you wolves for one day." He ignores my comment, simply looking down at me.

"Tell me, my little she-devil," he starts with a smirk. "Why does it feel to me that Sage just pisses you off more than anyone else?"

"I'm so sorry, but don't get ahead of yourself. That position goes to you. You irritate me the most. As for her, she's just a bitch that I don't have time to deal with." I roll my eyes.

"So... is there anything I can do to calm you down?"

His voice is low and raspy, sending pleasure rushing to my core. What? It's almost as if he's trying to calm me down. Why would he care when all he does is get on my nerves, too? My heart is pounding as my gaze meets his. I lick my lips slowly, trying not to focus on his. What does he even mean?

"Actually, there is. You can let me go."

"I had something else in mind…" he trails off.

"What do you mean?" I ask, suspiciously narrowing my eyes. He steps even closer, closing the gap between us. His chest presses against mine, his scent intoxicating me.

*Fuck, move back… I can't focus anymore.*

"How about I show you that you are far from filth?" He whispers seductively. My heart pounds, my core knots, and that familiar pressure settles deep within my stomach.

"I don't think that's a good idea," I whisper back softly.

"Anything between us is a bad idea. So, what's the big deal?" He murmurs. He's too close. "You want one up on Sage, don't you?" I frown. That's true… but… "Allow me to show you what I think of these," he whispers, finally letting go of one of my wrists only to curl his fingers under my chin, his thumb rubbing across my lips.

The temptation to kiss him just to piss Sage off is very strong, but at the same time, I want to just satiate the desire that burned within me.

One kiss. It would do no harm. Who am I kidding? Anything between us would do harm... but I've never minded a game of danger.

He still seems to be waiting, as if for approval. Doesn't the Alpha King simply take what he wishes for?

"Fuck it all," he murmurs before his lips crash against mine in an explosive kiss.

# Pillow Talk

## KIAN

$I$ CAN'T STOP MYSELF. ALL I want is a moment of her, to feel the way she tastes, to relish in the way she consumes me. Pleasure streams through me right down to my dick, making me twitch against her. Her soft moans vibrate against my lips, making me want to fuck her right now. Never had a kiss felt so good. I'm already hard for her. Right now, the way I feel… all I need is her, and I would give everything up to have it.

**Mark her, and she is ours,** Thanatos' voice comes through the link.

I plunge my tongue into her mouth, letting go of her chin. I tangle my hand into those gorgeous silk locks of hers as I explore every inch of her sweet, tempting mouth. Her arousal perfumes the air, and I let go of her wrist, wrapping my other arm around her waist and pulling her hard against me.

She reaches up, cupping her hand around the back of my neck as she kisses me back with equal passion and anger. She fights for dominance, yet I'm the Alpha, and that is not something I will give her. Our tongues fight against each other, mingling together, caressing the other's sensually yet roughly. I can sense her anger and frustration, but also her deep desire and want against my lips.

Our emotions fuel our kiss, my hand running over her slender waist and back. She gasps, and I realise my claws have come out, but even then, she doesn't pull away, kissing me back hard. The taste of blood fills my mouth, and I'm not sure if it's hers or mine. Fuck, she is beyond fucking perfect. I groan when she sucks on my tongue. The urge to rip her clothes off is taking over, and Thanatos is fighting for control.

**I want mate!** He growls.

I know he's losing it when he starts losing the ability to speak properly. In this state, he'd fuck and mark her. I pull away roughly, looking at her. Her lips are even plumper than usual, her cheeks hold a tint of colour, and her eyes are burning a dark red. My own are flickering to gold as Thanatos screams for control.

"Go," I growl at her. Her heart is pounding, and I know she wants to say something. "I said go!" I hiss, clenching my fist. Thanatos' hold is getting stronger. This is the only problem I have, having a wolf that is terrifyingly strong and one I know would wreak havoc if given the chance.

*My mate! How dare she walk away!*

She looks at me curiously before frowning deeply and storming down the hall. My eyes never leave her, falling to her ass.

**Cut it out, Thanatos, or I swear I'll send her far away where you will never get to ever see her again,** I warn coldly. Blood drips to the floor from my curled-up fists, my nails digging into my palms.

**You can't survive without her either,** he growls venomously.

**I can if it's meant to keep us from killing her.**

He doesn't say anything, and I know he feels guilty for what he wanted to do, but he doesn't understand it either. My own words ring in my head, and I frown.

Her safety over my own desire… is that what I just admitted to?

MORGANA

I walk to the bathroom, taking some pyjamas with me. I step into the ice-cold shower, which doesn't really help calm me down. The cold is pleasant, though, and I welcome it, remembering the cold weather from back home. No matter what I do, the inferno that he had set off inside of me is not quelling at all.

I close my eyes, leaning against the shower wall, and touch my tender lips softly. They still feel extra sensitive. His touch remains… I had kissed several men in my life, but Alpha King Kian Araqiel had a very different effect on me. Nothing felt this good… in fact, I had never thought anyone could make me feel crazier than Eroan did… but it seems even he had been surpassed. And what's worse…

Thinking of Kian doesn't disgust me.

I slide down the wall, sitting there numbly. This man is most likely responsible for my father's death, yet here I am, fraternising with him. But… getting close to him might just be the best option to get him to lower his guard… I can find out what exactly happened with my father…

Am I looking for an excuse to redeem him? I'm not sure. After a good while, I stand up, washing quickly. I step out of the shower, towelling myself dry and brushing my teeth before I slip on the pyjamas and return to the bedroom, only to see him sitting on the bed, his ankles crossed, a file in one hand and a pen in the other. He had already showered and changed… had I really taken that long? The curtains are drawn, and the only light is the bedside lamp that casts a warm glow around the room, one that tempts me to climb onto the bed and snuggle down…

I close the bathroom door slowly behind me and walk to the drawer, quickly running a comb through my damp locks. I can feel his eyes on me, but I ignore him. Putting the brush away, I finally turn to him.

"So… where do I sleep?" I ask, trying not to glare at him. Even just sitting there, he oozes arrogance and power. He raises an eyebrow.

"I knew you were stupid, sunshine, but I didn't realise how stupid. Where do people usually sleep?" He asks arrogantly, patting the bed next to him. My stomach flutters and I glare at him, not missing his remark. How can he act so normal? But I'm glad he is…

"Well, since I'm so stupid, why not let me go?" I mutter, getting into bed. *Oh god, this bed is comfortable.* I pull the duvet over me, only for him to place the file and pen down and turn onto his side, facing me.

"Why do you think I'll let you go? As I said, we have all the time in the world, and I assure you, you are not going anywhere," he says quietly.

My heart is thundering, and I know he can hear it. I hate this. I'm about to turn away when he reaches over, yanking the duvet off me, and, grabbing my elbow, pulls me onto my back.

"I was talking, little she-devil, and I don't like to be disrespected or ignored."

So, we are back to arrogant, irritating baby alpha mode…

"I don't really care. I want to sleep," I shoot back. Ripping free from his hold, I'm about to turn away when I'm yanked back around, but I'm ready this time.

I flip over, roughly pulling him with me, hoping to throw him off the bed, but he has other plans. He grabs me and rolls us over so I am under him. My eyes blaze as I glare up at him. I struggle against his hands, still holding my arms.

"I'm not weak, pup," I snap, flipping us over in a flash. My eyes blaze as I stare down at him. I'm strong, but so is the Alpha King.

"But I'm still stronger," he shoots back coldly.

Suddenly my back slams onto the bed, with him straddling my thighs. My heart thunders as he pins my arms to the bed. I'm very aware of the cotton fabric of the camisole clinging to my breasts. His gaze darkens, and his eyes leave mine, travelling over me slowly.

"Get off me." I don't move, knowing he is far too close to where that familiar ache had settled. Would it be so wrong to just fuck him once? Then maybe he'll let me go. He'll get over whatever sick fetish he has going on for him, and I can get out of here…

"Then answer my question. Why do you keep talking about leaving? I told you you are mine," he says coldly.

Our eyes are locked, and my heart is thundering. He leans down, the necklaces that hang around his neck brushing my breasts, and my heart pounds. I'm very aware of his package pressing against my thighs.

"I'm waiting, my feisty little blood rose," he whispers.

"Because sooner or later, you will get bored of me…"

**We will never let our mate go.**

I flinch when those words flitter into my mind, accompanied by the sharp shrill sound that always comes with the thoughts that flitter through me.

"Morgana? Are you okay?" Kian asks.

"I…"

**Our mate is hurting!**

I flinch again, clamping my hands to my head. What the hell is that? I didn't realise when he had moved away from me; the shrill, piercing sonic sound makes my head feel like it's about to burst.

"Morgana…"

His voice is distant, I'm not sure if it's as soft as it sounds right now, but his hand on my head is gentle. The other rests on my arm.

**Mate is in pain!** That deep, possessive voice comes again.

"Stop it. Stop talking…" I groan. It's coming from him… but…

My heart is thundering, and I breathe heavily, relieved when I realise it has stopped. My heart pounds, and I take a deep breath, realising he has his hand on my back, the other rubbing my arm.

"What happened?" He asks sharply.

I look up at him, about to answer, when one word from his thoughts echoes in my head.

Mate.

My heart thuds, a rush of cold realisation crashing down on me. Everything makes sense… the attraction he has towards me… suddenly, the man from the lake returns to my mind, and I look up at him sharply.

*Mine.*

That voice — it had been the very same voice that I heard in Kian's head… *No… This can't be possible…*

"Morgana, what the fuck is wrong? You look paler than fucking normal."

"Am I…" My hoarse voice leaves my lips. "Am I your… mate?"

## KIAN

Her words send a wave of emotions through me. How the fuck does she know that? I did nothing to hint… fuck… I swallow hard, my heart thudding as I stare back into those shocked eyes of hers. She's waiting for an answer I don't have. Well, one I can't give her.

"Don't give yourself so much fucking importance. How can a vampire be mated to a werewolf?" I ask with a scornful tone in my voice.

"Exactly, it's practically unheard of…" she whispers, placing a hand on her head, her hair curtaining her face.

I can't let her know. If she realises she has one on me… and if anyone else finds out… she could be in way more fucking danger than she could ever imagine. And above all, they would use her against me.

**Would you care or let her rot to her death?** Thanatos growls. Just the thought of her getting hurt…

I move back, my heart thundering. If anything happened to her, I'd never be able to forgive myself. The very thought is like a fucking bitch slap to the face. Somehow, I'm growing attached to her… this was fucking not the plan.

I remain composed, getting off the bed and walking over to the small fridge I have at the bottom of one of my bookshelves. Opening it, I grab a water bottle. Unscrewing it, I hold it out to her.

"Drink."

She looks up at me suddenly, her gaze going to the water bottle before she reaches out for it. It's then that I realise she's shaking slightly. She takes it, doing her best not to tremble. Our fingers brush, and the familiar rush of tingles courses through me. Our eyes meet before she moves hers away quickly, gulping the water down. A few trickles escape, trailing down her neck and in between her breasts… *I wouldn't mind lapping them up…*

**And I wouldn't mind licking every inch of her. Stop being a fucking pussy, man up, get our mate, and mate her!** Thanatos growls.

**When that happens, I'm fucking blocking you off,** I shoot back. He's becoming a fucking horny dog, and it's pissing me off.

**Everything pisses you off,** Thanatos shoots back.

She is about to place the bottle down when I reach over, taking it from her. I put the lid back on and place it on the bedside table.

"What happened to you?" I ask.

"Nothing," she says, frowning deeply. I want to push it, but something tells me that now is not the fucking time.

"Fine. Then drink and sleep," I say coldly, holding out my wrist.

**Not the fucking wrist! Let her drink from our neck, so we feel good!** Thanatos growls. He is the very reason I'm not going to allow it; I already feel him fighting for dominance. She looks surprised, her gaze dipping to my hand.

"What's the catch? " She asks suspiciously. I'm glad she's at least partially back to her normal self. I cock my brow.

"There's no fucking catch. Now drink, or you lose your fucking chance."

She smirks, "Okay."

She grabs my hand, opening her mouth. I watch as her fangs become even more pronounced, and she bites into my wrist viciously. A sharp sting of pain rushes up my arm, but it doesn't bother me. I know she did it on purpose, but I don't really care. I can deal with the fucking pain. My focus is on the way she's drinking hungrily, her eyes half-hooded, her hand gently holding mine. Her hands are fucking soft as if they had never seen a hard day in her life. I'm surprised she's good with weapons considering how smooth her hands are. Pleasure runs up my arm in delicious sparks, and I fucking feel it rush south.

*Think of something else, Kian, anything else but how she's making you fucking feel.*

After a few moments, she draws back and licks her lips. A trickle of blood remains at the corner of her mouth, and the urge to wipe it away is strong.

**Or just admit you need an excuse to fucking touch her. Let's do it.**

**Fuck, Thanatos.**

**No, fuck mate.**

I run my hand down my face, massaging my jaw. He really is doing my head in. I look at her as she licks her lips once more but still misses that corner.

"Can I ask a question?" She asks, looking at me keenly.

"That already is one," I say, gathering up my files and placing them aside. I'm not going to be able to fucking focus on anything with her around.

"Does your wolf… have a voice?" She asks, shaking the rumpled bedding out before getting in. I look at her sharply. That is not the question I was expecting her to ask.

"Yeah, he has his own personality and can talk." Shame though.

**Shut it, let me enjoy this. Our mate is asking about me,** Thanatos purrs.

I resist rolling my eyes as I drop onto the bed, laying back on the cushion. She is still sitting up, watching me, but there is something different in her eyes. A deep curiosity as if she is working something out.

"What's it like to have a wolf that speaks in your head?" I cock a brow, trying not to focus on that little smear of blood at the corner of her lips. Why the fuck is she so sexy?

**Because -**

**Shut it,** I cut Thanatos off and look at her.

"Like an annoying fucking conscience that never shuts the fuck up," I mutter. Her lips twitch in a small smile.

"I guess that would be pretty cool. You would never be lonely, no matter who you lose… your wolf is something that will always be there by your side. Kind of amazing."

"So, you're saying being a werewolf is amazing?" I remark as she slowly lies down again. She turns towards me, resting her elbow on the pillow and placing her head on her hands.

My heart skips a fucking beat when my gaze is drawn to the tops of her creamy breasts, which are spilling out of her top. I slowly force my attention upwards to that gorgeous face of hers. Goddess, she is fucking ravishing...

"I didn't say that, I just said it's cool. A person would never be alone, even if everyone they loved passed away," she replies softly. A flicker of pain flashes in her eyes, but it's gone as fast as it came.

"Maybe that's why you aren't a fucking she-wolf because no one would be able to survive two of you," I remark. Thanatos growls possessively.

**Oh, I could survive it. Whilst one rides Mini-Kian, the other one can ride our face-**

I frown, blocking him off and trying to push away the image he had planted in my brain.

"A she-wolf? Yeah, I don't think so. I'm glad I'm not one." She rolls her eyes, her voice saving me from my fucking thoughts. She drops onto her back, looking displeased. "There's nothing amazing about she-wolves anyway."

"Oh, yeah? Then why are you oozing jealousy?"

"Me? Jealous? I don't think so. Morgana Araton doesn't do jealous," she says airily. She's fucking jealous. It's now my turn to prop myself up on my elbow, smirking arrogantly.

"You're pretty easy to read, sunshine."

"I'm not. What's there to be jealous about? I'm the most beautiful woman in this kingdom," she states haughtily. "Now I'm going to sleep." She turns her back to me, and my lips twitch into a small smile.

My little she-devil is indeed jealous. I tilt my head, looking at her slender back and shoulders. Any man would enjoy their mate and their presence, feeling jealous and possessive of them, and I am no less. Even if she is a vampire...

I reach over, running my knuckles down her back between her shoulder blades. She gasps, her back arching at my touch and her heart thundering as she turns back towards me. I school my face into an emotionless mask. Sucking on the end of my thumb, I reach over and rub the corner of her mouth, removing the bloodstain from the corner of her lips. Her breath hitches, and her heart races as I cup her chin, my eyes meeting those deep red ones of hers.

"I agree. You are," I say before I move away smoothly, switching the lamp off and turning my back to her.

Right now, if she wanted to tear me to pieces, she probably could, and I wouldn't care. My emotions are a fucking storm, and is it wrong to simply relish in the fact that her scent envelopes and calms me so fucking much?

"Obviously," comes her airy reply, and I smirk, closing my eyes.

*That's my girl.*

# Shower Play

MORGANA

*I* DON'T GET IT. WHATEVER is happening between us… something had shifted since that kiss. I don't get what, but it had. As for those thoughts, I'm sure it was his wolf that I had heard. But what I can't get my head around is, am I really the Alpha King's mate? How could that even be a possibility?

One thing I am certain of is that he had been the man at the lake, and remembering that makes my cheeks burn and my core throb. That voice that had said 'mine' had been the very same as the voice I heard in his thoughts. I sigh deeply.

As a vampire, falling in love is something that doesn't happen often, but when we find the one, our beloved, the connection is there. My mother said your heartbeat would race, and no matter if you knew this person or not, when you laid eyes upon him, you would know he was the one. Perhaps it is similar to werewolves and mates… I'm not sure, but we would only truly love once. When we loved, we loved with a passion. I had been in a relationship once, but due to our different races, it wasn't possible. He was a prince, and I was a princess. Perhaps if we weren't people who were of such high rank, we could have gone somewhere far away and lived happily, just like he had wanted. It had been I who had refused and said we needed to end it, but it made me think, were our feelings strong enough? If they had been, wouldn't we have fought for it? There had been something missing... love.

I sigh deeply. I'm very aware of the heat radiating off the man behind me. The urge to lean against that warmth is tempting. They say a werewolf's love for his mate is beyond reckoning, that they cannot live without the other. I don't believe in that kind of love, especially since he clearly had a woman... yet, why am I the one in his bed? What are we? This connection I feel towards him...

I slowly turn over, my eyes falling on the dragon on his broad chiselled back. *Dear Lord, he is perfect...* I reach over, about to touch him, but... is he asleep? His breathing is even and rhythmic, but I'm not sure... I curl my fingers, retracting my hand.

*Our mate...* I can't get those words out of my head.

I close my eyes, sighing softly. I need to make him lower his guard around me. Play a game so well that he doesn't see what's coming, but he's so guarded. It will take time, but I have never been afraid of playing a dangerous game, and this is what this one is. A game of revenge, hate, and passion. One where I need to get close to the king and make him trust me before I make him pay for the crimes of his kind, but also make sure that I don't get so consumed in the process.

He turns over, and I snap my eyes shut, unsure if he is awake or not. My heart thunders when I feel his arm snake around my waist. My eyes fly open, and I stare into his face. His eyes are shut, and his breathing is still even. His head rests on his other arm, but even with just one arm, his hold is firm. My stomach is going crazy, and I don't know what to do. I lay there stiffly, trying to think, yet I can't with his body so close. The gap between our bodies isn't that big, and I know if I move even two inches closer to him, I'd be touching certain areas of his body...

Although I don't move, my eyes roam the plains of his hard, muscular body. Up close, I can see the faint scars that litter his body, and I know each one tells a different story. He's in his early twenties, yet how much has he suffered already?

I'm not sure when sleep finally overcame me or when I no longer cared that I was sleeping with the enemy. The urge to shuffle closer overtook me before I finally dropped off...

The sun is burning into my back, yet I don't want to get up. I feel so comfortable, cocooned so firmly in warmth and comfort. Yet whatever is touching my core is making me a little horny. God, I am a woman, after all, and I hadn't had a release in a while. Urgh… it feels good. My body wriggles a little, and a soft sigh escapes me when it throbs against me.

I freeze. My eyes fly open, realising that the cocoon is none other than the Alpha King, his arms tight around me, his head resting above mine, his leg between mine, and that thing pressing against me is…

God! I struggle in his hold, my heart thundering before I rip free and jump off the bed.

"Why were you holding me?" I snap. He smirks, sitting up, and my gaze instantly dips to the huge tent in his pants before I look back at his face.

"A mistake, I assure you," he answers arrogantly.

"Yeah, don't forget you are just a baby in my eyes," I lie. I know he hates when I refer to him as that.

"Stop calling me that, or I fucking swear I'll show you how far away from a baby I am," he growls, standing up as he comes towards me. His words send a knot of pleasure through me, but it's a sudden thought that pops into my head that makes me smile. If Sage smells his scent on me…

He narrows his eyes, instantly suspicious.

"What are you up to?" He asks.

"Oh, nothing at all," I answer, turning to my wardrobe. Scratch that, not *my* wardrobe, just the one that had clothes for me. This is not my place in any way. I turn to him just in time to see him adjust his pants and smirk cockily.

"You should get your precious Sage to take care of that," I mock, despite the sharp sting that rushes through me at my own words.

Instantly, his mood darkens, and I realise I shouldn't have spoken, but that's me. I don't really have a filter. I turn back to the wardrobe, only for him to grab my arm, spin me around, and slam me against the drawer.

"You're the fucking cause, so why don't you fix it?" He growls venomously.

"I'm not your fucking whore."

I don't know what happened, but the calmness that had fallen between us last night is gone. The cold reminder that we are enemies and that I am being held here against my will returns with full force. He smirks coldly, leaning closer, and his lips graze my ear.

"That's a good idea, actually. Maybe I should get someone who can actually satiate me to take care of me," he growls venomously. The sharp pain at his words is like a slap to the face, but I don't care. I had started it. If that's what he wants, then he can fucking carry on.

"Please do," I challenge.

"Don't start a game you can't play, little she-devil," he hisses coldly.

"A game you started…" I snap.

"And one I will fucking end."

His hand tightens around my throat before he slams me once against the wardrobe. Pain shoots through my head before he lets go of me. Turning, he storms from the room, slamming the door behind him with a bang.

I close my eyes, leaning against the drawers, massaging my throat. My heart is racing but not because of what he had just done… but the fact that he had gone. He had gone to another woman, but… I shouldn't care, right?

My heart thuds, and I'm fighting myself; my stubbornness, the possessiveness I feel, and the excuse I'm giving myself that I need to get close to him to escape. It would really make Sage happy if he went to her. That bitch needs to be put in her place…

It takes me less than three minutes to make my decision. Taking a deep breath, I exhale sharply. Fuck, I'm going to do this. In a flash, I'm at the door, my nose sniffing out his scent. I follow it, rush down the hall, and push open the door, freezing when I hear the sound of low groans coming from the door on the left wall. That bitch sure is fast.

I frown. I have no idea what the fuck I'm going to do or say, but, hey, when do I ever think, right? I storm across the room, ready to tear that whore to pieces. Yanking open the door, I stare inside, only to freeze at the sight before me.

Hot steam fills the room from the running shower, but my eyes are on the god inside it. Kian stands there, leaning against the wall with his hand wrapped around his huge fucking cock, looking incredibly deliciously sexy. My entire body tingles at the image before me, my core throbbing painfully, and I press my thighs together as our eyes lock. His sharp, sexy ones pierce into my own shocked ones.

Oh, kill me now… did I just walk in on the Alpha King jerking off?

And look him over?

Yep, and yep.

*Congratulations, Morgana, you really are ridiculously stupid…*

He raises his eyebrow and, to my shock, continues stroking his shaft.

"The cold's coming inside. If you're here for the show, close the door," he says huskily, making my core throb. I raise an eyebrow, trying to gather myself as best I can.

"I've seen many men, Alpha Kian. I doubt you will have anything to offer that I haven't seen before," I remark airily, confidently stepping inside and shutting the door. I walk over to the counter, perching on the edge of it near the sink basin, and cross my legs confidently. Since I had come running like an idiot, there's no choice but to ride this out.

A sexy, dangerous smirk crosses his lips, but he says nothing. Resting his head back against the tiled walls, his eyes locked with mine, he begins moving his hand along his thick, delicious cock.

Oh, fuck… I'm struggling to keep my gaze on his face. I can see what he's doing from the periphery of my eyes, but the urge to take it in completely is tempting. A low groan escapes him, and my heart skips a beat when I realise his gaze is no longer on my face but on my body. Is he imagining me? My stomach knots, and I know he'll be able to smell my arousal soon enough.

"Too embarrassed to look down, sunshine?" He murmurs.

"Like I said, I've seen it all before," I whisper.

Fuck, my voice came out so breathless. His arrogant smirk tells me he knows he's having an effect on me. It's so hot in here… why is the water at such a high temperature? I need air…

"Oh, yeah? How about you come in here and show me exactly what you know?" I never knew he could be so seductive…

I can't stop myself from looking any longer. Fuck, his huge hand doesn't look so big anymore. It's as gorgeous as the rest of him. Every ridge and muscle right down to his swollen mushroom tip makes me lick my lips. This man had indeed been favoured unfairly. How can any man compare?

"Like what you see?" His arrogant voice snaps my attention away from his cock. "Like I said, come join me."

"What's wrong? Does the baby Alpha lack experience?" I challenge, sliding off the worktop. If we were doing this… it's on my terms.

"Depends. I can't really answer that until I have something to compare to." His seductive voice makes my pussy clench.

"Good point," I say, walking over to the shower.

I step inside, keeping my face composed. My core clenches as the warm water drenches me, making the cotton fabric of my pyjamas practically see-through. With the way his eyes darken, I know he's getting a perfect look, but it's only fair since I'm feasting on him in all his naked glory.

I reach down, wrapping my hand around his dick, and bite my lip when I realise I can't even close my fingers around it completely. He swallows hard, and I smile sensually, gliding my hand along the length.

"You know, Alpha… right now… your life is in my hands. If I rip your dick off, my revenge is complete," I whisper. Despite my words, my hand runs along his length.

"Wouldn't be a bad way to die," he replies huskily, his words only making my heart thump faster.

"You're playing a dangerous game, Alpha." He cocks an eyebrow. The power that radiates from him shows me he isn't scared.

"Then let's play," he whispers huskily.

His eyes fill with a dangerous hunger that only gives birth to an illicit flame of pleasure that combusts within me. His hand tangles in my hair, the other slipping under my top and groping my breast.

My heart is pounding, but the moment he kisses my neck, I gasp, my heart banging against my ribcage. Obviously, he isn't scared by my threat. His hand slides my soaking top up as my hand runs along his dick, a moan escaping my lips. The pleasure I feel at his touch is immeasurable. I wonder if I had started the path to something far too dangerous… but it's too late. The big bad wolf has me exactly where he wants. Even though I have him in my hand, I don't feel like I'm the one in control. He throbs in my hand, and it only makes my own need grow. He sucks on my neck, making me cry out in pleasure.

"Seems like this pup knows what works already," he taunts. I grab his balls, running my hand along them.

"Oh, yeah? Well, you seem easy to please," I taunt breathlessly, wrapping my free hand around his neck and tugging him down a little roughly before sinking my teeth into his neck and making him groan. I feel him buck and smirk.

I'm going to win this one. He might be the Alpha King, but right now, he is in my control. I'm making him react. I suck on his neck slowly and sensually, my hand pumping his dick fast. His hand slips into my trousers, squeezing my ass while his other hand rubs my hardened nipple, making me moan.

"Fuck…" he groans as he begins thrusting into my hand. I extract my teeth, licking the wound slowly before trailing my tongue up his neck and to his ear.

"Does that feel good, Alpha?" I whisper, sucking on the lobe of his ear.

"You fucking know it does," he grunts, pleasure contorting his face. He only looks even hotter. His hand squeezes my breast harder, his other hand running between my ass cheeks, making me whimper. I know he's near. Even when he removes his hand from my ass and slips it down the front, massaging over my pussy, I struggle not to lose my self-control.

"You're fucking turned on, little she-devil. Seems like this inexperienced pup turns you on pretty easily," he growls huskily. His fingers find my clit, making my eyes fly open.

"Fuck!"

If I had any doubt left before that he was the man from the lake, it was gone. It is him; the way his finger knows exactly what works on my little button of pleasure is clear. He kisses my neck, sucking hard, and I feel my pleasure building. He groans.

"Fuck, that's it," he mutters, his own speed increasing as my pleasure builds.

"Oh, fuck, that's it… right there… fuck…" I whimper, parting my legs. My eyes sting as I feel like my entire body is burning with a dangerous illicit pleasure. The urge to tell him to fuck me is on the tip of my lips. "Fuck, Kian!"

"That's it, baby girl, tell me how good I make you feel," he murmurs, littering my neck with rough, burning kisses that I know will leave plenty of marks. Water pours down on us both, our scents mixing, and the feeling of being so close to each other…

I can barely focus on him anymore, my own pleasure consuming me. I feel him thrust into my hand. My own moans sound foreign to even me. His touch that doesn't move from my clit is making me crazy.

"Incredibly… fucking… goo- fuck!" I gasp when he delivers a sharp slap to my pussy before he continues his assault on my clit.

I can't come first… I am not going to- ouch! I gasp when he twists my nipple and pleasure tears through me as I reach my euphoric climax. My eyes sting, I can't breathe, and the pleasure I feel consumes me completely. Seconds later, I feel his release all over my hand, his delicious groan making me press myself against him. My hand weakly pumps his beast of a cock as I try to get my breath back. His now flaccid cock still makes me throb, and I run my hand over it just as he massages my extra tender pussy, and I whimper in pleasure.

"I won," he says arrogantly. His other arm is around my waist, holding my shaking body against his.

"Barely." I frown back, still breathless. A small smirk crosses that face of his, and he runs his hand up my pussy and stomach, making me suck it in,

"I will always win. No matter what you do," he promises arrogantly.

Leaning down, he is about to kiss me when the door to the bathroom opens to reveal none other than Sage. Her eyes are fixed on both of us, but the look of pain in her eyes is not something I was ready for. My heart skips a beat when Kian tenses. Letting go of me, he steps away and grabs a towel that was on the shelf next to us.

"Sage…"

She doesn't say anything. Her eyes glitter with unshed tears as she turns and runs from the room. Kian wraps the towel around him and is about to leave the bathroom, when he pauses to look at me. Our eyes meet, and for the first time, I see a different emotion in his eyes. Guilt.

He doesn't say anything as he leaves swiftly. I hear him call her, and I turn away, my lips quivering ever so slightly as I press them together. I'm confused; I had wanted to taunt her by displaying his scent on me earlier… but seeing her look so pained… I realise I'm the other woman here.

But it's Kian's fault. He's the dickhead she needs to drop and move on. He's the one who brought me here...

Now I understand his guilt. He felt guilty for hurting her, not for using me. After all, that's all I am to him, something to use.

My heart thunders loudly, my chest heaving as I try my best to calm the raging storm that threatens to wreak havoc all around me. I won't make that mistake again…

I think it's high time I took the elder Araqiel up on his offer.

# A Plan for Vengeance

KIAN

*W*HEN SOMETHING FEELS LIKE it's too fucking good to be true, it usually is. Although I know that she was trying to prove that she has a hold on me, I was still in control. Fuck, mate or not, her touch alone was my fucking undoing. Never had I had such a good fucking release, and that was just by her fucking hand.

When Sage entered, I wasn't expecting it. Although things are different now that I have found my mate... I still need her as my Luna. I need her to understand that she will be the Luna. If she went and told anyone about Morgana and me... that could ruin a lot more.

I had pulled away, grabbing a towel, yet the guilt I felt for just leaving her in the shower... I never thought I'd ever feel like this. Her face was emotionless. Her post-orgasm glow made her look even more beautiful... the innocence in those beautiful ruby red eyes of hers...

But I had to do this. I left the bathroom and rushed to find Sage.

"Sage!"

She is almost at the door when I grab her wrist and pull her back. There's nothing. I feel nothing when I touch her. Her scent does nothing for me either, but she's still a friend...

"Sage..." Her blue eyes, which I had once admired, now remind me that there is a red pair that I love more...

"What is it, Kian?" She asks softly, trying to remain composed, although I know I had hurt her.

"Sage, you will be my Luna."

"I know," she says, unable to look into my eyes. "But will I still be the one in your heart?"

**How can she fucking be somewhere she never was to begin with?** Thanatos growls. I frown. I can't even say Morgana means nothing to me… because she sure as fuck does.

"She's a vampire. There is no future for us regardless of whether I feel something or not," I say quietly, feeling my chest clench painfully. She gasps, her hands clamping over her mouth, and I realise I had indirectly admitted I feel something for Morgana. "It's a passing phase, Sage… it will be over," I add, knowing I was lying. There's no way I'd ever get over Morgana, right down to her fucking sassy nature… I love it. She isn't scared of me, she doesn't try to please me… she makes me forget reality…

"Why are you so infatuated with her? I don't know what it is… I know you have other women, but the vampire… she makes me uneasy. She sleeps in your room. She is different from the others. I love you, Kian. You're…" She looks away, frowning deeply.

I'm not hers for her to even make a claim on me. If it comes down to that… then I'm Morgana's. I frown deeply, trying to control my rising anger and the possessiveness I feel towards Morgana.

"Look, Sage… you will be Luna, but if you think you can stake your claim on me, it's not fucking happening. I belong to no one," I say quietly. "You are important to me though." I reach over and caress her cheek, but all I can think of is Morgana.

"Thank you… I just…" She doesn't complete her sentence, wrapping her arms around me tightly. I frown. I don't know what the fuck to say.

I move her away slowly. Regardless of the fact that she'll be my Luna, after messing around with Morgana, it's a bit of an insult to her to come here and allow Sage to hug me. I step back, and her eyes flash with hurt at my move.

"We've both got work to do. The guests for the summit will begin to arrive tonight. We need to make sure everything is in place," I remind her. She gives me a smile and nods before tiptoeing. She tugs me down, about to kiss me, but I turn my face away sharply. Her lips graze my jaw, and I hear her heart pound.

"Okay, Alpha," she whispers, her voice laced with pain, before she turns and walks out.

I sigh, frowning deeply. I close my eyes for a moment before I head back upstairs. Following her scent to my bedroom, I find Morgana in the bathroom. I can hear the shower is on and frown, glancing at my watch. I quickly get dressed, my mind replaying the moment from earlier... I don't know where we stand, but that had been fucking amazing. I pace my room, but she doesn't step out.

*So, she's avoiding me... fine.* My anger begins to bubble once again, and I glare at the door before storming out and slamming it shut behind me. *Two can play this fucking game.*

**Ajax! Get to my place and take Morgana to the kitchens,** I order angrily through the link.

**Got it, Alpha.** Fucking assholes.

**Why are you angry? Because you're a fucking pussy?** Thanatos asks calmly. I don't know why he's so fucking calm. Isn't he angry that she's avoiding us? **You walked away from our mate.**

I frown. Is he... upset? That isn't an emotion Thanatos knows. I don't reply. There's nothing for me to say.

Later in the evening, Luca, Ajax, Corbin, and I have just finished making a list of issues that needed addressing at the summit. Oliver is watching Morgana, but I told Andrei to make sure she takes it easy and to let her head to bed earlier than usual tonight. I hope she'll be asleep before I make my way upstairs.

"You can't keep avoiding Cain and Kai, Kian," Luca says, sitting back and sighing deeply. "Cain keeps saying he wants to dine with you. He said you have him blocked out."

"Yeah, I do, and it's going to stay that way. I don't have time to entertain his shit. If he wants to dine with me, then we can do so at the fucking dinners for the rest of the damn week," I say coldly, picking up my glass of champagne. Ajax raises an eyebrow.

"Also, the woman is causing a stir, no matter how much we tell everyone not to talk about her. Everyone knows that we have a vampire in our midst," he says quietly.

"And it's not just that; everyone's talking about her beauty, and apparently, she's quite the topic in the kitchens," Luca adds, and Corbin nods.

"She won't stay hidden," Ajax adds.

"I know... probably Cain being a fucking twat. He always has his nose everywhere," I growl.

"Then, what's the plan?" Corbin asks.

If anything, I only trust my Beta and my Deltas. When work is put aside, these are the men I'd sit and drink with.

"I don't know... I could introduce her as an asset... to show the summit that we have some power over the Sanguine Empire. However, if word is out that I went and claimed her as my slave, then that won't work." People would want to know why I wanted her so much as to make a treaty with the Sanguine Empire...

"And Sage was pretty quiet today," Luca says quietly.

I glance at him coldly. I know he has a special spot for Sage, being the previous Beta's daughter, and when Luca had won that title, everyone assumed they'd be mated. That didn't happen, and it's good. Sage has always had eyes for me, and Luca found a mate that he loves.

"Yeah, well, she needs to learn her fucking place," I say coldly.

"Can I say something, Alpha?" Ajax asks sharply.

"What?" I ask coldly, gulping some of my drink down.

"There's more between you and the vampire, but I don't know what it is..." he trails off, watching me calculatingly.

*She's my fucking mate, that's what...*

I don't reply, and none dare to speak when I don't answer. We sit for a short while longer, but when Oliver mind-links me that Morgana is in my bedroom, I decide to head back. I frown when I see Sage waiting at the door to my wing.

"What is it?" I ask. She gives me a small smile as if this morning didn't even happen.

"Well, I was thinking we could discuss some of the important bits for the summit. If you are introducing me as Luna, I need to at least be prepared fully. I don't want to embarrass you," she explains.

I frown. She has a point. I can't delay it with some of the guests already showing up.

"Sure, let's go to my office," I say curtly, motioning for the guards to open the door.

I step inside, and she follows. I head straight upstairs and into my office, inhaling Morgana's intoxicating scent that lingers around here. It's relaxing and comforting. Something I had begun to look forward to returning home to…

**Home. Where she is, fucker,** Thanatos adds.

My heart skips a beat, his words resonating in my head. I had never referred to this place as home before today… *I'm falling for my blood rose… fuck…*

"Kian…" Sage's voice snaps me from my thoughts. She comes towards me, and I turn away, slipping my hands into my pockets, not wanting her to touch me.

"Right, the main thing is making sure you know what's what when it comes to the rules and assets of the kingdom. They may or may not try to find fault in you. Several of the Alphas have daughters, ones they will try to represent to me as better choices," I explain coldly. She frowns, nodding.

"That's to be expected… but what if one of them is your mate, Kian?" She asks, her voice holding concern.

"There's no chance for that to happen. You don't need to worry."

I look at her, wondering if she has always acted so worried and fragile. I had always thought she was a capable woman, but now, comparing her to Morgana… Sage doesn't seem so strong anymore.

**Because our mate is strong enough to stand by our side as our equal.** Thanatos says the very words I was thinking.

**She's a vampire.**

**Doesn't matter. She is still our mate.**

*I know. I fucking know.*

"Okay, I'll make sure I have them all memorised. I know the Alphas who are part of the summit and their Lunas. I will accompany the Lunas and keep them entertained. But I do have one concern, Kian… I'm not marked. If you mark me, that will show we are one and committed."

I frown deeply, my eyes flashing as Thanatos's anger rages within me. I struggle to contain him, but it's futile as his voice leaves my lips, laced with pure blistering rage and anger.

"You know that I will never mark you. You are not our mate!" The power that emanates from me makes her flinch. The heaviness in the room devours all sense of air, and I know she feels suffocated.

"Thanatos…" she whispers, lowering her head. I try to push him back, but he refuses.

"You will never be ours," he hisses.

**Thanatos!** I growl. He scoffs, handing me back the reins.

"Sage," I sigh as she looks up, pain in her eyes. "We'll talk about the marking another time. You know we need Thanatos on board, and there's no way he will ever let me mark you," I suggest coldly.

Thanatos' anger rages higher, and I know he is getting angrier with each passing day. With Morgana close, his emotions are wreaking havoc. He wants her…

"Leave."

She looks at me, hesitating.

"Kian… can I spend the night? Just… to hold you? I need you," she whispers.

**Don't agree to her, Kian… you will hurt our mate,** Thanatos growls.

I need Sage as my Luna… it would only be to sleep. Nothing more.

"Fine," I agree coldly, slamming my walls up just as Thanatos' anger goes out of control.

MORGANA

When the door slams shut, I give it a few minutes before making my way back to the bedroom. I don't know how to feel. I don't know how to react. What happened shouldn't have happened, but the fact that he had used me and then run after Sage…

I'm done. No matter how much he tries, I'll refuse to allow him near me again. I have my pride.

I take out a fitted, maroon, crushed velvet, long-sleeve top with black leather pants and heels. I am not going to act like it had affected me, although it had greatly. I'll behave normally, and if baby Alpha- he is not a baby! That annoys me, too! I feel that after what happened, I can't keep calling him that. It doesn't matter. He's a spoilt brat who deserves a good beating! My mood just becomes darker with each passing minute.

The Delta, Ajax, is outside the bedroom when I am done. I don't miss the way his gaze flickers to my neck, and I know the marks are still there, although they'll probably be gone in an hour or so. I glare at him, and he averts his gaze smoothly.

I am not Kian's fucking plaything. How dare he…

With each step towards the kitchen, my chest heaving rapidly, my anger only grows. I told him everything I do, I do it with passion, and I do. I will be finding Cain today, one way or another.

The morning goes by swiftly, and due to the rush of people coming into the castle, everything is a little bit all over the place, so I take my chance. Discreetly, when the Araqiel family lunch is being taken, I manage to slip a small note under the plate.

'LET'S TALK – M'

I will leave the rest to him to find a way to contact me…

When the Omegas return, and nothing is mentioned about the note, I pray it ended up in the right hands. An hour passes, and when the dishes are brought back, I discreetly go over to help. Scraping the remains of the food into the bin and quickly shuffling through the plates, my heart skips a beat when there, underneath, is a tiny square of paper. I slide it into my sleeve and finish emptying all the dishes smoothly.

"Thanks, Miss," the Omega that I had saved the other day says. We hadn't really talked since then, and I'm not even sure of her name, but she had still gone to Kian for me. Even just the thought of him makes my heart clench painfully, and I press my lips together.

"Morgana, are you okay?" Andrei asks, concerned. To my surprise, he places his hand on my forearm. I don't think he even realised what he had just done. I feel my heartbeat quicken for a moment, remembering my uncle. His gesture reminds me of his concern.

I nod. Even if he really doesn't care, he's at least cordial.

"Yes, I am okay, just think I need a little air," I say lightly.

"Then take a break, go out if you need to. You have been working since morning."

I nod and place the plates down, walking over to the sink to wash my hands. I leave the kitchen and know that Ajax will follow. Well, let him carry on. I walk down the steps and sit down in the shadows behind a pillar, resting my head on my arms. Hopefully, he'll think I am just resting. I stay there for a few moments before I feel a shadow fall upon me. I look up to see Ajax standing there with an apple and a water bottle.

"You look pale. No pun intended," he says. I can't resist the smirk that crosses my lips.

"You're rather pale yourself," I tease, taking the bottle. He doesn't reply, stepping away, and I take the moment to slip the tiny piece out of my sleeve.

'THREE HOURS FROM NOW, RETURN TO THE SAME LOCATION AS LAST TIME. I WILL HANDLE THE REST.'

*Perfect…* I slip the square into my mouth and begin chewing it discreetly. I stand up, ready to return to the kitchen, and toss the empty water bottle into the bin, the paper joined discreetly. Now the next few hours would pass slowly, but I'm looking forward to my little rendezvous with Cain Araqiel.

Somehow, everything had gotten really busy. One of the huge gas cookers with several rings isn't working, and the kitchen is in chaos. There are people to feed and a shortage of cookers. The cooks bring out the portable worktop cookers, and I wonder if Cain had anything to do with the coincidental mishap.

The time is near, and I need to go out…

"Be careful with those eggs, Ben!" Andrei shouts.

"Where is the salt, you oaf?" Griselda growls at someone else. I fan my face, pretending to feel hot. It's warm in here, but that doesn't really bother me.

"Andrei, is it okay if I step outside?" I ask, putting on an exhausted expression, hoping he brought it.

"Ah, of course, dear," he agrees, seeming rather stressed as it is.

I give a small smile, making my way through the rush of people with Ajax right behind me. I hope Cain somehow gets him away because I have no way to do it. I walk to our meeting spot and slide down the pillar, resting my head back and closing my eyes. Ajax says nothing, and I hope I look tired enough to make it look real.

"Fuck…" he mutters. I open my eyes and look at him to see him frowning at me. "I have something to take care of. Don't try anything stupid because if you try to run -"

"You will find me right here. I'm not going to run. I've tried that, and it didn't work," I reply coldly, remaining calm. I don't want him to get suspicious. He nods before running off quickly.

I sigh, looking up at the darkening sky, when I hear a sound to my left. My head snaps to the side, seeing the man in the shadows. My heart thunders. Fuck... I didn't even notice him approaching. I'm about to stand up, but he stops me.

"Don't move. You may be watched from afar," he said quietly. "So, you came…"

I can sense the cruel amusement in his voice. He's happy I had agreed, and one thing is clear: if Kian is a sick bastard, this man is a bigger one. I can sense the cold, sinister undertone in his voice.

"You want to get back home, and I want Kian dead," he whispers coldly.

"If only killing him was so easy," I murmur, placing my head in my arms in case someone from afar sees my lips moving.

"You mean, how would you escape after killing him? That's why I am here. I came second in the duel for the title of Alpha King. I will be king after his demise. Kill Kian for me, and you will be free, Princess."

Kill Kian…

"Every day, in this spot, there's a niche in the wall here... I will leave you some vials of blood. You need blood to get stronger, and I will provide you with that. Kill Kian and avenge the death of your father." I freeze at those words, my heart thundering. So…

I swallow hard; Kian had been responsible for his death. Any questions I had for Cain are gone with that sentence he had uttered so casually.

"We will meet again, Princess, and I do hope that when I take the throne, we can work on a proper, fair treaty that can benefit both kingdoms rather than how my brother's ego is ruining so much for both kingdoms." His quiet, snake-like voice came. I scoff internally; I don't trust him either. The beasts are all the same, but right now, I have to choose what benefits me, and that is siding with Cain. "Daily, check for the blood. It will be here, and we will meet again in three days, same time."

"Fine. You have yourself a deal," I say coldly.

"You will not regret it, Princess Morgana. I assure you this will benefit us both. The Alpha summit begins tomorrow, and Kian will have his hands full. We cannot rush this. You will only have one chance. So, for now, bide your time," his quiet voice advises before he silently leaves.

Kian... I only feel anger at his name when he's not around, but I am his mate... I swallow hard. The connection I feel to him is going to be tough to ignore because, in his presence, I seem to lose myself.

I will kill him. When the time is right, I will be the one to rip Kian Araqiel's heart from his chest. I stare past the trees at the coloured sky, painted in warm hues by the setting sun. *Your days are numbered, Your Highness.* I smirk coldly.

He messed with the wrong woman, and so he will suffer the consequences. I am the start of a fire that he had ignited, a fire that now burns high with a vengeance.

# The Pain of the Bond

MORGANA

NIGHT HAS FALLEN, AND I am back in his bedroom. He is nowhere around.

After Cain had left, I had checked for the niche in the pillar, and, sure enough, there inside were four rather large vials of blood. I drank them quickly, placing the empty bottles back. If Kian gives me blood tonight, then I'll drink as much as I can. I need to get stronger. Cain is right; I need to be sufficient and at my best.

I am in bed now, but he never came. I stare at the ceiling, trying to sleep fruitlessly. Maybe I can do some snooping? I'm alone after all… this is Kian's room, surely there must be something about him here.

I push the sheets away and get out of bed. Turning the lamp on, I look around the room. I can't believe I never bothered to snoop before. The bookshelves catch my attention. Books, files, notebooks, journals…

*Oh, Morgana, you had an entire wall with information.*

I walk over to it, silently running my eyes along the shelf. *The Dragon's Fire… The Song of Doom…* My heart skips a beat as I realise there are many fiction books here. Did he actually read these? One would think he only studied war and battle tactics with his lack of personality! I let my fingers run over the spines of the books.

*His Forbidden Love.* The title catches my attention, and I smile. Taking it off the shelf, I skim through it. So, the king actually reads love stories… I smirk in amusement. Well, he must believe love is fiction because he sure doesn't have any emotions.

I place it aside and return to the shelves, noticing the journals that sit on the highest shelf. Well, too bad I can reach. I'm not short like his dumb Sage. I tiptoe, straining to reach them before using my powers to pull them towards me. I smirk as I look down at the first one, only to frown when I realise it's locked. Really? I take a few more off, displeased when I realise each one is locked. Great.

I peer around the sides, but the only thing on the leather covers are dates. Last year… four years ago… does the Alpha actually keep a journal? I replace them, thinking I'll look for a key another time. Surely it's around here somewhere.

I hear a distant door shut and quickly replace the books, save the love story. I hurriedly go over to the bed, sitting down and pretending to read, but no one comes. Strange.

I become immersed in the book, and for a while, I forget all my troubles. The book is bittersweet, two people so in love, yet they are not meant to be. With each page, my heart thumps, wanting to know what will happen next.

*No, you dimwit! Don't push her away!* My heart thunders, and I snap the book shut, huffing.

"Men are so stupid!" I hiss, "Stupid book! I hate books!"

But I know I will be returning to that book soon enough. It must be far past midnight, and, for the first time, I wonder if Kian is even going to return. Why am I so restless? I know I want to see how he reacts after what happened, but then the way he had gone after Sage -

Sage.

My heart thumps. How could I have been so stupid? Of course, he's probably with her.

Are they here? I get off the bed and walk to the bedroom door. I know I shouldn't, but I can't stop myself. I follow my nose, and his scent becomes stronger the further down the hall I go. My silent footsteps pad quietly on the floor. Why does this feel painful? My stomach is twisting, and I feel sick with dread.

I stop outside a door, and sure enough, two scents that are familiar come from this room. So, he is with Sage… my heart clenches painfully, and I wish this feeling would go away.

The urge to open the door is too strong, and before I can even comprehend what I'm doing, I turn the handle silently. Unlike the first time I did something like this, the sight in front of me is far different, and I feel like something is being ripped from my chest. My heart thunders, and I can't breathe as I look at Kian. He lay on his back with his arms under his head with Sage snuggled into his side, her hand on his bare torso.

Why is this fucking hurting? I hate him.

I back away from the door, my entire body trembling.

*Breathe, Morgana…*

Turning, I walk down the hall and back to his bedroom. It hurt… a lot…

I shut the door silently. Trying to breathe, I pace the room, struggling to calm the storm I feel inside. It has to be the bond… only something so strong could cause me such pain.

## MANY YEARS AGO

*"Mother! Tell me the story about the prince and princess from different kingdoms again!"*

*"Settle down, my love. You should have been asleep long ago!" Mother scolded.*

*"Mother, please, I love stories!"*

*"Now, which one?" She sat on the bed, scooping me into her lap, and I giggled, looking up at her.*

*"The one with the werewolf," I whispered. Those monsters were not allowed to be spoken of, but I loved this story. It was our secret. "Please, Mommy." Her tinkle of laughter made me smile as I stared up at her in anticipation.*

*"Long ago… there was a beautiful elven princess. Like vampires, she had a betrothed… someone she would marry and love until the end of time…"*

*The warmth in the room and the glow of the lamp illuminated Mother's dark locks. It made me relax into her as she continued,*

*"He was part beast, yet he loved deeply, so deeply that she no longer cared what he was. When she was with him, she was consumed by his very presence. The connection between them was undeniable. That night, when she confessed her love for him, he told her that she was his destined one, his -"*

*"Mate!" I exclaimed, my sleep vanishing. "The, what, Mommy?" She laughed, her red eyes full of warmth.*

*"Then… he marked her."*

*"And then…"*

"Then… I will tell you what happened next when you are older," Mother said, tucking me into bed.

"But, Mommy! There must be more! I want to know how he told her he loved her!" I whined.

The undeniable pull of the mate bond.

The bond is said to be between werewolves… but there were rare occasions when a werewolf was mated to another species.

Why me? My heart twists as I realise that he must have come to the palace because I was his mate.

"You're mine!"

Those words of his… I can't forget. The possessive tone in his voice, his anger and rage. But is the bond really that strong? He doesn't care for me, so why didn't he just leave me where I was happy? Why is this hurting?

He killed my father… I would never be able to forgive him for that, but something about Cain is clearly off. I need to know exactly what happened that night. Did he kill my father directly, or did he get someone to do it? He had been in the Sanguine Empire that night. I myself was witness to that. I also know, deep down, that when I'm with him, I forget everything else. Is it just the mate bond making me try to justify that maybe there was more to it?

I look at the bed. I can never sleep there again. I have my pride. With trembling hands, I turn away from the bed and walk to the window. I sit on the ground, staring out at the moon.

*I was not yours for you to create this bond, Selene.* I glare at the moon, hoping she heard.

As sleep finally overcomes me, the last question that tumbles in my sleepy mind is: *How does one destroy such a powerful bond? Surely there must be a way?*

Before sleep welcomes me into its fold, the last image that fills my mind is of Kian and Sage sleeping together. Hell hath no fury like a woman scorned… yet that is nothing compared to mocking Morgana Araton.

*You have played your card, and now… it is now my turn.*

KIAN

Sleep hadn't been great, and although I did fall asleep in the end, I didn't want to be here. Thanatos was hammering against the wall I had put up, and the risk of him taking over was consuming me. From the moment I got into bed, I told Sage I was tired and not to talk. She had obliged, and I was glad for it.

Now, my eyes snap open just as the sun is rising, and I frown down at Sage. I ease out of her hold slowly and get up. Thanatos needs Morgana, or more like I need her to calm him down.

My heart skips a beat when I notice the open door. There are only three people in my wing…

*Morgana.*

*Fuck.*

I get up quickly and leave the room swiftly, walking through the hall down to my room. Opening the door, I look at the empty bed. A book lay open on top of the messy sheets. Her scent is strong, but for a second, I panic.

I step into the room, my heart racing when I see her. She's sitting on the floor leaning against the window, her legs bent under her and her arm wrapped around her waist. Her breasts rise and fall, and those plump lips of hers are parted slightly. There is a sadness to her, and her hold seems vulnerable.

*She saw… fuck, she saw…*

I clench my jaw, feeling Thanatos' growl of rage echo through my head from behind his wall. I know he's furious that I hurt her.

I crouch down before her, my own fucking emotions a mess. How is someone so delicate so strong? How much will she take before I end up breaking her? Her mind is in turmoil, I can sense that much. I reach over, stopping inches from her, almost as if one touch might shatter her. What am I doing? What do I want to do?

Thanatos' struggle is growing, and I fucking hope he calms the fuck down before the Alpha meeting.

I wrap my arms around her shoulders, knowing that when she's asleep, nothing can wake her. She's a deep sleeper. I slip my other hand under her thighs, standing up slowly so as not to disturb her, and carry her to the bed. I try not to focus on the sparks that rush through me, sparks that soothe both Thanatos and me… I missed her…

I place her on the bed, but just then, her eyes snap open, and she pushes me away with such force that I stagger back. She gets off the bed as if it burned her, glaring coldly at me.

"Did I give you permission to touch me?" She hisses.

As much as I want to remind her that she belongs to me, I don't think I have that right at this moment. I feel guilty already…

"You were on the fucking floor."

"And is that any of your concern? From here on out, I want a separate room, or the cells will do," she states coldly. I frown.

"You are not leaving this room." She scoffs, crossing her arm as she walks over to me and stares into my eyes.

"Oh, I am. Bring your woman here where she belongs. Don't test me," she hisses. Fuck, if I thought she was going to be upset… I was way fucking wrong. She isn't upset or jealous, she's fucking pissed.

"You are not leaving this room," I say coldly, my eyes flashing. "That's my fucking order." Her lips curl in a cold smirk.

"Oh, yeah? And what's going to stop me?" She challenges. I clench my jaw; I'm fucking struggling to contain my anger and Thanatos right now. Is she really doing this?

"Don't push me unless you want to be bound again," I growl.

"Oh? Do you really think you can do as you wish? I'm done with your games, Kian. Either accept what I ask for or I assure you I have plenty of ways to get what I want!" She snaps.

"Morgana! Do not, and I fucking mean, do *not* push me," I growl. Thanatos is clawing at the wall, and I'm not sure how long I'll be able to hold him back. She raises an eyebrow.

"I will do what I want. You may be a king, but I am a princess, and I am not less than you, nor do I fear you. You may think you're the king, but to me, you are nothing."

Her words cut deeper than anything ever had in my life. None of Cain's mockery growing up… none of the insults that I was not good enough… the fact that I had to prove myself against someone six years my senior from the day I could fucking walk… nothing. But her single sentence cut fucking deep. I swallow hard, trying to focus on her, but the beautiful woman before me holds so much hatred in her eyes that it fucking stings. What's worse, it was my own fucking doing.

She smirks, now walking towards me, and for a moment I don't understand why. Until Sage appears in the doorway.

"Kian…" she trails off, seeing Morgana approaching me. Morgana smiles, and I know for a fact that she's up to no fucking good.

"Finally… you're here. Look, I'm asking your Alpha to let me either move to a different room or even the cells, but he's refusing," Morgana says with a mocking pout, looking at Sage. "I wonder… what hold do I have on him that he can't simply let me out of his sight?"

Fuck, she's messing things up. I narrow my eyes. What is she even insinuating?

"Morgana," I warn.

She closes the gap between us, locking her arms around my neck. My heart fucking races at her touch, and I'm not able to stop myself from looking at her lips. She licks them slowly, and my eyes flash.

"Aww, will you look at that? Your woman is right here, yet you can't even behave in her presence," Morgana whispers seductively. She presses her body against mine, and I feel myself throb. *Fuck.*

"Morgana…" I growl, gripping her waist, trying to stop her from fucking turning me on even more. But when she presses herself fully against me, I can't even hold her away. I fucking love it. The sparks, the illicit desire to fuck her senseless… "Don't," I breathe dangerously.

"Are you an enchantress or something?" Sage spits, walking into the room.

"I don't know…" Morgana hums. She leans over, her nose brushing mine, and the urge to kiss her is strong. "Want to kiss me, Kian?"

Her voice is soft, seductive, and I fucking want to do a lot more than kiss her, but I am not going to do this with her right now. My eyes flash, my emotions a storm; her words, that look in her eyes, her scent…

Before I can even reply, her lips meet mine in a sensual kiss, sending sizzling sparks through me. I throb hard, but before I can react or kiss her back, she pulls away, smirking coldly.

"See… he can't resist. So, either you tell him to move me elsewhere, or deal with this and a lot more," she says harshly to Sage.

My heart is thundering, struggling with Thanatos, whose anger is only growing with the mess she had made of my emotions. She has a fucking hold over me and she knows it…

"How dare you…" Sage glares icily at Morgana. My eyes flash.

"Sage!" I growl. No one is allowed to speak to her like that!

"Kian, she -"

"I said enough!" I hiss.

Morgana simply smirks, running her fingers through her silky black hair. She now whirls around and takes hold of Sage's chin.

"Seems like he has a favourite... you should really feel hurt," she taunts, batting those lashes of hers. "Tell me, is there anything special about my touch?"

"There -"

Sage is cut off when Morgana's lips touch hers. A gasp leaves Sage, her cheeks flushing as *my* mate kisses her. My eyes fly open. Jealousy and anger rip through me like a fucking tidal wave, and any control I had left on Thanatos is gone. A fucking million emotions course through me at the sight of her kissing someone else other than me, and I rip her away from Sage, pushing Sage away roughly.

*"Mine!"* Thanatos and I thunder together, glaring at Sage, who flinches.

*Fuck...*

The final straw of control snaps, and I'm thrown to the back of my mind as Thanatos takes control.

# BREAKING POINT

THANATOS

*I* AM DONE. IF THIS fucking pup is going to hurt my mate, then I will show him who the fuck the true Alpha is.

The moment Morgana put those soft lips against Sage's, my anger snapped. It disgusts me when Kian kisses her, but it disgusts me even more to see my mate kiss this bitch!

"Kian... Thanatos..." Sage whimpers, staring at me.

"You heard what I said! She. Is. Mine! And if Kian cannot be fucking man enough to admit it, then I will!" I hiss. I grab her by her neck, wanting to rip her to pieces.

**Thanatos, don't! You can't tell her about Morgana!**

*Why? Ashamed of her?*

**No! I don't want to risk her in any way! If anyone finds out -**

**Fuck off, I'm fucking in charge here!** I hiss back, slamming my walls up. I hope he enjoys the fucking treatment. He's a fucking dick. If he can't accept mate, then he doesn't deserve mate! She is mine!

"I-I'm sorry, Thanatos..." Sage whispers, looking at me. I drop her roughly. Filth!

"You will live this time because you mean something to Kian... but stay far, far away or I will end you!" I hiss.

"Yes, Alpha." She bows her head, her entire body shaking with fear as she turns to leave, unable to look me in the eye.

"Oh, and one more thing," I growl. She freezes, and I step closer. "If you repeat anything that happened here to anyone…" I leave my threat hanging. I hate her.

"Never, Alpha," she whispers before she turns and leaves the room, breaking into sobs as she runs down the hall.

I smile coldly, turning to my lush little mate. Finally, we meet again. She looks delicious, standing there with those perky, lush tits of hers pressing against that silk night top.

"Thanatos…" she says quietly. She looks alert now, her eyes wary and any playful taunts are gone.

Fuck, that voice sounds so fucking good, and I want to hear her moan my name under me. Hmm, I am still tempted to bend her over and spank that ass of hers for pissing me off.

"What is it, my little mate?" I purr, closing the gap between us. She is wary of me, and I cup her jaw, gazing at those lips of hers.

"Why did you… take over?" She asks calmly. I smirk dangerously.

"Oh, Kian was being a fucking dickhead," I purr, grazing my nose along her cheek.

"I agree…" Despite her calm voice, her heart is racing. Jealousy rears its head once again.

"You are not to kiss anyone else," I growl, my eyes blazing with anger as I stare into those ruby orbs of hers.

"I… was proving a point," she explains softly. I smirk, rubbing my thumb along her plump lips, hearing her breath hitch.

"Not afraid of me, are you, my pretty little thing?" I purr, stepping closer. Oh, she fucking is.

"Not at all," she replies, brushing my hand away. I admire her bravery.

"Good, because you are my brave little mate."

I wrap my arms around her tightly, nuzzling my nose into her neck. Ah… she smells so fucking good... how I want to mark her.

"Hmm, so we are mates." She says it as if she already knew this.

"Yes," I murmur, ignoring Kian's trying to take back control. Oh, she feels good pressed against me. "Now how about you be a good little mate and let me have a taste of that sweet little cunt of yours," I growl, squeezing her ass as I nibble on her neck.

Suddenly, her hand meets my face as she fucking slapped me hard across the face, pulling away from me, shocking me to silence.

"Don't you dare think that just because I'm your damn mate that I'm going to do as you wish! You and Kian have done nothing to earn my trust, and you think you can use that kind of language with me?" She snaps. I smirk, seeing the faint blush on her cheeks as I regain myself. I enjoy her feisty behaviour, so I will forgive her slap for now...

"Oh? You didn't like it... I thought women loved men being filthy animals, and I am an animal," I growl, advancing on her.

"Thanatos... this is not a joke. Stand down," she warns.

I smirk, "Challenging me, my little mate?"

"No, asking," she says firmly, placing her hands on my chest, stopping me. I smirk coldly.

"Fine, one kiss then. It's the first time we are officially meeting and talk-ing..." I request, caressing her cheek with my knuckles. My piercing gold eyes glare into hers. I hope she is smart enough to not disobey me. "You know... unlike Kian... I want you..." I murmur, pressing myself against her. I hope she can feel how fucking hard I am for her.

"One kiss," she agrees quietly.

I smirk arrogantly. Of course. One kiss. She leans over slowly, and I smirk. *Oh, we are going to kiss, but on my fucking terms...*

I suddenly grab her wrists, spinning her around and pushing her down onto the bed, pinning her wrists to the bed. Before she can even fight me, I slam my lips against hers in one fucking crushing, sizzling, rough kiss. Fucking delicious sparks rush through me, so fucking strong that for a moment I am able to ignore Kian trying to breakthrough. That fucking idiot needs to learn his lesson.

As for our mate... fuck, she is delicious. I kiss her roughly, yet passion-ately, assaulting her mouth in a bruising kiss. Pleasure rushes to Mini-Kian, and I really want to put him to use. Since I won't be able to mate her in wolf form, as she has no wolf, I'll have to make do with that tiny thing.

**It's not fucking tiny,** Kian growls in the distance.

Oh, it fucking is. Compared to mine, anyway...

**Thanatos, reign it back, you're hurting her,** Kian growls.

**Like you haven't hurt her, I'm not hurting her!** I shoot back angrily. She is struggling, but I'm sure she's enjoying the game. I keep her pinned under me, straddling her thighs. She moans and whimpers against me, but I don't let go.

**Thanatos, fuck, stop it!** Kian thunders.

The pleasure of devouring my mate is intense. I ignore the fucking asshole, but when the first taste of blood fills my mouth, I freeze and move back. I look down at her. Her heart is thundering, her eyes burning with rage. I notice how my hands are crushing her wrists extremely tightly, and I feel guilt twist inside seeing the redness around her bloody lips. She's breathing deeply, and I can see the hatred in her eyes.

Fuck, I had just hurt our mate, too.

KIAN

The moment Thanatos becomes wracked with guilt, I take over. He doesn't argue, curling up in my mind, and I'm not sure if I actually heard a whimper.

I get off Morgana slowly, frowning at her bruised wrists. I reach out for them as she massages them, turning away from me.

"Sorry, I shouldn't have let him -"

"Please. Don't act like you care. He, at least, isn't as bad as you," she spits coldly. That makes Thanatos perk up a little.

"Morgana…"

"Fuck off, Kian," she shoots back. My name on her lips sounds fucking good, but not when it's laced with so much hatred. "I want a separate room," she hisses.

"No." I fucking need her here with me.

"No?" Her eyes flashing. "Listen to me, Kian… I am not your fucking plaything. I am no one's bitch, and either you agree, or I swear I'll rip my fucking heart out right now."

I narrow my eyes at her. That look in her eyes… I know she'll do it, too. She knows what she is to me and how to hurt me. I'm sure she'd go to any level. Despite how passive my face is, my heart races at those fucking words.

"Don't push me, Morgana. My word is - "

"I will do it. Don't think that I am just playing, I'll do it, and we both know your infatuation with me is far too deep to let me die so easily," she hisses coldly. No…

"Morgana… don't do this. If this is about Sage, nothing happened, or I assure you, you would have felt it," I say quietly. Her eyes blaze as she glares at me, scoffing.

"Don't give yourself so much importance! I am not your toy! I want my own room, even if it means the cells!" She hisses again. I grab her by her upper arms, wishing she fucking understood. "Do you really think I care? Do whatever you want with whoever you want, but I will not be one of your dolls," she says dangerously. I frown. I need her.

**Then fucking tell her,** Thanatos hisses, despite the sadness that radiates off him.

"What do you want from me, Morgana?" I ask coldly. Right now, I'm willing to bargain with her, but I don't want her out of my sight. Not to mention, Sage probably knows Morgana is my mate… I need to tell Luca and the others.

This had to happen today. Fuck, with the first summit meeting soon, I need to be in the right fucking headspace.

"I want you to stay the fuck away from me," she hisses.

"Anything but that."

"Let me go." I close my eyes.

"Anything that doesn't include you leaving or staying away from me," I elaborate, my eyes flashing as I look at her. I don't miss the sharp, calculating look in her eyes. She's thinking it over…

"I'll tell you… tonight. But promise me you will give me what I ask for," she says coldly. I hesitate. Only a fool would promise something fucking blindly.

**Agree, you fucking idiot.**

I don't trust her… but I had fucking hurt her enough.

"You have my word," I reply coldly, clenching my jaw. She turns her back on me, and my gaze dips to her ass. Frowning, I look away. I had hurt her when I didn't mean to. Whatever she asks for, I'll give it to her as long as it means she won't leave me… "Stay here for today. You need to rest," I say quietly.

Not waiting for a reply, I leave the room, shutting the door behind me. I'll have my blood sent to her, but I can't risk letting her drink from me directly when neither of us were in the right fucking frame of mind.

I get washed and dressed quickly, pulling on a white button-down shirt and black pants before I make my way to the main castle and towards my office, mind-linking Luca and my Deltas to join me there as soon as possible. I need to tell them about her. Now that Sage knows more than enough, I can't leave them in the dark any longer. Ten minutes later, the four men are looking at me expectantly. I have no fucking clue how to start this fucking conversation.

"Kian, the meeting is in an hour. Are you seriously making us stop for whatever you need to tell us that you are not even able to tell us?" Luca asks. Clearly, he has been trying to deal with last-minute preparations and is fucking stressed out.

I sigh, looking at all four of them. Reuban is still out at the border, and there's still no clue about who is behind the attacks. Oliver, Ajax, and Corbin watch me silently, waiting for me to speak whilst Luca has now proceeded to start biting his nails. What the fuck is his problem? He's fucking more annoying than a first-time dad waiting for his pup to be born.

"Chill the fuck out. If you want, you can leave," I growl. He's acting worse than a fucking grandma.

"Sorry, man, but what is it?" He asks, glancing at his watch.

"Morgana…" They exchange looks, obviously confused by my words, or lack thereof. "The reason I brought her here, the reason I have kept her in my room… the fucking reason I need her…" I trail off, sitting back in my chair. Yeah, still, none of them click on. "She's my mate."

Idiots.

Their reactions are all different. Luca blinks, stunned. Corbin stares at me, completely shocked. Oliver gasps, and Ajax nods slowly as if it makes sense.

"Whoa…" Luca murmurs after a moment.

"Interesting," Ajax remarks.

"So… the vampir- I mean, Morgana is our Luna?" Oliver asks in a hushed tone.

"No," I state quietly. That simple word stings.

«A vampire mate…» Luca murmurs. His face is pale.

"This can make people question your role as Alpha King…" Oliver murmurs. I scoff, my eyes flashing.

"I'm the fucking strongest, it gives them no fucking basis." I growl, "And I am not making her my Luna." I hate that. The pain that fucking eats me up inside.

"But without your Luna… your wolf will only begin to lose his sanity," Luca muses quietly.

"But I'm keeping her by my side, am I not?" I ask coldly.

None speak. I know it's fucking crazy and messed up.

"I have a suggestion," Ajax says, massaging his jaw as he paces my office.

"What is it?" I ask. Luca sits down in the chair opposite, clearly too shocked to care about time anymore.

"Why not say you are taking a woman from the Sanguine Empire as your partner to create peace between the two kingdoms? We know the power of an Alpha wolf... you need your fated mate... you won't be able to resist her for long," Ajax says, "and take Sage as your Luna, too. That way no one can question it."

"Co-Lunas?" Oliver asks, raising an eyebrow.

"Many kingdom's leaders have more than one woman by their side. Call it what you want, but it can show that you will have good ties with the vampires. We are more powerful, but a peace treaty can help us in many ways as well."

"We already agreed to a cease-fire when I took her as my slave," I remind him coldly.

"I'm saying build an actual alliance with them. They have control of the dams on the water we need, and we have the produce and crops they need. If we actually agreed to talk, we could become stronger Alpha," Ajax explains quietly. "You yourself have said that once." That is true... I don't care if anyone thinks I'm weak, I want what was best for my people. In the end, in any fucking battle, it's the civilians that suffer.

"He isn't wrong," Oliver murmures, "but a vampire Luna..."

"Sage will also be his Luna, guaranteed to give him a werewolf pup. This way, his mate stays by his side, and no one will ever need to know that she is his mate..." Luca says it as if it all made sense now.

Yeah, I'm not fucking Sage again. Knowing it will cause Morgana pain, I would never touch her. Besides, I don't want her... not anymore. This option seems too good to be true. If my men think it's good, then why not? My heart is racing, and Thanatos has perked up.

**Let's do it, Kian. These are your advisors, and they have way fucking more sense than you,** Thanatos growls. They all seem to be agreeing with one another. But it feels too fucking easy...

"She's strong, she is the type of woman that could actually be an asset to the king," Corbin says thoughtfully.

"I don't actually not like her… she's good with the Omegas, witty, sharp, and smart," Ajax adds seriously. My eyes flash at that. Hearing him compliment anyone is something he rarely does. Jealousy and possessiveness flare inside of me, and I clench my fist, letting my aura roll off of me.

"She's mine," I growl dangerously.

"Yeah… we get that…" Luca says gently, trying to calm me down.

"She is," Ajax agrees, lowering his head in submission. My heart thuds as one thing comes to my mind.

Will Morgana agree?

It would mean me admitting to her how I feel… the thought that I could actually have her…

"If she's your mate, Alpha, then you need her," Oliver says quietly.

**Yeah, we fucking do, and these fools seem to have realised that quicker than you,** Thanatos growls.

**You're allowed some happiness, Kian, even if it is unconventional,** Luca's voice comes through the link.

**Oh, yeah? That's fucking interesting coming from you… aren't you always team fucking Sage?** I remark.

**I'm team you first. If she's your mate… then Sage isn't in the equation. But if you still plan to make her your Luna on the side, then you need to tell her how it's going to be.**

**Yeah…**

**So… Morgana… does she like you?** Luca asks, smirking. I glare at him. Yeah, my ego is not going to let me fucking admit that she fucking hates me…

"That's none of your fucking concern."

"I think they 'like' each other," Ajax adds with a tiny smirk.

**Alpha the meeting is waiting for you,** one of my men link. I stand up, looking at them all.

"What we spoke of stays here. I will announce what I need to when I feel the time is fucking right."

"Understood," they reply in unison.

I take a knife from my desk and grab one of the glasses from my wine cabinet before slashing my hand. I keep the knife pressed there, letting the blood flow into the glass. All eyes are on me, but I couldn't care less. Once the glass is full, I let the wound heal and wipe my hand clean.

"Oliver, take that to Morgana," I order.

Not waiting for a reply. I leave the office. I walk down the halls towards the courtroom. I'm ready for this meeting and any shit they throw my way because they fucking will have crap to say. My footsteps make the only sound that echoes in the silent halls.

My mind is on my blood rose, and the fact that I hate vampires. It's interesting how I forget all of that when it comes to her. I know my father may have died at the hands of vampires, but it isn't like it was Morgana who had done it... is there a chance for us?

**Oh, we fucking can have a chance. Mate tastes good. Now, when will I get to taste her pussy?** I internally groan. He's going to fucking mess me up.

**Fuck off, Thanatos.**

**I still haven't forgiven you,** he grumbles.

**And you almost hurt her,** I reply quietly. I know he feels guilty for it, but I need him to be fucking careful next time.

**So that means if I'm gentle, I can spend some time with her?** He asks, sounding like a fucking puppy. I frown... Thanatos in control is dangerous.

**If she agrees,** I say quietly.

**Okay! Ask mate soon!**

Yeah, he really is a fucking animal...

He growls menacingly but I simply ignore him as a small smile crosses my lips. A sliver of hope for a future with my she-devil glimmers bleakly and I will grasp on to it. Maybe, just fucking maybe, we could have a future.

# THE FIRST SUMMIT

MORGANA

THE MOMENT HE LEAVES, I begin to ponder what to ask for. What would be beneficial for me? I want more than just my freedom; I want revenge for my father's death… I need a lot more… I'm pacing the bedroom floor when a knock makes me look up.

"Enter."

The door opens, and Delta Oliver is standing there with a glass of blood. From what I can smell, it's Kian's. My heart skips a beat.

"For you, Lady Morgana," he offers politely. I raise an eyebrow. Lady? Since when does he address me so kindly?

"Thank you." I take the glass. "Please close the door after yourself." I'm not in the mood to entertain anyone. He leaves me alone, and I sit down on the bed, staring out the window.

What do I ask for? Him to cut Sage from his life? Oh, as tempting as that is, I need to choose something beneficial. I want nothing more to do with him or his beast. I sigh, sipping the blood, when an idea pops into my head. I swirl the blood in the glass slowly as a small smirk crosses my lips.

"Perfect," I murmur.

## KIAN

The moment I enter the hall, everyone stands and lowers their heads toward me. I let my aura swirl around me, displaying my power. I am the king here. Taking my seat, I lean back, power and arrogance exuding from every pore in my body, despite how casually I sit. I rest my elbow on the arm of the chair and look at each Alpha one by one.

This meeting is like a pack of hungry wolves waiting for their next fucking target. Each one here is hungry for more status and power, wanting to be in my fucking spot. Everyone wishes to be the Alpha King, but I doubt that most of them even understand the fucking meaning or responsibility of this position.

"Let the meeting commence," I announce quietly. My voice carries to every corner of the room, and the Alphas all take a seat.

"With permission, Alpha King Kian, may I go first?" Alpha Phillip asks, bowing his head to me. I give a curt nod, and he stands up.

"As you all know, my pack is on the borders, not far from the Black Dawn Pack," he begins. He hesitates, but I can hear the desperation in his voice. "We offered a lot of help as ordered, but it's drained our resources, too. There are certain things we need; supplies are short, and I know we got our allowance for the season, but - "

"For helping a neighbouring pack, I thank you. As for any help you need, put in a request before the week is over, and you will be given what you need," I interrupt. He gives me a small smile of appreciation and sits down.

"I don't think that's fair. When there was the attack from the rogues last year, you told us that the damage - " My eyes flash as I glare at the man who had spoken.

"For one of the strongest Alphas, you sure as fucking petty. Rogue attacks are the norm, and you should have the correct measures put into place. These attacks are different, and unless you want to send some men to the border for extra fucking patrol, keep your mouth fucking zipped," I say coldly.

A tense silence flits through the room before another Alpha looks at me.

"Alpha, what are we going to do about the attacks? We are still unsure who is behind them."

"I have sent out a team, and it is one of the things I want everyone to contribute to. I want squads of men from every pack to strengthen the border defences." My eyes skim over them all. "Over the next few days, I will discuss these plans further and in detail." I can tell which ones are reluctant and which ones are willing to protect this kingdom. "I will get to the bottom of this, but as a kingdom, we all need to do our part."

"What of the humans? They're just living leisurely, they - "

"They're humans, far weaker than us. Let them stick to what they do best. Fae or Vampire, do you really think humans would stand a fucking chance?" I growl. "It would only result in unnecessary deaths."

"But it can't be vampires, right? Did you not create a treaty with them?" Another Alpha cuts in.

"A cease-fire, but each kingdom has those who don't follow the law. We can't relax over a simple treaty when there is nothing to show for it. I don't trust them, nor the Fae," I explain quietly.

"Alpha Kian… is it true there may be war?" The eldest Alpha in the room spoke. In his late fifties, he still looks younger than his age, but compared to a lot of these fucking assholes, he is wiser. A rustle of unease spreads through the room, and I stay silent, my face not giving anything away.

"If war comes to us, then we will show them that we are ready. As for starting it… there are no plans."

I frown. The rumours that the Fae are making an alliance with another species worry me, but I'm not going to let my people know that. If I show my worry, then it will only negatively impact them. As long as I, as king, remain confident, my men will remain strong. It's a fucking domino effect, and I am the fucking starting piece.

"So… the chances for war are low?" The Alpha repeats.

"I didn't say that. We should be prepared for the worst, however, what I said is that war will not start by our hand," I reply firmly. Our eyes meet, and the Alpha nods.

They begin talking amongst themselves, discussing the pros and cons as I remain silent, frowning deeply as I let them debate it out. The problem is, at the moment, we are four species which are either neutral or hostile… yet there is no good relationship between any… but if two kingdoms unite… that fucking puts us at higher risk.

The talks shift to the water situation and then to the demand that were-wolves have separate schools from humans.

"No. It's not going to happen," I interrupt coldly.

"We are above them, Alpha Kian."

I scoff, "How? In what way?"

"Intelligence, for one."

"Considering fucking pups who mind-link and use it to cheat in tests? Intelligent indeed," I scoff again.

"That... that isn't fair; they are just kids. Your new method was rather extreme..."

"What? By giving them a dose of wolfsbane before tests? Not extreme at all. It's called fairness," I say icily. "Our people are one, and I don't care how shit's done in other kingdoms. We will not divide the humans and werewolves. That's where it starts before we begin to believe we are better... just the way it has come to my attention how Omegas may be treated. Just because we are stronger does not give anyone the fucking right to hurt those weaker than us..."

**But you can hurt mate...** Thanatos remarks.

I clench my jaw. Yeah, I did fucking hurt her... kept her tied up, tossed her in a cell... hurt her emotionally... yeah, I'm a fucking hypocrite... but I'm going to do better from here on out.

"Alpha?"

"Alpha Kian."

I look up, being brought out of my thoughts, and I blink.

"This kingdom will continue to treat its people with equality and respect," I say clearly. My voice carries powerfully across the room, my decision absolute.

"There is still the food chain Alpha. If we are stronger, we have - "

My eyes flash as I glare at the man who spoke. I stand up, my aura swirling around me like a fucking tornado. The last fucking thing I need is a civil fucking war or tension from within the kingdom.

"I'm the fucking king here, and if you want to defy anyone, remember that I stand for those who cannot fend for themselves," I growl.

Casting one cold glare at the table, I turn away. This meeting is over for the day. I'm fucking done. Those who cannot fend for themselves...

Right now, it's my mate who is alone in this fucking place. I have treated her unfairly. I'll make it up to her because even if my father was killed by a vampire, it had not been by her hand...

## MORGANA

"The King said to get changed. Tonight you will dine with him."

Those are the words the Omega girl says before she asks if I need help getting ready. I decline her help and decide to get ready by myself.

I hadn't been able to go down to the courtyard for more blood, but it's fine. I need to be careful, so I spent the day searching this part of the castle. Although most of the doors were locked, I still had a look around. I hadn't managed to find the keys to the journals, much to my disappointment, but I still have this room to search more thoroughly. Wherever that annoying Alpha had hidden them, I'll find them.

I know what I want from him, so I decide to use my allure and looks tonight to keep him distracted and hope he'll agree to what I'm asking. I know I have a hold over him with the mate bond, and something tells me that if I want, I'll be able to bring Thanatos forth. Unlike his human counterpart, he is much more smitten with me. However, that, too, can be dangerous, considering how rough he had been last time.

Isn't it funny that I, a vampire, am mated to the Alpha King? I wonder, if I really wanted to, would I be able to bring him to his knees and have him yield to me? Oh, I know I have the capability to. If I want, I can make anyone fall in love with me. I can be so sweet, despite how psychotic I am, too.

I just showered and now stare at my large array of clothing. *Now... what is the perfect colour to bring a man to his knees?*

Red.

I choose the sexiest dress from the wardrobe. Slipping it on, I just about get it zipped up. It's tiny; with my height, it just about covers my behind, and my legs are on full display. I apply some smoky eye makeup, deep red lipstick, and finish off with some highlighter. After putting on some heels, I curl my black locks before running my fingers through them. Finishing with a touch of fragrance, I look in the mirror for a moment. It feels like I am Morgana Araton, Princess of the Sanguine Empire, once again.

What have I become? Stuck in this place as a captive. I'm losing my identity with each passing day.

I push the thought away and glance at the time. The Omega had said dinner would be served downstairs at eight p.m. How strange; from what I had thought, isn't he meant to be dining with his guests for the next few nights? I guess I'll ask him...

I leave the room and make my way downstairs. The smell of delicious dishes wafts through the air, but it's something else that makes me stop in my tracks. Kian is leaning against the bannister of the staircase, arms crossed. He looks incredibly handsome in more formal attire. His bulging muscles strain against the fabric of his shirt. A few buttons are left open, showing off the necklaces that always hang around his neck. His intoxicating scent overpowers everything else, leaving me feeling slightly lightheaded.

He turns, glancing up at me. I don't miss the way his heart begins to race. His eyes darken with desire as his gaze trails up my body, and I fight to keep my heartbeat steady.

He's doing it again. His gaze alone plays with my emotions. My stomach is fluttering like crazy, and that familiar ache settles in my core... but this man is not going to touch me again. Not after how he played and used me last time. I just have to remember that.

I walk down the steps, my chin held high and my hips swaying. Yep, I'm just being a little bit sexier than normal, and my hair bounces around me. I stop when I approach the bottom. Reaching out, I place a finger under his chin, trying not to gasp at the sparks that rush through me.

"Never seen a woman before?" I ask mockingly. He raises an eyebrow, his gaze dipping to my breasts. My satin dress leaves a lot of cleavage on display.

"Not one as beautiful as you. You look… ravishing," he says huskily, his deep voice sending a shiver of pleasure down my spine. My stomach flutters, but I am not going to let him get to me. I let go of his chin and toss my hair over my shoulder.

"Obviously," I state. I'm confused. After what happened with Sage, is he really going to continue this?

"This way."

He steps ahead and leads me down the hall. I had come here earlier, so I know exactly where the dining room is. However, the room that had been dark and empty earlier is now warmed with dimly lit lights. There are a few candles in the centre of the table, along with some fresh flowers and a variety of dishes set out. The table that is large enough to seat eight has only two places set, one at the head of the table and one to the right, meaning we were sitting side by side. I frown when Kian pulls the chair out for me. What is this? I narrow my eyes and take a seat.

"It's surprising to see you have manners. I mean, to come from keeping me tied up for days to holding out a chair? How sweet," I say coldly as he tucks my chair in. He doesn't reply, frowning slightly as he takes his seat.

"Do you prepare your snarky comments in advance, sunshine, or do they naturally come to you?" He asks, picking up the bottle of champagne and pouring two glasses. I smile sweetly.

"Oh, they come naturally. Especially when I'm around dimwits," I say innocently. He cocks a brow and smirks.

"At least you're entertaining."

"Oh, I'm glad you see it like that," I say, picking up my glass.

He does the same, clinking it with mine before knocking half of it down in one go. Is it wrong to admit that he is irritatingly handsome? Everything he does captures my attention, and if he wasn't such an annoying asshole, maybe - just maybe - I would have fallen for him.

"Indeed. Now let's dine before you actually end up pissing me off," he suggests, gesturing to the food. I smirk.

"That is the aim," I tease haughtily, taking a sip of my wine.

A short while later, we have food on our plates, and silence falls. Although I can feel his eyes on me often enough, he at least lets me eat in peace.

"So, did you think about what you wanted?" He asks, breaking the silence.

I really do jinx things. Why do I do this?

"I did. If I am to stay here, then I want to actually do something. I'm a person, not just a doll that you are keeping," I start. I need to phrase this like I'm simply bored, not as if I have double intentions.

"Do explain," his arrogant reply follows.

"Back home, I was part of my father's court. I am good when it comes to battle strategy and - " I stop when he smirks. "What?" I ask, glaring at him.

"You? Good with battle strategy? Have you forgotten that your every attempt at escaping has not been thought out? I mean, if the Sanguine Empire relied on your strategic methods, I'm surprised they're not already all dead," he mocks. I clench my jaw, my cheeks heating up. He's not wrong… but mocking me like that!

"Hey! That was me acting on emotion. I am not stupid; besides, we don't die easily!" His smirk only grows, flashing his perfectly white teeth.

"So, the fact that they didn't die is due more to their resilience rather than your perfect battle plans? I'm not sure I want to risk my men's lives." I glare at him, and he chuckles, sending a small flutter of butterflies twirling inside of me. He leans over, and my heart thunders when his hazel eyes meet my own. "Seems like you're not the only one who gets under the other's skin," he murmurs.

*Don't let him get to you...*

I glare back at him, doing my best not to let my gaze fall on those plush lips of his that are so good. He licks his lips, moving back, and I let out a small breath.

"Why not test me? In strategy, planning, knowledge, hand-to-hand combat, and with weapons. If I do prove myself, then you don't have a reason to refuse," I suggest, returning to my food. He's silent for a moment.

"Fine. I will test your knowledge first. Let's see what the Sanguine Empire has taught their daughters."

"More than what the Clair de Lune Kingdom has taught theirs."

No matter what he says, we are at least treated more equally to men; we are allowed to fight, be part of battles, the court, and much more. Yes, there is still the aspect that we had less power...

"We shall see about that tomorrow," he remarks. I do not miss the lingering gaze on my body. Men...

"And weren't you supposed to be dining with the visitors?"

"I can do as I want, and, as promised, I wanted to hear what you desired," he replies arrogantly. He confuses me. Sometimes I feel he isn't too annoying, and then he goes and pulls some stupid move. I won't fall for this, not again.

"Does your precious Sage know you're here dining with me?" I ask, unable to resist. He frowns at that.

"She knows who you are to me, so she would understand."

"I don't know if you're the idiot here or if Sage is just stupid," I admit, shaking my head.

"I don't see why you have an issue either way. The Sanguine Empire's men have many women at their side, so why are my personal relationships any different than that?" He asks coldly. I cock a brow, Mother's story returning to my mind. I smile faintly.

"Because I thought your kind were different... if there was one thing that I actually respected, it was the love and respect of the mate bond. Where a man loves and cherishes one woman forever," I admit quietly.

An emotion I can't read flashes in his eyes, and is that also sadness? I'm not sure; it was gone as quickly as it had come. He reaches over, taking hold of my chin.

"Tell me, Morgana, does it hurt when I'm with someone else?"

"Oh, please, don't turn this around on me. I'm just saying I thought the mate bond was more, but clearly, it holds no value to - "

I'm cut off when he leans over, claiming my lips in a sizzling soft kiss that sends a wave of pleasure rushing through me. The taste of the champagne lingers on them, but before I can even pull away, he moves back. His eyes meet mine.

"It does hold value… way fucking more than I can ever tell you."

# HIS PROPOSITION

MORGANA

*I* GLARE AT HIM, KNOCKING his hand away and hating the tingles that he left on my lips.

"Don't touch me," I hiss, slamming my fork on the table as I push my chair out and stand up, crossing my arms.

"Morgana." His deep voice is low. I do my best to ignore the way it makes me feel and turn my back on him. Right now, I don't want to see the arrogant jerk. I feel the heat from his body behind me and quickly turn around, raising a finger in warning.

"Don't touch me," I warn.

"Morgana, can we talk? Man to woman, without our race, rank or anything else coming in between?" He asks quietly.

"The Alpha King wants to talk?" I scoff.

"Please." I narrow my eyes at him. Now what game is he playing?

"Talk. I'm listening," I say, moving away from him and perching on the windowsill, crossing my legs. I resist a roll of my eyes when his eyes trail over my legs, his eyes flashing gold. "You have five minutes," I inform him, tapping my foot. He runs his fingers through those tight curls of his, and the urge to touch the tight ringlets is tempting, I won't deny that.

"Fine…" He steps closer. Looking down at me, he plays with a bracelet he's wearing. "Look, you are my mate. I won't fucking deny that I do want you by my side…" I look at him sharply. Yes, I know that he wants me for sex. "As… my Luna," he mutters. I see the guilt in his eyes and wonder if he's feeling bad about Sage again. My heart skips a beat when I realise what he's saying. *As his Luna. What?*

"Excuse me?" I ask, shocked.

He smirks sexily and places his foot on the ledge next to me, resting his elbow on it as he leans down. His intense gaze pierces into me.

"You heard me. I want you as my Luna by my side." I try not to let those words make me feel lightheaded.

"Won't your people have an issue with that?" I ask suspiciously. "Something is definitely off about this."

"I talked to a few of my men that I'm closest to… it seems you've impressed one or two already." His eyes flash, and I smirk. Is he actually jealous?

"Aww, is the Alpha jealous?" I whisper, leaning forward slightly as I stare up at him, batting my lashes, knowing I'm giving him an eyeful of my breasts.

"You're mine. As much as you hate me, it doesn't change that you are mine alone," he says possessively, sending an odd rush of pleasure to my core.

Yes, I am seriously messed up. I hate him, I hate the way he's treated me… yet I get satisfaction in the pull he has to me… the way he can't resist me… the way he thinks I'm his…

"Anyway, I want you to be my Luna. However… this kingdom won't accept you if I say you are my mate…" He moves away, and I can sense the conflict in him. I become serious, too, frowning at his back as I wait for him to continue and try not to look at his ass. *Damn, this man is fine…*

"They know of the treaty I made with the Sanguine Empire… I was thinking if I introduced you at the summit officially, let them know that I'm taking you as my queen, it would work in both my favour and theirs. Mine to know I have my mate by my side and theirs to know that we have the princess of the Sanguine Empire by our side, which will ease their restlessness about the attacks that are occurring in our kingdom and perhaps let them feel assured that it may not be vampires. A political union to calm the rising tensions."

It's too much to take in. He wants me as his queen? But more than that, what gets to me is the mention of attacks on the kingdom. If their kingdom doesn't stop us from getting supplies, there wouldn't even be any conflict…

Suddenly, the plan for revenge seems to falter. What if... what if I did accept this position? What if I could actually benefit from helping my people? I know Azrael's spur-of-the-moment submission to Kian was out of fear. He's a coward; even his agreeing to peace is just a way to make his own life easier. What he needed to do was wager and talk about conditions because we need supplies and crops, but instead, he just agreed like that and gave his own sister away.

I know Cain offered me an escape and a peace treaty if Kian was killed... but to be completely honest, I don't have concrete proof that Kian killed my father or had him killed. I need to ask him that. I need answers, and above all, I need to make sure I don't rush my decision...

What would a true ruler do? Seek revenge or help their people? I smile internally. Oh, Father would be disappointed if I even pondered on that. No matter how hard the right path is or how difficult it is, we must walk it... right? I do want revenge for my father's death, and I will seek out the truth...

If he's offering me the position of queen, I should take it. Whatever decision I make, ultimately, this will benefit me. I'll get to be closer to him, if I need to kill him, I'll be able to lower his guard if I accept this position... I wanted in on the strategy of the kingdom; I would have more power as a queen rather than as a slave that is kept in the kitchens or bedroom. My only fear is that I might become too emotionally invested. Would I be able to defy the mate bond pull?

"Kian..." I turn towards him, seeing he is observing me intensely. "If I'm queen... it does not mean you get a pass to become intimate with me." I narrow my eyes, and he smirks.

"Of course not." Although he said it, he's smirking like an asshole. Does he actually think he'll get more? "So, do you agree?" He closes the gap between us, and I hate how my heart races.

"That soon? I don't think so. We have a lot to discuss, starting with Sage." That makes his mood darken. He frowns.

"What about her?" He asks.

"Does she know?" I ask, raising an eyebrow.

"Does it matter? She knows you are my mate. Her opinion doesn't matter." I frown, shaking my head.

"Well then, I decline your offer." I cross my arms and turn my back on him.

I would *never* be the other woman. I would never steal someone else's man from them, mate or not. If Kian wants to do this, he needs to do it the proper way. Even if we are just going to be a business deal, although I know he wants more, I have my own plan. I also know there is a chance that something may happen, and if it does… I am not going to be a sidepiece or be the woman who is using another woman's man. Yes, I made the mistake once, but I couldn't do that to someone.

"Look, Sage is nothing to me, not anymore. I won't lie; to start with, I thought I'd get over this, over you, but I can't, and I'm not going to shy away from that. I fucking want you and you alone. Since you've come here, I have not kissed or fucked anyone else. You don't need to worry about her." I cock a brow, whirling around. Is he for real?

"Do you really not get it? This isn't about me worrying about something happening between you two! This is me not liking the fact that you are trying to play two women! She was here first, and hell will freeze over before I ever agree to be the other damn woman…" I trail off, my heart thundering, when I realise that he is staying silent.

Fuck. How could I have been so stupid? He *does* want me to be the other woman… fuck.

"Kian, you didn't have any plan of getting rid of Sage, did you?" I ask quietly. He looks away, and for some reason, that really fucking hurts. Damn it, why the hell does he have this hold on me? Hiding my hurt, I shake my head. "No, I refuse. I will never accept you as my king," I state coldly.

He frowns deeply, closing the gap between us and cupping the back of my neck. His thumbs caress my cheeks, and tingles course through me. As much as I want to close my eyes and relish in the warmth of his embrace, I can't.

"Morgana, look, hear me out. People will want a werewolf Luna… if I want you - " I pull away roughly, slapping his hand away.

"It's all or nothing when it comes to me, Kian. The rest is your damn choice. If you think that I'm going to agree to this, then you really don't know me! Besides… who said I even want you? Carry on pleasing your people. Make Sage, who *wants* you, your queen! Because I will never be yours," I snap, anger flaring inside of me. I'm done with him.

I'm about to leave when my gaze falls on the necklaces around his neck. My heart thuds when I realise one of the several chains holds a few tiny keys. Are they for the diaries? Remaining smooth, I toss my hair and turn away, storming out of the room in anger, but I don't get far. Suddenly, he grabs my arm, slamming me up against the wall. I gasp at the impact. His entire body is crushed against mine, sending my stomach fluttering crazily as he presses my wrists to the wall.

"Don't say that. If Sage is the fucking problem, then fine... I'll end it with her."

His words shock me, and my heart thunders. I don't get it... why does he seem so desperate? I narrow my eyes, looking into his hazel ones, and try to hear his thoughts. The shrill sonic sound fills my head, and then I am past it.

**... can't lose her, I fucking need her, Thanatos...**

**We do need mate; this is the best decision! Now, apologise!**

I almost smile at that; Thanatos really is the sweet one.

"I want you, Morgana. Fuck the fact that you're a vampire or that you have a fucking attitude that pisses me off. I still want you," he murmurs, making my core knot.

My chest is heaving, and I'm very aware of his body against mine, aware of his hard muscles, his firm abs, and the bulge in his pants. He leans closer, and I turn away, but he isn't fazed. His lips touch my neck, sending a rivet of pleasure through me. I bite my lip. Why is my body reacting this way? I just...

He sucks on the skin softly. A sigh escapes from my lips as his brush my neck, but he doesn't push me further, pulling away. His eyes meet mine, and it throws me off to see the emotions in them.

"I'll talk to Sage first thing in the morning. You can take my room. I'll take another."

He turns, walking towards the entrance door. My heart is racing, and my legs feel weak, but above all, the realisation that he had just agreed shocks me the most.

*He's choosing me.*

# TRYING TO DO BETTER

KIAN

*I* CAN'T FUCKING LOSE HER. The moment she was ready to walk away, I couldn't stop myself, I need her, and so I promised her something I know is going to throw the entire fucking summit into chaos. But… she's worth it.

We had a fucking messed up start, but I can't fucking continue. Each day, my resolve is breaking, and I'm pushing her away. If she wants to be my one and only, officially, then that's fine… I don't get women; it's not like I am going to cheat on her. I'll deal with the Alphas and the backlash this is going to cause. Yes, the timing is fucking off, but if this could solidify the treaty between her kingdom and mine, it may ease the council's wrath.

**She is strong,** Thanatos growls encouragingly.

**I know. She's already fucking broken me down.**

**I have a complaint,** Thanatos grumbles as I strip out of my clothes, shifting into wolf form.

**You always fucking do.**

**Mate looked so sexy tonight. Why didn't you eat her for dessert? You are a bad date.** I mentally cock a brow.

**Seriously, as much as I want to eat her out, she'll probably snap my neck if I try.**

As we break into a run, he laughs, and I relish the wind that rushes through my fur, mind-linking Corbin to keep an eye out so no one breaks into my quarters. Although I have guards posted all around, I still want someone I truly trust around her. I'm not sure what they'll think of this, but I'm too fucking close to losing her.

**Sage.**

**Kian?** Her hopeful voice answers.

**I want to talk to you first thing in the morning. Meet me on the west side.**

**Oh, okay. I'll be there. I hope you're okay, Kian. You weren't at the dinner…**

**I'm fine. See you tomorrow, Sage.**

I cut the link, thinking, *I'm going to do this.*

I return home and slip into my bedroom. She had changed out of that fucking dress that had me hard for her. Her gorgeous hair is still in its curls, but her flawless face is free of the makeup that had made me fucking want to tell her I'll fucking worship her day and night as long as she stays by my fucking side. She's wearing a satin nightdress. One arm is draped over her stomach, and the other one is curled into a fist, tucked under her chin. The bedding is a fucking mess, which means she's been asleep for a while. My she-devil doesn't know how to stay in one spot when she's asleep. I smirk slightly, thinking, *I could get used to this…*

I take some boxers and pants, then slip silently into the shower. Would it be wrong to just sleep here tonight?

**No, not at all. Sleep here.**

**That in itself tells me it's fucking wrong… I promised her I'd take another room.** Wow, I'm fucking becoming a wuss…

**No, you just love mate.**

My heart skips a beat. Is that it? Have I fallen for her? Her sly smile and that spark in her eyes when she's up to no good flash in my mind. The burning passion in her eyes when she wants to fucking kill me. The way she has self-respect… I smile slightly. Life isn't so bad when you have a feisty queen to keep you entertained.

I step out of the shower and dry myself off before pulling my pants on and leaving the bathroom. I walk over to the shelves, grab my journal, and walk over to her before bending down and placing a soft kiss on her lips.

"Dummy Alpha… mh…"

I cock an eyebrow, smirking. Seriously, is she fucking insulting me in her sleep too?

**Yes,** Thanatos's sleepy voice answers.

I don't reply to that, hiding my smile as I leave the room. The feeling of her lips lingers on mine. Entering my office, I take a seat at my desk, unlock the journal, and begin to write my latest thoughts. I don't put everything on paper, not trusting that it may end up in the wrong hands, but there's nothing wrong with mentioning certain stuff without names.

Morgana… I look down at the paper. I've never been good with fucking words, but everything becomes a lot easier when you have a pen or brush in your hands.

*… It's been a while since she's come here, and without even trying, I'm falling for her. She's just like a rose in full bloom; beautiful, perfect, and armed with her thorns…*

I keep Thanatos blocked off as I write down how the fuck I feel. The hope that there could be a future grows stronger with every fucking word. I know I need to make it up to her, but I want to get inside her head, want to know exactly how she thinks, what's on her mind and what pleases her without fucking showing that I want that.

I place the journal aside after re-locking it and take out some reports I need to handle. The situation is becoming worse. There's no clue as to who the fucking culprits are, but my people are suffering. I'm doing my best, but two-thirds of the kingdom share borders with other kingdoms, leaving most of it easy access. Thanks to the heavy woods that border most of my kingdom, one-third is joined to the sea, but even that has its own fucking share of issues.

I sit back, staring at the ceiling. The Elven kingdom is the only one I'm sure is not involved. They are aloof people who keep themselves to themselves, but they are strong.

I massage my jaw, returning to work. Thanatos is asleep in my mind, and I'm doing my best not to think about Morgana. It's fucking strange for a woman not to want me, and, on top of that, my mate. That red dress fucking threw me off big time with the tempting back details. All I had wanted was to fucking rip it off her, and now I can't fucking get her out of my head…

I stand up, walking over to my window and staring out at the darkness. The odd light is on here and there in the courtyards below, but at this time, most people are asleep.

If worse comes to worst and I need to leave to check out the border myself, what about her? Is this what it feels like to have a fucking family? That you'll always be so fucking worried about them? I need her safe. She's my fucking strength right now. I know if anything happens to her, I'll lose my fucking shit.

I return to my desk and get back to work despite the worries that flit through my mind.

The following day, I get dressed before heading out to meet Sage. She is already there, clearly having gotten up extra early to dress up. She smiles at me, her heart racing as I approach her.

"Good morning, Kian. Did you sleep okay?" She asks, concern clear in her eyes.

"Yeah, I did." As we both begin walking, I slip my hands into my pockets and fix my gaze on the rising sun in the distance.

"What did you want to talk about?" She asks, brushing a strand of her hair off her face the moment we are a good distance away from the castle.

"About you becoming Luna…"

"Ah! I talked to several visiting Lunas yesterday, and they seemed to approve of your decision. We - "

"I can't. I know it's a dick move of mine, but I can't make you my Luna, Sage. I'm fucking sorry." Her heart is thundering as she looks at me, and it's almost as if I can see the damage I'm fucking doing to her inside.

"Kian… please don't say that… I…"

"Look, you know Morgana is my mate… and I really can't refuse her. She is the only one I want, Sage, and she isn't fucking wrong; I'll just be hurting you both by continuing this game." Her racing heart is thundering, and she's shaking as she runs her fingers through her hair.

"Kian, please don't do this," she begs, now gripping my arm. "I love you, don't make me Luna! Let her be Luna, just… at least keep a little spot in your heart for me."

I look down at her, feeling guilty for doing this to her. For the last few years, she's been there for me, and I always knew her feelings were far stronger than mine, but I still took advantage of that, not caring. Now, with Morgana in the picture, I know how it feels somewhat. I sigh deeply, placing my hands on her shoulders.

"Look… there's still hope you may find your mate. You haven't felt his passing, have you?" I ask quietly. Usually, even if we haven't met our mates, if they do die, we feel it. She shakes her head, brushing her tears away.

"No! I… I rejected him for you!" She breaks into sobs, covering her mouth as she tries to control herself. Her words shock me.

"Why didn't you ever tell me or even consider asking me before you did that?" I ask coldly. Fuck, I didn't know that. "Who is he?"

"He was from another pack… but I… I couldn't lose you," she whispers. "I love you, Kian. I always have."

"It seems our feelings don't match, or I would have been able to defy my mate, but I cannot. Whatever we had, Sage, is in the past. From today onwards, I am your friend at most. Don't cross that line because by now you should know if anything hurts Morgana, I won't tolerate it," I say icily.

"But, Kian… what about what we had?" She whispers.

"I would say cherish the memories, but in all honesty, that will just fucking hurt you more. I'd say throw them out and don't let this stop you from living your life. Move on, Sage. From this point forward, we both are to walk different paths."

"I… but… please, Kian."

"My word is final, Sage. I won't be telling the council that Morgana is my mate, so I expect that to stay between us. However, I will be introducing her as my soon-to-be queen." I turn away. This conversation is over, but her next words make me stop dead in my tracks.

"Please… No! Kian, please! I'm pregnant!" Her words ring in my head. I turn to her sharply.

"There's no proof you are," I say coldly.

"I am, I haven't had my periods, and I have been feeling really nauseous!" She exclaims, coming over to me. "Just give it a few weeks, you will be able to hear the heartbeat!" My heart is thumping fucking hard.

**No… I don't care, we cannot go against our fucking promise to mate!** Thanatos growls.

**I know. I fucking know…**

But that's my pup…

I step away from her, frowning as the news swirls around me like a fucking storm. I can't hurt her. I can't do this. Not to Morgana.

"I will support you through this pregnancy, raise that child as my own… but I made a promise, Sage. I can't fucking break it," I say quietly.

It's at that moment that I realise no matter what is fucking thrown at me, I'll keep my word to her.

"Kian, we are having a baby!" Sage sobs, grabbing hold of my arm.

"Sage… look, we can't do this anymore. I told you I'll support you, but nothing more. Besides, until a heartbeat is heard, this is just a baseless assumption."

**Good,** Thanatos growls.

"I love you, Kian!"

"And I love Morgana!" I snap, my heart thudding when the words leave my lips.

Fuck.

Thanatos chuckles, **Oh yeah, fuck indeed. You admitted the truth.**

Sage seems to have frozen in shock. Her eyes which are filled with hurt and betrayal, are fixed on mine. I frown at her, pulling out of her hold.

"Now you know. I hope you understand that. As I said, I'll be here for you regarding the pregnancy and the child, but nothing more. You may stay in the castle as you are, and you will be given guards. However, don't try to come between Morgana and me," I warn her coldly, my eyes piercing into hers.

Turning, I walk off, but I don't get far when I see Kai standing there looking shocked. *Shit, don't tell me heard…* Fucking hell.

"What you fucking heard stays between us," I growl, walking off. I don't have time for this shit.

"Kian… Morgana, is she the - "

"Whatever she is, you can fucking keep the fuck out of it," I growl.

"Alright… well… I had some… never mind, you're right, it's not my business," Kai says, frowning.

*Yeah, I'm not fucking interested…*

Heading inside, I don't know what to think of it. Is it a lie? She was desperate. I don't think she would have waited to tell me such news if she was… maybe it is a lie. We haven't been intimate in a while. If she is, then

I'll be able to hear a heartbeat very soon. I'll get someone to keep an eye on her discreetly, and if this is a lie, then she'll be punished for it.

**And if she is pregnant?**

**Then I'll take care of her as promised,** I reply curtly.

**Just the pup!**

**It would just be a cordial relationship. I will not hurt, Morgana. Don't worry,** I reply coldly.

And what about Morgana? Do I tell her? No… I won't tell her until it's confirmed. One thing I know about Morgana is that she's unpredictable. Who knows if she'd agree to give me a chance if I tell her Sage might be pregnant? So there's no point in announcing it until I know for sure.

Speaking of… I'm meant to test her skills soon. Let's see what my little blood rose is capable of.

We are in my inner courtyard, an area surrounded completely by my wing, so it's just the two of us. The large castle walls block off most of the sunlight, and this particular one has many trees to give us extra shade.

I glance at her. She is dressed in black flared pants and a fitted white top. Her long hair is pulled into a high ponytail, and she's spinning the two long swords she had chosen. As dangerous as passing her weapons might be, I can handle her if she tries something.

**Mate would never hurt us!** Thanatos growls.

**She is capable of anything,** I reply with a small smirk.

"What are you smirking at?" She asks suspiciously.

"Just wondering if those scrawny arms of yours will be able to handle those swords." That makes her glare at me.

"I am a lot stronger than I look, baby Alpha." I cock my brow.

"Oh yeah? You are yet to prove it," I taunt.

Her eyes blaze with anger. She is before me in a flash. I raise the staff I'm holding. My aim is to test her, not hurt her. She spins around, sliding one sword under as I jump back. It's clear she is aiming for the kill, though.

"I don't play. I fight to win," she whispers. My gaze falls to her lips. As much as I want to simply pull her close and claim them, I'll soon be gutted if she keeps this up.

Soon we are a blur, her striking, me blocking, and sometimes I'll aim a hit, but she is perfect. Her every move is fluid, and she's ready to counter at any second. She keeps her defence up at all times. The only thing she leaves open a rare few times is her left hip. I guess that's where I'm going to aim to end this.

"Not getting tired, are you, sunshine?"

"Not at all. Don't get too cocky," she shoots back icily.

Teasing her is indeed fun. I realise I haven't given her any blood again... I guess it's time to end this now. I spin around, knocking one of her swords aside and hit her side with my staff. She gasps, not expecting that as her weapon falls from her grasp. I yank the other from her grip and grab her wrist, spinning her around. She gasps as I pull her against me, caging her against my body.

"I win," I whisper from behind, my eyes falling to her rising and falling chest.

She turns her head towards me, struggling to free herself from my hold, only making me close my eyes as I try not to focus on her ass pressing against my dick. The sparks are already sending a storm within me.

"You cheated," she says, displeased, her voice breathless and so fucking hot.

"Oh, I assure you I didn't..." I murmur, running my hand down her stomach. Tossing the staff aside, I brush my other hand up her waist. Goddess, I fucking want to do so much to her...

"Well, the sun is out. That slows me down, too," she pouts. "I demand a rematch!" Don't tell me she's a fucking sore loser? I smirk.

"Never realised you were a sore loser, Princess." She glares at me, but I simply flash her a smirk, pressing my lips to the base of her neck. Her breath hitches, and I hear her let out a soft sigh. "But you weren't bad. Impressive actually. You only need a little work on keeping this part covered." I tap her hip, and she gasps. I smirked: These sparks, this feeling, she can't ignore them forever.

"Impressive you saw that on your first match with me. It has always been my weakness, but usually, people won't pick up on it unless they have fought with me several times," she admits.

"I'll work with you," I promise. Her heart thunders, and I smirk. *I promised to make you mine and I meant it.* "So... I talked to Sage..." I whisper. She tenses, and her heartbeat quickens.

"And?" She asks. Although she tries to sound nonchalant, the beat of her heart gives her away.

"And I made it clear that the only one I am interested in and want... is my mate," I whisper, sucking hard at the corner of her neck. Yes, those feelings are far fucking deeper, but I can't tell her yet.

"And who said your mate wants you?" She replies haughtily.

"I'm not sure... does she?" I ask, letting my hand trail down over her stomach. Her heart only beats louder with each passing second as my hand inches into the band of her pants.

"Kian..." she whispers warningly.

"I'm yours, little she-devil. Let me show you the fucking stars," I murmur.

My hand slides lower as she bites her lip. Fuck, I haven't even touched her yet... but these sparks are fucking messing with my head as well. My hand brushes over her panties, and she gasps. Oh, she feels so fucking good. I massage her over her thin panties before pushing them aside. I missed this. I could fucking touch her day and night and never get bored of this...

"Fuck!" She moans the moment my finger touches her clit.

With my free hand, I cup her breast, massaging her, waiting for her to pull away...

I massage her pussy, smirking to find her already wet for me. I'm already fucking hard for her, and the scent of her arousal hanging in the air is making me come undone. Goddess, she's fucking fine. I run my hand along her pussy before thrusting two fingers into her already dripping core.

"Fuck!" She gasps.

She turns her head towards me. The storm of emotions there tells me she's fighting this, fighting the bond or whatever the fuck she's feeling, and as much as I want to fucking make her come right here, I want her to beg for it...

I can't focus on anything but the fact that I wanted her. My own dick pressed against her ass, it's fucking hard, and I faintly hear myself growl. I want to mark her and fucking mate her.

It takes all of my willpower to slide my fingers out, rubbing them over her clit as I kiss her neck hungrily. Squeezing her breast hard, I slide my fingers out of her trousers and slip them into her mouth, wrapping my other hand around her throat.

"I'll wait, wait for the day you beg for more, and you will," I whisper huskily, fucking throbbing hard when she wraps her lips around my fingers and runs her tongue along them sensually, her eyes locked with mine. Fuck, she is so fucking tempting. "And when you do… I'll make sure I make you feel so fucking good that all you will want will be to be tied to my bed whilst I fuck you senseless day in and day fucking out."

# A Diamond Ring

## MORGANA

HIS WORDS MAKE HEAT travel through my body. As much as I hate him, I can't deny that he holds an incredible pull over me. He knows it, too, just as I know I have a hold on him. It's a two-way thing. Riddled with our egos, our emotions, this bond and our hatred, we're stuck in this constant battle of wills and desire.

It threw me off knowing he had told Sage he wants me. He is openly admitting to what he desires. I don't understand him at all. He's cold, yet hot. He's a jerk, yet at times he can be... dare I admit it, charming. I hate him, yet I want to be in his arms. I want to see the darkness in him, yet I want to be his dirtiest fantasy, too. He consumes me like an addiction I should never have tasted, one I can't refuse.

His lips meet my neck once more, and I bite my lip, my core throbbing. His hand around my throat tightens for a second, and I am very aware of his cock against my ass. If he wasn't so damn sexy, I had a feeling I might have succeeded in killing him already. His strong arms wrap around my waist, and, for a moment, neither of us moves. I close my eyes, relaxing into his hold. A dangerous move. If he wanted me dead, I'd be dead, but then again, he has had many chances to kill me.

"Dare I ask how Sage took it?" I ask as his lips graze my neck.

"As expected, but I made it clear we are done," he says, moving away from me. He turns me towards him, frowning. "I will be announcing you as my queen at the summit today… and I will introduce you at the dinner tonight." He looks away. I know he's conflicted about something.

"What is it?" I ask, resisting the urge to cup his face. He looks at me and sighs.

"They may be under my reign, but they are fucking dickheads. They will look for ways to make remarks or bring you down. Let alone if I bring you in front of them. I am putting you in danger… I know I put this forward to you, but if you want to pull out - " I place a finger to his lips, my heart thudding as I step closer.

"I've dealt with one jerk, a few more won't make a difference," I tease, tracing my finger lightly over his soft, plump lips. His eyes flash, and I smirk, moving away.

"I think you should introduce me at this summit. You yourself said that you want to introduce me as an asset. Not to mention, what better way to test my knowledge than in front of an audience? Introducing me on your arm tonight will give people the impression that I'm just your arm candy. Let me come to this summit. Let them know that your chosen queen is so much more than a mere woman," I suggest, staring into his hazel eyes. I see a flicker of emotion I can't place before he smirks coldly, taking hold of my chin.

"Should I trust you?" He asks. "Behind that gorgeous face of yours, what are you thinking?"

"You shouldn't trust me. I may look like a dream come true, but we both know I'm a nightmare. However… it's your call," I challenge seductively.

I have no plan to play up at the summit. I'll win his trust, get the answers I want, keep in touch with Cain, and then make my choice slowly and wisely.

"Fine," he agrees as I smile sweetly. He narrows his eyes. "Fuck, you're going to be the death of me."

*Oh, I am.*

"So, I can come?" I asked.

"Yes…"

Reaching into his pocket, he takes out a box. I frown and step back, my heart thundering the moment he flips that box open. Inside, upon a silk cushion, sits a large, diamond gold ring. In the middle sits a large ruby surrounded by many small clear diamonds. No… this is not what I was expecting. I look up at him to see him watching me. Despite how emotionless he looks, the storm in his eyes isn't fully masked. Fuck, he's taking this so seriously…

"This is one of the Araqiels' most prized jewels. It is also the ring that the first king gave to his mate. We may have lost a few places in between, but the first royal was from my bloodline… the colour is just so perfectly you, I thought it was befitting. Since we are going before the council, I was hoping you'd wear it."

An engagement ring. Oh god, this is not what I was thinking. Yes, he said he was going to make me queen, but this…

He picks the ring up, and it glints brightly. Slipping the box back into his pocket, he looks at me, waiting for an answer.

"Well, since we need to appear real… don't go getting ideas," I say haughtily, holding out my hand.

"I'll try not to," he replies, taking my hand. I can't deny the sparks that rush through me at his touch. He slides the ring on; it's a perfect fit. "As if it were made for you," he murmurs, raising my hand to his lips. He kisses it softly, and I purse my lips. Oh, no wonder he had Sage pining for him. He is charming indeed.

"When is the summit?" I ask.

"In an hour," he replies. "You will have enough time to get dressed - "

"Forget getting dressed, I need you to tell me the issues that will be addressed. I don't want to enter there looking like a complete nincompoop." He looks surprised at my words before he nods.

"Perfect."

"Then, let's not waste any more time."

Our eyes meet, and we both nod. An agreement is made without an argument, something rare for us, but it feels good.

I walk alongside Kian as we head towards the summit, a place that women do not usually attend. It shocks me how this kingdom's power is completely in the hands of men. Today is a large summit; many of the visiting Alphas, Betas, or Deltas will attend as well. I know something is up from the way

Kian's Beta and his two Deltas that are attending keep exchanging looks as they flank us.

"You know, it's rude to mind-link when someone else is present," I state, giving them all a sweet, dangerous smile, one I have been told looks quite creepy. That's the aim, though.

I'm wearing a red, high-collared top with fitted sleeves paired with black pants and heels. My hair is in a fish plait, and although I wore some eyeliner and red lipstick, I kept the rest of my face make-up free. Small studs are in my ears, and the huge ring Kian had given me sparkles brightly on my finger, something all three of Kian's men noticed.

He had given me blood, but he had put it in a glass. I'm not sure why the change, but I wish I could sink my teeth into that perfect neck of his.

"Ready?" Kian asks me.

"For anything," I reply. Our eyes meet, and his gaze flickers to my lips. "Good."

Leaning over, he presses his lips against mine. Pleasure flows through me; the taste of his mouth makes me want more, but he moves back, leaving my heart beating wildly.

Ajax opens the door, and we step inside; Kian's hand is on the small of my back as all eyes turn to us. Everyone in the room stands; I can feel the power that rolls off these men, something I realise always surrounds Kian, yet I'm so used to it, to him, that I never even let it get to me. Now, in this room where all eyes are now on me, curiosity, anger, disgust, confusion, interest, and suspicion mix together as we walk to the head of the table.

Luca pulls out my chair, and I sit down, giving him a small polite smile as Kian sits in the large chair by my side. I glance over at him, realising he truly is the Alpha in the room. The power that exudes from him is a turn-on alone. I look away from him and hold the gaze of a few men who are looking at me, making sure they look away first.

Kian had told me a few things that were causing problems for his kingdom and the basic issues that would probably be brought up. What moved me the most was when he talked about his people… that emotion, that protective instinct of his, the way his eyes burn with worry that he tries to mask. It's unnerving to see this side of him.

"This is…" an Alpha starts.

"That is the first thing we will discuss today. As you all know, I have brought a woman from the Sanguine Empire home. However, what you may not know is that she is no ordinary woman. She is the princess of the Sanguine Empire, sister to their king, and a woman whose reputation surpasses the borders for her wit, beauty, and intelligence," Kian says clearly. His aura radiates off him, and I know he is giving a silent warning that if anyone dares defy him, they will be punished. "I present to you Morgana Araton, the soon-to-be Luna of the Midnight Eclipse Pack and the future queen of Clair De Lune."

As expected, the room erupts in whispers, gasps, and a wave of questions that swarm through the room.

"Are you all fucking done?" Kian asks coldly after a moment.

"Your Highness, are you sure about this? I mean… this is no small fete. Yes, Lady Morgana is indeed a beauty, but she is a vampire," one man says, bowing his head apologetically.

"Which would mean your children could be hybrids or even vampires," another adds. Kids with Kian? Okay, these people are thinking too far ahead. Who said I'm going to be sticking around?

"And? It's not like my son needs to take the throne. If he doesn't turn out to be a werewolf, it isn't an issue," Kian says coldly. Once again, he's shocking me. I'm not used to this side of him.

"Can we ask why you chose a vampire woman when there are many daughters of Alphas available?"

Kian looks at me, and although only his Betas can probably see, he takes my hand in his. I'm about to pull away, but he holds it tight, lacing his fingers with mine. I look at our combined hands. The stark contrast between our skin makes me smile softly; opposites in every way, yet we fit so perfectly. My heart skips a beat when his thumb brushes my knuckles, and I smile. I'm the milk to his chocolate, together just like that delicious hot chocolate drink I love. I smile at the thought. That's kind of cute.

I look up, realising I'm getting suspicious looks, and smile extra sweetly, turning to Kian when he begins to speak.

"What better way to settle unrest between two kingdoms than a marriage?" He asks coldly. "As you all know, the attacks on our borders may or may not be due to vampires. However, if we decided to work with them and come to an agreement where both our kingdoms could benefit, then why not?"

"You do know, King Kian, your father was killed by a vampire?" Another asks. My eyes snap to Kian, my heart thudding at that. Sure, I had heard the rumours, but really? Kian frowns.

"And? Does one vampire's actions account for the rest?" He asks coldly.

"Has she cast a spell on you that you are so blinded?"

"Your father was killed before you. He, too, tried to bring peace. Do you want to go down the same path and die in the process?"

"Morgana Araton is known for her battle skills, too. Are you allowing one in your bed? Do you trust her?"

"My King, we respect you and your decisions. You have done nothing but prove how capable you are of this position and how the well-being of your people matters to you, but to allow a woman of the Sanguine Empire to be by your side... losing you at this critical time would be catastrophic for the kingdom."

"You won't fucking lose me. I know how to protect myself. As for Morgana, I trust her," Kian says, his eyes now meeting mine. My heart thuds, yet the sudden guilt that slithers through me makes me uneasy.

*Don't trust me, Kian, don't be so foolish.*

I frown in concentration, trying to hear their thoughts. I try not to flinch when the shrill sound erupts in my head before their words follow.

*He's stupid...*

*He's going to die and leave us to rot. Why would he agree to this?...*

*Something isn't right, this is madness...*

*We can never bow to a vampire queen...*

*Kian cannot remain on the throne if this continues...*

There is no one who is on his side, and as much as I have my own issues, I am not going to let him do this alone.

"Alpha Kian may be taking a risk, yet he's doing it for his people. The Sanguine Empire needs crops and produce that sadly do not grow on our lands, and the Clare De Lune kingdom needs the water that my people are withholding. I understand that seeing a vampire in this position might be alarming, frightening even, yet remember what your king is capable of," I say clearly, and instantly, silence falls as all eyes turn to me. "Alpha Kian has not only defied all odds and taken the position as Alpha of Alphas, despite being the second born, and he was only nineteen at the time. Despite his birthright and his status, he challenged it all and demonstrated himself as far superior to all of you. Are you really questioning the one man who has gone against everything to prove himself? Has time not shown you that he will do anything for his people? Taking me as his future bride only shows he would go to any lengths for the betterment of his people. I am not of this kingdom, yet even I can see the love and compassion he has for his people, no matter how cold and ruthless he may act. Don't judge his actions until you have a reason to conclude." My voice doesn't falter, remaining strong as I stare each of the Alphas in the eye. I can actually see Kian's arrogant smirk on that annoying face of his. As the men begin to converse quietly, a lot calmer now, Kian leans over, his shoulder brushing mine as I feel my heart skip a beat.

"Impressive," he murmurs, those sexy hazel eyes of his staring into mine.

"Obviously," I reply airily. "I am M-"

"Morgana Araton and you are fucking incredible."

# ᏟHE ᏁICHE IN THE ᏢILLAR

MORGANA

Two nights have passed since that day. I attend the dinners in the evening and the summit meetings during the day. However, it troubles me a lot. Kian doesn't push me further; he sleeps in another room, and although he sometimes teases me or kisses me unexpectedly, he doesn't go further than that.

I haven't seen Sage again. In the evenings, the visiting Lunas try to show that they were more than me, although I instantly put them in their place. When it comes to knowledge, I am not lacking, and I make sure I make that clear. Also, many werewolves, especially the single ones, have their eyes all over me. Some of their thoughts disgust me, but unless I want my truth to be known, I have to pretend I can't hear them.

Above all, it's Kian's and Thanatos' thoughts that make me blush, especially Thanatos'. On top of that, he also wants to meet me again. I often hear him begging Kian to allow him, with Kian refusing, saying he had hurt me, so not yet. It is rather fun to hear them have their friendly banter.

With each passing day, I feel torn. I still want to ask Kian about my father's death; I would try to read his thoughts when I do, but something keeps making me hesitate. As if I don't want to know....

We had written a message for my brother, and I hope we hear back. If he doesn't reply, I'm tempted to go there myself. I may have issues with Kian, but not his people. If this could benefit both kingdoms, I want to see it through before I make any huge decisions regarding revenge.

I'm allowed to roam freely as long as someone is with me, and I manage to sneak back to the alcove. Sure enough, there is a note from Cain awaiting me asking me what I'm planning, and some more vials of blood. I drink them down, but even that feels like I'm cheating. Kian often asks me how much I need, and he always fills me a glass. Still, I take it, and I leave a note telling Cain that nothing has changed; I am simply doing what we had planned, but with each passing day, the guilt inside of me is growing.

Today the ongoing summit is regarding some internal issues between packs, so I decide to skip it. I walk to the kitchens with Ajax following. I know they, too, had been shocked that Kian had completely ended it with Sage, but, being King, none of them questioned him. I think my being his mate overrules every other argument. Apparently, the idiots had wanted him to have two Lunas... they had put the dumb idea in their dumb king's head! Men are indeed stupid.

"Lady Morgana, are you going to the kitchens?"

"I told you, it's Morgana, and yes, I am," I answer.

I miss the banter. It's a place I had been treated well. Upon entering, the kitchen falls silent, and all eyes turn to me. A few women look utterly shocked, and some look rather jealous, to my surprise, but then again, Kian is very sought after.

But there is one man my eyes seek, and I smile when I see him.

"Ah, Morgana! I mean, Lady Mor-"

"Morgana is fine. Andrei, tell me, did you miss me?"

"Ah, yes... there's no one faster at slicing those vegetables than you. You were very passionate about it." Of course I was. When you imagine chopping baby Alpha to pieces, you begin to slice and cut with passion. I smile.

"I'm glad to hear it. So, want me to cut some now?" He looks startled at that, glancing at Ajax.

"No, no, I'm sure you have so much to do. Congratulations on your engagement to the king," Andrei says, his eyes falling on the hand that holds my ring, a ring that is beginning to weigh on my finger and soul.

"Well, I don't think there's anything wrong with keeping myself busy," I say, going over and taking a knife along with a bowl of peeled potatoes. "What are we doing? Dicing or slicing?"

"Ahh… we are cutting them into cubes," he says, hurrying over. "This size."

"Okay."

I smile, getting to work. I make sure to finish the potatoes before I go for a stroll in the garden.

"Can you at least give me some space?" I complain to Ajax.

He gives a curt nod, and I wander ahead, wondering if anything else is in the alcove today, but with Ajax around, it's going to be hard to retrieve them. I wander around before slowly sitting down beneath the pillar and closing my eyes, taking a deep breath.

"Do you wish to return home?" Ajax asks.

"No, I like sitting here. It's soothing," I reply.

It isn't a lie. With the clattering from the kitchen, the laughter and mirth, along with the hustle and bustle of everyone preparing food for the entire castle, it's welcoming. The shade and the slight heat from the sun make me feel tired. In an odd way, I enjoy that heavy, drowsy feeling. It's perfect.

I hear Ajax move a little distance away, and I open my eyes a crack. I'll bide my time before I check the niche. A good twenty minutes later, when Ajax moves away a little to check on something, I manage to slowly get up and peek inside. I don't have time to grab the blood, but there is a small pouch beside it which I quickly pocket and sit down once again just as Ajax returns. He looks suspicious for a moment before shaking his head.

"Do you want to return?"

"Sure," I agree, stretching before I stand up and lead the way back towards the entrance to the castle.

I head to Kian's quarters and am glad to be left alone. I make my way upstairs and take out the pouch. There's a small vial and a square folded note. My heart thunders as I unfold it.

'I'M GLAD TO HEAR WE ARE STILL IN AGREEMENT. I HAVE INCLUDED SOMETHING THAT CAN START OUR PLAN. READ THE INSTRUCTIONS, AND GOOD LUCK. I KNOW I CAN RELY ON YOU; FREEDOM AND VICTORY WILL BE YOURS.'

I fold the paper, my heart thundering as I stare down at the tiny vial, my chest rising and falling. I know what this is… but why am I hesitating? This is what I wanted, right?

## KIAN

Night falls, and Ajax just told me Morgana spent half the day in our bedroom, or should I say hers? Right now, I'm not so sure what to call it.

We have another dinner to attend, but if she doesn't want to come, then that's up to her. I'll ask her, though, if she wants to attend. I mean, I wouldn't mind just spending some alone time with her... but she is keeping me at a distance, and I'm not going to push her boundaries too much, not unless she wants me to. Although it is fucking hard to resist her. I've always taken what I wanted, and this time, trying not to is taking all my fucking self-control.

I knock on the bedroom door, but there is no answer. Frowning, I open the door to see the bathroom door is shut and a ray of light seeping in through the bottom. Guess she's getting ready. A black dress lies on the bed, and it reminds me of the first time I saw her. She had looked ravishing that night…

I walk over to the bed, letting my gaze linger over the dress. Just then, the bathroom door opens, and Morgana steps out. My eyes widen as they trail over her, blood rushing south. I feel myself throb fucking hard. I was not fucking expecting this.

She looks fucking breathtaking. Her scent, mixed with expensive fragrance and bath products, envelops me as my eyes rake over her creamy skin, clad only in a black strapless bodysuit that hugs her tiny waist and emphasises her breasts, making them half spill out... and those perfect lush, sexy thighs.

She's wearing heels that only add to how fucking sexy she looks, and her hair is curled and tumbling around her shoulders. Her dark, alluring eyes and red lips complete the look of a sex goddess, one who is staring at me in surprise.

How can I fucking stay away from her when she is begging me to fucking take her right here…? I advance towards her, and her heart thunders as she slowly inches backwards.

"Kian... have you not heard of knocking?" She asks, crossing her arms. I smirk. Despite how calm she's trying to act, she's nervous.

"I did, but I'm fucking glad you didn't hear," I growl, smirking when her back hits the wall behind her, making those lush breasts of hers bounce.

**Ah, rip it off and let's devour those breasts,** Thanatos growls. Would it be so fucking bad to give in to his wishes?

"Oh, really... what's the matter? Never seen a woman before?" She asks, her eyes trailing over me.

"Not one this fucking hot," I murmur.

"Well, shame we have a dinner to attend," she says, firmly pushing me away, but I pull her close, yanking her against my chest.

"I'm the fucking king. If I don't want to attend, I don't have to," I remind her, not missing how she bites her lip. Oh, she can fucking feel me hard for her. I squeeze her ass, making her whimper, her hands going to my shoulders.

"And I don't see any reason you should skip," she whispers, her gaze dipping to my lips.

"That reason is right here, being a fucking temptress," I reply, leaning closer. "Give in to me, sunshine... you know you fucking want to."

Our hearts beat as one. This pull towards her... no matter how much she fucking defies it, I know she wants me.

"Just one kiss..." she agrees quietly.

"Sure."

We both know that's a lie. In a flash, I have her on the bed, kneeling between her legs. My lips crash against hers in a searing kiss. Sparks explode through us, and the feel of her lush lips against mine sends me out of control. My eyes blaze as I plunge my tongue into her mouth. She moans against me, her arms tightening around my neck and her hand twisting into my hair. One leg locks around mine whilst her back arches off the bed.

Both of us fight for dominance. There are so many fucking emotions coursing through us, but right now, desire and the need for each other are fucking reigning supreme. I break away from her lips when she gasps for air, kissing her down her neck and between her breasts. She whimpers in pleasure, her back arching higher as I move lower, kissing her over her bodysuit and down to her hot core. Her arousal is fucking intoxicating. She is beyond fucking perfect. I kiss her inner thighs, sucking and caressing each spot passionately.

"Fuck!" She gasps when I lick her inner thigh along the side of her black bodysuit, satisfied when I see the buttons. Yanking it open, I glance up at her. Her eyes are half-closed, but she isn't resisting. Pushing it up, I look down at her perfect pussy. It's fucking beautiful.

"You're fucking beautiful, my little rose," I whisper huskily, pressing her leg open slowly and watching as her wet folds part to reveal her moist core. Oh, fuck. I could worship this pussy day and night...

I bend down. Her thudding heart pounds as I squeeze her ass, but the moment my lips press against her core, she whimpers, and I can feel her internal struggle.

"Relax… don't fucking think. Just enjoy the moment," I murmur before I part her lips with two fingers and place my tongue flat against her entrance, slowly running it up to her clit.

The moment my tongue touches her, she cries out, her hands twisting into the sheets. If anything had tasted good in life, it no longer compares. I have never had anything this fucking divine in my mouth. She's fucking sweet, addictive, and fucking lethal all in one. This is a drug that I never want to give up.

"Oh, fuck!" She cries out the moment I whirl my tongue around her clit. "Fuck, Kian!"

Her moans are fucking music to my ears, and with each stroke of the tongue, her salacious sighs only make me throb harder. I plunge my tongue into her, loving the way she reacts to it.

"That's it, Kian… fuck, that's it, don't stop…" she whimpers.

I know she's fucking gone. The only thing she can think of now is the fucking pleasure I'm inflicting on her. I shove two fingers into her slick, delicious pussy, making her whimper.

"Oh, baby, that's it."

She moans as I begin fucking her with my fingers hard and fast, continuing my assault on her clit as I fuck her with my digits. Her cries become louder, her juices trickling out of her until I can feel her tighten even more around my fingers. Fuck, she's tight. I can't wait to be wrapped up inside of her.

"Oh, fuck, Kian! I'm coming, God, I'm coming!" She cries out as her orgasm rips through her, her body arching off the bed as she screams out in pure ecstasy. "Fuck!" She whimpers, grabbing onto my bicep. Her nails dig into me as she cries out in complete bliss, a second orgasm rippling through her, and her juices begin squirting out of her.

I move back, watching the way her body reacts. Her breasts are almost spilling out of her corset, the beginning of her dusky pink areolas peeking out from the top. My gaze snaps down to her pussy as I continue to fuck her with my fingers, watching her juices drench my hand and the bed beneath her so fucking perfectly.

"Ouch, fuck!" She breathes, her back hitting the bed. Her entire body quivers with pleasure as she comes down from her high.

I slide my fingers out, bending down and lapping up her juices. This is my fucking need, and I'm not going to let it go to waste. I lap it all up hungrily, wanting so much fucking more. She whimpers, trying to close her legs, but it's a little late for that. I run my tongue lower past her pussy and between her ass cheeks, making her heart thud as I lick up every trace of juice. My tongue brushes against her back entrance, and her entire body shudders. I smirk deviously.

*Oh, my little she-devil. I'm going to play with this body in every fucking way. I will ruin you in such a fucking manner that you won't ever want another man...*

I move back, grabbing a towel that lay on the bed nearby, no doubt from when she showered a little while ago. First wiping my face, I then wipe her between her legs, which are still trembling. She's breathing hard, a hand to her lush curls, and her eyes half-closed. I smirk, leaning over her.

"Now, tell me. Do you want to stay in bed, or shall we attend dinner?" I growl in her ear before placing a kiss on her lips. She whimpers, and I know she can taste herself; I rub my fingers between her legs as I kiss her slowly.

"Dinner..." she murmurs.

"Good... although I think I'm fucking satisfied. I've never tasted anything so fucking good. All I want to do is have you sit on my face so I can eat you out until you fucking pass out," I admit quietly. Her eyes widen, and I give her a killer smirk. "What's wrong? Cat got your tongue?" I tease.

"Just a big bad wolf, but don't get used to it," she whispers.

Yanking me closer, her lips crash against mine in a hungry, passionate kiss that takes me by surprise, but I'm not going to fucking complain. She slips her tongue into my mouth again, and this time I let her because, fuck, I'm already losing control around her. I love her attempting to be dominant; even if she'll never win that battle, she's still my fucking temptress.

# ꞱPOISONED

### MORGANA

*M*Y CHEEKS REFUSE TO stop burning. Even when I cleaned up and got dressed to come down to dinner, my heart was still racing. My core is throbbing and tingling; every time I think of what happened, I feel it knot with pleasure. My entire body feels heightened. I don't know what that is, but seeing him look so good in all black, with a few buttons open, and the way he had pulled me close… fuck, I lost all control. Even then, he didn't expect anything in return, seemingly satisfied with pleasuring me.

That arrogant, cocky smirk remains on his face as we head downstairs. His every action confuses me, messing with my head. Although I carry the tiny vial with me, I'm not sure I can go through with this.

Why do I feel like he's genuinely trying? No… I know he is… but I really need to ask him about my father's death.

"Luna Morgana…" someone calls, and I turn to see none other than Cain. My heart thuds as he smiles politely, lowering his head. "I knew there was more to you than just my brother's slave."

"Cain," Kian spits venomously. Never have I heard such hatred in his voice than at this moment. His hand tightens around my waist as he pulls me back. The tension between them is palpable. The rush of guilt that I feel gets worse when Kian moves me behind him as if he doesn't trust Cain anywhere near me.

"I only wanted to congratulate my new, soon-to-be sister-in-law, brother," Cain says, looking Kian straight in the eye.

I can feel so many eyes on me. The slinky black dress that clings to my figure only makes me feel extra bare with all the attention on me. Every night had been like this, but this is the first time Cain has approached. Something tells me he's reminding me of the little gift he had left me...

Soft music plays in the background as we walk through the crowd to the table at the head of the banquet hall. I can feel Kian's anger radiating off of him. The moment we sit down, I reach over, placing a hand on his leg and giving him a look. He looks back at me coldly, yet he seems to calm down a little. He picks up one of the glasses of wine and downs it in one go. Every day, different Alpha couples are at our table. Today, there are four different couples, two on my left and two on the other side of Kian.

"You look beautiful, Luna Morgana, yet I see you aren't marked," the woman whom I know by the name of Estella, Luna of the Moonstone Pack, comments.

"Well, we are in no rush. Our union requires work and promise. There are much more important things to do than mark one another."

"A mark is a sign that you are committed," she replies, a fake smile on her face.

"We will be having an official crowning ceremony. This is the future queen. She deserves the best," Kian adds, his eyes flashing, although he doesn't even look her way.

"Of course, Your Highness," she replies, his powerful aura making her lower her head.

I smile sweetly before looking ahead. As the food is being brought in, I remember the vial. The note said it needs to be added to food... this is going to be so hard. Is it even the right thing to do?

The vial is slipped into my dress where I can reach it easily, but with so many eyes here, will I manage? I scan the crowd, my eyes landing on Cain. He has his arm around a woman who I know is his mate, kissing her neck, but his eyes meet mine, and he gives the tiniest of nods. Oh, he knows I'm planning on doing this, which means he'll cause a diversion.

I continue eating, feeling rather distracted, but every time Kian's hand brushes my leg or grazes my arm, my entire body tingles with pleasure. I feel as if I'm lacking air. I try to listen to him. With each passing day in his presence, I can tell he is a good king, and that just makes this harder. No, I can't do this. Not until I have answers -

I hear something smash and a gasp. A woman's shriek is followed by the entire hall becoming hushed.

"I'm sorry!" An Omega whimpers. She's standing by Cain, whose eyes are blazing. It seems she had dropped a hot dish all over his mate. How sick is he? Did he just use his own mate as a distraction?

Kian is up in a flash as Cain is ready to strike the Omega. Everyone turns to the commotion, and, without thinking, my heart thuds as I discreetly take the vial out and tip it into Kian's plate, watching it fizz before it blends in with the sauce. Slipping the bottle under the table, I let it roll to the floor, then slide it away from me discreetly. The guilt tightens in my chest as I look at Kian, who is arguing with his brother.

"She should be punished! She burnt my Luna!" Cain spits.

"It was an accident; she is a child," Kian growls. I look at the girl. She's barely eighteen, and it's clear she is terrified.

"It was a mistake. Just fucking leave," Kian hisses, grabbing his brother by the collar.

"Siding with a mere Omega over your brother, tch. What a fucking loser," Cain hisses before grabbing his Luna's hand and pulling her from the room. I frown. Cain as king? That would be a horrible decision. I really need to think this through.

"I'm so so sorry, Your Majesty. It won't happen again," she whimpers.

"It's fine. Be careful next time," Kian replies coldly.

He returns to his seat, and instantly everyone begins eating and talking once again, although many are casting Kian glances. He sits down, pouring himself another glass of champagne and downing it in one go. He picks up his fork, and my heart thunders as he swirls it around the plate and is about to eat it when I place my hand on his thigh. I can't do this, but how do I stop him? The fork is approaching his mouth -

"Feed me!" I request suddenly. He raises an eyebrow, clearly not expecting that. The Luna on the other side chuckles.

"That is sweet. I am glad that your union will be more than just political."

Kian looks at his fork before holding it out to me. I smile and take it, my stomach twisting as I do. I have no idea what that vial held... but I can't support Cain, not without knowing the truth. Kian smirks.

"What are you up to?" He asks quietly.

"Why? Don't you trust me?" I ask, reaching for the champagne bottle. I pour myself a glass and am about to place the bottle down when I knock my glass into his plate on purpose. "Oh, sorry!" I exclaim, praying it looks like a genuine accident. All eyes turn to me as I quickly grab a few napkins, patting Kian's arm that I had also splashed.

"Are you okay?" He asks, and my heart skips a beat.

"Perfectly."

I take a seat again as an Omega quickly comes to clear it up. I glance at the plate, *Thank God...* With relief, I sit back and begin eating. Kian is given a new plate, and soon conversation begins flowing once again.

I eat slowly, my body suddenly feeling feverish. My skin feels clammy, but the worst part is the feeling that my insides are suddenly on fire. My heart races dangerously fast, and my vision is becoming blurry. Shit, is it the drug? But I didn't even have much... what was it anyway?

"Morgana, are you okay?" Kian's voice asks, echoing in my mind. I look at him, coughing slightly, accompanied by the strong taste of blood in my mouth. "Fuck! Morgana!"

I look at Kian, trying to form words. My entire body suddenly starts shaking, and I can't breathe. My heart squeezes painfully as if someone is digging their claws into it.

"Morgana..." His voice is distant. *"Get a fucking doctor!"*

The worry in his voice... he cares for me...

I feel him lift me up. Is that my heart beating or his? What is that ringing in my ears? The wind is rushing through my hair... is he running? Where is he taking me?

"Hold on... fuck, don't close your eyes... I won't let anything happen to you..."

*Why do you care?* I want to ask him that... would he still care if he learned that I tried to poison him?

This pain...

"Don't, fuck, don't.... Help her!... Hold on, baby girl, please fucking hold on."

Shouting... Kian's panic... his fear... why is it so strong? Why is it hurting?

I can't hold on....

"No, fuck no..."

"Her heart rate's dropping..."

"Sorry...."

"*No!*"

Strong arms wrap around me, a racing heart... soft lips press against my burning chest...

I can't...

Sorry...

It's my fault...

My eyes flutter shut, and I can no longer refuse the darkness that welcomes me into its hold.

KIAN

Never have I felt as fucking helpless as I do right now. The moment her body started shaking, and I felt the odd pain within me, I realised something was incredibly wrong. Seeing the blood that she coughed up and hearing her heart racing too fucking fast had made my emotions take over. The fear of losing her ripped me apart like I had been pushed through a fucking shredder. *I can't lose her, nothing can happen to her.*

My entire fucking exterior crumbled when I ran from the hall as fast as I fucking could, commanding every doctor in the palace to be ready to receive her. I was terrified of losing her. Her delicate body convulsed in my arms, blood dripping from her mouth, and tears of pain clung to her lashes. I tried to keep her fucking awake, but her heart was skipping beats and slowing down. At times I couldn't even hear it. My own was thudding violently. Thanatos was frozen in shock within me. Even when I rushed into the medical wing and told the doctors to help her, I couldn't think of anything but my precious Blood Rose.

*Fuck, hate me all you want, just don't fucking leave me.*

I didn't care that I was losing control as I roared at them to save her no matter what. She had lost consciousness, and her already pale skin was even more ghostly.

"There's nothing we can do... her heart's fading too fast..."

"No, you will fix this!" I thunder.

"Alpha, please, we will try - "

"I swear, if anything happens to her, I will kill you all!"

"Alpha, please calm down. It looks like she's been poisoned. We need to pump everything from her body, but she isn't strong enough to fight it. It is lethal," one of the doctors explains. I don't even notice when Luca, Corbin and Ajax arrive or when they start holding me back to allow the doctors to deal with Morgana.

Shit, she needs to make it. I can't lose her…

"There must be something! Just fucking save her," I growl helplessly.

I don't even recognise the fear and desperation in my voice as I pull free from my men and rush to the bed, caressing her clammy forehead. *Fuck, wake up!*

"Alpha… perhaps marking her might help," the doctor suggests, making my eyes snap towards him.

"Mark her?"

"Yes, marking may be the only way, My King. I know she is not your fated mate, but there's still a chance - "

"I'll do it," I cut in.

She is my mate. She has to survive this. I look down at her, my heart racing with the fear that's eating me up.

*I need you.*

**Mark her,** Thanatos growls.

I stare into her perfect face. I will not leave her at death's door.

*I can't lose you.*

I reach down, threading my hand into her hair.

*I don't care if you get angry at me… but I fucking need you to live.*

Without even a shadow of a doubt, my eyes blaze gold, and my teeth elongate as I bend down, sinking them into the corner of her neck. I don't care about the eyes that are on me. All I want is for my queen to return to me. Her heartbeat faintly accelerates, and my eyes flutter shut as I bite into her neck, marking her.

A rush of power courses through me like a searing blast of heat. The sparks that I feel when I touch her now feel like a strong, pleasant voltage of electricity. The pain she is in hits me a thousand times stronger, almost as if we are one entity. Fuck…

"Alpha, please move back. We need to pump the poison from her stomach," one of the doctors says urgently. Luca yanks me back, but I can't focus.

*The only thing that I need is for her to live, please… I'll take her place.*

"Come on, Kian," Luca mutters, dragging me from the room. The last thing I see is the doctors crowding around her, shouting commands to each other as they work together.

"She'll make it," Ajax says firmly.

I can't think straight, and when the door slams shut, cutting off my view of her, I feel as if someone has just shoved their hand into my chest and twisted it painfully. Morgana...

My back hits the wall as I stare at the door.

"Kian..." Luca's voice is fucking distant.

*Don't talk to me...*

"She will be okay. You marked her. You're strong, and so is she," Corbin says quietly.

*I don't know about that...*

The way her body was -

"Kian!"

I don't even bother turning when Sage comes running towards me. *Fucking go away.*

"Are you all right, Kian?" The moment she touches my arm, I pull away, glaring at her.

"Don't fucking touch me!" I hiss. She looks tearful and concerned, but the anger that's bubbling inside of me is fucking suffocating.

"Kian... I'm worried about you. She'll be okay, I hope - "

"Did you do this, huh? Did you think that getting rid of her was best for you?" I shout, grabbing her by the neck.

"Kian, no..." she whimpers, tears spilling down her cheeks.

"I will find out who did this!" I shout, glaring at Luca as I drop Sage to the ground roughly. "Now, get the fuck out of my sight!" My gaze snaps to the rest. "Get her the fuck away from me, and I want everyone from the fucking Omegas to every wolf in the entire fucking castle under house arrest until I know who did this!" I hiss.

Corbin doesn't move as the other two signal for him to stay with me. Luca tugs Sage away, and I'm fucking glad. I'm ready to kill. I look at him, my eyes filled with fury.

"Tell me, Corbin, how many fucking people are in this castle?"

"Over a hundred or so..."

"Yeah? And do you think you joining them might fucking be better?" I hiss. His face drains of colour. He nods, quickly turning and hurrying off.

The fire of vengeance will not be fucking quelled until I have revenge for my woman. Glancing at the door, I place my hand against it. *Please be fucking okay.*

I don't know how much time passes, but it feels like fucking forever. I want to go in, but I know I would only get in the way. My only reprieve is that the pain is fading, which means things are getting better.

*Please fucking be okay.*

The moment the door opens, I'm before it in a flash.

"Alpha, come inside," the doctor says. I step inside to see Morgana lying there. Two drips are connected to her, along with a heart rate monitor.

"How is she?" I ask, closing the gap between the bed and me and taking her slender hand in my own.

"Luckily, alive. Marking her helped a lot. I think, as king, your mark was indeed strong…" he murmurs. I know what he means; the mark is almost like a true mate's mark. Well, she is mine. Of course, it would fucking help. Her lips are slightly parted, her breathing weak but steady. My gaze dips to her neck, where my mark is mostly healed.

"We managed to remove the poison, but the toll of it will take some time to recover from. We are, of course, not so well rounded with a vampire's healing process, but as long as she is drinking plenty, I'm sure she'll recover sooner," he explains, checking her pulse.

"Hmm. Do we know what the poison was or how it probably got to her?"

"Most likely, she took it orally. The concentrated level of it makes me think she digested it shortly before it took effect. Personally, there is one thing that concerns me…"

"What is it?" I ask, caressing Morgana's cheeks. The strong surge of sparks and the incessant need to pull her into my arms is hard to fucking ignore.

"If… a werewolf took it, they wouldn't have made it," he says quietly. I frown, looking at him sharply. "Alpha, the poison, from what we gathered, contained obsidian nightshade and blood wolfsbane. Both are herbs that are lethal to our kind and - "

"And are banned from our kingdom completely."

"Whoever brought this poison into this kingdom… they had this planned out, yet, what concerns me is, was this poison really for Lady Morgana, or was it intended for you?"

# A Discovery

KIAN

**N**IGHT FALLS, AND ALTHOUGH I want to question every fucking person, I can't leave her. So I have the entire fucking castle searched, every room, guest or not, I don't care. If someone is trying to poison Morgana or me, they will pay. For hours, nothing has been discovered, but then Luca tells me they have found a vial under the banquet table. After testing it, it had indeed contained the poison, but how it had gotten there is still fucking beyond me. So far, no other clue has shown up.

Sighing, I stare at the ceiling. I brought her back to my room once the doctor checked her over a final time, and she was stable. The rest is up to her. I'm just making sure she gets the rest and blood she needs. I took the hospital gown off and pulled one of my shirts onto her, doing my best to keep her covered. I keep seeing flashes of her at the dining table, the way her body -

**Stop it, Kian,** Thanatos' growl comes. He's been so fucking silent, too. The shock that we might have lost her is still fresh in our mind.

**I'm fucking trying, Thanatos.** I pull her against my chest, burying my nose in her neck. **She might be angry we marked her,** I murmur in my mind.

**We did it to save her!** He shoots back possessively. **Mate loves us!**

**I don't know if she does…** I admit quietly. But even if she doesn't, I'll fucking make her fall for me.

I don't know when I fell asleep, but I wake up when I hear Morgana's startled gasp. Her heart begins to pound as she looks around as if trying to comprehend what happened.

"You're okay," I say quietly, loosening my hold on her slightly, just enough to make sure she gets the air and space she needs. She sits up, and I place a hand on her back, supporting her, and she gasps again, her heart thudding as she pulls away from my touch.

"W-what was that?" She asks hoarsely.

"Hey, relax. You're okay. You were poisoned," I explain softly, feeling fucking guilty. I should have taken care of her… instead, she almost fucking died.

"Poisoned…" She mutters, her heart thudding loudly; she raises a shaky hand to her forehead. Her emotions are a mess, and she looks distraught. I pull her into my arms, making her heart race once more. "Why is your touch different?" She asks weakly, her head hitting my chest.

"Good different?" I ask, staring down at her. Thank the fucking goddess that she's okay.

"Intense…" she whispers. Looking up at me, her eyes are a light red.

"You need blood." I don't mean whatever the doctors had tried to give her, but to actually drink.

"You didn't answer." Her gaze falls to my neck. I look down at her, my fingers combing her hair.

"You were going to die… the poison was lethal, and you were too weak to fight it," I begin quietly. "So… I marked you to give you the strength you needed to fight." Her eyes stare into mine, and for a few painful seconds, she stares at me blankly.

"God no…" she whispers, her heart thundering as she tries to pull away. That fucking stings.

"Morgana…"

"No… no… who told you to mark me!" She cries out, pulling herself to the edge of the bed and away from me as she feels her neck.

"It was that, or you would have fucking died!" I growl.

"Then you should have let me!"

Thanatos growls. **Mate shouldn't be angry...** he practically whimpers. Yeah, well, he doesn't get human emotions.

"You can hate me all the fuck you want, but I won't let you die," I say dangerously.

"Because you need me?" She asks quietly, her eyes blazing with anger.

"Yeah, I fucking do. I don't give a shit what anyone thinks. I know I fucking hurt you, the way I brought you here and the way I treated you, but I..."

**Say it.**

"I think I've fallen for you," I admit quietly just as she staggers off the bed, the shirt barely covering her ass. Her eyes widen as she stares at me, her heart thundering.

**Fucking wuss,** Thanatos mutters. She shakes her head.

"That is a mistake," she whispers.

"It isn't," I disagree immediately, getting off the bed as well.

"It is... dammit it, don't you get it? I told you..." she trails off, placing a hand on the bedside cabinet weakly.

"I don't care what you told me," I say, walking around to her. She rolls her eyes, and I almost smile at the fact that, despite how weak she is, my sassy queen is still inside her.

"You are indeed a fool," she says. "Is loving someone that easy? You and Sage were such a precious little couple, and now you think you can just fall for me? Seriously?"

"Can we not fucking talk about her?" I growl. "That was nothing compared to what I feel for you. Can you stop being so fucking stubborn and get back to bed? You almost died. You need rest." With those words, I lift her bridal style and place her on the bed, adjusting the pillow under her head. I look down at her, not missing the way her eyes are locked on my chest. Does she know how fucking tempting she is? I'm fucking glad she isn't arguing.

"You need blood." I drop onto the bed next to her, and she cocks one of her perfect brows.

"Yes, I do. However, shouldn't you pour me a glass like you usually do? And who gave you permission to sleep here?"

"I did, and I'm too tired to grab a glass, so..." I arch my neck to the side, giving her access. My eyes lock with hers.

"Don't risk it. I'm thirsty," she whispers.

"I don't mind the risk. We both know that just being with you is fucking playing with fire, isn't it?"

"Oh, one hundred percent," she whispers, shuffling closer. She reaches up, her heart thundering as her fingers graze the back of my neck. Fuck, her touch feels good…

"Do your worst," I whisper seductively.

In a flash, she has me on my back as she straddles my bare stomach, sinking her teeth into my neck and sending a strong sting of pleasure through me. The entire fucking situation is fucking hotter than ever. The level of pleasure mixes with the strengthened bond, those fucking sparks sending desire rushing through me. Her bare core is pressed against my abs, making my dick throb. The euphoric pleasure I feel as she drinks my blood turns me on even fucking more. My hands slide to her hips, holding onto her tightly.

Her soft moan… the way her hand runs up and down my neck… there's just something so fucking mind-blowingly sexy about it, but the breaking point comes when she grinds against my stomach. My eyes blaze, and I bite back a moan. *Fuck.*

"Carry on fucking grinding on me, and I swear I'll fuck you right now," I mutter.

Her answer is to suck harder on my neck, her nails digging into my skin and the tempting scent of her arousal fragrances the air.

**Complete the bond! Mate with her!** Thanatos growls. Oh, as much as I want to… she needs to recover.

I can sense her intense desire as she moans against me. I grab her naked ass, glad I didn't put any fucking panties on her. She whimpers against my neck and momentarily pauses feeding from me, her back arched as she presses herself against me.

"Fuck, Kian…" she gasps. I tangle one hand in her hair, yanking her close as I kiss her neck, sucking hard.

**Alpha, are you awake? This is urgent,** Corbin's voice interrupts.

"Fuck," I growl. Of all fucking times now?

**What the fuck is it?** I growl back.

**We may have found something…odd,** Ajax says quietly, and he sounds urgent. As much as I'm enjoying this, if this involves whoever poisoned Morgana, I need to know…

**Coming,** I say coldly. I kiss her neck one final time before pulling away forcefully.

"You need rest," I whisper huskily, staring into her deep red eyes. Reaching up, I wipe her lips clean. Fuck, she is so damn sexy. She looks curious for a moment before she nods and quickly gets off of me as if just realising what happened. "I need to go attend to something. Get some rest." She smirks, glancing at my fucking hard-on. "No, I didn't mean that," I say, giving her a look. "We both know you're fucking turned on as well, sunshine, but I think you need to rest and keep your energy up," I add arrogantly before grabbing a shirt. Surprisingly, she doesn't reply. I glance towards her. She's just sitting on the bed, looking thoughtful.

"Kian…"

"Hmm?" She seems to hesitate and shakes her head.

"Never mind."

"Sleep."

I leave the room and ask the boys where they are. I make my way out to the courtyard behind the kitchens, frowning. What the fuck is this about? All three of my Deltas are there, along with Luca, talking quietly.

"What is it?" I ask, walking over. They exchange looks; something tells me I'm not going to like this.

"Can you fucking tell me? I don't have all day," I growl.

"Kian, we were searching everywhere as ordered, and Ajax found these in the niche in this pillar," Luca says, quietly pointing at one of the large pillars. I don't even glance at it, instead looking at what he has in his hands. Several bottles of…

"Blood. Human blood," Ajax says quietly.

"There are about eight small bottles in total," Oliver adds.

My heart races and my head feels like it's fucking squeezing. There is only one person in this entire castle who would need blood.

"This is… Lady Morgana's favourite spot. She always sits here when she's resting," Corbin adds as if he doesn't want to believe it.

**No…** Thanatos growls. **Lies!**

The pain of betrayal that is now fucking consuming me is powerful. I can't deny that there were times when she hadn't drunk from me, and her eyes were a lot darker. I also knew my men wouldn't lie to me. Once or twice, that thought had come to my mind, but I never pondered on it. Sure, they didn't find out who fucking poisoned her, but there is someone aside from me who is giving Morgana blood. Meaning she was in contact with someone else…. There are only a rare few who I actually trust here, too.

"When you're watching her, have you ever seen her take anything from here?" I ask, looking at the narrow niche. It's so fucking deep that no one would ever think much of it, it's just a slight damage in the architecture.

"There are moments when we aren't constantly watching her, especially when she isn't moving and just wants to rest. Like earlier, she had stood up the moment I got distracted and then wanted to head straight to your wing, saying she wanted to stay there," Ajax says, frowning coldly.

"I see. Place the blood back exactly how it was, and I want someone to discreetly keep an eye on this spot constantly. I want to see who comes here... Morgana included," I order emotionlessly. I do not want them to sense how I'm fucking feeling. But the way I feel inside... I have my walls up, not wanting her to sense anything from the bond, but it fucking hurts. I thought I was trying to treat her better, but clearly, it was not fucking enough.

**Maybe when you hurt her to start with, you pushed mate to look elsewhere for blood,** Thanatos adds.

**I don't know... let's return home.** I don't want to talk about it.

I head inside, not knowing how the fuck to feel. Alongside the betrayal, I'm also angry. Entering the bedroom, I see she's fast asleep. She had put on some shorts, and her legs are tangled in the blanket, one hand under her cheek. I frown. Now there are fucking things on my mind.

I can't sleep, so I decide I'll go start questioning everyone in the goddamn castle. The culprit who tried to poison her or me is still here, and I intend to find them.

The sun has risen, but even when noon comes, I'm not done. Going around and questioning everyone is no small feat. I'm now at my brother's quarters, and the fucking asshole is just sipping his tea as if the entire situation is amusing.

"It's a shoddy job, Kian. If it was me, do you really think I'd leave room for her to make it?" I growl warningly, and he sighs. "It wasn't me. You would know if I was lying, wouldn't you? After all, you are the Alpha," he spits, clenching his jaw.

"I am, but we both know there are many ways to defy that. I don't trust you, Cain. I also know you came back for a reason, not just to play happy families. Heed my fucking advice; if I even get a slight suspicion about you, I swear by the goddess herself I will kill you," I warn coldly. His eyes blaze as he glares at me with open hatred.

"Don't threaten me, Kian! I am still your brother!"

"Brother, friend, or whatever, hurt Morgana, and I will kill you. Now where the fuck is Kai?"

"Out," he hisses, but he is smart enough not to argue further.

**Kai, where are you?** I ask through the mind link.

**Training grounds, brother.** I frown and head that way. Although I don't believe it was Kai, I still need to question everyone. I see him running laps and approach him. He slows down and walks over to me, lowering his head slightly.

"Kian."

"You know why I'm here; did you have anything to do with what happened to Morgana?"

"You know I would never hurt her. She's yours, Kian," he says quietly.

"All the more reason to hurt her," I reply coldly. He looks away, and I can sense hesitancy within him. My eyes narrow. "What is it?"

"Nothing… I mean… have you asked Morgana?" He asks attentively. I frown.

"Asked her what?" Kai doesn't reply immediately; he just simply shrugs.

"I know we aren't close, Kian, and it's not my place, but I wouldn't trust Morgana completely. I'm sorry," he says quietly before turning and jogging off, leaving me feeling completely cold.

Another blow. Another fucking wave of betrayal… *What does Kai know? Is Morgana really involved in something?*

**No, mate can't… mate is ours!** Thanatos growls.

I know if we ever discover something about her, it will destroy him completely. I hope, for all our sakes, it isn't true. Fuck…

There is so much crap to do. I had cancelled the summit meeting for today as well. I think everyone needs to fucking clear their heads. Just then, none other than Reuban mind-links me.

**Alpha, can we talk? It's urgent. I am waiting inside your office.** He's back? Which means he has news.

I return to my main office swiftly. The door is flanked by two guards. Upon entering, I shut it behind me to see Reuban sitting there. He looks exhausted. It's clear he came straight here, as he is dressed only in a pair of pants.

"You have bad news," I state.

"I do. I came alone and as fast as I could."

"What is it?" I ask, sitting down in my chair.

"Another three packs have been attacked in a matter of days. The attacks are increasing. We are losing more people. Several younger she-wolves and human girls have been taken... things are a lot worse than we thought, Kian," Reuban says, his voice heavy. I frown; this is not fucking good.

"I wouldn't have returned if I didn't trust that the news may not get to you. We are losing far too many men. Playing defence alone isn't enough. Also, it is the Fae, that is confirmed. There have been three occasions where the description has matched, and the victim survived to tell us... and, you know, with their speed... it's definitely lone attackers who are sliding past the defences."

"Are you sure?"

"Yes," he replies with complete confidence. "As you ordered, if things looked bad and it was the worst-case scenario, I have already ordered our men to clear out all civilians from the borders, and they have started moving them all. Some will come to the palace and other cities around the capital. We can't deny it anymore or ignore it... we can't stop war because we are already at war."

I know he has seen a lot; I can see that from the haunted look in his eyes. I frown, standing up and walking over to the window. War.

"If you are the one who is saying that, then it's true. You are one of the most passive of my men. You have always been against war," I say quietly.

"I am, but we can no longer refuse to acknowledge it."

"Hmm. I have extended the hand of friendship to the Sanguine Empire in hopes that we can declare peace and help each other's kingdoms grow. If we are at peace with them, then it means we can deal with the Fae without any other kingdom getting involved." Turning, I quickly fill him in on how Morgana is my mate and what had happened last night. "I hope they agree. This might be ideal, considering they are neutral with the Fae."

"I hope so because things are already bad," I reply quietly.

"What is your command, Alpha?" He asks.

I frown deeply. I have to announce to the kingdom that war is upon us, which means I need to take Morgana as my queen, and I need to lay out our battle plans.

"Give me a day. I need to make plans. Get some rest. I will fill the other four in, and then tomorrow, we will announce it at the summit. It's good that you returned at this time. With them all here, it'll make spreading this news a lot easier."

"Understood."

"A job well done, Reuban," I say quietly. He gives me a half-smile.

"Yeah? Well, I don't know about that, but thank you, Alpha." He lowers his head before leaving my office. Can shit get any worse? I'm left in silence, pacing my office.

**We will win,** Thanatos growls. **Those Fae are dangerous and need to be dealt with once and for all.**

**Yeah, they fucking do, but they are also fucking strong. War is going to cost us greatly.**

**Yes. I know you don't want that, Kian, but inevitably it needs doing.**

**I know… but you know how many women will be left without their mates, children without their fathers, and, in some cases, even mothers…**

**It is understandable, but as a king, you have to have thick skin. Death will happen. You will have to hold yourself together for your kingdom,** Thanatos murmurs. I frown.

**I know, and I fucking will, even if I don't like it,** I reply coldly.

We both fell silent, the shadow of war lurking above our heads. As much as I want to go upstairs to check on Morgana after what I discovered, I'm delaying it. The pain that she may have fucking betrayed me is still strong. Although maybe I deserved it, it still doesn't make me feel fucking better.

I go back to my desk and begin working on some matters that need attending to. I am immersed in my work when there's a knock on the door.

"Enter!" I call out. It opens, and Luca stands there, slightly breathless.

"A reply from the Sanguine Empire," he explains, holding up a black envelope with a red seal. He looks as nervous as I fucking feel. He comes over, and I break the seal, flipping it open.

I skim over it, my heart racing as the words I read ring in my head. Things just got one thousand fucking times worse.

"What does it say?" Luca asks quietly, nervousness and anticipation clear in his voice.

"They declined our offer and have joined hands with the Fae Kingdom Onis."

# A Truth Under the Setting Sun

MORGANA

Guilt is eating up at me. I had almost poisoned him... I could have killed him... Even if I backed out at the last minute, it doesn't change the fact that I had tried.

I run my fingers over the mark that now binds me to him, a mark that guarantees how serious he is about me. If he had wanted, he could have left me to die, and he would have been free of me. I still remember the panic and fear in his voice as he rushed me from the hall and the concern in his eyes when I woke up. With the bond now connecting us, I can feel the emotions from him... Kian may even love me. No, I'm sure he does. When I drank his blood, those intense emotions...

I place my head in my hands, feeling exhausted, and not only physically. I need to tell him. Even if he gets angry... we need to talk, and I really need to ask him about my father, too. These emotions inside of me... I don't know how long I can fight them. I just need some clarity before it's too late...

With renewed resolve, I decide to talk to him when he returns today. Getting up, I take a shower and decide to make myself look a little present- able. I look like death itself, and that's saying something for a vampire. After showering, I spend a good twenty minutes selecting the perfect outfit.

I don't know why I want to make an effort, but... maybe if he gets too angry, I can calm him down with my charm. Yes, that's the reason. It has nothing to do with how I love the way he looks at me as if I'm a treat he wants to devour…

After slipping on some red lace lingerie, I choose a chiffon ivory blouse that is slightly sheer, showing off my bright bra underneath. With the top's dipping neckline that reveals an ample amount of cleavage, it looks rather sexy. I then choose a red suede pencil skirt that falls to my mid-thigh and finish off with a pair of black stilettos.

Once my hair is dry, I decide to style it in a little quiff that I pin back, leaving a few strands out to frame my face and the rest falling down my back nicely. I then get to my makeup, settling for black winged liner and red lips. After applying some shimmer to highlight my face and a touch of blush to give me some life, I'm almost done. Finally, picking out some earrings and a dangly necklace that falls between my breasts, I'm satisfied with how I look. My gaze falls to the ring that Kian had given me, a ring of a promise…

I'm going to tell him, no matter what.

Noon comes and goes, but apart from the doctor and a few Omegas to give me food, Kian doesn't come. Even the guard in the hall simply says he's busy.

It's now sunset, and I'm beginning to worry. I feel anxious in the pit of my stomach. Where is he? And how come he didn't even come to check up on me? Sure, he didn't need to but… did something happen?

I feel restless, even going for a walk outside, but I feel uneasy and return soon after, instead pacing around the large halls, trying to occupy myself by looking at the paintings on the wall. I'm now down the hall on the first floor at the large balcony, staring out at the setting sun when I hear footsteps, and Kian's familiar scent reaches me. I turn, my heart pounding despite trying to remain calm as I remember our moment from earlier before he had left. He stops when he sees me, and his eyes trail over me, darkening as he drinks in my appearance.

For once, I don't know what to do with my hands. So instead, I place them on the balcony behind me, crossing my legs as I perch on the edge. The moment Kian's gaze goes to my breasts and the hunger fills his eyes, my stomach knots. He walks towards me, like a predator coming for his prey, so I lean back until I can't anymore.

"Any special occasion for you to look so fucking sexy, sunshine?" He asks huskily, his legs on either side of mine. His hand trails up my bare thigh, making my heart pound violently.

"No…" I sound breathless. I frown, looking at him closely. He looks exhausted… and is that worry in his eyes? "What happened?" I ask sharply, all my nervousness gone.

"Why do you think something happened?" He asks, burying his nose in my neck, making me gasp. His strong arms pull me up against him, wrapping them around me tightly and caging me against him. I can sense the storm of emotions that he is trying to suppress. Concern fills me, and I run my hand through his hair, caressing the back of his neck.

"Kian… I can sense it. What's wrong?"

"Nothing for you to worry about," he murmurs, kissing my neck softly.

I shiver in pleasure. The pressure between my legs is growing, so I press my thighs together. I need to focus… but how can I focus when Kian is pressed against me so perfectly, his manhood pushing against my core? All I want to do is give in to all the dirty thoughts that are consuming my mind, but before I do anything crazy, I need to tell him the truth and ask him, too.

"Please tell me," I request, pulling his head back and away from my neck. My entire body is leaning against his arms. If he lets go, I'll probably tumble to the floor.

"War is upon us, Morgana… the attacks that we've been facing were the Fae, and I just got a reply from your brother," he says quietly.

"What did he say?" I ask, my heart thudding at the revelation that Kian had just shared.

"He refused. They had joined sides with the Fae Kingdom." My eyes fly open, anger rising within me as a huge aura swirls around me. "Whoa…" Kian mutters. I take a deep breath, trying to calm down.

"Sorry. That bastard! Allow me to return to the empire. I'll rip his heart out and make him pay."

"Why are you so upset? If war comes, it means you have a high chance of being able to return. Isn't that what you want?" I feel a sharp pang inside of me. Why is he saying that?

"Do you want me to go?" I ask quietly, confused at his odd question. He frowns.

"I already told you I want you by my side… I have fallen for you, Morgana, and when an Alpha cares for someone this strongly… it never ceases. Do you still wish to see my ruin?" Why do I feel like there is more to this?

"Are you giving up hope?" I ask softly. "Do you think we can't survive this war?"

"I won't lie. If we do win, it will be barely. Two kingdoms against one gives us a very huge disadvantage - "

"Then let's reach out to the Elves!" I suggest suddenly, my heart racing as the idea comes to me. I pull out of his arms, brushing a strand of my hair back. "The Kingdom of Elandorr will never say no to us." He frowns, crossing his arms sceptically.

"They won't fucking care. They are far too arrogant to get off their high horses. No one will touch them, so why do you think they'll help?" I smile confidently, snapping my fingers.

"Because I am friends with the future King, Prince Orrian." That seems to surprise him. He narrows his eyes suspiciously, staring at me.

"Friendship alone isn't going to guarantee them sacrificing their people for us." My cheeks flush slightly, and I hope he doesn't notice it.

"We… we have a past. He promised me that if I ever needed him, he'd be there." Kian's eyes flash, and I see a spark of jealousy in them.

"Care to explain that past?" I roll my eyes.

"Seriously, Kian? After Sage, do you even have any right to ask me?"

"Yes, I do," he growls. Despite the seriousness of the situation, I can't resist a smirk.

"Well, I couldn't wait a hundred years for my little baby Alpha to be born, now could I?" I can't pass up the chance to tease him. He is rather amusing when he gets angry.

His eyes flash, and the powerful aura that swirls around him tells me I pushed him too far. In a flash, he is before me, slamming me against the wall on the left, his hand wrapped around my throat. The glowing hues of the sunset behind him only add to how powerful the man before me looks at this moment.

"Do I need to remind you that I am not a fucking pup?" He growls.

I bite my lip. I actually wouldn't mind that… but… I need to tell him first. Kian's gaze dips to my lips. The anger and rage within him only grow, but now it is laced with desire and lust.

"As much as I would love to… I need to tell you something." I admit softly, firmly trying to push him away.

"Make it fast…" he whispers huskily, pressing his body against mine.

"I poisoned the food," I blurt out. Kian freezes, his heart thudding as his gaze snaps to mine.

"What?"

"I… I was meant to poison you… but I couldn't go through with it… so I took it myself," I whisper, my stomach churning with nerves so much I feel sick. Never have I felt so worried about something I had done as I do right now, staring into the raging golden eyes of an Alpha king ready to kill…

My heart thunders as I stare at him, ready for him to unleash all his anger upon me. His eyes are blazing, but within them, it's as if a hurricane has been unleashed. The calibre of the emotions in those golden orbs devour me completely, so strong I can't make them all out, the conflict, the anguish, the pain, the anger, and so much more than I can even comprehend. Although the urge to read his mind consumes me, I'm too terrified of what I may hear that I refuse to. Instead, I wait for him to crush my neck in his grip and do his worst.

"I acted impulsively… I don't know why I did it. I know it's a little late, but I'm sorry for trying to kill you… or hurt you… I didn't really know how much damage it would do…" I mumble lamely.

"So, you decided to stupidly just eat it yourself?" He asks coldly, his voice trembling with unbridled rage.

"It was a spur-of-the-moment decision… I didn't think it out," I shoot back, despite knowing how dangerous it was. "But at least I didn't let you take it." Hurt and anguish are the emotions that I can sense the strongest through the bond.

"And you thought you'd risk your own fucking life?" He now cups the back of my neck with his thumbs on my cheeks.

"It was that or you…" I remind him, having no idea where this is going. His eyes return to hazel, and the sheer level of emotions in them tugs at my heart. It's painful, so fucking painful, that I can't breathe…

"Then I would fucking rather it have been me," his husky, hoarse reply admits.

My eyes widen as I stare at him in shock, trying to figure out what he had just said. Our bodies are moulded together as one, our hearts pounding.

"What?" I ask hoarsely.

"You heard me, my fucking crazy she-devil. I'd rather you had poisoned me than yourself. You are the craziest, most reckless, dangerous, insane, psychotic woman I have ever fucking met, and I'm probably just as fucking crazy to have fallen in love with you," he says, making me gasp. His words ring in my ears, my heart skipping a few beats.

He loves me.

"You told me not to trust you from the start… disclaimer included, and I'll still take it. So, try to kill me as many times as you fucking want. I don't give a fuck. You're still my lethal desire."

With those words that render me speechless, he yanks me towards him, crushing my breasts against his chest. His soft plush lips meet mine, but it's different from anything I've ever felt before. His lips caress mine sensually yet painfully slowly as if he's trying to memorise every part of them. Time seems to stand still. My heart is fluttering, and I feel lightheaded at the intense emotions that pour into the kiss. The taste of his minty mouth, the feel of his body against mine, his scent, everything is beyond perfect. At that moment, I realise that this will never be enough, one kiss will never be enough.

I don't know when I begin to kiss him back. My eyes flutter shut, and my mind is blank apart from how this feels. His hands leave my neck, one tangling in my hair, the other all over me, feeling every inch of my back and ass with a need and intensity that makes my legs feel weak.

His kissing becomes harder and hungrier with a fervent need that I have never felt from him before. The hunger, desire, and love that is filling me so intensely are from him. His emotions. His tongue slips into my mouth as if he doesn't want even a millimetre of space between us, and I don't, either. We are two opposites made to be one…

I run my hand up his chest, locking my arms around his neck, and arch myself even more into him, moaning as he throbs against my stomach. I hook my leg around his, and his hand cups my ass, squeezing it as our kiss becomes hungrier and rougher, changing from something slow and sensual to something illicit, awakening those indecent desires within me once more.

I have to pull away, gasping for much-needed air. Even then, Kian isn't done placing kisses down my jaw and neck, making me shiver as another rush of tingles courses through me.

"Fuck…" I whisper, breathing heavily, still trying to recover from that mind-blowing kiss. I gaze out at the setting sun through hooded eyes, my heart pounding rapidly. I know that I will never forget this moment, and as much as I'm tempted to yank him to the bedroom… we still need to talk.

"Kian…" I breathe. He inhales deeply, and I know he can smell how turned on I am.

"Fuck…" he mutters, forcing his head back, but he still doesn't let go of me. "What is it?"

"I have a few questions… and I'm sure you want to know where I got the poison from. Don't you think we need to talk first, especially if war is coming?" I ask, trying to clear my mind. At least tell me if he killed my father. I need to know. He looks down at me, now frowning, as he takes my chin in his fingers.

"Good point… but, really, a little fun to distress would have been fun…"

"Maybe later… if we're still up for it," I suggest, leaning up and brushing my lips against his softly. His eyes darken, and I know he'll hold me to it.

"Let's go inside," he says, glancing down towards the open balcony. I nod and follow him, still feeling very giddy and weak. "By the way… you will be punished for what you did." I blink, not expecting that.

"Oh… I thought I might be," I sigh, pouting. Our eyes meet, and he smirks devilishly at me. Something tells me he doesn't mean the cells.

He opens the bedroom door and steps back, allowing me inside first. I walk over to the bed and sit down, feeling emotionally exhausted.

"I have one question first, Kian, and I want an honest answer," I say, leaning forward. His gaze falls on my breasts, and my stomach flutters at the way he licks his lips. If I'm lethal, then he's deadly.

"Go on."

To my dismay or pleasure, depending on how I look at it, he begins to remove his shirt right in front of me. My heart thumps, and I suddenly feel the huge room is far too small. His eyes snap to mine, hearing my racing heart, and he doesn't look away, removing his shirt and tossing it aside so damn sexily. Just imagining him stripping completely makes my stomach knot with anticipation, and I have to do my best to focus on the conversation at hand. I bite my lip, trying not to admire his god-like body that is begging to be worshipped. I close my eyes.

*Focus, Morgana.*

"You were saying?" He asks arrogantly, and I can hear the amusement in his tone.

"Did you kill my father or have anything to do with it in any way? Organised it, commanded it, or know anything about it?" I ask quietly, opening my eyes. It's going to be his word against Cain's and everyone in the Sanguine Empire who assumed it was the werewolves. His brows furrow as he removes his belt and shoes, his eyes on me.

"I didn't, and it was not something that had ever been put on the table, even by the other Alphas in the council. I have never talked to him, however, shortly before his death, he sent me a letter requesting a meeting. I won't lie, I wasn't planning on replying to it. The only time I entered your kingdom was - "

"The night you saw me in the lake…" I finish. Our eyes meet, and he smirks.

"Exactly."

"That's the night my father died. Remember those bells? They signalled an emergency."

"That in itself should have been proof that it was not me. I was with you," he says quietly. I shake my head.

"It had to be someone powerful. My father's personal guard was an enchanter, and no ordinary person could have done that," I explain and begin pacing. Then who was it?

"Then there's a possibility it was someone within. It's not uncommon for them to be taken off guard. I'm assuming your father was powerful. Perhaps he wasn't expecting the attack; if it was someone close to him, he would never have seen it coming." He sits down, rubbing the back of his shoulder, leaving me to let the words sink in, words that ring in my head. Why had I never considered that? Azrael always wanted to be king…

No… was that it?

"… Morgana?"

My head is pounding, and my chest hurts. I clutch it, the shrill sound filling my head. Dozens of voices fill my head, the agonising sounds making my head feel like it's about to explode. One voice stands out from the rest.

**Mate! Help mate!** Thanatos growls.

"Morgana? Look at me." Kian's firm yet soothing voice comes, but it's too far away. Strong arms wrap around me, but I can't focus. How could I have been so stupid?

# Something More

KIAN

THE MOMENT SHE SEEMS to have gone into shock, I quickly lead her to the bed, grabbing some water and holding the glass to her lips. They don't move, almost as if she doesn't notice the glass there. Her heart is thundering as if what I told her was something that was far too shocking. I place the glass down, wiping the water from her lips with my thumb before running my fingers through her silky hair, telling her to talk to me.

From the moment she had told me about the poison, the fact that she had changed her mind was fucking enough. She's sassy and fucking crazy, but her honesty is something that shines through. No matter how impulsive she is, she does everything from her heart...

I look up at her, rubbing her knuckles on my knees before her. Her asking me about her dad fucking surprised me. I mean, I know my father's death had its circumstances, but for her to actually think I killed her father...

"Morgana."

Leaning in, I claim her lips in a kiss, biting down on her bottom lip. That gets the reaction I want from her. She gasps, breathing heavily as if she had just gotten back the oxygen supply that she needed. She looks at me, brushing the strands that framed her face back. She looks so fucking good tonight, and I wish we didn't have so much fucking crap going on. Then I could do a lot more to her...

"He said… you killed him… God, I'm so stupid." She places her head in her hands, giving me a fucking eyeful of her breasts.

**Who told mate that?** Thanatos growls.

"Who said that?" I ask, frowning. She looks up at me, biting her lip almost as if unsure if telling me was wise.

"If I tell you, you need to promise me you will stay calm and act wisely." I cock a brow.

"Are you actually fucking telling me to stay calm, sunshine? After how fucking reckless you yourself are?"

"Please," she says, running a finger down my jaw. My eyes flash, and I won't fucking lie, the sparks that rush through me only make my already hard-on even fucking more painful. She stands up, walking over to the window and sighing heavily. "At the start, when you were making me work in the kitchens, someone reached out to me, telling me that if I helped them kill you… they would promise me my freedom, and I would have revenge for my father's death. They also left me blood in a niche in one of the pillars down behind the kitchens."

Despite the fact that her planning against me from the start leaves a bitter taste in my mouth, I'm pretty fucking glad she's at least telling me about the blood. I didn't want to have to ask her about the blood, but if she hadn't mentioned it, I would have had to.

"The poison was just… it was just stupid of me, but despite my doubts, the fact that he had so smoothly said that you did kill my father…"

I frown while listening to her. My eyes are on her slender back, and her sexy plump ass looks so fucking good in that tight skirt. If I thought she needed a fucking punishment before, she definitely needs one now.

**Yes, I agree,** Thanatos growls. Ever the fucking horny dog. **You thought it first,** he grumbles as I make my way over to her.

There is one person whom I don't trust… but I need her to tell me that.

Even Kai's words not to trust Morgana return to me, a part of me wonders if she had told me the truth, knowing I had figured something out. But that isn't possible.

"Will you give me a fucking answer to who that is, or shall I take a guess?" I ask, wrapping my arms around her from behind. Her breath hitches, her heart pounding as she leans into me. I press my lips against her neck, loving the way her body reacts to me, those delicious sparks, and the way her ass is pressed against my fucking dick. "Cain," I whisper quietly, my lips brushing her ear.

Her face snaps to face me, those large ruby-coloured eyes staring into mine. I know I hit the fucking nail on the head. Thanatos' murderous growl reverberates in my head, and my eyes blaze gold. Morgana turns her body completely towards me, locking her arms around my neck tightly.

"Kian…" I clench my jaw, trying to calm the rage within me. "Forget him for now. You can decide calmly on what to do next," she whispers.

"Don't fucking tell me to calm down when I'm fucking pissed," I growl, tugging her head back as I stare into that gorgeous face of hers.

"Then I might have another way to calm you down," she whispers, one of her hands running down my chest and abs, leaving pleasure coursing through me in her wake. The moment her hand cups my balls, I'm fucking taken to another fucking level of need and desire. Her lips meet my neck as she massages my fucking cock.

"Fuck," I groan, yanking her head forward and slamming my lips roughly against hers.

I will never get enough of her, that's for fucking certain. She's a fucking temptress, and she has me exactly where she fucking wants. She begins to unbuckle my pants and unzips them. I won't fucking lie, I need the fucking space. They are too fucking tight right now.

She pulls away from our kiss, breathing heavily before she crouches down. Tugging my pants down, she deftly slips her fingers into my boxers and slides them down as well. Her eyes darken with desire as she looks at my dick. The need for her is fucking uncontrollable, and knowing where this is going…

*Fuck, that's my girl…*

Teasingly, she runs her fingers along my shaft, rubbing her thumb along the tip as she licks her lips. Her eyes are hooded with lust as she looks up at me.

"Want me to suck your dick, Alpha?" She teases in a sexy voice, sticking her tongue out and running it along my tip. Goddess…

"Without a fucking doubt. Now, be a good little girl and suck that cock as if you were fucking hungry," I growl huskily. A seductive smirk crosses her lips.

"Your wish is my command," she breathes seductively before she presses her tongue to the base of my shaft, running it right along to the tip.

One of my hands tangles in her hair as I groan at how fucking hot this is. The way this feels, the pleasure is so fucking big. I want to do everything with this woman; fuck her, love her, and fucking live my entire life with her.

One of her hands fondles my fucking balls, teasingly rubbing that sweet fucking spot right behind them. The pleasure from her simply teasing me is so fucking good that I can't wait for her to have those lips around me.

"That's it, baby girl…" I grunt, unable to hold back my groan of pleasure.

She licks every inch of my dick before wrapping her lips around my tip, making me suck in a sharp breath. If she had looked fucking sexy before, she looks even better now. Those plush red lips stretch around me, and her arousal perfumes the air; it smells so fucking intoxicating, a perfect sign that she's enjoying this as much as I am.

*Oh, yeah, that's it…*

A wanton moan leaves her lips, humming against my dick as she takes more of me in, bobbing her head as she sucks me. I'm not able to control myself and begin thrusting into her mouth. This image of her on her fucking knees with my dick down her fucking throat is fucking hotter than the sun.

"Skirt up, Princess. Spread those legs and touch yourself like the dirty little temptress you are," I command huskily.

I smirk when I see the faint blush coating those porcelain cheeks of hers. She does as she is told, and I almost fucking come at the sight of her ass in a tiny thong. She parts her legs, never stopping her rhythm as she throats my dick and reaches down between her legs. The moment her lids close halfway, I know she found her fucking clit.

"That's it," I mutter. My fucking release is near, but I'm trying to hold off, wanting to enjoy this for as long as possible. The pleasure I feel is too fucking perfect. "Fuck, you're good…"

Her eyes never leave my face, even when I tighten my hold on her hair and begin fucking her mouth harder and faster. She's fucking good. Even when I hit her throat, choking her, she doesn't gag much, taking it all and moaning like she never wants to fucking stop. I don't want her to. Her hand is on my thigh, unable to keep her balance as I assault her mouth roughly, feeling my release build.

"Fuck… that's it," I growl just as I yank out roughly.

My orgasm shoots through me, coming all over her neck and breasts. The pleasure I feel makes my mind go blank, and it feels like I just fucking see stars. My entire body is fucking shaking, and the groan that escapes me is fucking louder than I had ever allowed myself to be. I couldn't hold back. Riveting aftershocks thrum through me, and the urge to bend her over and fuck her senseless is strong.

The moment I recover a little, I look down at her. She's gasping for breath, her sore-looking lips parted as she breathes heavily. Leaning down, I yank her up, crashing my lips against hers hungrily. She clings on to me; even when I reach between her legs, delivering a sharp slap to her pussy, she simply whimpers with pleasure and parts her legs for me. I give her another sharp tap, making her moan louder, locking her arms around my neck. I massage her between her soaking lips, teasingly rubbing her clit before giving her another tap. She gasps, whimpering with pleasure.

"Fuck, Kian, that's it…" she whimpers.

"Are you going to be a good girl from here on out, my little she-devil?" I growl huskily in her ear, kissing her sensually.

"Yes…" she moans as I tap her pussy again before slamming two fingers into her, making her whimper even louder as I begin fucking her with them hard and fast. Fuck, she feels so fucking good. Her cries of pleasure fill the room, and I don't care who the fuck hears; she is mine, all fucking mine.

I feel her tighten around my fingers and deliver a sharp tap to her ass just as I slam my fingers deep into her, making her orgasm explode through her. Her juices coat my fingers as she moans in pure ecstasy, her entire body reacting to it. Her orgasm makes her shudder, and the moan of pleasure that leaves her makes me fucking hard again. She gasps, now a trembling mess. I grab her around her waist before she collapses and lift her bridal style, carrying her to the bathroom. She looks a fucking hot sexy mess right now, but the urge to tell her that we got this takes over.

"Morgana… I know we're fucking different… but we can work."

"No, we *will* work," she says, smiling like the minx she is. "Even when I misbehave…" She traces circles on my neck and chest, looking at me seductively.

"I'll just punish you," I murmur.

"I like the sound of that," she whispers before I begin kissing her once more.

## MORGANA

Last night had been magical. Although we had just kissed a little more, showered, and got into bed, there was something about coming clean and being honest. Knowing that he hadn't been behind my father's death had lifted the weight within me. It meant I was willing to give in to these emotions…

My core still tingles when I remember taking his dick in my mouth. I wouldn't mind waking him up like that every morning. There's something so sexy about looking at that view of pure ecstasy on his face. Kian is an emotionless, stoic person, so whenever I get to see that side… he is everything one could want and more, and, despite his arrogant nature, he cares for me. No, loves me.

Today, I get dressed in black pants and a strapless floral green satin wrap top that shows off the top of my breasts. My hair is in a high pony, and I wear a few delicate necklaces, dangly earrings, a few bracelets, and rings. I won't deny I love the way he can't stop looking at me, that struggle with his self-control when I bend down to slip my heels on. I feel… happy and as if I belong here. I guess I do, with Kian. I'm not a fool to deny that. I just hope we can find a solution to this war.

We don't talk about Orrian again, but he is willing to reach out to them. I smile just thinking of the way he gets all possessive. Is it wrong that I find it amusing?

It's early morning, and we are in his office with his four Deltas and Beta. Each one seems to be unsure of what to make of me as Oliver closes the door slowly, his green eyes fixed on me, almost as if he doesn't trust me. I'm perched on the arm of Kian's chair, and I frown, trying to read their minds.

*After what we found… is Kian actually trusting her?* Luca wonders.

*She's in cahoots with someone… this is weird…* Ajax thinks.

*She's dangerous, I don't trust her.* Corbin's thoughts.

I frown, looking at Kian sharply. What had they found?

"So, do we have a plan?" Ajax asks, his gaze once again going to me. I remain passive, thinking I would let Kian tell them what is needed.

"There're a few things that we need to discuss, and we will start with the fact that Morgana has been in touch with Cain, who told her I killed the previous vampire king and hence made her want revenge," Kian explains quietly, his voice cold and emotionless. All of his men look shocked at that.

I feel a little stupid, thinking their reaction is enough to make it clear that Kian had nothing to do with that.

"Cain… so…" Luca looks at Kian, and I know they are mind-linking.

"He left the poison in one of the pillars outside, along with blood," Kian says icily. Although he isn't holding me responsible, I know the fact that Cain had tried to get me still causes him anger.

"Then why have we not arrested him?" Corbin asks, running a hand through his hair as his eyes flash.

"We're going to keep an eye on him, and this time I mean a proper one. I want to know what else he's fucking up to. I won't get him to talk, no matter how much I fucking torture him. I feel he's planning more," Kian says. I look at him. This is my chance to redeem myself…

"Maybe you can arrest him. If you trust me, that is… I may not look like it, but I am a vampire who has abilities that even my brother does not have. Something my father wanted me to keep a secret," I begin. I know these men trust Kian and he trusts them. Sharing my secret is not an issue. "I can read minds, somewhat. It's not easy and often I get only snippets but…" I trail off as all six men look at me, trying to register what I had just said. I bite my lip looking at Kian.

"Read anyone's mind?" He asks, narrowing his eyes.

"It's how I knew I was your mate. I heard Thanatos and you speaking," I explain quietly. Luca whistles, letting out a sharp breath.

"Whoa…" he mutters.

"Fucking hell… anything else you want to share, sunshine?" Kian asks coldly, raising an eyebrow. Despite his tone, his eyes hold that glint that is reserved only for me.

"If there is, I'll let you know when I remember," I reply haughtily. Our eyes meet, and I watch his gaze dip to my lips and breasts before he looks away.

"Read my mind then. Can you do it willingly or is it randomly?"

"Often willingly, sometimes it happens on its own. If I'm overwhelmed, I kind of lose control of it and hear an influx of voices," I reply before focusing on Kian. "You need to think of something," I murmur, placing my hand on his shoulder. The shrill sound erupts in my head before I push past it, probing his mind.

*Like how fucking sexy you look in that top? Although I do prefer you naked.* **Mate looks good. When can I play with mate?**

I blush lightly. What?

"Did you get anything?" Kian asks, his face emotionless. I give him a pointed look.

"Really, do you want me to say that out loud?" I ask before leaning in towards his ear. My lips brushed against his lobe, and I love how his heartbeat quickens. "Tell Thanatos soon…" I whisper seductively, and if we were alone, I would have run my hand over his manhood. He turns towards me, his blazing eyes meeting mine.

"That's proof enough."

"So, when you need me to, I can get the information from Cain… however, to start with, how about we set up a trap? It would be better if you allowed me to leave him a note to meet him somewhere. I think I could get him to speak out. That way you can hear it for yourself and not have to rely on my word alone, as I know your men may not trust me," I suggest, looking at the five men. Apart from Oliver, the rest look away, whilst Reuban frowns. Kian takes my hand, kissing my palm before threading his fingers with mine and resting our combined hands on his leg.

"That sounds like a better plan. However, if I say you are to be trusted, then no one else has a fucking say," he said coldly. I know that's a warning to his men. "As for the letter from the Sanguine Empire and the news of the Fae Kingdom Onis, there's something Morgana has suggested that might be our best shot," Kian continues, now frowning. I can sense his displeasure and smirk.

The men listen seriously as Kian begins laying out the plan of going to Elandorr. I add my input here and there but leave it to Kian for the most part.

"That might be risky…" Ajax says, "you going alone…"

"We need to do this discreetly, without anyone being alerted. After the summit, you can just put it down to the two of us needing some alone time before the coronation. With the preparations in full swing, everyone will be too busy to focus on us. As usual, have food delivered to our quarters and try to make it out as if you are seeing us at times. Perhaps even have a dinner here one evening. Let's just keep it fucking believable," Kian says, frowning.

"But you two are travelling alone. Are you sure, Kian?" Luca asks worriedly.

"I'm strong enough, and it's not the first time I've been to a different kingdom alone," he reminds them coldly. His voice holds power and finality; I know that's the end of the discussion.

"And I don't mean to sound disrespectful to the Luna… but after what she attempted… is it wise?" Ajax asks. I can't deny him being concerned for his king is fair, but the surge of anger that lashes through me, anger that does not belong to me, tells me Kian thinks differently.

"Care to fucking say that again?" He hisses, his voice overlaying with Thanatos'. He is about to stand up, but I place my hand on his arm.

"It's fair for them to worry, Kian. They aren't wrong," I say quietly. I won't betray Kian, not when he trusts me. I would never humiliate him like that again. If he could trust me, then I wouldn't break that trust.

Ajax lowers his head to us, and I shake my head at Kian.

"Relax, they only care for you. I am not here to cause rifts," I say, now looking at Ajax sharply. "The elves are an ancient race, and they are powerful. If we have them on our side, this war can be stopped early, and, if not, then we go for the win. Besides, do you not have faith in your king? We all know he could kill me if I did try something." Kian clenches his jaw, but his men seem to find this reasonable enough.

"And you are willing to go against your people?" Reuban asks calculatingly. My heart skips a beat, and I look at Kian.

"I hope that they surrender or join me. I can promise them a better future. If my brother dies in battle, then I'm sure his soon-to-be born heir will make a fine king, but until he comes of age, I will become ruler by default. If that happens, we can make amends between both kingdoms. Then, by the time my brother's offspring is of age, they can rule. That is, of course, if it comes to that…" I turn to Kian, who is sitting there with a thoughtful look on his face.

"So that's the plan." He says, "At the summit today, I will announce that war is upon us, that the Fae and vampires have joined hands, and that Morgana and I will be wed soon enough. We will also plan the journey to and from Elandorr. It will take us a minimum of two weeks. You five will hold the fort in my absence."

"Understood," they all say in unison. Confidence and determination is clear on their faces.

I look out the window as they begin discussing the chances that Elandorr will help, but I know Orrian will. We may have ended our relationship, but we are still friends.

I stand up, walk over to the window, and stare out at the kingdom. The sun is up, and it all looks so peaceful. Past the palace grounds, the gorgeous hills, rivers, and woods spread out along with the huge cities built around them. This alliance isn't only for Kian, it's for my father, who had reached out to him. Something deep down within me tells me that my father wanted to extend the hand of peace. Not only will I help the people of Clair De Lune, but also those of the Sanguine Empire, those who are innocent despite their ruler's sins.

I turn back when the men exit the room and see Kian rubbing his neck again. He's tense, that much I can see. I walk over to him and place my hands on his shoulders.

"You're so tense…" I murmur as I begin massaging his muscular shoulders and neck.

"Hmm."

I press harder, satisfied when he groans slightly, rolling his neck. I slip my hand into his shirt, massaging him firmly and feeling the knots.

"Relax, handsome, you're really tense…"

"Yeah, I won't fucking deny that. We will deal with Cain before we leave," he murmurs, reaching up. He pulls my head down, kissing my lips sensually for a long moment, before relaxing back and allowing me to carry on.

"Sounds like a plan. We will get through this, Kian. One step at a time," I say, frowning slightly.

"Yeah, we will," he agrees with confidence clear in his voice. He groans slightly, and I bite my lip. God, he sounds so sexy. "You're fucking good with your hands, sunshine."

"I'm good with a lot more than my hands," I reply seductively, leaning down and flicking his ear with my tongue.

"Oh, I fucking know," answers his husky reply. Grabbing my wrists, he pulls me down and my heart skips a beat. We didn't put a label to us, but we had somehow become more. I tighten my arms around his neck, kissing his cheek.

"So… I heard Thanatos wanted to meet me…" I say teasingly.

"He fucking does, but I don't trust him."

"Hmm? I can handle him. So, whenever you're ready, I don't mind," I say, returning to massaging his shoulders.

He had confessed his love to me… yet, I hadn't expressed my feelings vocally. Soon I will, too.

# ʜatred & ᴊealousy

MORGANA

THE WEEK PASSES, AND the summit is over. Everyone has left, and with them, the talk of war spreads through the land. Everyone is working together, and the army is beginning to prepare for the upcoming war. People are coming to the palace as well as to the inner cities for shelter. The palace will be busy getting accommodations set up, and I know it's the perfect time for people not to notice our absence, as I know our journey is going to have to be discreet. I just hope we get through the mountains that led to Elandorr with ease, as no transport will pass through there.

Today is the night I'm meeting Cain. I left him a note in the pillar two days ago and hope that he falls for it. Kian had gone out on a trip today; well, that's the façade we are using, as I had mentioned in the note that I heard he's leaving the palace, and we should plan our next step. Although he and Luca had left the palace with some men, they'll sneak back and be lying in wait.

I've just finished talking to a dressmaker about my wedding dress and am out for a walk. I don't even feel it's fair to have a dress when war is at our doorstep, but a strong and confident royal couple carrying on as usual gives hope to the kingdom and its people.

I'm walking through the courtyards, dressed in a long pale pink maxi dress with my hair pulled into a simple bun, with Oliver following me at a distance. It's strange how I had made a habit of walking in the sun so often since being in Clair De Lune. Unlike the Sanguine Empire, where it's colder, it's warmer and sunnier here. I sit down near a pillar, something that is somewhat of a ritual. I'm meant to act completely normal, so I chose the same spot near the pillar that has the niche. I close my eyes, appreciating the shade, when the sound of women talking reaches my ears.

"…baby coming, are you excited?"

Isn't that Liana, Luca's mate?

"I'm excited, I guess. I mean, it's painful, too. One day I will have to explain to this child its parent's dynamics." My stomach sinks, and my heart thunders at that voice. Sage? Pregnant? What is she going on about? I don't move, trying to calm my racing heart and straining to listen to the conversation.

"Kian still loves you, Sage, even if it's not the same way he loves Morgana. You will still be the mother of his first child," Liana says sympathetically.

Sage is pregnant? I feel as if someone has slapped me across the face. How… God, does Kian know? Would he still have chosen me?

"I know, and he has promised to be here for me and raise this child alongside me. He wants me to reside in the palace so we are close, but I don't think I have space in his heart, Lia," Sage says, sounding broken. Kian knew…

The instant worry I had over whether he would have chosen me or not if he'd known… well, this hurts just as much. It means he knew but didn't bother or consider me important enough to share it with. My heart feels like someone is crushing it, and I feel cold.

"You will still be the mother of the future Alpha," Liana replies firmly. "So, have you asked him if he likes any names? Is he going to take part in your appointments?"

"Not yet, but I'm sure he'll be excited to choose a name or two." Sage laughs. "What Alpha doesn't want to see their future heir growing inside?" Their voices fade as they move away. I stare at the ground, my head spinning. Kian is about to become a father… with his ex…

I don't know how to feel. I hate that I wish she wasn't pregnant. With a child, it means she'll always be around. Then I also feel guilty for destroying what they had. I was the child of a king's mistress, and I hated how I was treated; do I want that for another child? No. I feel betrayed… Kian didn't think I was important enough to confide in. I wrap my arms around my knees, burying my head in them. It hurts…

Above all, what stings the most is that Kian hadn't told me….How could he do this? I thought we had an understanding that we were a couple. How long has he known for? And for a moment, I had thought he perhaps didn't know.

Right now, as much as I want to get angry and do or say something, my mind is drawing a blank about what I should do or how to react. It's just so painful.

Sure, Kian and I have been intimate, but we have not gone all the way. Is there a reason behind that? I'm sure he has a high sex drive, so why hasn't he taken it further? Yes, we've had a few moments, like in the shower this morning, but he won't go all the way. Why?

Suddenly, it doesn't feel like everything is good between us. I stand up with a heavy heart, checking the niche as planned, and there lay a simple square of paper along with the vials of blood. I open the square of paper, staring at the words on it.

'SEE YOU SOON'

Night falls, and the moon is shining through the narrow window. I'm in the small tower room on the fourth floor, a room that we had decided on as the location so no one sees us. It's empty for now, but the freshly painted walls and the boxes show it's being organised for another family to occupy. We need as many rooms as possible, and every empty room is being put to use.

I haven't seen Kian since morning, but I trust that he is hidden somewhere near. We just have to be discreet in case Cain is watching. My entire day has been in turmoil. I still don't know what to feel. All I can think is that Kian hadn't told me…

Oliver had approached me soon after, saying to relax and that everything would be okay, a message he forwarded from Kian, who could sense my turmoil through the bond. I just wish I could block him off completely, but I'm not sure how. Well, at least he thinks it's tonight's meeting that is messing with me.

"You are restless," a voice whispers in my ear. I spin around, my heart thundering. I hadn't even heard him enter. I look at Cain, dressed all in black, his dark eyes glinting. He chuckles morbidly.

"I am restless. Even if Kian isn't around, I had to sneak past Oliver," I hiss smoothly. His smirk vanishes, and he nods.

"Indeed, let's make it fast. Our meeting isn't ideal," he says. His snake-like silky voice makes me want to shudder. His eyes fall on my mark, and I see him frown. "He's marked you, yet you still want to betray him?" We knew this might come up. I'm not a fool.

"Without my consent," I hiss resentfully. "Besides, I almost died thanks to him."

"Ah… the poison. How did you end up consuming it?" It's clear he doesn't fully trust me, either.

"Kian fed me a spoon of his food. With the other Lunas sitting there and encouraging it, it wasn't easy to refuse. I didn't think it would affect me either," I retort as if it angers me.

"Ah… Kian does care for you. I heard he ran from the hall shouting for someone to help you. It's funny, considering he has never seemed to hold two ounces of emotions within him."

"Well, I guess I know how to win people over," I say, feeling guilty just saying that. "What is the next plan? It's getting harder for me to come down to the pillar. If I keep going to the same spot, it's bound to become suspicious."

"That's understandable. I was thinking your wedding would be the ideal time…"

I zone out of what he's saying, trying to read his mind.

*… precious to Kian…. To think she thinks she's two steps ahead and that I trust her…*

**Oh, I love how you think,** a deeper voice growls.

He doesn't trust me, so I need to get to this fast.

"Cain, how do you know that Kian is the one who killed my father?" I ask.

*I don't even know who killed that old fool.* His thoughts filter into my head.

"I heard of the plan. He wanted nothing more than to kill the vampire king. He kept it top secret, not wanting anyone to find out. Of course, that makes sense. Otherwise, there would have been a full-out war."

"But you found out."

"Of course. I have my ways."

"And why do you want him dead?" I ask. "Apart from wanting this throne." His eyes glint, a cold smile on his face as he observes me.

"So, you no longer trust me…"

*She's planning something, Cain...* his wolf's deep voice warns.

*Let her. I plan to destroy Kian, with or without her. In fact, killing her first would be the perfect blow.* My heart skips a beat, but I'm ready if he tries anything.

"I want my rightful place as king. I would make a far better king than that fool," he says quietly. "Don't you agree, Morgana?"

"Of course, and you promised me my freedom," I say, trying not to let the fact he wants to kill me show. I really was a fool to believe him.

"Then you would love to be a part of my revenge, correct?" He asks in his smooth snake-like voice.

"Of course," I answer confidently.

"Tell me, Morgana... a little bird told me you asked Kian to feed you at that dinner," he murmurs, stepping closer. My heart skips a beat.

"Whoever told you that lied," I say defiantly.

"Oh? Well, the thing is, as much as I'd love to trust you, I no longer do. So die!"

My head snaps towards him just as he lunges at me, a dagger in hand. He's before me in the blink of an eye. I gasp when I hear the knife impaling flesh, the thumping of my heart in my ears, and smell the blood that fills the air. I stare at the back of Kian's head, my heart thumping wildly. I'm yanked back by Luca, but my eyes are fixed on the blood dripping to the ground. Why the fuck did he have to jump in the way?

"Really, brother?" Kian asks, his voice cold and dangerous.

I pull out of Luca's hold and rush to his side, a little relieved to see the dagger had just gone through his hand and not his body. He yanks it out, tossing it to the ground before slamming his brother to the ground.

"We both know that I am stronger, Cain, or do you want another example of the fight for the title of Alpha King?" Kian growls. Luca is next to me, moving me back once again.

"He's hurt," I whisper, my heart thundering, and the concern I feel for Kian fills me fully.

"He is also the Alpha King, the strongest of our kind. The dagger is poisoned, but with nightshade. It was to kill a vampire, not a werewolf," Luca explains quietly. "Have faith in him."

"So, she has changed sides." Cain hisses, "She was willing to kill you, Kian!"

"She was, but she didn't. I have forgiven you several times, too. Your attempts on my life never cease, yet I fucking let them slide. But this time, you tried to attack my mate," Kian hisses.

"Mate?" Cain's smirk falters, and his eyes blaze with rage as he glares at me venomously before he gets to his feet again.

"Mate," I confirm coldly, raising my hand and blasting him to the ground with a force of my power. "Any questions for him, Kian?"

"Did you have anything to do with the vampire king's death?"

"No," he spits, lunging at Kian.

I probe his mind, but he truly doesn't know. Perhaps it was really Azrael… my stomach twists at the thought, and for a moment, I can't focus on the blur of punches, slashes, kicks, and blocks. Unlike us vampires, their fighting style is messier, more animalistic. They don't care about the mess or ripping each other apart.

Kian is indeed stronger; their shirts had been ripped off, and both are bloody and wounded, but I can see that Cain had more injuries. I feel a little better realising that I had never been weak in comparison to Kian; it's just the fact that Kian was my opponent and, being the ultimate Alpha, he is stronger.

The memory of Sage and Liana talking earlier returns, and I feel the pain eat up at me once again. Will I lose him? Do I even have him?

*Stop it, Morgana. He promised to marry you.*

"What did you think you would achieve by attempting to get rid of me?" Kian growls, slamming the bloody body of his brother to the ground, his hand tightening around his throat and his claws elongating. "Answer me, or I swear I will rip you to fucking pieces!"

"I wanted to be king! Is there something so fucking wrong with that? I am the elder brother! I am the firstborn! The fucking Alpha!"

"I gave you the fucking choice to take those who wanted to follow you and create your own fucking pack," Kian growls.

"They didn't want that!" Cain spits, trying to shove Kian off him, but my man is far stronger. There's actually something sexy about seeing him unleashing all his anger. The power that rolls off him is suffocating, but I don't mind lacking air if he's the one cutting it off. A thin layer of sweat coats his body, and I find myself admiring him, despite the situation.

"Have you been in touch with the vampires or Fae?"

"No."

I narrow my eyes, pushing through the barrier into his mind. No, he wasn't...

***Kill him! Use the poison!*** His wolf growls. ***Now is your chance!***

My eyes snap to his hand that is inching towards his pocket. I rush forward, slamming my foot onto his wrist.

"He has poison in his pocket!" Kian's eyes flash as he reaches into his brother's pocket and takes out the injection that Cain was carrying.

"I'm tempted to use this on you... wouldn't that be ideal?" Kian asks dangerously, squeezing his neck. "Now, talk. Where did you get this fucking poison from?"

"And why should I tell you?" Cain spits as if not even bothered that his brother could rip him to shreds at any moment.

***Like I'd ever tell you about the traveller,*** I hear him think.

"What traveller?" I cut in.

***How the fuck does she know about the human?*** Cain thinks, sounding panicked.

"It's a human."

"How are you doing that?" Cain growls. Reaching down, I slap him across the face.

"That's for trying to stab me," I say icily. Kian smirks, looking at me with a glint in his hazel eyes.

"That's my girl."

My heart skips a beat, but the pain of Sage's revelation remains. He leans over, claiming my lips in a hot, deep kiss for a moment before pulling away, leaving my heart a pounding mess.

Kian turns back to Cain, his eyes cold once more. He asks him a few more questions, but I don't get anything else from his mind. It's clear that his only goal was to kill Kian and become king. His hatred comes from the fact that Kian was always stronger and better at everything, no matter how hard he tried. Their father loved Kian more, and it's clear that he had nothing to do with his father's death.

"Take Morgana back to our room. Once I'm done with this fucking asshole, I'll be there," Kian says, glancing at Luca and me. His eyes soften ever so slightly. "Are you okay?"

My heart skips a beat at the question that was directed at me. I nod and force a small smile before turning away, not missing the way he frowns in concern.

An hour passes, and he still hasn't come. I take a shower and change into black lacy lingerie, along with a black knee-length silk gown. After covering my entire body with a soft silver shimmer and a touch of fragrance, I apply red to my already cherry-coloured lips and a touch of eyeliner before I get into bed, dimming the lights so it casts a warm glow around the bedroom. I need to see something… to check if this works.

When Kian returns, I don't turn but pretend to be asleep. He comes over, the smell of blood and sweat mixing with his intoxicating scent. He leans down, his necklaces brushing my shoulder as he places a soft kiss on my forehead before going to the bathroom. Ten minutes later, when he steps out of the bathroom with only a towel around his waist, I sit up and give him a small smile, letting my gaze trail over his body. I want to know if I push him, will he take it forward?

"Hey, handsome," I greet him, playing with a strand of my hair.

"I don't trust that smile, my little she-devil."

"You shouldn't."

I motion for him to come to me with a finger. He smirks, coming over to me, about to bend down to kiss me, when I yank him onto the bed, pushing him onto his back and straddling him.

"Someone's in the mood for something," he replies arrogantly, slipping his hands under my gown and squeezing my ass. His eyes darken when he realises I'm in nothing but lingerie.

"One hundred percent," I whisper seductively, raking my hands down his chest before sitting back and slowly tugging at the sash of my gown. I hear his heart race and watch the way he swallows and licks his lips when I slowly let the gown slip off my shoulders sexily, revealing my creamy breasts. The sheer lingerie does nothing to hide my hardened nipples. I let my gown fall to my wrists, leaning forward and placing a feathery kiss on his lips. "I want you to fuck me." I stare into his eyes, my heart thudding when I feel him tense. *Please don't deny me.*

I lean down, cupping the back of his neck as I press my lips to his. He kisses me back, sending rivets of pleasure through me. I sigh softly, but before I can deepen the kiss, he tugs me back by the hair, sitting up and wrapping his arms around my waist tightly. I bite my lip feeling his hardened dick press against my ass. I don't get it; it's obvious he wants me… so why is he refusing me?

"I'll take that as a no," I say quietly. The stinging pain of his rejection is like a harsh slap across the face.

"Don't say that. I love you, Morgana."

"Then why can't you take it further? We are to wed soon!" I snap, letting my frustration seep into my voice. I try to get off, but he holds me in place. "Let go of me, Kian!"

"Not until you hear me out."

"Fine. Give it your best shot." I glare into his eyes, my chest rising and heaving as my anger builds within me. He leans over, burying his head in my neck and inhaling deeply. I can hear his beating heart and wonder why he refused me.

"If we mate, it will completely seal the bond. We become one."

"And? I thought you loved me, and I..." *Love you...* He runs his fingers through my hair and gives me a cold smirk, leaning back.

"I do, and it's because I do that I don't want to risk your life. The mate bond means we will be connected in every way; emotions, pain - we live as one, and we die as one. We are at war, Morgana. If we complete our bond, and I am killed..." My stomach twists as I realise what he is saying. My eyes sting with tears that I refuse to allow to fall, his words rocking my entire being.

"I would die too," I complete his sentence quietly. I stare into his eyes, realisation hitting me like a tonne of bricks. The only reason he's not taking the next step is for me...

"And as much as I want to fuck you day in and day out, I don't want to risk your life. I would never be able to forgive myself if anything happened to you. You are my fucking life source, feisty temper and all."

With those words, he pulls me against him, his hand tangling in my hair as he kisses me like there's no tomorrow...

# Her Anger

KIAN

*I* DIDN'T WANT HER TO question it, but I knew sooner or later, it would come up. Seeing her looking so fucking seductive made me want to fucking tear every item of her skimpy clothing off and fuck her senseless. But that dark thought that if I ended up fucking dying, I might end her life with mine, that isn't something I was ready for.

She kisses me back with equal passion, her heart thumping, swirling her hips against my dick as she slips her tongue into my mouth. It seems like my little rose wants to be in control. We both know that's not how it works, but I love her attempts. I suck on her tongue, relishing in the sparks of the bond and the fucking pleasure that makes me throb harder.

Satisfied when she sighs into my lips, I break away, wanting to fucking go down on her and eat that pussy of hers out, but I know there's something else bothering her, too. I had sensed it through the bond, and I want to know what it was.

I suck on her neck, allowing her to get her breath back while grabbing her breasts and thumbing her nipples. She whimpers, arching her back and giving me better access. Fuck, she is a temptress. I'm finding it so fucking hard not to take her right now.

"So, how about you tell me what was on your mind all evening? Or why you were pretending to sleep when I came in..." I ask huskily. She frowns, clearly displeased at being caught.

"How did you know?" She asks. I smirk cockily.

"Because I'm not fucking stupid."

"My heart was steady. Even when you kissed me…" She doesn't look impressed. I don't think I'm going to tell her she sleeps like a fucking animal when she's actually asleep. It's cute. I smirk.

"Well, nothing gets past me," I reply, tapping her ass.

"What is with you and my ass?"

"I actually love your ass, and I'll be doing a lot more than just spanking it," I murmur. Anal doesn't count as completing the bond, does it?

**No, let's do it,** Thanatos purrs.

Damn, I'm not sure. Not that I had ever wanted to try it before, but there's something about Morgana that makes me want to fuck her in every way possible, and I intend to.

**And I want to as well. I'll borrow little Kian for a bit,** Thanatos remarks.

**Fuck off.** I shut him off, not wanting to have him fill my head with even more explicit thoughts.

She looks at me suspiciously. Oh, when the time fucking comes, she'll be up for everything. I know that because she's just as fucking kinky as I am. Kissing her once more, I place her down on the bed and walk over to the wardrobe, taking out some boxers. After slipping them on, I go back to the bed, push back the covers, and get in.

"Take the fucking gown off and come here," I command. She raises an eyebrow.

"I'm not sure I should. Since you refused me, then I should refuse your order," she replies. I cock a brow, leaning over. I tug her on top of me and rip her gown off. "Kian!"

"That's better," I say, admiring her fucking perfect body. She is everything that one would fucking want… *Fuck, this is going to be a fucking mission.*

"So, tell me. What did you do with Cain?" She asks, brushing her finger along the curve of my abs. Once again, she avoided answering my question. Well, I'll entertain her for now, but I will get my answer.

"I just tortured him a little to see if he had any more information, but he didn't. He will stay in the fucking cells for the rest of his fucking days."

"Killing him would mean the end of his mate," she says, stopping her tracing of my pecs.

"Pretty much. Although I have ended men, I try not to if they are mated," I explain, although she knows I'm not happy with that.

"That's admirable, knowing that you at least consider their mates."

"As a king, they are still my people regardless of the fact that their mates are fucking dipshits." I begin tracing circles on her ass, satisfied when she lets out a soft sigh.

"Who knew the arrogant Alpha king had a heart?" She whispers. Bending down, she kisses my neck softly. At the same time, I feel the pang of pain that courses through her. I grip her elbows, pulling her back, frowning deeply as I look into her red eyes.

"Morgana, what is bothering you?" I ask coldly with a warning in my voice that I ensures she knows I am done playing games. I want an answer from her, and I want it now. She takes a deep breath before getting off of me and settling into the bed beside me. I pull the blanket over her long, sexy, lush legs.

"Is there anything you need to tell me, Kian?" She asks me quietly. I frown; I have told her everything.

"I'm sure you've been in on everything going on, sunshine."

**Mate is mad with us,** Thanatos growls.

**Yeah, I can tell, and I have no idea why.**

"Okay, then, then there's nothing?" She asks, lying down with her back to me. My eyes fall to her shoulder blades and her slender waist. The urge to yank the blanket off and take a look at her ass almost distracts me from the situation at hand.

"Morgana. Answer me properly," I growl, wrapping my arm around her waist and pulling her against me, kissing her shoulder.

"If you can't remember something so vital, I don't know if I should laugh or be irritated," she bites out, that same pang of pain rolling off her.

**What have you done to hurt mate?**

**Not now, Thanatos,** I growl.

"I'm tired, Kian. Let me sleep," she whispers.

"Not until you tell me what's fucking worrying you," I growl. She sighs in frustration.

"Sage!" She snaps, turning and glaring at me. "She's pregnant, and you didn't think to tell me?" Fuck, I forgot.

"Morgana, look - "

"No, tell me, Kian, since when have you known?" She asks, her chest rising and falling in anger.

"That day I cut it off with her," I admit, knowing I had fucked up.

"Wow. Just fucking wow." She glares at me, pulling away from my hold. Hurt and betrayal are clear in her gorgeous eyes.

"Morgana, look, I didn't want to tell you until I was sure if she even is. I don't really believe her," I explain coldly, keeping a tight hold on her arm as she tries to pull away.

"Oh, really? But you told her you'll be there for her. Why would you say that if you were not even sure if she was pregnant?" She shoots back.

"I told her *if* she was. Morgana, fuck, it doesn't matter, it changes nothing between us."

"Doesn't it? Isn't Sage the better option, knowing you two are having a - "

"She is not a fucking better option, Morgana!" I hiss.

"Yet you were fucking okay to fuck her and get her pregnant but can't touch me?" She shouts, pushing me away and getting out of bed. Her ass jiggles, and I really fucking hate how she's distracting me right now. I just want to bend her over and take her right here. "Just leave me alone, Kian." I clench my jaw, my anger raging through me as she turns and glares at me.

"I have never wanted to fuck anyone as much as I want to fuck you, Morgana! You know my reason!" I growl, getting off the bed and advancing towards her, my eyes blazing.

"Really, just in case you might die? Then don't die!" She shouts back, glaring at me.

"Fine, you want me to fuck you? Then I'll do exactly that!" I growl, grabbing her by her arm and tossing her onto the bed, watching her breasts bounce. Her heart pounds, her blazing eyes locked with mine. I smirk slightly, seeing the fire of desire in those gorgeous ruby orbs of hers.

I don't break eye contact with her. Both of our hearts are racing with anger and desire. I know that no matter how much I want to wait, I can't. I need to show her exactly what she means to me, and I fucking intend to. I bend down, wrapping my hand around that slender throat of hers.

"Even if you beg for me to stop, my sexy she-devil, I won't," I warn her huskily, staring into those eyes of hers that are burning with lust and a hunger that I know is going to be my undoing.

"Good," she whispers before our lips crash against each others in a kiss fuelled by passion, lust, love, hunger, anger, frustration, and irritation. A kiss that is just so perfectly us.

*Fuck, tonight I'm going to fuck her until we pass out…*

MORGANA

My heart is thundering as Kian kisses me, his hands raking over my body, touching, groping, and massaging every inch of me. His lips don't leave mine. The tingles that course through me are like shots of electricity, and my entire body feels extra sensitive.

He rips my bra off, the strap burning my back when he yanks it free. Everything with Kian is rough. The pain that mixes with pleasure is something I savour but never knew I would. I had never been with a man who is as unpredictable and rough in bed as Kian. Where other men treated me like a goddess and aimed to please me, Kian does what he wants, treating me roughly yet so fucking perfectly, worshipping my body with unmasked raw hunger and emotion.

I like to fight for control, but Kian refuses to let me win. I love how he knows he can make me feel so good without giving in to my every whim. I love the way he manhandles me, treating me like a doll, and I love being his plaything.

He yanks me to the edge of the bed, his eyes on my breasts before they travel lower, the animalistic hunger in his eyes consuming me entirely. It's the first time I'll probably be completely naked before him, and it's at that moment that I realise this is it. The sealing of the bond… of us completely becoming one…

Our eyes meet; the intensity of our emotions is raw in them. His hand tangles in my hair as he kisses me passionately, making me moan.

"Fuck…" he growls when I run my hands down his chest. I pinch his nipple, making his eyes flash as he grabs my wrist. "Behave," he growls before taking my nipple in his mouth and biting down hard.

I smirk, arching myself into him and crying out at the mix of pain and pleasure. I can't help whimpering loudly as he slaps the other breast before grabbing it tightly. My core is throbbing, and I can feel the wetness there. He switches to the other breast, latching onto my other nipple and sucking hard before he begins placing rough, open-mouthed kisses around my breast, at times leaving hickeys. The pleasure he's inflicting upon me is heavenly. My pussy clenches in a need that only he can satiate.

"Fuck, Kian…"

"That's it. Call my name, baby girl," he growls, beginning his descent down my stomach before moving to my waist and biting down on my smooth skin. "I won't be leaving any part of this beautiful body unmarked tonight."

"Fuck…" I breathe, our eyes meeting for a moment before he kisses my lips hungrily, only to then continue his assault on my body, nipping, sucking, and licking me between my breasts, down my lower stomach, and around to my inner thighs, but he's avoiding the one area that is begging for his touch. "Don't tease," I moan as he licks and sucks my inner thighs. I reach between my legs, wanting to satisfy that ache, when he grabs my wrist.

"Patience, my little she-devil…" He kisses me down my legs, making me whimper in pleasure before he grabs me and flips me over. "Fuck…"

He delivers a sharp tap to my ass before playing with my thong, tugging it even tighter between my ass cheeks and delivering a sharp tap to the other cheek. He grabs my breasts from behind, kissing and sucking my neck. I cry out, feeling his dick against my ass. Fuck, this feels good. I gasp when his tongue runs along my neck, sucking on the tip of my ear. God…

His hand runs down the planes of my stomach, yanking me up onto my knees, and I gasp when I feel the sharp edge of his claw.

"Do you like pain, my little she-devil?" He growls, nibbling on my ears. I gasp, feeling his claw pierce my skin, and my core clenches in anticipation.

"Yes," I murmur, my cheeks burning as his finger goes lower, slicing through the thin fabric of my underwear. My breath hitches, and he chuckles at my nervousness.

"I need this pussy intact," he growls, ripping the rest of my underwear off and parting my lips with two fingers. "You're dripping wet, Princess."

"Do you blame me?" I shoot back.

Reaching behind, I grab his boxers and tear them off, too, before running my hand over his perfect cock. He chuckles breathlessly, one strong arm wrapping around my breasts as he gropes and palms one of them. His other hand runs between my lips, making me gasp. Delicious pleasure runs through me at his touch. My legs tremble as he finds my clit. Oh, fuck…

"Look how your body reacts to me. No matter how fucking angry you are, you can't deny me," he murmurs, rubbing his dick between my ass, only adding to the pleasure that is consuming me. I reach behind, squeezing his muscled ass. God, do I love him. I'll tell him tonight…

I gasp when two fingers are thrust into my pussy, making me cry out. Reaching down with his other hand, he begins rubbing my clit hard and fast.

"Ouch, fuck, that's it," I moan. All I can think of is how good this feels. I never want it to end. Fuck. "Oh, god, that's it. I'm coming," I breathe, feeling my climax building. Fuck, oh, fuck!

The moment I'm about to come, Kian bites into my neck, making me cry out as a powerful orgasm rocks my body, sending off jarring shock wave after shock wave of pleasure through me. I moan loudly, not bothered by the sound of my juices squirting everywhere. My head rests back against his shoulder, his cock throbbing between my ass, but he doesn't stop his assault on my pussy until I've ridden out every ounce of my orgasm.

He lets go of me, and I fall forward onto the bed, whimpering when he taps my ass before giving it a squeeze. Bending down, he kisses the small of my back, lifting me up by the hips before he positions himself beneath my pussy. I blush when his tongue flicks out, and he begins to roll it over my tender pussy.

"Fuck, Kian!" I moan, lifting my still weak body up. Reaching behind me for balance, I brace my hands on his chest. He taps my ass as he pleasures me. He's so good… he knows my body so well. I grind my hips against his face, reaching between my thighs and tangling my hand into his tight curls.

"That's it, baby, eat my pussy," I moan in pleasure as another orgasm begins to build. Before I can come, he lifts me off and drops me onto the pillow.

"Now you're ready for me," he growls. As much as I want to play with him, I want him inside of me.

"Fuck me, Kian." I pull him down, kissing his lips passionately. I can still taste myself on his lips, mixed with the fresh minty taste of his mouth.

"You taste fucking good, don't you," he murmurs. I reach down between us, wrapping my hand around his dick, and bite my lip at the size of his girth. "Now I'll destroy this pussy in such a way that you'll only want me to ever fuck you," he growls possessively, pressing his swollen tip to my clit and rubbing it sensually before he presses at my entrance.

"Good, I- ahh!" I cry out when he rams into me. I can't breathe for a second, feeling the immense pressure as my body tries to adjust.

"That's it. Just breathe," he says with an arrogant smirk on his face. I glare back at him, despite how much I need this. The sparks that are rushing through me and that knot of pleasure in my core are begging for more.

"Told you that thing is a monster!" I groan, grabbing onto his shoulder and locking my arms around him tightly.

He smirks arrogantly, slowly pulling half out and thrusting in once again. A low guttural groan leaves his lips, and it only makes me even wetter. Fuck, he is so sexy. He's anything but gentle, thrusting into me deep and rough.

"Ouch! Fuck, that's it… slowly…" I groan in pleasure.

"I don't do slow." His cocky reply comes before he begins slamming into me hard and fast.

I gasp, unable to even speak with his rough thrusts. I look up at him through my hooded eyes. He's the picture of sinful perfection. My eyes dip to where he's pressed my knees to the bed, taking in the way he's looking at me, the way his body meets mine, the sound of our skin meeting, and the smell of sex hanging in the air. If I die tonight, it will be worth it…

I close my eyes as my pleasure begins growing. My words are incoherent. The only sounds that escape my lips fully are the cries of pleasure, over which I have no control.

"You're fucking beautiful," I hear him murmur, my heart pounding with the emotions of this moment. I look into his blazing eyes that are unmasked, the intensity of his emotions consuming me. Pulling him down, I kiss him deeply.

*I love you. I don't want to ever lose you.*

Almost as if he understands, he threads his hand into my hair, burying his nose in my neck as each thrust hits that sweet spot deep inside of me. This is what heaven feels like… never has sex felt so good. Fuck…

"Kian!" I cry out just as my orgasm rips through me. I feel a surge of power rush through me, mixing with my orgasm and making my vision darken for a moment. Fuck, that was….

I whimper just as Kian pulls out, and I feel his seed come all over my inner thighs.

"Morgana…" He groans, letting himself down on top of me and running his hand through my hair as my entire body trembles from the strong orgasm that had rocked it.

"I…"

I look up. There's so much I want to say… but why is everything getting darker? I want to tell him that had been mind-blowing… but I also want to tell him…

"I love you, Kian…" I murmur, my voice sounding distant and fading away. I see a small, rare smile cross his lips.

"I know you do," his faint voice follows as my world goes blissfully dark…

# IT'S YOU

MORGANA

*I* OPEN MY EYES, FEELING the sun warm my skin through the gap in the curtain. I'm alone in bed, but the sound of the shower running reaches my ears. The bathroom door is ajar and a waft of steam escapes into the bedroom.

I feel refreshed, despite the ache between my legs. I raise an eyebrow, smiling slightly as I remember last night. I bite my lip, closing my eyes as I press my legs together at the hot memories. No man could ever compare to Kian. The way he looks at me, the way he kisses me, the way he fucked me…

My core throbs as I remember our night of passion, one I won't ever forget. He is definitely a beast in bed, yet through it all, his emotions were so obvious. I can't forget that raw, primal hunger and passion laced with love when he looked at me last night.

I sit up, looking down at my naked body. The love bites he had marked my entire body with are mostly gone; only a few faint marks are left behind from those that had been deeper. I brush my hand over the one on my breast. He truly had marked me in every way…

The shower turns off, and my stomach flutters, knowing Kian will come out at any minute. I clutch the bedsheet to my breasts, knowing I probably look a mess. Sure enough, Kian steps out with a towel around his waist, looking like the king he was. His eyes fall on me, and they blaze gold like a beast wanting to devour his prey. I wouldn't mind being his prey right now.

"Morning. Slept well?" His voice sends a thrill of pleasure through me.

"Actually, yes," I admit, leaning back when he approaches. My heart is thumping when he bends down and kisses my lips deeply. Pleasure erupts through me, and I sigh against his lips, my cheeks flushing when I feel that ache in my core.

"You're turned on, sunshine," Kian murmurs, breaking away from my lips.

"As are you," I reply. I don't need to look down to confirm my statement.

"I won't fucking deny that." He runs his fingers through my hair as my gaze dips to the tent in the towel. Would it be so wrong to pull his towel off and take him in my mouth? "As much as I wouldn't mind that idea, go shower. Breakfast awaits us." My eyes fly open.

"How did you know what I was thinking?" I ask suspiciously, looking into his gorgeous hazel eyes.

"Those large eyes of yours were staring at my towel like you wanted to fucking devour me," he replies with an arrogant smirk, making me roll my eyes.

I get out of bed, running my fingers through my hair. I can feel his gaze burning into me, yet I have to admit I'm surprised at his self-restraint. I get to the bathroom before I grab the wall. My legs definitely feel weak! I shower quickly. Are we actually going to have breakfast together? That isn't something we really did.

Despite the looming threat of war, I feel happy and complete. Stepping out of the shower, I brush my teeth and apply a little moisturiser to my skin. Taking another towel, I dry my hair and exit the bathroom. To my surprise, Kian isn't dressed, still only in his towel. I raise an eyebrow.

"Weren't we meant to be going for breakfast?" I ask.

"Yeah, we are." He comes over to me and takes my towel that I had been drying my hair with from me, tossing it onto the ground and kissing me once before moving away.

"Kian…"

"Let's go." He takes my wrist, making my heart skip a beat.

"I'm not dressed!" I protest.

"I can see that." He says it as if it was obvious. He leads me out to the hall and down the stairs, but he doesn't take me towards the dining room. Instead, he goes down the opposite side.

"Kian, where are we going?" I ask curiously when he stops outside a door.

"Really, my little she-devil, have you not heard of patience?" He asks, raising an eyebrow.

"No, you should know that by now."

He smirks, snaking an arm around my waist and yanking me into his chest, making it suddenly hard to breathe. My heart bangs against my ribcage as the sudden proximity gets to me.

"I do," he says.

He pushes open the door, and the scent of lavender, camomile, vanilla, and coconut fills my nose. A cloud of steam wafts in my face as he leads me in. Soft instrumental music is playing in the background. I look around, realising we are in a dimly lit room. The walls and ground are made of stone.

My eyes fall on the huge hot tub in the middle. A scatter of petals dances on the surface of the water. A tray containing breakfast floats in the water, filled with a variety of food. Candles and flowers line the edge of the tub alongside wine, two glasses, and a platter of fruits and chocolates.

For a moment, I simply stare at the scene before me, blinking slowly. The surge of emotions that overwhelm me renders me speechless. The very fact that Kian had done this for me… I swallow hard, feeling his intense gaze on me. I take a shaky breath and turn my gaze to him. Past that emotionless look on his face, I know he's waiting for my reaction. He raises an eyebrow.

"Are you scared of water?" He asks mockingly. I smile, rolling my eyes as I lock my arms around his neck.

"No, I'm just scared of where the usual Kian has gone. This… it's…" My teasing smile vanishes, and I caress the back of his neck, stroking his jaw with the other hand. "It's perfect… I wasn't expecting something so sweet and thoughtful… not to mention so romantic. I didn't know you had it in you." He tilts his head, a small smirk crossing his lips.

"Yeah, I don't do this sort of thing... and I assure you, I'm still the same Kian. I know several ways to remind you of that," he replies, tapping my ass hard, sending a wave of pain and pleasure through me, clearly satisfied when I whimper. "So drop the towel and get in."

"Good idea," I say, yanking his towel off him just as he tugs mine off me, making me laugh. My eyes widen when I see a small smile cross his handsome face; it's gone as soon as it had come, but it leaves me feeling breathless.

His burning gaze trails over my body. I turn and walk to the tub slowly, making sure to sway my hips a little more, feeling his emotions through the bond. I smirk, satisfied at that. Stepping into the tub, I brush my fingers through the water, enjoying the warmth. Kian gets in seconds later, pulling me against his chest and sending my heart racing once more.

"You look fucking beautiful," he murmurs, his arms pushing my breasts up. "You're glowing, baby girl." I smile softly, despite the knot in my stomach, feeling his hard dick press against my ass.

"I would say that was half your doing with the sex, but I am rather beautiful regardless," I say airily, turning my head to look into his sexy hazel orbs.

"I couldn't agree more. You really are something else."

"I would rather say something special. Something else makes me think I'm crazy."

"We both can admit you are fucking crazy, too," he says, making me glare at him. My stomach flutters when he picks up a truffle from the platter. "Special alone doesn't fucking cut it. You're way more than can be described, my wild temptress," he whispers, placing the chocolate truffle to my lips. I bite into it slowly, my eyes locked with his, watching how his darken and the hunger that is clear in them.

I tug the chocolate from his fingers, holding it between my plump lips and pulling his head down to mine. He smirks, leaning forward and slowly biting onto the other half of the chocolate. His lips graze mine as I slowly turn in his arms, trying to ignore his shaft that now presses against my core. Delicious, intense sparks course through me. I don't know how I ever survived without him.

We slowly move back, both of us eating the chocolate, our eyes locked. He leans over, running his tongue along my lips, licking up any excess chocolate before he arches his neck to me, a silent command to drink. After last night I need it, too. I feel tired.

"You know… this is a sign of submission," I tease, placing a soft kiss on the corner of his neck, feeling his body react to my touch.

His next words take my breath away. His hands run down my back, one hand squeezing my ass sensually.

"I know it is, but if there's one person I'll ever fucking submit to, it's you."

KIAN

The emotions in her eyes are fucking intense, and it feels strange yet fucking right. The way I'm able to express how I feel to her. The fact that I, who had never ever submitted to my father, who had been my Alpha, am willing to bend for her.

**The power of the bond and love,** Thanatos murmurs.

I know he's already a fucking goner. Something tells me he'd be even more willing to kneel before her.

**Of course, to lick that pussy of hers.**

Her heart is racing as she closes the tiny gap that remains between us. I bite back a groan as my dick rubs against her. Wrapping her hand around the nape of my neck, her fingertips graze my hair. Her breasts press against my chest, and once again, I fucking appreciate her height. My dick perfectly nestles against her pussy.

"I love you, Kian," she whispers seductively, rubbing her pussy against my dick. *Fuck, I'm going to come if she continues that.* "I want you to fuck me whilst I drink from you."

I don't need to be told twice. Settling into the tub and having her straddle me, letting the water reach up to our chests, I reach down between us and press my tip to her opening. She moans when I rub against her clit before she slams down onto me, making me swear. Before I can even relish in having her wrapped around me once again, her fangs pierce my skin, making me grunt at the surge of pleasure that rushes through me.

She moans against me, and I squeeze her ass as I begin fucking her slow and deep. Each time I'm almost fully out, I ram back into her, not even able to stop the groans that leave my lips. There's something so fucking erotic about her drinking from me as I fuck her. Every suck seems to tug at the pleasure within me, making it pool in my cock. We keep going as she drinks sensually, meeting my thrusts halfway, only adding even more intensity.

"Fuck, Morgana," I breathe, feeling even Thanatos' desires lace with my own.

I speed up slightly, but it's taking all my fucking control not to pound her hard, knowing she won't be able to drink if I do. I rake my hand down her back, loving the way her body reacts to me.

Soon I can't even focus on anything but how fucking good this feels, barely able to realise what's going on as the state of pure pleasure and bliss consumes me. If heaven fucking exists, this is what it is. If there's a reason to live, this is it. She had become that fucking addiction that I was never going to get enough of.

I can feel her insides tightening around me, her moans and whimpers becoming louder. My eyes blaze as both Thanatos and I are consumed by the immense euphoria that courses through us. Wanton moans leave her lips, her nails digging into my skin. She gasps, breaking away from my neck. I take the chance, biting into her neck right over her mate mark and sucking hard just as her orgasm shoots through her, making her let out a deliciously horny scream of pure satisfaction and pleasure. Her walls clamp down on me and set off my own orgasm. I barely manage to pull out as I come, letting out a groan of satisfaction.

Hers in the midst of pleasure is the most beautiful voice I had ever heard and all I ever wanted to hear.

"That was perfect, hot chocolate," she whispers breathlessly, locking her arms around my neck tightly. Hot chocolate? I don't mind the sound of that. I know it's her favourite discovery of our kingdom. I guess so am I.

"It fucking was," I growl huskily.

**It was, and I'm awaiting my turn,** Thanatos growls.

I'm not so sure. Usually, we werewolves mate in wolf form at times, so our wolves can connect, too. However, Morgana is not a werewolf. To allow Thanatos control of my body…

**I won't hurt mate! He thunders.**

I can already feel his need for her growing, the desire to ravage her stronger than ever. As much as I'm a beast, Thanatos is a true beast, and I don't think Morgana is ready for that.

**We'll see,** I say before kissing Morgana's plush lips.

"Let's get some breakfast into you now," she suggests, her deep red eyes full of concern. "I drank a little more than I should have. Are you okay?"

Am I fucking okay? I'm way better than fucking okay.

"Perfectly. I think that's the type of morning I want every fucking day," I murmur as she gets off of me and reaches for the tray that is floating around the other side of the tub, pulling it towards us.

"Me too," she whispers before pouting. "Although… there is another type of morning I want at times…"

"Oh?" I ask. "And what is that?" She picks up a berry and places it to my lips as she straddles me once more.

"To wake you up to my lips wrapped around your cock," she says coquettishly, sticking her tongue out sexily and flicking it against her top lip, making me almost choke on the damn berry. Her eyes look so fucking sexy. I feel myself harden, and she smiles faintly like the vixen she is.

"You really are a fucking tease," I say, trying not to let her see the effect she has on me, especially when she takes a cherry between her teeth. We both know she fucking knows the effect she's having on me. Smirking, she breaks off a piece of the sandwich, feeding me.

"You know you like it." She says, "Now, be a good little boy and eat. Or should I say, big boy?"

"Fuck…" I groan when she rubs against me teasingly.

"What's wrong? Too distracted to eat?" She teases.

"You fucking know that," I growl, grabbing a glass of juice and gulping it down.

She laughs at that, her entire face lighting up. I caress her cheek, allowing her to feed me that fucking sandwich that is only sticking in my throat, thanks to her being a fucking tease…

I kiss her neck, making her sigh before I dip my finger into the chocolate bowl and place it to her lips. Her eyes lock with mine as she slowly takes my finger into her mouth, licking it clean slowly. I slip my finger out, my eyes blazing as I yank her towards me, wrapping my hand around her throat as I kiss her fucking hard. This desire and passion within me really aren't ever going to be fucking satiated.

We fight for dominance, the hunger for one another fucking strong. Neither of us cares about anything but the other. I could kiss her for fucking forever, but she needs air. I let up as she gasps for air, the scent of her arousal strong in the air again. Her eyes meet mine, and I simply lick my lips, breathing hard before placing a teasing kiss on her mouth and holding her tightly.

After a moment of getting her breath back, she moves back slightly, my dick still pressing against her pussy, although all I want is to be buried inside of her all over again.

"When are we leaving for Elandorr?" She asks, pouring us both a glass of wine before she passes me one.

"At dawn. Supplies and clothing will be waiting for us outside of the pack grounds," I explain, clinking my glass with hers before taking a sip.

"I see." She nods. "Then what are your plans for today?" I frown, knowing exactly what I'm going to do today. My mood darkens, and she frowns. "Kian…"

"I have a few things to take care of, one regarding Cain and… Sage," I said, hating that she was fucking brought up. Morgana tilts her head, placing her glass down.

"It doesn't matter if she's pregnant. I know you're mine. I will treat that child well because it is yours - "

"*If* she even fucking is. I don't think she is," I say, coldly cutting her off. I don't know, it just feels too fucking coincidental.

"Have you listened for a heartbeat or had a scan even?"

"She's had a scan without me actually knowing, but from what Luca said, it's healthy. She had pictures to prove it. I know she's been trying to get in touch with me, but I have made it clear I don't want her around me. The thing is, we do have enchanters in this kingdom. They are rare… but there are certain spells that can deceive a person or make something appear as it isn't."

"What are you insinuating?" She asks, frowning.

I sigh, "The thought came to me when I was discussing the plans about making sure it looked like we are still around in the castle, and Luca mentioned someone Liana knew who could cast illusionary spells, saying perhaps we could get him to cast a few for us so some members of staff hear or see us. I refused, not wanting to risk even this enchanter knowing. But the fact that he knows Liana… there's a high chance Sage knows him, too. They are friends, after all," I explain, downing the last of my wine. Morgana nods slowly, and I know she understands what I'm saying.

"So you think… she's… lying?" She asks, stunned.

"There's a high chance. We'll find out today because I've invited an enchanter of my own to confirm her pregnancy, or lack of," I say coldly. Yeah, I don't trust her, not one fucking bit…

# A Revelation

KIAN

*I*HAD SPENT ALL MORNING and most of the afternoon making love to Morgana, leaving her thoroughly satisfied before I told her to rest because, even if she is a vampire, I know I had fucking drained her. Not that I regret it; she's a fucking drug.

Her words of accepting this pup, if there is one, showed what a queen she really is. But if there is one woman I want pups with, it's Morgana. Hopefully, we can think of that once the war is over and I've had some quality time with just her first…

It's now early in the evening, and I'm in my office with Ethan, the enchanter I had mentioned to Morgana earlier. Although a few enchanters reside in our kingdom, there aren't as many compared to those in the Sanguine Empire.

I had told Luca to bring Sage, Liana, and himself to my office. I will get my answers, and if Liana is involved…

I strum my fingers on my desk impatiently. All I want is to have Morgana in my arms.

**With Mini-Kian buried in her pussy,** Thanatos adds.

**Fuck off… and stop calling it fucking mini. I swear if you tell Morgana that's what you call it…**

He scoffs, **I'm sure she'll find it funny.** He purrs hornily at the thought of her, once again pushing the image of her with her legs spread open to the forefront of my mind, making me groan inwardly as I feel myself twitch. Fuck…

Luckily just then, the door opens, and the trio enters. Sage is smiling, her eyes on me, yet I simply remain emotionless. I don't want anything to do with her. Luca seems to notice the enchanter before the women. He seems confused, and I don't blame him, considering he knows I wasn't planning on using one, and I hadn't told him why I had called them here.

"Kian, how are you?" Sage asks. She had tried to get in touch with me a few times, but I ignored her every time, not needing her useless pleading and begging.

"Perfect," I smirk coldly when her gaze falls on my neck. Several marks Morgana had left just before I left our room litter my neck and haven't completely faded yet. "Meet my friend, Ethan." The women now seem to notice the man, who just seemed to blend into the surroundings. He bows his head of black hair politely.

"What is this about?" Luca asks, shutting the door behind him and motioning for the women to take a seat, standing behind Liana's chair. I close my eyes, and sure enough, I can hear that extra heartbeat aside from ours. Now, the moment of truth; is it real or all just a façade?

"Oh, he's just going to make sure that our pup is healthy. Ethan is extremely good with many kinds of magic. He's even good at seeing illusionary spells, especially in the art of deception," I explain coldly, turning my mocking gaze on Sage, who, to no surprise, looks pale; her lips are pressed together tightly, her heart thudding loudly. "Ethan?"

"Yes, sire," he murmurs, stepping forward, his long, gangly legs crossing the room swiftly. He reached into the pocket of his long coat, chanting something in the foreign tongue, and tossed the handful of herbs over Sage.

"I… stop! Don't!" Sage whimpers, fear and panic rolling off her.

I observe them all; Luca is frowning, and Liana looks confused. When Sage grabs her stomach, she looks at her sharply. So, she wasn't in on it… at least that means I don't need to punish her.

The chanting stops, and with it, that small heartbeat vanishes. I close my eyes, feeling a wave of relief rush through me. No matter how fucking sure I was that she had been lying, there had been a part of me that still knew it was a possibility.

"Did the fair lady know she had been enchanted and that there is no pup?"

"What… Sage?" Liana whispers, shocked. Sage looks terrified, turning to me as she jumps up from her seat.

"Kian… Kian! I only did it because - "

"How could she…?" I hear Liana mumble, sounding dumbstruck. I guess a friend's lie and betrayal fucking does hurt.

**Lies! She upset mate! Kill her!** Thanatos growls.

"Throw her in the fucking cells, and she is to remain there until I say otherwise," I order icily, standing up.

"No, Kian! Please, I love you!" She cries out.

"We're done here," I said coldly.

"At your service, My King."

"Thank you, Ethan. Luca, show him out and pay him well."

"Yes, Alpha…"

"Have two guards escort her to the cells," I add, making my way to the door, but before I can even reach it, she grabs hold of my arm.

"Kian, please!" She sobs, tears streaming down her cheeks. "I love you, I sacrificed everything for you! Please, my love! Please, for what we had, please have mercy on me!" I rip out of her hold, yanking the door open, my eyes blazing as I glare at the guards.

"Escort Sage to the cells." I hiss.

"Kian, no! Please, I love you!" Sage wraps her arms around me from behind, only making me angrier. I rip her arms off me, and the guards grab her.

"Yes, Alpha," one of them says.

"Wait," a familiar voice interrupts.

Everyone falls silent, and we turn to see Morgana dressed in a floor-length silk nightgown, her hair braided and her face an image of seriousness. She looks as regal and breath-taking as ever, yet the calmness and power I can sense from her seem to affect everyone.

"I am wronged! Kian, please!" Sage cries.

I walk over to Morgana, and she instantly wraps her arms around my neck, calming the raging anger of both Thanatos and me.

"So, the pregnancy wasn't real?" She asks me quietly, her sweet, intoxicating scent consuming me.

"It wasn't," I answer coldly, turning my gaze back to Sage. "She'll be punished accordingly for lying and deceiving her king and Alpha." My aura surges around me. As much as I want to rip her head off, I stay in place, my hands on Morgana's slender waist.

"As your Luna… can I decide her punishment?" Morgana asks, much to my surprise.

**Yes! Let mate rip her head off!** But unlike Thanatos, I'm not sure that's Morgana's plan.

"It better be harsh," I say quietly. Morgana sighs heavily.

"I don't like Sage, I never have, since the day she showed up at your bedroom door," she said. I feel the pang of hurt from her, my guilt returning as I remember what I had done that day.

"Kian, please! Don't listen to her! I love you; she's trying to act all innocent - "

A thunderous growl rips from my throat, sounding completely animalistic as I glare at her murderously.

"Do not, and I mean *do not* fucking disrespect your queen!" I hiss, Thanatos' voice overlaying with my own, making everyone but Morgana and Ethan flinch.

"It's okay," Morgana says, placing a kiss on my jaw before she moves away and walks towards Sage, motioning for the guards to unhand her. "I'm not going to play the 'oh, it's okay, let's forgive her, she's hurting' card."

Sage's eyes widen, and it seems she had been expecting exactly that. I won't fucking lie, I even I thought that.

**See? Mate is good!** Thanatos chuckles proudly.

However, Morgana's next move takes us all by surprise as she raises her hand, slapping Sage across the face hard. Sage gasps, clutching her cheek as she stumbles under the impact. I almost smirk. That's my fucking girl.

"What you did was disgusting and low," Morgana says coldly. "I understand you were desperate. You love him, and seeing another woman take away what you always thought would be yours would surely hurt, but I won't apologise for that. Kian made his choice, and he ended it with you. Yet, to cause conflict in a useless attempt to win him back? You played such a game…" She shakes her head as everyone remains silent, watching her. "Why are you so hung up on a man who doesn't even treat you well?" She asks Sage, her voice softer. "You are more than that. A man is not enough to destroy yourself over."

"I love him."

"And so do I! You trying to manipulate him with this fake pregnancy has angered me. I know he has made mistakes… and for that, I don't feel being thrown in the cells is fair," Morgana says coldly.

My eyes widened in shock. I was not expecting that… neither was Sage or anyone else.

"Banish her from the palace and this pack, strip her of her rank, and make her an Omega for life," Morgana orders, her eyes blazing as she turns away from Sage, who looks shell-shocked. "That is for lying to your king."

Sage lets out a scream, about to collapse to her knees, but the guards catch her, keeping her upright. Tears stream down her cheeks, realising her life is forever changed. Perhaps she thought she would have gotten out of the cell… no, she wouldn't have if it had been my choice. This punishment is not as harsh as mine, but it is also a strong and befitting punishment.

I look at the woman who is my fucking all, and our eyes meet. I give her a small nod, proud of her. She really was made to be queen, and it's high time I did my queen's bidding.

**Who would have thought the Alpha would become a fucking puppy,** Thanatos snickers.

**Fuck off,** I growl in response, but to an extent, I would do as she wished; I'd let her take charge over some matters… Yet there are certain aspects of our relations that I will always remain dominant. After all, even if I am the Alpha male, she… she is my fucking equal.

I step forward, cracking my knuckles before stopping a few feet from Sage.

"I, Kian Araqiel, King of Clair De Lune and Alpha of the Midnight Eclipse Pack, demote you, Sage Oakwood, to the rank of Omega and expel you from the Midnight Eclipse Pack for your crimes against your king and queen. Effective immediately."

A piercing scream fills the air as I feel the pack link break between us. The final connection I had had with Sage is gone for good.

MORGANA

I wonder if my decision for Sage to be removed from the pack was far too harsh or if it was fitting. Either way, her deceit appalled me. However, I'm not one who can say much; I tried to kill Kian, too. The guilt of that decision will always remain in my mind, and I know that I'll always regret it, even if I didn't go through with it. I had thought it.

The following morning, we leave the castle discreetly. I'm wearing black boots that reach my knees, fitted black pants, and a skin-tight black halter top. I have two long slim swords slid into my belt with a few small knives slipped into my boots. My hair is in a braid, falling down my back, and I have a black jacket which is also filled with poison-tipped little daggers.

Kian, on the other hand, looks incredibly handsome in black pants, boots, a top, and a jacket. He's carrying two large bags and refused to allow me to carry anything extra. He has a sword, a crossbow, and a few other weapons on him, too. We are equipped with whatever we may need, from lightweight food for Kian, I will stick to blood alone, to antidotes and poisons just in case, and poisons that could be used against Fae.

The weather is rather warm as the day goes by. I remove my jacket, feeling Kian's intense gaze burn into my bareback.

"Like the view?" I tease, placing a hand on my ass.

"Like is a fucking understatement," his deep, sexy reply answers.

I smile faintly as we continue walking. At the start, we had run as fast as we could, putting plenty of distance between us and both the castle and the main city. When I asked why he didn't shift, he muttered something about not trusting Thanatos around me. I really think he needs to trust his wolf a little more. I can handle myself perfectly well.

We continue on, not missing that the further away from the centre of the kingdom we get, the emptier the land becomes. We even come across a few burned-down towns and many that had become ghost towns, with their people heading to the capital and to safer places.

"It's been eleven hours since we left. We've travelled pretty far. Let's take a break," Kian says, looking down at the forest that looms in the distance.

From our position on the hill, we can see the area around us clearly. The dense forest covers a large part of the border, and once we pass it, we have a river to cross before reaching the mountains. It is past these mountains that we will cross over into Elandorr. That part will be rather hard, considering we'll probably be intercepted. I only have the words in the elven tongue that Orrian told me to use if I ever needed passage to his kingdom. I don't know their meaning, but I hope they work. I'm leading Kian into something with just my words, and by all means, I don't want to let him down.

"Is it safe to? What about patrols?" I ask, looking around. Kian places the supplies down by a tree and looks over at me.

"They won't come around here. Making it through these forests is almost impossible. Besides, this part of the kingdom has been emptied. The patrols are set to the east. If anything comes from the forest, they won't make it far," Kian murmurs.

"I see…" I sigh softly, the weight of the situation and this quest weighing on my shoulders.

"When we reach those trees, I intend to shift and run through the forest until we reach the other side," he says quietly.

"But, Kian, isn't it vast? Can we really make it through by just - " He places a finger on my lips, spinning me into his arms.

"I'm an Alpha, my little she-devil, and I assure you I have the stamina of many wolves combined. Travelling alone in these woods is easier, hence how the fae are entering. I'd have crossed many borders in a short time. We will take a break here and then find somewhere to stay for tonight. Tomorrow at dawn, we will enter the forest, and I doubt we will get proper sleep after that," he says before kissing me sensually.

I nod when we break apart. I trust him. This is his land, and he knows it better than I do. If he said he'd be able to, then I knew he would.

"So, we have the entire afternoon to find shelter and rest," I say more to myself as I scan the area. There are a few hills, bushes, and trees. Then, in the distance, I can make out some buildings. "There's a town not far out. Should we go there?" Kian looks at me before nodding.

"Our eyes aren't as good as a vampire's, but that would be the home of the Jade Oak Pack," he says, his hand squeezing my ass.

"Then shall we go there?"

"Sure…"

"What's wrong?" I ask, looking into his eyes, concerned.

"Thanatos wants to spend time with you… and I'm to shift tomorrow. I'd rather he does it before then… but I don't know - "

"Really, Kian? Do you think I can't handle him? I am Morgana - "

"Araton, my fucking incredible mate and future queen of Clair De Lune. You can handle him," he finishes off for me. I smile proudly.

"See, you're learning, and just like I handled you, I can handle him," I promise, cupping his face. That frown on his face is extremely deep, and I know he's concerned. "Trust me," I whisper softly.

He sighs, wrapping his arms around me and pulling me against his firm chest before he kisses my shoulder softly. I sigh, softly nuzzling my nose against his neck.

"I do. It's him I don't trust," he murmurs, planting kisses up my shoulder and onto my neck.

"Relax, we will be fine," I say, although it is still something I can't wrap my head around fully; it's almost like two personalities in one body. Kian's eyes burn into mine, his thumb rubbing over my lips.

"If you do decide to have fun, make sure he doesn't push you more than you want," he says quietly, making my eyes fly open and my cheeks burn.

"What? I mean, isn't that… Isn't that…" For once, I can't form words, despite the nervous butterflies that had already settled in my stomach. He smirks, cocking a brow.

"He's a part of me, and you are tied to him as well as you are to me. I assure you, we are both very different in many ways."

He squeezes my ass before delivering another tap to it. He definitely likes my ass. I bite my lip, clinging to his shirt tightly. God, he is so damn sexy.

Something tells me meeting Thanatos is going to be far from boring…

The town where the Jade Oak Pack once resided is one of the few that had been cleared out before they had been attacked.

"Are we just going to break in?" I ask as we stop outside a large inn in the ghost town.

"I'm the king, sunshine, I own the entire fucking place," Kian says, breaking open a lock on one of the doors before entering the inn. A pleasant scent of strawberries and camomile fills my nose, and I inhale deeply. It's clear they had cleaned and locked up before going.

"I don't think they would like it if we just came in like this."

"We aren't going to fucking ruin the place," Kian remarks, locking the door.

I look around; the setting sun is peeping through the gaps in the windows, casting a pleasant glow around the large hall. If I didn't know the truth, I would never have thought that such a peaceful place had been deserted due to the threat of war.

After searching around, he finds a bunch of keys and leads the way through the halls and up the stairs. I shake my head; he really has no care that we're breaking in. He stops outside one of the doors and checks the number on the keys before trying one. It clicks, and he pushes the door open, letting me enter first. I look around the room. It's simple yet extremely welcoming, or perhaps after all that running, I'm just tired.

The floors are wooden floorboards, and the walls are covered with floral wallpaper. A large bed sits to one side of the room, and there is a vanity table with a stool. Save that, the only other things in the room are the small table by the bed, a small window with the curtains drawn, and a small door that Kian opens and looks inside.

"There's toiletries and towels. Run a bath, and I'll join you after I go see if there's any food that we can have and save what we have packed." I smile. Oh, a bath sounds good!

"Perfect, don't take too long. I'll be waiting," I whisper.

He kisses me passionately, sending off a wave of sparks through me before leaving the room.

I enter the bathroom, looking around. It's clean and welcoming, with wooden floors, panelled walls, and a decent-sized tub. I look at the toiletries that sit on the shelf in small travel-size bottles, selecting two bubble bath ones and adding them to the water before I begin to undress. I hear the bedroom door open, and Kian's familiar scent fills my nose just as I peel off my trousers. I turn when I hear the door being pushed open wide.

My heart skips a beat when I look at the man before me. A sexy smirk curls at the corner of his lips, his arms crossed over his muscular chest as he leans against the door frame, his eyes blazing gold and a pout settled on that handsome face of his. His entire demeanour is different, and I know before he even speaks that this isn't Kian.

"I was a little impatient to wait any longer. I hope you don't mind," Thanatos' deep sexy voice comes before a devilish smirk crosses his face as his eyes rake over my body, and a glint of pure carnal hunger burns in his eyes. "Hello, my beautiful little mate."

# HIS OTHER SIDE

THANATOS

*I* HAD WAITED FAR TOO long to meet our mate properly. Kian is being a selfish prick. We find some dried food, drinks, and pastries and bring them up when I ask Kian to let me take control. Reluctantly, he agrees, warning me not to push her and to remember that tomorrow we have a long journey.

Her eyes are wide as she stares at me when I greet her, and I smile slightly. Oh, teasing her will be so much fun…

"Hi… Thanatos," she says, her voice breathless.

I walk towards her, and she steps back in nothing but those tiny black panties and bra. It frustrates me. I want to see her tits completely, see those hardened nipples and suck them until they're sore. Why do humans bother with clothes? Seeing mate naked all the time would be heaven. Oh, tonight is going to be fun, indeed.

"Are we bathing together?" I ask her. Reaching over, I hook a finger into her panties, playing with the band as I look down, peeking at the smooth skin of her pubic bone. Ahh, I can't wait to see Mini-Kian buried within her from up close. I will make her all raw and sore.

"I guess we are," she answers, her heart pounding as I carry on playing with the string of her thong.

"Good."

I growl in approval, ripping that tiny piece of fabric that holds no purpose but to tease me. She gasps. Her eyes widen when I follow up by ripping her bra off, too. I rub my thumb over the red mark I left on her skin where the fabric chafed her.

"I do apologise," I murmur, leaning down. I smirk as I slowly run my tongue along the light cut, satisfied when she sighs. "Now, next time we are together, I expect you in nothing." She raises an eyebrow.

"I thought Kian was bossy," she remarks, crossing her arms. Despite the fact that she is pressing her thighs together, the sweet hint of her arousal already clings to the air.

"You haven't seen anything yet, little mate," I growl, running my fingers over her hardened nipples. I can't wait for her to have our pups so I can milk these, too. I smirk, snaking my hands around her waist and looking into her deep red eyes.

"I get that feeling with you," she whispers, reaching for the hem of my top and pulling it off.

I smirk, allowing her to undress me. I could get used to this every fucking day, but Kian the asshole wouldn't allow me the luxury. I had shut him off completely. He can watch, but this is my time with mate.

She watches me sharply even when I am fully undressed. I step into the tub, pulling her in. I can sense the way she's observing me. I make her straddle me because although I want to talk to mate, I want to feel my cock against her delicious little cunt.

"Now... tell me. Are you happy?" I ask her, admiring her round breasts once again. That takes her by surprise, and she smiles softly, nodding.

"Extremely," she says, tilting her head and slowly beginning to un-braid her hair.

"Good. Kian is stupid and took forever to accept you, but he's a human." I grip her hips and move her over our cock.

"He isn't stupid," she pouts.

"Well, you should know I love you and that I loved you before him," I say, my emotions surging up through me as I stare into her eyes. This has been something I've wanted to tell her for a long time now.

"Really?" She asks softly, her eyes full of emotions as she locks her arms around my neck.

"Yes. So, how will you reward me for always loving you?" I ask. She bursts out laughing,

"You're so cute," she smirks. I frown.

"How the fuck am I cute? Kian is the stupid cute one. I'm the Alpha," I state. Humans are a little strange because I have no idea what is on her mind as she watches me, a small smile on her lips.

"You're cute," she repeats before kissing me softly. "Thank you for loving me when I never thought we were even possible."

"There's only one way I like to be thanked, and I'm sure you know exactly what I mean, little mate," I growl huskily, throbbing against her.

Her heart thuds, and she slowly tugs me closer, claiming my lips in a deep kiss. This is fucking good, but I'm the Alpha here. Twisting my hand into her silky black hair, I kiss her harder, dominating her completely.

Now, this... this is more like it...

"Fuck, Thanatos!" Morgana cries out as I pound into her relentlessly.

The scent of her arousal mixed with sex and sweat is divine. I hadn't been able to contain myself, cutting our bath short and bringing her to the bed because once I'm done, she'll need a shower all over again anyway.

I can tell she needs blood from the scarlet shade of her eyes, and Mini-Kian is indeed very large for our tiny mate - I can see the toll my pounding is taking on her. I pull her head up, kissing her hungrily as her orgasm rips through her, making her scream against my lips.

"Now, that's my good little mate," I purr, pulling out of her just before I come, something Kian had told me was necessary because we are at war. Stupid Kian, but even then, I will respect his wish. We are one, after all. I still believe it is our job to protect mate, and mates' job to have pups.

I'll impregnate her as soon as this war is over, I've decided.

She's breathing hard, and although I had gone extremely easy on her, she looks tired. I reach for Kian's jacket that I had taken off before I went to the bathroom and take out a small knife. I smirk, holding it up to her.

"Now... how about a little knife play?" I ask.

She looks at me curiously, despite clearly being exhausted. I smirk, holding my arm out and creating a deep cut on my forearm.

"Drink, little mate," I growl, watching her get onto her knees, sticking her tongue out and running it up along my arm. Pleasure courses through me, and I smirk, watching the wound heal up. Pulling her up, I kiss her, and she kisses me back, the taste of my blood lingering on her lips.

Taking the knife once more, I create a cut down the centre of my abs. She bites her lip, bending down and running her tongue from the base of my stomach and up along the cut, making me fucking throb. Reaching down, I squeeze her ass before delivering a sharp slap to it. She whimpers, biting her lip as I create an incision along my Adonis belt. She looks up at me before she runs her tongue along the cut, lapping up all the blood, but this time our little naughty mate begins sucking and licking me sensually.

Oh, yeah, this feels good….

I groan in pleasure, Mini-Kian hard and ready for another round, but it seems she has another idea. She runs her tongue lower, her hand fondling my balls. With the other, she takes the blade from my hand. Giving me a devilish smile, she taps my leg, motioning for me to widen them.

"Can I play?" She asks, running her fingers along my inner thighs, sending off waves of pleasure.

"By all means," I growl.

She sits back, motioning me forward. I oblige, raising an eyebrow when she cups my ass and pulls me forward until my knees are on either side of her shoulders. She raises the knife, taking it to my inner thigh. I feel the blade cut into my skin, making a long incision along my inner thigh, not as deep as the ones I had made, yet still pleasurable. The moment her tongue flicks out, running along it, I feel myself throb hard, groaning as she does the same to the other side. Oh, yeah, *fuck*, that's our good mate!

She whimpers in pleasure. Tossing the knife aside, I feel her tongue run along my balls. My hand shoots out, tangling in her locks as I throw my head back when the pleasure rocks through me.

She opens her mouth, taking Mini-Kian into her mouth and moaning as she begins to suck me off. A blazing surge of pleasure courses through me. I tangle my hand into her hair and begin thrusting into her mouth. I groan as I grow faster and rougher.

**Slow the fuck down,** Kian growls, cracking down the walls I had raised.

I look down at her, easing up a little. My eyes soften as I push past the hunger that consumed me. I do love mate, truly…

I groan, feeling my release nearing. My movements become faster, yet I control the force behind them, pleasure consuming me. I don't want to injure her…

"That's it…" I groan, not caring to keep my voice down. Her moans and the feel of my cock in her mouth feel too fucking good. I actually don't care that I can't mate with her in wolf form. This is very good… very good indeed… "Fuck, Morgana!" I growl as I shoot my load into her mouth. She swallows it down, sucking on my cock and milking me for all I have. I breathe hard, swearing as I pull a now much smaller Mini-Kian from between those plump lips of hers with a small pop. Fuck…

I move back so I am straddling her hips and pull her up against me, breathing hard as I bury my nose in her neck, inhaling deeply. My mate. My precious little mate.

"I love you, Thanatos," she says softly.

I tense, moving back, my heart racing as I stare into her eyes. My emotions are storming through me. It's almost as if she knows the deep-down fear I have within me, one I don't even let Kian see.

"Even if I don't have a wolf counterpart, you are both one, and I love you both," she says, softly cupping my face, love clear in those eyes of hers.

Now those words make me very happy. I don't care that she has just swallowed my seed; tugging her close, I kiss her hard.

"I love you, too, my beautiful mate," I whisper huskily before pushing her down, ready to devour that pretty little cunt of hers.

I've changed my mind; I won't let her sleep tonight…

MORGANA

Kian had not been wrong. Thanatos is a beast. Last night he gave me orgasm after orgasm, my body feeling overly sensitive to the point of being painful, yet he didn't stop, murmuring his love to me in between eating me out. I don't think he realised that even if he wasn't pounding into me, he was still tiring me out. However, I wouldn't have changed anything. I loved every moment of it, and somehow I feel like I had become even more complete with Kian. Thanatos is a part of him – a part of me.

It had been special, and the love that he was so desperately trying to show pulled at my heartstrings. He had ended by letting me drink from his neck before whispering goodnight and that he'd come back soon to 'feast on my pretty little pussy.' He had gone, and when Kian returned, kissing my forehead and shoulders, clearly concerned, I whispered that I was fine and I loved him before falling asleep in his arms, fully content.

Today I'm barely able to walk, but after a few glasses of blood and a soak in the bath, we leave. It's good that I'm riding on Thanatos' back today because I don't think I would have been able to continue on foot for so many hours.

Kian smirks at me when I finish getting dressed, pulling my hair into a high ponytail.

"So you clearly enjoyed your time with Thanatos." He snickers annoyingly. I glare at him, despite the smile I try to hide.

"Actually, I did, and whilst making love… I heard something interesting in his mind."

"Oh?" Unlike me, he isn't dressed, only wearing a towel around his waist as he's going to shift very soon.

"Yes, it was rather funny to hear him refer to something as Mini-Kian," I say, bursting into laughter. That makes him shut up. He clenches his jaw, pulling me into his arms.

"There's nothing mini about it," he growls.

"I know, but I still love the name," I assure him, breaking into another fit of laughter. He watches me, and I see a small smile cross his lips, making my heart skip a beat. "So, does Mini-Kian want to come out to play?" I giggle.

"Keep at that, and I assure you, if it comes out to play, you won't be walking for at least a week," he growls, taking hold of my hand and kissing it softly.

"And after last night… I barely can," I admit. He pulls me close, kissing my lips softly.

"I love you, my little she-devil. I'm afraid riding on me all day might just make you a little sore, and not in a good way, but we need to do this," he says, brushing his thumb along my cheek.

"I can handle it," I promise, giving him a tight hug before we step outside.

Kian locks the inn door with a padlock, although we know if someone wants to break in, nothing will stop them. Placing our luggage down, he takes a deep breath. This is it…

He shifts into his huge wolf, and I pick up the bags, slinging them onto my back before climbing onto his huge back. I entwine my hands into his fur before he breaks into a run, making me gasp. If running on feet is fast, this is even faster. His paws barely touch the ground. I know that this is going to be one tiring ride, but I'm ready for it.

Although there is a way to avoid the forest and reach Elandorr faster, it would be more noticeable, and I know Kian had thought over everything before deciding on this. I just hope our journey will be pretty straightforward…

A few hours have passed, and we are travelling through the forest. Apart from the stray animals that cross our path, a few snakes, and a poisonous nettle, we have a fairly smooth journey. I use my ability to knock a few wild animals away, those that Thanatos didn't rip to shreds. I wish I could tell him to take a break, but I know he knows exactly what he's doing. The moment the sun begins to dip in the sky, I become wearier of our surroundings.

"Kian, how long until we reach the edge of the forest?" I ask softly.

All I can see is the dense forest of trees in every direction. Closing my eyes, I try to hear his thoughts. The usual shrill sound fills my head, but what I hear makes my heart thunder.

*… bide our time, it's getting darker, and then we will attack.*

*Kill the Alpha first…*

The voices are so soft yet so sinister that it sends a cold shiver through me. We aren't alone… but where are they? I close my eyes, trying to focus on my surroundings. I need to tell Kian. I lean down to his ear. How do I tell him without being heard?

"Not alone," I whisper so faintly I'm not sure he heard. I close my eyes as I try to read his mind.

*… What? Morgana, can you hear me?*

"Yes," I murmur back.

*We aren't alone?*

"No."

*An enemy?*

"Yes."

*Try pinpointing their location. Once we get something, I'll attack. The fact that we can't sense them… it's Fae…*

"Okay," I murmur, caressing his fur and remaining calm.

We both knew this might happen. After all, from the attacks, we know Fae are moving through our kingdom. I could throw some daggers and see if any hit anything or…

My gaze falls to Kian's bow that is on my back. I could use the knives as my first attack and follow with a few arrows. Luckily, the blades have poisoned tips, perfect to use against Fae. I stroke Thanatos' fur, hoping he understands me. I need him to keep moving.

"Keep running," I murmur, slowly removing a few knives from Kian's pouch. I close my eyes, trying to focus on reading the minds of those around me once again.

*…on it, you attack from the left. The sun is almost gone. Let it set then.*

*Make sure the poison hits first.*

*Understood, Falian.*

I take a deep breath. Now is the time to use my speed and capabilities. Several daggers are at the ready, and I know I have one chance. Taking three daggers in each hand, I spin around, throwing them in all directions. I hear a grunt and see a stain of blood, raising my hand as a blast of light comes rushing towards us from the left. I slam it back with a wave of power, taking the bow up as a tall, slender man with dark hair and glowing eyes appears, holding his own bow and arrow.

"Oh, so you knew?" He whispers. I don't entertain the enemy…

"Kian, keep running!" I order, now sensing several presences. Fuck, they must have been following us for some time!

I raise my bow and begin shooting arrow after arrow as fast as I can. A hundred years of practice is a long time to perfect the art. My hands are a blur, each arrow aiming to kill, shot with precision and power. However, the Fae are fast and powerful. Another, which has the power of fire, keeps sending spiralling balls of flame towards us. Kian growls, and I know he wants to turn around.

"Kian, on three," I murmur. That would give me enough time to jump off his back. "Three!" I shout.

I do a backflip, landing on my feet before drawing my sword and slicing the head of one of the Fae straight off. I blast another back with my hand before appearing before him in a flash. He knocks me back, the ground trembling as roots erupt from the ground, wrapping around my entire body and slamming me to the ground brutally. Pain spasms up my back, knocking the breath from me.

Kian bites my attacker's head off and rushes towards me, only for a Fae to intercept him. I break free, blasting the tree roots back and grabbing the sword I had dropped moments earlier, just as another Fae with blazing red hair and eyes raises his own.

"Let's dance," he says, flashing me a deadly yet beautiful smile.

"I will let you lead."

He smirks, his sword suddenly coated with fire. He spins it, lunging at me in a fluid movement. His move remains beautifully elegant despite the clear aim to kill me burning in his eyes.

"How kind of you; a vampire working alongside a werewolf, marked by one… you chose the wrong side, my lady," he says, his silky voice laced with darkness. I spin around, drawing my other sword as well, and block him before taking the offence.

"I chose the correct side. It is you who did not!" I spare myself a moment to see Kian tearing through the Fae, even with their powers. He is powerful, yet I can see how fast they are… no ordinary werewolf could last against so much.

"Care to share a name, my beauty?" He murmurs.

"None of your damn business!" I snap icily.

I send a blast towards two who are working on creating a huge ball of fire to throw at Kian, knocking them backwards before I manage to nick the man before me across the cheek. His eyes flash, and he hisses, darting forward. At the last moment, I realise he is aiming for my weak point, the very same point that Kian had said I needed to work on…

I barely manage to knock his sword aside, plunging my own straight into his chest. His eyes widen, but just then, I feel a searing pain rip through me. A scream escapes my lips as agony makes my entire body convulse. I fall to my knees as the man falls face forward, dead. I look down at my body, clutching my waist, and see the dagger that is impaled in my waist. I yank it out with shaking hands, looking at the darkened blade. Poison…

A menacing growl rips through the air as I see Kian stumble. No… the mate bond connects us. He's feeling my pain…

Through stinging eyes, I look around, seeing only two Fae remain. I am Morgana, Queen of Clair De Lune and the king's mate, and I will *never* give up.

I force myself to my feet just as Kian pounces on one of the two, ripping him to shreds. I raise my sword, gripping my waist with the other hand,

and, with everything I have, I throw it towards the final Fae, who is heading towards Kian, crackling electricity swirling around his hands. My knife impales him just as Kian turns, shifting back to human form, his eyes on me.

I give him a small smile, hoping he understands I'm okay, before I topple face forward to the ground, the smell of blood and dirt filling my nose. The searing, excruciating, overwhelming pain pulls me into its folds…

# ḢIS ṂOONLIGHT

KIAN

Y ENTIRE BODY IS wracked with pain, and my eyes snap to Morgana. She's hurt!

**Mate!** Thanatos groans, his panic and worry bleeding into mine.

"Morgana!" I shout, rushing to her side as fast as I can as she falls face forward to the ground. "Fuck, no!"

I won't let this pain get the better of me. I need to help her. The Fae around us are dead, yet I know more could come at any moment. They had already infiltrated our kingdom.

I rip Morgana's top from her waist. Fuck, how did they figure out her weak spot so fucking quickly? It isn't even big, but it's clear these men knew what they were doing. Skilled and powerful.

**Fae are fast, and some even have the ability to see the near future, hence giving them the upper hand in battles,** Thanatos says, worry clear in his voice.

**Yeah.**

I look into her eyes. I pull the dagger out; nightshade… wolfsbane, and silver. Something that could hurt us both. There's something else, too, but I can't make it out. I place it down, seeing her skin take on a blue-grey colour around the injury. Fuck, this is not good. Bending down, I begin to suck the wound, spitting out each mouthful of blood and poison. I'm trying to remove what poison I can, but it's not fucking enough.

**It's too strong, Kian... that won't work. It was on the blade alone, which means it was strong,** Thanatos grunts.

My heart races as panic and fear consume me. I look down at my beautiful rose. Her chest is heaving, her face scrunched in pain, and her heart is beating dangerously fast. I suck another mouthful out desperately but to no avail.

I jump back and rush to the nearest Fae, searching or hoping for something that may help. There is nothing but more poisons. I toss them to the ground, the anger seeping through me getting stronger with each passing moment. Each body holds nothing of importance nor anything that looks like an antidote.

Fuck!

Wait! The antidotes we brought with us! My heart is thumping as I rush to our bags, my hands fucking shaking as I rummage around until I find the vials. The fear, worry, and panic that I feel are coursing through me, wreaking havoc. My head is pounding, and my chest is clenching. It's almost the same as the day she had been poisoned at the dinner.

*Fuck... Morgana, be okay...*

**She will be okay! She's fucking strong,** Thanatos growls as I rush back to her, pouring one of the vials onto her injury. She whimpers, and I lift her head, slipping open her mouth and slowly pouring the antidote in, a few drops at a time.

"Come on, baby girl, swallow..." I murmur, my heart thundering.

Although it only takes a few minutes, it feels like hours as she finally takes the entire antidote. I hold her, kissing her neck softly and rocking her gently. There's nothing more I can do...

*What the fuck do I do...?*

I pause when I think I hear something in the distance. I close my eyes, honing in on my surroundings. I sense a faint chill of darkness. Something is approaching fast. Is it more Fae?

We need to go.

I shift, the sound of bones snapping and reshaping filling the air for a few seconds before I am in my wolf form. Nudging Morgana onto my back, I make sure she is firmly draped over before I grab our bags in my mouth and break into a run. Staying in this forest is equal to a fucking death wish.

I need Morgana safe. There are far too many things out here that could harm us. I have already failed to protect her. Again.

The guilt that I feel overrides the pain in my side; it's eased up a little. I just hope the antidote fucking works. I won't stop running until I reach the other side of this forest, no matter what.

I run faster than I ever have, the passing trees a blur in my eyes. I'm the fucking king, and if anyone can make it through here, it's me.

Time passes. The pain in my side is still there, yet I don't let it bother me. However, my muscles are screaming for a reprieve, but I don't stop.

For a while, I can sense something following us, but I only push myself further, outrunning whatever it is until I can no longer sense it. Even then, I can't be sure. Any other time, I'd have stopped and faced it, but I have Morgana, and she still has not awakened. I'm relieved that her heartbeat is a lot steadier than before.

Finally, I see the trees beginning to thin. I push further, bursting out through trees, leaving the forest and its dangers behind. The sound of the distant river whispers in my ears, and the urge to go for a drink tempts me. My throat is parched, and I'm exhausted after hours of running, but I need to find a safe place to stop to rest. Night has already fallen, and the moon is high in the sky, although it is half-hidden by a thick layer of clouds. I look back towards the forest. The ominous darkness that seems to envelop it feels almost visible. Now to find shelter…

I turn away, padding down towards the river; the terrain is rocky here, so I make my way down carefully, making sure Morgana is firmly on my back. I guess this is where we'll rest tonight. There are some bushes and the odd tree that we can rest under, although I know I won't be able to sleep knowing we are out in the open.

I place Morgana's slender body down gently. She looks even more fucking fragile like this. Her luscious lips part slightly, her breasts heaving with every breath she takes. I shift back into human form and brush her hair back.

Looking at her waist, I can see the wound looks almost blackish-grey now, and it's spreading across her stomach. Whatever else was on that dagger, we don't have the antidote to it. I wish I had grabbed the dagger to examine it further or some of that poison they carried, but I hadn't thought of it at the time.

I take out another dose of the antidote. There's no harm in giving it to her. I feed it to her slowly, as I had earlier, wishing she would wake up soon. I kiss her lips, feeling those sparks dance through me. *Please be okay, my little she-devil.*

Placing her down gently, I move away and take out some pants from the bag, taking out one of the water bottles and pouring it over her wound that has almost closed up. I then take out a bandage and a square cloth, apply some balm on it, and place it on the wound before wrapping her waist with the entire bandage. I pull her onto my lap, burying my head in her neck.

"Wake up, sunshine…" I murmur, inhaling her intoxicating scent.

It fucking hurts inside. I feel so fucking lost without her awake. I'm already missing her sly smiles, her sparkling devious eyes and the way she -

**Kian, stop it,** Thanatos growls. **You need to stay strong for mate.**

**I know… I just… I need her, Thanatos. I feel fucking lost.**

**That's the bond. We need her because she is a part of us,** he says softly.

I understand what it means now: without one, the other won't survive. There is no way that I could ever live without her. I cling to her tightly, trying to suppress the emotions that I feel inside.

**Kian, you need to eat and drink,** Thanatos says quietly.

**I'm not going to, not until she wakes up.**

Fuck this! I need to continue. Maybe they will be able to help her in Elandorr….

**If you become weak, Kian, who will take care of her? Focus!** Thanatos growls.

I frown. I know he has a point… fine. Sighing heavily, I reluctantly place her down, gently covering her with a thin blanket and walking over to the water, where I begin drinking my fill. Once I'm done, I refill the bottles and return to Morgana. I eat some of the food we had brought before I slice my wrist and place it to her lips, letting the blood flow into her mouth.

*Fuck, wake up, Morgana…*

The blood trickles out of her mouth, so instead, I raise my wrist to my mouth, sucking some of my blood into my mouth before pressing my lips to hers, slowly letting it pour in. Sparks course through me, and I hold her even tighter, only moving back when she swallows all the blood. I stare into her face, one hand behind her head, the other holding her close, and it's then that I see her eyes flutter slightly. My heart begins racing, feeling Thanatos leap with excitement, too.

"Morgana! Come on, baby girl, wake up," I say hoarsely, giving her a slight shake. She moans, whimpering when she moves slightly and flinches.

"Take it easy, beautiful," I whisper, my heart pounding. Relief floods me when her eyes finally open, and she stares up at me, looking confused and delirious.

"I… where… where am I?" She asks weakly.

"You're safe," I say, pulling her against my chest. Thank the goddess she's okay. If anything happened to her…

The weight that had been weighing down upon me lifts slightly, but I know she still needs help.

"I… Kian?" She whispers weakly. I move her back gently, looking into her pale red eyes.

"What is it, my queen?" I whisper. She smiles slightly at that.

"I… you need to… if I don't make it… tell Orrian… I - "

"You will fucking make it, and you will be the one to speak to the fucking elf," I growl, my eyes flashing.

"I know… but in case…"

Her eyes flutter shut, and she loses consciousness once more.

Fuck this, I am not going to rest any longer and waste fucking time. We will cross the river and mountains. I'm not going to fucking stop until I reach Elandorr. With renewed willpower, I stand up, get dressed fully, and pick up the bags before lifting Morgana onto my back. We are going to get her help, no matter what.

I stare up at the mountains in the distance. If we rest, we should be there in another three days… but I'll make sure I get there within a day. My eyes flash, and I know Thanatos is with me. For our mate. Her wellbeing is our fucking priority, even if it's the last fucking thing we do. We will see this through, one way or another.

Night turns to day, and day turns to night once more. I only stop to give Morgana blood and to eat and drink. At times, I shift, and at others, I walk.

Morgana opens her eyes a few times, but she is weakening despite how much blood I'm giving her. She's able to stay awake for longer, but she isn't able to do much more than cling to me weakly. She keeps apologising for the burden she's become. What she doesn't damn realise is that she had fought like a fucking queen, protecting my back as she held her own by my side.

"We're almost there," she whispers. Her eyes have never looked so washed out as they had this morning, her face ashy and her breathing laboured. "I'm sorry... you must be so exhausted." I can feel her guilt and anguish through the bond, along with her helplessness.

"Really, sunshine? Not with that again. You fought like a fucking warrior goddess, and I assure you, watching you was a fucking turn-on." She lets out a weak laugh, kissing my neck softly.

"Only you would think that," she murmurs.

"I think you're underestimating your beauty," I reply, making my way through the snowy mountain.

The possessiveness that rises at the fact that this prince is her ex makes me frown. I am curious to see what the dickhead looks like, what had been so appealing about him that she had chosen him. Someone who had been befitting enough to capture my woman's attention...

"You're getting jealous and angry," she murmurs. Perks of the bond; it works both fucking ways.

"I'm not," I deny trying to block my emotions from her.

"You know, you and Thanatos are the only ones I love," she whispers, her head resting on my shoulder, exhaustion clear in her voice.

**Mate mentioned me, too, she's fucking perfect,** Thanatos growls.

"Well, he's happy you remembered him," I remark, tilting my head and kissing her forehead.

I pause, staring out at the mountains. We are out of Clair De Lune, we crossed those borders when we passed the river. Right now, we are in unclaimed land, but a few miles forwards, and I'm sure we will reach the borders of Elandorr – a place I had never been to, said to be full of magic, splendour, and beauty. Yeah, well, I hope they're as strong and welcoming to match their kingdom's fucking appeal.

"I can feel the magic... we're nearing the border," she whispers. I pause.

"Already? I thought it was a few miles out? Then again, I've only ever scouted this place to get a scope on my kingdom. I've never come too far out."

"Hmm, I can feel the veil…" she murmurs, pressing her lips to my neck once more, placing soft kisses along it. Fuck, is it wrong that even in this state, she's still fucking turning me on?

"Do you want my first appearance in front of the elves to be with a fucking hard-on?" I growl, slowly easing her off my back and into my arms, bridal style, then kissing her neck. She gasps, grabbing onto my jacket weakly.

"It wouldn't be a bad sight," she whispers, looking into my eyes. I press my forehead to hers.

*Fuck, not much longer, and you'll be okay…*

I kiss her lips deeply, forcing myself to keep control rather than devour her when she is already so weak.

"Is the veil a barrier or just a concealment spell?" I ask as we continue forward.

"Both." She replies, "We won't be able to cross it until we are granted permission. There's a reason Elandorr is the only kingdom said to not welcome anyone in."

"Yet you think this guy will allow us in?" I ask, now able to sense the magic myself. She smiles faintly.

"He will." She says this with complete confidence.

I am doing this on her words, but even if she is wrong, I won't hold it against her. I just hope that even if he doesn't offer us help, he'll at least help heal Morgana.

Another hour passes, and I can actually feel the power in the air. I'm beginning to lose focus on my sense of direction. It's colder and icier; I can actually feel it biting into my bones.

"I thought the barrier was somewhere here," Morgana whispers weakly. Her breath is coming out in a puff of white mist due to the cold.

"I think we're already in it…" I murmur. She looks at me, and I stop.

Elves have hearing and sight that is more than impressive. They must be close enough to hear us…

"We seek passage to speak to the rulers of Elandorr," I say loudly.

Morgana looks at me before motioning for me to place her down. I frown but do as she says, supporting her body that she is not able to hold up by herself.

"I have been welcomed into the kingdom of Elandorr by His Royal Highness, Prince Orrian, himself. I have a message which he told me would grant me passage!" She says as loudly as she can.

I hear the soft rustle of something shifting around us, and then it feels like everything stills. It's almost as if the very air around us is waiting.

"What message?" A strong melodic voice asks.

The cold seems to lift, and the haze that had seemed to have settled around us thins out. Trees that are in full bloom are scattered around, ice droplets frozen on the coloured leaves like jewels glinting under the sunlight. As far as I can see, these tall, elegant trees cover the area, but they are spread out, each one having its own area. In the distance, I can see some sort of gate made out of white wood and silver filigree patterns.

I look at the three men, who have unmounted their white horses and are walking towards us. Each one is dressed in the finest threaded clothing one could find, the type you would wear on a special occasion. Silvery white fabric with embroidered threadwork, with fine chainmail and grey pants underneath. Each one holds a long sword in his belt and carries a bow and arrows. Their hair is similar shades of light blond to one another's, worn in thin braids from the front with the rest left open. Their eyes are all light icy blue, pale green, and light brown. Each one is tall and lean yet built with a regal air to them.

"Aal rai'ash hara si oren dashe saara ki Orrian aal Elandorr nayash!" Morgana says clearly and confidently.

Her words fucking hit me hard, and I feel as if I've been doused in icy water. I feel as if someone has just stabbed me through the fucking heart. I clench my jaw, swallowing hard as I exhale sharply. My eyes snap to Morgana, her words echoing in my head and my eyes blazing as my emotions surge through me. Does she know what she just said?

"We yield to our future queen," they say, bending one of their knees before us, each one placing a fist on his heart and lowering his head to Morgana.

Morgana's eyes widen in shock, turning her head towards me. I know she realises that her words held a meaning she wasn't expecting, and the way those words had hit me hard.

"I… no… I don't… I don't know what I said…" she explains, worry filling her as she clenches my top.

"I come home to my beloved with the gift of his promise under the white sky of the mountains of Elandorr," I say quietly. The words sound sour in my mouth. They may not have meant much, but in the elven tongue, he had given her no less than the gift of a promise of love and a proposal. I hadn't been so sure before, but it's clear now that their relationship had been far deeper than I had thought.

"Kian," she says softly.

I'm fucking trying my best not to show my anger when she is already unwell, but it's hard to contain it completely.

"Kian - "

"We will take you to the prince," one of the guards says, motioning for Morgana to take his horse.

"I'm okay, Kian will hold - "

I lift her onto the horse, getting on behind her. No matter how fucking hard this is, I'm not going to shut her out, despite the urge to take a break and clear my head. My heart is thundering with rage and anger. My instincts are telling me to rip this fucking asshole to shreds when I see him, but I'm sure even Morgana wouldn't forgive me for that, I think bitterly. She is mine, and I'll be damned if this fucking Orrian so much as looks at her in the wrong way.

**Kill him,** Thanatos spits, his anger like a fucking tornado in my head. I hold her firmly in my arms as I guide the horse after the other two men, my eyes blazing gold.

"Kian, listen to me…" she whispers.

"Save your energy," I say, unable to look at her. I know it was in the past, but it fucking hurts. Yeah, I'd had Sage, but something tells me this bond between them was fucking deeper.

"Kian, I…" She swallows, and I wrap one arm around her tightly.

The men watch us sharply, and my eyes flash. The urge to kiss her right here overcomes me, and so I do, placing my lips to her neck softly. She sighs, and I realise her heart is pounding as it always does when I touch her, making me feel fucking guilty that I got angry over something that wasn't really her fucking fault.

"I didn't know what - "

"Don't. Let's meet this prince," I say, my voice barely able to contain the anger that burns through me, and I know the elves can sense it, too.

She doesn't speak after that, realising I don't want to talk. As guilty as I feel for it, staying silent is the best way for me to be able to control myself.

We ride for a short while through the snow and trees when the sound of a galloping horse makes one of the men signal for me to stop. I tug at the reins, my other arm around Morgana's waist. The moment the man pulls his horse to a stop, leaving a flurry of snow in his wake, and jumps from it, I know he's the fucking prince.

He has long ash-blond hair that falls over his shoulder, reaching halfway down his back. Two braids are woven alongside the side of his head in the elven style, and a crown rests on his forehead. Dressed in a white tunic and light grey pants, he oozes power. His icy grey eyes widen as they stare at Morgana. The intensity of his emotions makes my gut twist and my anger flare.

"Moonlight… it's good to see you again."

And the fucking cherry on top is that Morgana's heart begins to race…

# Decades Old Past

MORGANA

T HE MOMENT I UTTERED those words, I felt Kian's intense hurt and anger before he slammed his walls up and blocked me off. That hurt more than the pain that consumed me – his unspoken barrier that shunned me. I don't know if it's the state I'm in, but his silence is eating up at me. I do my best to try to calm my emotions, but I know with his walls up, he won't be able to sense my emotions anyway.

Kian… I'm too exhausted to argue, but I can't bear to see him like this. I love him, not Orrian. I just wish I could show him that… right now, I'm far too weakened to even reason with him.

One of the men motions for us to stop, and I hear the sound of thundering hooves before a white stallion comes galloping towards us, with none other than Orrian himself upon it. He hasn't changed at all, despite it being a few decades since we had seen each other. His long blond hair is still as perfect as ever, his angled jaw and those flawless features so true to his kind, yet he stands out from the rest.

"Moonlight… it's good to see you again."

"Morgana, Orrian," I correct quietly. I can't let him act like we're not over, especially when I know Kian's temper. I didn't like him flaunting Sage in front of me, I won't do that same.

He frowns ever so slightly, his gaze flickering to Kian before his eyes dip to Kian's arm, which is wrapped around my waist firmly, my breasts resting against it.

"It's good to see you too." Before I can speak further, Kian speaks.

"Can we skip the pleasantries? She was poisoned on our journey here by the Fae. She isn't well and needs to be attended to," he says coldly. I can feel his power exuding from him, and I don't miss the look of curiosity in Orrian's eyes before he nods and mounts his horse.

"Let's head to the palace immediately!"

"Kian…" I start as both men nudge their horses into a gallop.

"Hmm?" He hums, his eyes fixed ahead, blazing gold.

I reach up, using all my energy to drag my limbs that feel like heavy lead. My hand almost touches his face before I can no longer reach for him, and it drops back into my lap. My eyes sting with tears, but before I can voice my pain, I feel my vision darken. No matter how painful my body feels, it's nothing compared to the agony in my heart…

I'm conscious but unable to open my eyes when Kian lifts me off the horse as we come to a stop. I feel his lips press against my forehead and his finger brushing away my stray tear.

"Bring her inside, I'll have our healing mage look at her," Orrian is saying. "Will you not share your name? I can sense you are powerful and a werewolf, yet you are here with a vampire."

"Kian Araqiel. The Alpha King of Clair De Lune," Kian's ice-cold voice answers. His anger is palpable, and I wish I wasn't so helpless.

"Kian Araqiel… no wonder I can sense the power from you," Orrian's softer voice follows. "Here, place her down." I hear the rustle of bedding before I am placed on a very soft bed, sinking into it. If I wasn't already battling trying to stay awake, it becomes much harder now.

"Sire, you called?" A woman's voice comes.

"Yes, healer, she has been poisoned."

"You may give us some privacy," the woman says.

"Come, Alpha King Kian."

"I'm staying by her side; she is my mate," Kian hisses.

A silence falls between them. I hear the woman sigh as she whispers something, and then I feel a coolness wrap around my body.

"I wish to be alone. You may both leave. I need to focus on what I am doing. This poison is spreading and wrapping around her heart. I can feel its evil tendrils sinking deeper into her soul - negative energy will not help me..."

"I won't leave her," Kian repeats.

"Your energy is affecting me," the woman says calmly.

"She is safe here. Come, you need rest, too. I assure you Morgana is safe," Orrian says quietly.

My heart clenches as I feel Kian move away. He didn't kiss me goodbye...

He and Sage together didn't hurt as much as his behaviour is hurting me now...

I finally let myself fall into darkness. The last thing I hear is the woman murmuring something, and I feel a strong pull rush through me as if she is ripping something from inside of me. Then I lose consciousness.

When I come, too, I feel... alive. I lay in bed, realising I am now washed and dressed in a slightly sheer shimmery organza nightdress with thin straps. My hair had been washed and braided whilst I lay in a luxurious, comfortable bed. The silver moonlight shines through the sheer curtains on the windows, and the lamps that light the room are dimmed. From what I can tell, the walls are made of shimmering white rocks. The floor is marble, and the furniture is all made of intricate gold and silver filigree vines with patterns intertwining through the wood.

The pain is gone, and I feel completely normal, much to my surprise.

Kian! Where is Kian?

I kick the bedding off, rushing to the door and pushing it open. I can smell him faintly, my stomach knotting as I remember his anger. I need to explain to him...

I cross the small hall and push open another door, my heart beating like a drum.

"Kian!" I call, the brightly lit room blinding me for a moment.

His seductive scent hits me before I see him seated with none other than Orrian. A tray of food is before them; they seem to have been having a serious conversation. Both men look at me, but it's when their eyes fall on my body that I realise my clothes are sheer. Under the dazzling lights of the chandelier in this room, every curve and part of my body is on display.

Before I can even cover my breasts with my arms, Kian growls, his eyes blazing. He's before me in a flash, pulling off the ivory shirt he had been wearing and placing it around my shoulders. His jaw is clenched, but the moment I reach out, grabbing his face in my hands, his eyes flash, and his hands go to my waist, my heart thundering.

He slowly looks into my eyes, and I can see the emotions that he is trying to hide from me. I wish he could feel how I felt about him. His eyes soften, and he is about to lean down. My heart skips a beat, yearning for something, some sign that we are okay, but before he can do more, we are interrupted by Orrian.

"It's been a long time, Morgana," he says, breaking our moment.

Kian looks down at my body, his eyes darkening with anger and desire before he takes his shirt and slips it on over my head. I smile faintly at that. My baby is getting rather possessive… but it's to be expected. This is the first time we are running into an ex of mine. We have just gotten here, but he's already raging. I resist a smile. Is it bad that I found it a little amusing?

"Orrian, it has been a while. A few decades?" I ask.

I won't flirt or anything because my heart belongs to Kian, but even simply talking to Orrian seems to anger my handsome man.

"I guess I'm the only one who remembers the exact number of days, months, and years since our parting," he says softly, standing up. He towers a few inches above Kian, yet the power and aura that rolls off Kian makes him ooze with dominance, unlike Orrian, who has a strong yet calming aura.

Orrian holds his hand out to me, and I take it. For a moment, I remember our time from long ago, the moment we broke up and the final promise he made, leaving me with those words of his. He kisses my hand softly before I tug it away, feeling Kian's anger.

"I have a complaint before I share my issue," I say, glaring at him. "Why did you give me those words without even telling me what they meant?"

He smirks, "Oh, it's always fun to tease you, Morgana."

"Oh, really? Well, next time, if my beloved Kian tries to rip you or your men to shreds, I won't hold him accountable," I inform him, wrapping my arm around Kian's' bicep and pressing myself against him. Hopefully, I've made it clear to both men to whom I belong. I feel his surprise. I look up into his gorgeous hazel eyes, my heart thundering as our gaze meets. The fear of him pushing me out again stings as I remember his anger.

"Beloved?" Orrian asks, his voice full of surprise.

"Mates," Kian adds dangerously. His voice is so cold. His hand cups my neck, brushing the collar of his tunic down so Orrian can see the mark that branded my skin and claimed me as his. "So I'd appreciate it if you threw out any thoughts you have of her from that head of yours. Morgana is mine."

Orrian looks stunned, but the frown that settles on his face moments later makes my stomach twist with unease. Orrian isn't the type to frown often.

"So, you marked her, knowing that you would not outlive two centuries... you cut her life span short so selfishly?" My heart skips a beat as I look between them.

"Orrian, no, it's not - "

"It is like that. You would live for thousands of years, Morgana, like me, yet he claimed you and shortened your life. We all know that werewolf mates die alongside their other halves. Yes, you could have claimed her, but there was no need to mark her. How could you be so selfish?" He asks Kian quietly.

No, it's not like that.

I look at Kian, who clenches his jaw, his eyes blazing yellow. I know he had never considered that. The guilt and regret that I can see in his eyes that he tries to hide from me squeeze at my heart, knocking the air from my body.

*Don't ever regret marking me, Kian.*

He turns away from me, pulling his arm free from my hold and swiftly leaving the room. The door shuts behind him with a loud thud, leaving me standing there feeling more alone than I ever have in my entire life.

My eyes blaze with anger as I spin towards Orrian, ready to unleash my wrath upon him. He raises an eyebrow, crossing his arms.

"I only stated the truth, Moonlight," he says, looking into my eyes.

"Orrian... he marked me to save my life! And even if that wasn't the reason, I would have wanted him to!" I insist, glaring at the taller man, who is unphased by my anger, but that's Orrian; calm, collected, cold even to many. Yet he had lowered that wall for me, but when he's stuck on a way, he's as stubborn as an old man.

"I won't understand why you would agree to something like that. Regardless of whether it was your wish or not," he says. His voice, as always, is powerful and deep with that cold edge to it.

"Don't be so stubborn or fixated on your thoughts, Orrian… I love Kian, a level of love that I have never felt before," I say quietly, knowing that was a hard blow. "I love him more than I can ever explain to you. There is no life for me without him." The look in Kian's eyes… that guilt… I don't want it there.

"The Morgana I knew would never throw her life away for love," he says, his eyes calculating. I glare into his eyes, my chest heaving.

"Throw my life away? *He* is my life! And, no, I'm not the Morgana you knew long ago. This Morgana knows what she wants and has found where I belong! I found a love worth dying for!" I say dangerously.

My dark eyes meet his icy grey ones, and, like always, his are guarded. Orrian is the one person whose mind I am not able to penetrate. He is powerful, strong, and even now… parts of him are a mystery. Memories of long ago flash through my mind as I think back to the day we parted…

OVER THIRTY YEARS AGO

*The sun had set, and the crescent moon was glowing in the sky, making the sea sparkle like a thousand jewels. The sand beneath my feet was welcoming and soft. I leaned back against Orrian's firm chest and closed my eyes, letting the coolness of the night blanket my skin. I wore a backless red silk dress that fell to my ankles with a slit from the thigh down.*

*"The night is so welcoming," I murmured, sighing when his lips brushed up my neck, sending pleasure rushing through me.*

*"You are my light in the dark, my moonlight," he whispered. My heart clenched, and I knew he was waiting for an answer… the answer to the proposal he made a few days ago… "I know your answer," he said quietly, his voice like a whisper on the wind. It was almost as if he knew what ensued within my mind.*

*"I'm sorry, Orrian," I said, slowly tugging out of his arms, turning to face him. "I know what being your queen will mean… to never step out of Elandorr for my entire life."*

*"Elandorr is huge, Morgana, you won't be stuck within the palace walls," he said, reaching over and caressing my cheek. I looked down.*

*Orrian was nearly 900 years old. I wasn't even 100 yet… I had barely lived, so how could I promise him that…? And our families… I didn't see this working.*

"And what about our families?" I asked quietly.

He smiled slightly, knowingly even, as if he understood something I didn't. He looked to the moon before his face became passive.

"I guess you are correct… we are just not meant to be. Perhaps parting ways is best for the both of us," he said, caressing my cheek with his hand. My heart clenched as I stared at him. Would he not even fight for me? Were we not enough to fight for?

"You're okay to… end this?" I asked, surprised. I had almost expected him to argue. No, the life of an elven queen was not what I wanted, but… was our love not enough? The pain that rushed through me felt like the bitter waves on a stormy night, and I bit my lip. Orrian glanced at the sky and smiled slightly, his icy grey eyes softening ever so slightly.

"Do you know why I love the night?"

"Hmm? Because you can escape from your duties as a prince," I replied. He raised an eyebrow.

"Partially, yes," he said, "but it's because the moonlight reaches every corner of our lands. It is never far, and it returns every night to where it belongs, casting its light to the darkest of places." I frowned. Typical of Orrian, never to speak straight up. I rolled my eyes.

"Very poetic, my prince," I teased.

"Only stating a fact, my lady," he replied. "We will part ways, but if ever you need me or my help, know that the gates to Elandorr will forever remain open to you. If ever you need passage to my kingdom, then utter the following words; Aal rai'ash hara si oren dashe saara ki Orrian aal Elandorr nayash."

"Aal…?" I didn't understand the elven tongue.

"Repeat after me…Aal rai'ash hara si oren dashe saara ki Orrian aal Elandorr nayash."

"Aal rai'ash hara si oren dashe saara ki Orrian aal Elandorr nayash…"

"Remember those words. Repeat them to no one unless you need to use them, and they will grant you passage," he said softly. He stepped closer; at six feet six inches, he towered over my five-foot-eleven frame.

"I'll remember them, and I'll hold you to it," I said with a pout. "I might need a place to hide if I piss Azrael off." He smirked ever so slightly.

"Oh, anytime. I wish you all the best, Morgana… the last few months have been special, but I think we both knew it was going to be fleeting," he said, running his fingers through my hair. My heart ached. I always knew a future *would have meant many difficulties, and being an elven queen wasn't something I could do… but…*

*He looked down before hesitantly looking into my eyes. His eyes were filled with more emotions than I had ever seen before in our time together.*

*"What if we ran away? Far from these - "* I placed a finger on his lip and shook my head.

*"No… Orrian, you have far too many responsibilities. You cannot throw that all away for us."*

*"I can," he replied quietly.*

*I looked down. Maybe… but what about when the elven court came after him and wanted his head? The elven kind was ruthless, strong, and their rules were absolute… I knew that the elves would never be able to accept a vampire queen. I couldn't let him risk his life. He had several siblings whose eyes were fixed on that throne. The chance to try and kill him would be something I was sure some of them would love to do…*

*"No, I think it's better we end this," I said, trying to hide the pain in my chest.*

*Orrian would always be my first love. That first kiss… that first taste of forbidden pleasure… but we were never meant to be. Our love story was magical and more of a short-lived dream than something that could ever be real…*

*He didn't reply, cupping my face and pressing his lips to mine. Pleasure rushed through me, his lips as warm as his eyes were cold as they caressed mine like they were something so precious. I closed my eyes, wrapping my arms around his neck, my fingers playing with his long hair.*

*I'll always remember you, Orrian… I love you…*

"You wouldn't understand the meaning of the love between Kian and me," I say coldly, glaring at the man before me. I do not want to disrespect our past… but it doesn't compare to what there is between Kian and me.

"Do explain how cutting your entire life short is a good idea?" He replies coldly.

"Why do you care if I live a hundred years or a thousand?" I snap, but the moment the words leave my lips, I regret them. I look away from his emotionless face and take a deep breath.

"Regardless of the fact that we ended things, Morgana… you are still dear to me," he says, his voice emotionless yet soft. I swallow, exhaling sharply.

"I still consider you a friend, Orrian, yet I can't let you get in the way of Kian and me… I love him more than anything, and I do not appreciate you making him feel like he did something wrong."

"I'll keep it in mind," he says, his jaw clenched. His nostrils flare slightly, but apart from that, I feel nothing more from him. His emotions and thoughts are closed off.

"Thank you." I remember that we are here for his help. "Did Kian say anything about why we came?"

"No. He isn't much of a talker, is he? Perhaps it's his pride, or maybe that's the way he is. Alphas are known for their arrogance, after all." I roll my eyes.

"And all elven princes are as annoying and sarcastic as you, aren't they?"

"Well, not really. I like to consider myself unique," he says with a slight air of confidence.

"Unique indeed." I narrow my eyes. "We'll talk tomorrow... but I need your help." He looks up at me and nods, clenching his jaw.

"I promised you that I will always be there for you... I intend to keep it in whatever way necessary. Good night, Morgana. I'm glad you are feeling better."

Not waiting for a reply, he turns and leaves the room. I look at his back. His shoulders fit his shirt snugly, and that air of power and status surrounds him.

The moment the door shuts, I sigh heavily and decide to go find Kian. I hate this conflict between us. I don't waste time going the way Kian had left, and I find him standing on the balcony, the doors open with a cool wind blowing through them. His hands are braced on the marble rail, and my heart skips a beat at the very sight of him.

"Kian..."

# OUR LOVE

MORGANA

*H*E TURNS HIS HEAD slightly when I call him, but he has his walls up. I can't sense his emotions. I walk towards him, my heart squeezing painfully. I wrap my arms around his bare waist tightly from behind and rest my head against his back, relishing in the tingles that course through me like a storm I welcome.

"You are my world, Kian. I don't see life without you. I don't want a life without you... I don't want to live a day without you. I love you more than anything, so don't ever feel guilty for making me yours because even if you didn't do it to save my life, I would have wanted you to mark me anyway," I say. I can feel his heart racing, and my own is no less. He doesn't answer, and I feel a sting of hurt. "Kian... we love one another. I'm not meant to feel like you will shut me out at any time. I don't like this. You are the only one I will ever love, you or no one. You know that." I don't bother hiding the pain in my voice. I hate showing my vulnerable side, but I don't like the walls he built around himself.

Those words seem to get to him; he removes my arms from around him, turning to look at me, but rather than speaking, he pulls me against his chest, wrapping his arms around me tightly and burying his head in my neck. I curl my arms under his, placing my hands on his broad shoulders and closing my eyes.

"I didn't think… I never ever took into account what marking you meant."

My heart thuds. His words were so quiet I barely heard them. The pain I feel inside is ripping me up, and a tear trickles down my cheek.

"I know," I whisper. He tenses and pulls back, frowning as he stares into my face.

"Are you crying?" He asks, almost as if he is far too stunned to believe it.

"Of course not! I don't cry," I say, brushing my few stray tears away. His gaze softens, and he smirks, making my stomach flutter.

"Oh, yeah?" He asks, rubbing his finger along my damp cheek.

"Yeah," I say softly, staring into his gorgeous hazel eyes. Reaching up, I cup his face, brushing my finger along his stubble. "Kian… stop feeling guilty. It hurts seeing you like this, and I don't like getting sentimental," I pout.

"I literally cut your life short… you're the one person at the top of my fucking list to protect, yet I already took away your - "

"You are my life! Stop it, Kian! If you really want to make up for it, then don't waste even a moment… don't shut me out," I plead, unable to hide the pain when I say those last words. His eyes flash with guilt as he threads his fingers through my hair.

"I'm not shutting you out. I just fucking needed to control my own emotions," he says quietly, rubbing his thumb along my lips. "I'm sorry… I just fucking love you."

"I know, and I'm yours. You are the only one I want… and Thanatos, too," I add with a smile. I know him well enough to know that he'd complain if I didn't mention him.

"You really do fuel his ego," Kian says, his arm snaking around my waist, the other squeezing my ass as he presses me hard against him. I bite my lip, looking up at him seductively.

"Want me to fuel yours?" I ask, running my hand down his abs, my core clenching in anticipation. He smirks but shakes his head.

"No… tonight it's about you," he says huskily, not waiting for a reply as his lips crash against mine in a deep kiss.

Pleasure rushes through me, but it's the moment he lowers his walls, and the intensity of his emotions hits me hard: the desire, the possessiveness, the overwhelming affection and concern underlied by a hint of guilt and sadness. But above all, the deep love, appreciation, and need for me.

I moan against his lips as he kisses me with everything he has. My heart is fluttering, and I feel dizzy, but it's perfect. My arms tighten around his neck as I kiss him back with equal passion and love. He then lifts me up, bridal style, his lips not leaving mine as he carries me back through the archway to the bedroom and places me down in the middle of the bed before he climbs on top of me. I smile ever so softly, sinking into the soft mattress, but the moment his lips touch mine again, my back arches, pressing myself against him as that ache between my legs grows.

"I love you, sunshine," he whispers, kissing my neck before he tears off the shirt he had put on me earlier, his eyes darkening with approval as he looks down at me in nothing but the shimmery gown. "You're mine."

"I am yours," I agree seductively before yanking him towards me and kissing him hard. I am his, and I want him to always remember that no matter what, that will never change...

He tears my nightgown off me, kissing every inch of my body sensually. My body is begging for more, yet he takes his time. Even when I take his pants off, the most I am able to feel of him is his manhood rubbing against me at times. I reach down, stroking his shaft, and moan softly. God, do I want this inside of me.

He fondles my breasts, sucking hard on my neck, making me groan in pleasure.

"I told you, tonight is about you," he murmurs, grabbing the torn night-dress as he flips me onto my stomach, tying my wrists behind my back. "I know you can break free... but if you do... you won't get anything tonight." My core throbs, and I bite my lip.

"I'll behave," I pout, moaning when he runs his tongue down my spine. I shiver as pleasure tingles through me.

"Good. That's my girl," he whispers seductively, grabbing my hips as he lifts me up onto my knees and parts my legs. I gasp when he runs his tongue between my ass cheeks, pleasure shooting through me as that tongue works its magic.

"Fuck, Kian!" I moan, wriggling my ass.

He delivers a light tap, his tongue rimming my back entrance. I bite my lip, fighting back a moan. His tongue goes lower until it reaches my pussy, licking me teasingly before he moves back. If my hands weren't tied, I would have turned to look at him, but my body is supported by my shoulders and cheek that is pressed against the bedding. I gasp when he slips two fingers into me, sending another wave of pleasure through me.

"Oh, fuck! Kian…" I whimper as he slowly begins fucking me with them. I tense when I feel his little finger press against my back entrance.

"Relax…" He whispers, "Trust me…"

I do trust him. His finger circles my back entrance, slowly pressurising the area, and I bite my lip. His fingers that are slowly fucking me help take the edge off of the pain, the pleasure making me let out a wanton moan.

"Oh fuck baby…" I groan when his small finger finally penetrates me. The pressure is intense, and if I didn't know, I would have thought it was something a lot larger.

"That's it, baby girl, relax," he groans. I can tell he's turned on, despite not letting me even touch him. He kisses my ass, his hand fucking me slowly.

"Aah, god… Kian…. Fuck…"

It feels good, different but good. I like the feeling of being completely full. The forbidden pleasure makes me throb harder. I whimper at his slow assault.

"One day… I'm going to fuck this ass of yours," he growls huskily, making my stomach knot. I couldn't imagine him ever fitting, but the pleasure I feel makes my head fuzzy, and I can't think straight. He speeds up slowly, my moans getting louder.

"Faster, baby." I whimpered, "Fuck me, Kian. I want you."

He slips his fingers out of my pussy, yet his finger remains in my ass as he positions himself at my entrance.

"Oh, fuck…" I groan. The moment he thrusts into me, I cry out, my body taking a moment to adjust to his girth. I don't think I'll ever be prepared for how big he is. He slips his little finger out, replacing it with his index finger. I gasp when he slips it inside of me, the pain making me tense for a moment.

"Tell me how you want it," he orders huskily,

"Hard and fast," I whimper. He taps my ass in approval.

"That's my girl," he growls before he begins fucking me, one hand holding my bound wrists as he speeds up, giving it to me hard and fast. His finger moves faster inside of me, along with his cock that is buried inside of me.

The pleasure is inexplicable. My whines of pleasure are loud, and I sound horny as I beg for him to fuck me harder. I can't even recognise myself. My moans are loud and horny, but I don't care.

I feel myself nearing when he tugs me up by my hair, pulling me onto my knees as he continues to fuck me. His other hand squeezes my boobs hard before he begins rubbing my clit. I spread my legs, whimpering as pleasure erupts inside of me, my orgasm tearing through me like a huge tidal wave, and I faintly hear myself scream his name as my juices coat my inner thighs. His arm wraps around my waist, supporting me as I tremble from the aftershock. He slips his finger out of my ass, making me gasp. He squeezes it gently before giving it another light tap and wrapping his hand around my neck.

"Fuck, baby girl…" His moves become faster, rougher, and with a few more thrusts, he comes, groaning against my ear. "Fuck!" Kian growls, pulling out. I realise he had come half inside of me, his seed mixing with my own release. "Shit, I'm sorry…"

"It's okay…" I whisper, thinking he always pulls out… I turn, looking at him, curiosity at his actions that I never questioned now filling my mind. "Why are you worried?" He looks at me, cupping my face with one hand as he presses his lips to mine.

"We are at war… if you end up pregnant, it will put you both at more risk." I feel the worry and fear from him, and I smile gently.

"One time won't get me pregnant. Us vampires don't get pregnant so easily," I assure him as he lays us down, untying my wrists. I locked them around his neck and kissed his lips.

"I don't want to rush you," he says quietly, cupping my chin and kissing me deeply. We break apart, and I bite my lip.

"Don't worry so much," I say. "If you ask me, you're just scared that perhaps there's a little Morgana in the works, and she'll make your life just as much hell as I do." For the first time in our time together, an actual smile crosses his face and remains. His eyes soften as he caresses my cheek.

"That would actually be perfect…"

My heart skips a beat, and I realise, despite his cold exterior, Kian wants a family, and I would be the one to give him that. Is it wrong to secretly hope that maybe, just maybe, I will get pregnant soon?

"I love you, my little she-devil."

"I love you too, baby," I whisper, cupping his face as I kiss him once more…

Last night had been magical. Something about just letting our emotions out felt... special. We are both strong-minded and strong-willed; for us to just let our fears and thoughts out like that... well, it isn't something we often do. I guess, unknowingly, Orrian did us a favour.

This morning, a maid brought us food and ran us a bath. We bathed together, and I won't deny that we made love once more. Once we had eaten, gotten dressed, and finally left our suite, we were led to Orrian's office, or what looked like a huge meeting room. Like the rest of the castle, it is vast, all made of marble and white stone that seems to shimmer. An oval table with many chairs stands in the middle.

Orrian himself is there, seated at the head of the table, dressed in all white with his crown set on his head. Today his hair is braided fully, with only a few strands left out to frame his face.

"Morgana, Alpha Kian, I hope you slept well," he says emotionlessly.

"Yes, we did."

I lace my fingers with Kian's. He gives a curt nod and motions for us to take a seat. I take the seat next to Kian, ready to put my request on the table.

"I know you didn't come here for old times' sake. So would you like to share how I can help you? Although I have an idea," he says, looking at us.

"It is I who has asked Kian to come here. As you know, my brother has joined hands with the Fae Kingdom... and they have made it clear that they are ready to destroy Clair De Lune. I know we have not spoken in years, but you once told me you would always be there if the time arose. I know perhaps it's cheeky of me to request this, but for the children of our kingdom, for our men and women who will surely lose their lives if this war takes place... will you help us in this war? We reached out to Azrael, but he refused to back down. We were meant to be at peace since I was taken to Claire De Lune, but he has simply turned his back on that treaty," I explain, my anger blazing. Kian's hand on my leg calms me slightly, yet I am still angry, unable to calm the raging storm within me.

"I was willing to look past the murder of my father, which was at the hands of the vampires, to make things better for the people of both kingdoms, but they completely refused. I am putting my pride aside and asking you, as the king of Clair De Lune, for your help," Kian says. Despite his words, the power radiating off him is a clear reminder that he is indeed a king, one who is willing to ask for help for his people. An honourable king.

"At what cost? What are you willing to give up for our help?" Orrian asks, his calculating eyes on Kian. Kian's eyes blaze, yet when he speaks, his voice is still level.

"Anything but my people and my queen," he says icily. Orrian smirks ever so lightly, yet there is no humour in it.

"Then what can you offer us?"

"How about you put it on the fucking table what you want instead of going around in damn circles?" Kian suggests coldly. Typical of Orrian to do that… Kian, on the other hand, is very straightforward.

"Nothing… I promised Morgana to help her, and it's clear that she sees Clair De Lune as her home," Orrian replies, his voice emotionless and cold. I can feel Kian's intense gaze on me when I stand up, bracing my hands on the table.

"So then… will the arrows of Elandorr fly for Clair De Lune?" I ask quietly, looking into those icy grey eyes of his.

"I am not yet king, but as the crown prince, I command thirty percent of the elven army. My men and I will ride for the queen of Clair De Lune and victory." His words make my eyes fly open in surprise. He himself is going to participate?

"And if ever Elandorr needs the king of Clair De Lune to help you in any way, we will be there," Kian offers. Both men look at each other, and Orrian nods. It's clear Kian is not going to accept his help without promising something in return.

"I am glad we have got this sorted. Tonight, Father has organised a party to welcome you both, the first werewolf king and queen of Clair De Lune to step into this kingdom. He knows you are friends of mine… I would appreciate it if we kept it at that," Orrian says quietly.

"Obviously, it's the way I'd prefer it too," Kian says, his voice cold and passive. Orrian gives a curt nod.

I'm glad this was sorted. Thirty percent of the army is a large number and will help greatly. As for Orrian not wanting his father to know about us, I like it like that. After all, I don't want more conflict. Besides, I only want to be known for what I am. Kian's queen. Orrian's and my relationship had been a passing secret and would remain that.

"What are the plans? Do you have a battle strategy?" Orrian asks Kian.

"My men say the Fae army is gathering. Within a month, they will move in. My men are also preparing, leaving some squads to protect the people with the enchanters. The way they will attack is through the western woods, using the trees as cover, not the ones on this side. It also makes it harder for us, considering the passage through that area is hard to surpass. So, I was thinking if we get there first… we take the forest as our own and meet them there," Kian explains, his eyes calculating. His hand once again laces with mine, resting on my thigh.

"A good plan, but you will have to move faster. I think you mean these forests?" Orrian pushes a map over to Kian, who cocks a brow.

"It is interesting that you have such detailed maps of my kingdom," he comments, glancing up at the elven man.

"We are always prepared. Knowledge is power."

"Yeah, that forest," Kian says, frowning slightly.

"Then how about we block it off? Divert the battle to this open plain. If we take this stance, then they have to travel through the mountain pass, narrowing their entrance. Less troops at once," Orrian suggests, tapping a certain area of the map.

I listen. I have to admit the men know what they're talking about. I nod, understanding perfectly well how that would give us an advantage.

"Unclaimed land…"

"The best place for a battle to take place," Orrian says. I pulled the map closer, tilting my head.

"Here. This is where we will wait." I tap a finger on the map. Both men look at me curiously. It's just an open area, not far from the narrow mountain pass.

"Why there?" Orrian asks.

"Because the arch of Olen is there," I explain, mentioning the arch of pure ice in the mountain pass.

"Don't tell me you want to target that…." Kian says keenly. I smile in approval that he understands.

"That is exactly what I'm saying. We bring it down. It will help us kill off many at the same time." Kian smirks and nods.

"Impressive. For once, you are thinking ahead before acting," he mocks lightly, despite the look of approval on his face. I roll my eyes.

"That's what you're there for, to fix things after I mess them up. What's the need to think when you do enough for us both?" I reply airily.

"I guess that's fucking true," Kian agrees, cupping the back of my neck as his lips meet mine in a passionate kiss. We're the perfect power couple;

I'm not going to deny that. We break apart, my heart still pounding from his touch as Kian gives me one of his sexy smirks.

"We will set out first thing in the morning. When should we expect you?" Kian asks.

"Two weeks. I will have my men ready within a fortnight."

"I will let my own men know to expect you. I will keep your assistance a secret. I do not want the enemy to know." Orrian nods.

"Perhaps us staying hidden until the battle might work out better."

"Orrian… if you take your army… won't it weaken you inside Elandorr?" I ask suddenly. I know his other brothers want the throne, and each holds a portion of the army, with Orrian having the most. He raises an eyebrow.

"Then let's hope that I don't lose many," he says, clearly unphased. I frown but nod. No matter what, I would be grateful to him. We discuss the path and how this will work when I frown at something Kian just said.

"Why will it take us over two weeks to return home?" I ask.

"Because we will go to the Sanguine Empire," he says, shocking me, and Orrian, too.

"Why?" I ask, staring at him.

"To speak to your brother, once and for all. Let's see if we can prevent this war… they are your people, too," he says quietly. My heart thrums loudly as I stare at him. His words make me smile faintly.

"I never knew my handsome Alpha could be so thoughtful," I tease.

"I had no fucking idea either," he replies coldly, and I can't help but giggle at that. He really is perfect!

"Well, I think we have our plan in place. We will discuss the details after lunch," Orrian adds.

"Perfect," Kian says.

I smile. Tonight's dinner will be the last light-hearted fun we are going to have in a while, so I will make the most of it.

# THE BEAUTY OF THE MOON

KIAN

*I* HAD REFUSED TO WEAR the elven-style clothes; they are a little too fucking feminine for me. I choose to opt for the most suitable pants and shirt I had packed. I did accept some boots and a belt, though. I don't need a crown or any extravagant crap to make it clear that I'm the Alpha King. I'm wearing a black shirt, black pants, and boots that are dark brown.

I'm a little annoyed that Morgana had been pulled away from me to get ready, or rather, I had been removed from our bedroom. Two hours have passed, and I have not seen her still. I'm ready and pacing the hall, with none other than the pretty boy as company, who is obviously in all white. Maybe I'm being a little fucking petty, but, yeah, I'm not going to wear the same colour as him. I look at him, having a question that has been at the front of my mind, and one I may not have the chance to ever ask again...

"What is it, Alpha Kian? You certainly wish to ask me something," Orrian says, almost knowingly, that emotionless expression set on his damn face.

**I don't like the fucker,** Thanatos growls.

**That makes two of us,** I reply before raising an eyebrow at Orrian.

"You clearly still have feelings for her... so why did you let her go? Morgana told me that you both ended things on good terms. Both agreed that parting was best."

"We did because she didn't see herself as queen. I offered to run away with her... but she refused that option, too, saying I needed to go back to my kingdom. I realised then that her feelings were not strong enough. She was looking for an excuse," he explains quietly. I look at him sharply.

"So, you accepted that?" I ask. I don't get it. When you love someone greatly, don't you fight with everything you have for them?

"When you love someone that deeply, you realise that the greatest thing you can do for their happiness is let them go. I hate to admit it, yet the Morgana I knew was nothing like the one who loves you so deeply now. I can see it in her every move, her every gesture, and her every gaze. I'm sure you could confine her to your palace, yet as long as she has you, she will be happy," he says, and this time, despite his best efforts, the bitterness seeps into his voice. It's then that I fucking realise that there really is nothing that could come in between Morgana and me. "I let her go because I realised her love for me was not strong enough... but I still had hope that one day things could be different. Clearly not... she has moved on and has found true happiness."

"Yeah, she has." A tense silence falls between us, and just then, two elven women step out of the bedroom, bowing to us.

"Your Highness, your queen is ready," one of the women announces, a proud smile on her face as she looks at me.

I glance at the door, my heart racing a little, before I give a curt nod and walk towards the bedroom. I want to see her.

Pushing open the door, I stop in my tracks when I see her standing there. Her back is to me as I slowly take in what she is wearing. A sheer net dress with silver beads, gems, and embroidered patterns along the bodice and over her sexy ass seems to be the only thing keeping her modesty. It has a corset back that leaves part of her back bare and makes her tiny waist look even smaller. I can see her legs through the thin fabric, and there is a huge trail that spreads beneath her. She looks breathtaking, and I haven't even seen her completely. Her hair is up in an elegant updo. It's at that moment that she turns.

**Beautiful...** Thanatos murmurs in awe.

I know he is lost for words, as am I.

Like the back, the embroidery mainly covers her breasts, waist, and stomach, dipping down slightly. Underneath, she wears a skin-coloured satin bodysuit. Her cleavage is partially on show, and a soft silver shimmer covers her body, adding a tempting glow to her already flawless figure. Her lips are lighter than her usual deep red, yet her make-up is smoky and dark. A few tendrils of her hair are curled, framing her face. A silver diamond necklace wraps around her neck, and matching earrings hang from her ears. A crown sits on her head, and she wears a few rings that sparkle when she moves her slender hands. Her glittering nails also capture my attention when she lifts her skirts slightly, turning her body. Ethereal and fucking ravishing... she looks out of this world, almost unreal...

She's always beautiful, no matter what she does, wears or doesn't wear, especially when we make love... but seeing her dressed up like this... she feels like a dream that, if I reach out to her, she may just vanish.

"I never knew the power and beauty of the moon could be challenged so easily..." I say huskily, struggling to find my fucking voice. I clear my throat, but luckily she is admiring me and doesn't tease me. Her eyes finally meet mine, and she smiles faintly.

"I am, after all, the Alpha King's mate. If not I, then who else can challenge the beauty of the moon?" She asks airily before laughing. That laugh... that fucking tinkle of happiness that makes me feel fucking crazy inside. I close the gap between us, my hands snaking around her waist and pulling her against me.

"Fucking right, no one can, but tonight even the moon holds nothing in comparison. You look... beautiful doesn't cut it..." There really aren't any words. She tilts her head, smiling softly as she gazes into my eyes.

"I've been called beautiful all my life... but to hear it from you... it's something so different. More so... your eyes speak so much deeper," she says softly, her smile fading as she leans up, pressing her plush soft lips against mine. Delicious sparks rush through us, and I tighten my hold on her. Our lips move against each other's in perfect synchrony. We were, after all, made for one another...

I break away when I feel myself getting fucking hard, my eyes flashing as Thanatos pushes himself to the forefront. I allow him to, knowing he wants to compliment her.

"You look ravishing, little mate, and it will be my pleasure to help you undress tonight," he says, his deeper voice overlaying my own. Morgana smiles.

"I like the idea of that," she says with a wink.

Thanatos growls, yanking her back into my arms and kissing her once more, this time with a deeper hunger and thirst for none other than our mate...

A short while later, we head to the grand hall where this party is being hosted. I don't often feel fucking short, but in this throng of people, I'm pretty average in height, with a third of the men being taller than me. They are all as pale as one another, yet not as light as Morgana. The hair on the elves ranges from light brown to almost white. Morgana and I stand out with her dark hair and my dark skin, but I think I like it. We aren't one of them anyway.

The king has pure white hair, and his eyes are light green. He is a little taller than I am and is seated upon his throne emotionlessly. It is rumoured that he has been king for over one thousand and eight hundred years. How did he do it? Do they never tire of life? Is immortality a gift or a curse?

**A gift! Imagine being immortal and fucking mate every day forever,** Thanatos says. My chest squeezes at that, the reminder that she won't live forever...

**We'll be together after we die,** I tell him softly, turning to Morgana, who had been busy looking around the luxurious sculptures that are spread across the hall. That beautiful smile graces her lips.

"What is it?" She asks, placing her hand on my chest.

"Let's make the most of the night."

I pull her into my arms, about to kiss her, when I feel the presence of the king himself approach. Morgana and I both turn. I lower my head ever so slightly, maintaining eye contact, and the king does the same, whilst Morgana lowers her head graciously, the jewels in her ears tinkling under the light.

"King Kian. I never once thought that your people would even associate with us."

"Isn't it the elves who stay to themselves?" I ask, raising an eyebrow. He nods as if thinking about this for the first time.

"Indeed, perhaps. It seems my son has more plans for the future of our kingdom. You two are friends. Perhaps you can advise him to choose a woman for himself…" he suggests, glancing at Morgana. "Although… I'm surprised that a werewolf chose a vampire."

"Who said I didn't choose a werewolf first?" Morgana asks, raising an eyebrow. I smirk slightly. "Race is of no importance, Your Majesty. If the bond and love are there, then what more does a person need? I'm sure Orrian is just waiting for the right person."

"Perhaps… sometimes, more than choice, you need to see what is best for the kingdom," the king says, looking at an elven woman who is talking to a few others, a crown upon her head. She is dressed pretty extravagantly, and I realise he probably wants this woman for his son. Well, good luck, although the fucking fossil needs to get a move on…

**Haha, fossil,** Thanatos snickers.

"A couple with a strong bond and connection is the most important thing for a kingdom, Your Majesty. Trust me," Morgana says, her arm curled around my forearm and her breast pressed against my arm ever so temptingly. My eyes dip to her creamy boobs. I can't wait for tonight.

"I can't agree more. At one point, I was planning on taking a queen for the sake of it, yet there was no approval or excitement there… but with Morgana… I knew she'd do great things," I admit, looking at my woman with such pride that I realise you really couldn't just settle for anyone but the one you love.

**She will do great things… especially with Mini-Kian,** Thanatos adds, not very fucking helpfully, as all I can picture now is Morgana on her knees. I swear, I do not want to have a fucking hard-on right now.

"Very true… perhaps I am rushing him," the king says.

"Considering your life span… I'd say yeah. You probably are," I agree, making Morgana smile. The king nods, giving me a narrowed look.

"Well, enjoy the feast. For someone who is so young, you seem wise," he says, gesturing to the hall.

"We don't live as long, so we've got to get a move on with the time we have. Thank you, not only for this banquet but for allowing us into your kingdom and treating us well," I say seriously.

I'm not a trusting person, and I'm excellent at reading people, yet surprisingly, despite the prince's past with Morgana and the fact that this is a reserved person, I know I can trust them. When the war is over, I will surely pay Orrian back.

"Let's dance," Morgana whispers in my ear, her lips sucking on the lobe of my ear. I resist a groan. I look at her, cocking a brow.

"Anything to see that gorgeous body of yours move," I growl huskily, wrapping my arm tightly around her tiny waist and kissing her hard.

She gasps, locking her arms around my neck as I bend her backwards, kissing her passionately and not caring who is around. One hand cups her thigh, and the feel of those delicious sparks courses through me as we kiss. I let her up, smirking at how shocked and flustered she looks, one hand on her crown.

"Wow…" she says breathlessly, her cheeks coated with a faint blush. Well, it seems I can catch my little she-devil off guard, too.

"Now let's dance," I say, leading her to the dance floor where other elven couples are dancing gracefully. "I think they are a little outdated on dancing," I murmur, making her giggle.

"Dare we turn the heat up a few notches?" She whispers, moving her body sensually against mine.

"Sounds like a plan," I reply seductively.

I really have to fucking focus not to get turned on. I smirk, spinning her out before pulling her back against my chest, my hand on her stomach, the other running down her arm as she rubs sensually against me, making pleasure fucking rush through me. We get a few looks, but really, I don't give a fuck, too lost in the goddess before me. I spin her around, and she lets go of my hand, twirling, before she runs into my arms once more. I lift her, spinning her around, unable to keep the smile from my lips, seeing that happiness on her face. The lights above glitter off her clothing and jewellery as I slowly lower her, moving slowly to the music.

*I'll fucking give anything to keep that smile on your face. I promise to keep you happy…* Even knowing what tomorrow and the following few weeks mean… I will cherish this fucking moment…

*I love you.*

# A Queen

MORGANA

THE FOLLOWING DAY, AFTER breakfast, we set out before the sun is even up in the sky, having packed more supplies and a good number of antidotes just in case. We are given two horses, although Kian isn't too keen on it. Orrian says it's better for us to ride them until they tire and then reserve energy. Agreeing it would help a little, we take the horses.

I am dressed in pale grey pants, a fitted long-sleeved top, and a hooded cloak. Despite them being from the elves, we made sure they just looked simple, with no elven thread-work on them, not wanting to let my brother know where we were coming from. Kian, on the other hand, refused to wear anything of theirs, and I have to admit it's rather amusing when his ego gets in the way.

We are now at the borders of Elandorr, and although Orrian will see us again in a few weeks, he stubbornly wants to come to see us off.

"Thank you to you and Elandorr for everything," I say, looking down at him as I hold the reins of my horse in one hand.

"I wish you all the best on your next venture," Orrian says, getting off his horse and walking over to mine. I glance at Kian. hoping he doesn't get irked, before I look down at Orrian and raise an eyebrow.

"We don't need luck, but let's see how welcoming Azrael is." I glance at the seven men who flank Orrian. I had learned that these are some of his most trusted men.

I'm still shocked that Kian wants to try to help the Sanguine Empire for my sake, but it only shows that he is a true king and one who deserves the title he holds.

"It is the first time you stepped into Elandorr, and I fear it may be the last. The next time we meet, it will be as allies on the battlefield... you will be the queen of Clair De Lune, and I will simply be your ally..." he says. This time, I can see the emotion in those eyes of his. His sadness, wistfulness... the eyes of a man who had lost so much.

A sharp wind blows past us, sending both his hair and mine flying, but we don't break eye contact. He needs this closure, so I will allow him to say what he needs. We can do at least that much in return for all he is offering us.

"An ally and still a friend," I offer quietly. He nods, giving me a smile that holds no happiness.

"I know you won't appreciate me saying this, but you will always be my Moonlight. I want you to know that, although I can tell that you are content and truly happy," he says quietly, looking at Kian. It may have been a few decades ago, but it's clear that Orrian had held hope that one day I would come to him.

"Let me go, Orrian, from your heart. Make space for someone more, someone who can return the love that you have to offer. I was never yours," I say softly, wishing he finds the same love that I hold for Kian. He looks down and nods.

"I once thought you were the one for me. Perhaps we could be, but you weren't mine. It's true. You never were mine. I can see that Kian is the one who has given you happiness that I never could. Goodbye, my Moonlight... for the next time we meet, I will not address you as such." I nod and offer him a gentle smile.

"Thank you. In decades to come, you will remember the woman who was just a passing moment of your life and laugh that you ever thought you could never love again because I believe that you will find her. The one who becomes your all," I tell him quietly, and I mean it.

"Or him," Kian adds with a cold smirk. Orrian raises an eyebrow, and I look at Kian.

"Well, whichever works. Orrian is rather pretty."

"Thank you very much. At least you can admit that I am good-looking." Orrian frowns slightly.

"There's a difference," Kian replies with an antagonising smirk. I think I see the faint glimmer of a smile on Orrian's face as he and Kian grip each other's forearms and shake before Orrian moves back. "See you soon."

Orrian nods, and, with a final smile at him, I turn away. Kian and I nudge our horses into a trot, passing through the veil and beyond the borders of Elandorr. The wind rushes through my hair as I nudge the horse into a gallop, making sure to stay ahead of Kian, only for him to take the challenge and try to outdo me. However, I am definitely the better rider.

"Seems like I'm better at horse riding than you are, my love," I taunt with a small smile on my lips.

"Well, I don't really see the need for me to know how to ride. Thanatos already finds this insulting. We don't ride other animals when we can fucking shift," Kian says, turning to me. Our eyes meet, and I smirk.

"Well, just admit that I am better at it," I say haughtily.

"You are, I won't fucking deny that, but then again, you're pretty good at riding regardless of what it is," he replies with a smirk, looking me over. "But don't let it get to your head, sunshine." I roll my eyes, despite my stomach fluttering at his words. "Cat got your tongue?"

"Just a wolf," I reply in the same tone before I become thoughtful. "Kian... you once said it was a vampire who killed your father. How can you be so sure?" He frowns deeply. Our horses are now at a steady trot, and the mood suddenly becomes serious.

"I witnessed my father being killed, but I was helpless. I saw the vampire... Father was fucking confused, saying he didn't understand when all he wanted was peace... but the vampire didn't care." His voice is cold and filled with a burning rage.

My heart is pounding just listening to him. Unlike me, having assumed that a werewolf killed my dad, he knows it was a vampire. I reach over, placing my hand over his comfortingly, sensing the excruciating pain through the bond, although I knew he was trying to mask it.

"You saw it?" I ask, shocked. Kian looks ahead and nods.

"He had released a poison in the air, and I remember breathing in whatever crap he had concocted, barely able to walk or keep my eyes open. It's all a haze, or I would have caught his scent. I just lay there, watching him kill my father, slowly... painfully... as if it was entertainment for him. My father signalled to me to stay the fuck down, and you know what? I did. Like a fucking useless coward." He is angry and even disgusted with himself.

"Kian… you did what was right." I say softly, "You were in no shape to fight."

"He tried to use his Alpha command on me, but when that didn't work, he warned me that if I got up, it would be the end of the entire kingdom," he continues. I know it's hard for him to say. I stay silent, my heart aching for him. "I would never have tried for the fucking title of king, but my father had wanted me to, saying that Cain could not become king, that he was not fit for it. All I wanted was to just live happily… but he reminded me of his wish as he was pinned to the ground, unable to move. I simply watched, watched my father die…"

"Pinned him down…" I muse. Does he mean with powers? But that's rare…

"There is something about that vampire that I'll never forget," he says quietly, his jaw clenched.

"What is it? Maybe we can find him," I ask softly.

"The colour of his eyes. There is only one vampire whose eyes are as dark as that killer's," he says quietly, now turning to me. Our eyes meet, and I understand his silent statement. As mine…

Dark… mine are the darkest. There is no one in the Sanguine Empire whose eyes are as dark as mine…

"There's no one… not even Azrael," I murmur.

"I did take a look when I came. None of the officials had that colour eyes, only you, but the vampire was a man," he says, frowning.

"I'm sorry… it must have been hard to look at me." He cocks an eyebrow.

"When you're that fucking hot? You're rather easy on the eyes, although my cock gets hard at the sight of you," he says, now smirking arrogantly. I raise an eyebrow.

"Oh? Well… that's good, because I like Mini-Kian being hard for me," I giggle. He frowns at me, and I know for a fact that Thanatos must be laughing.

"The two of you fucking annoy me," Kian growls.

"Yet you love us," I remind him, and just like that, the mood lifts. "Race you to those hills!" I shout, snapping my reins and galloping off ahead.

"That's cheating, little she-devil!" Kian growls. I laugh as the wind rushes past me, the sound of galloping hooves loud in my ear.

"Then you can punish me later," I tease, not slowing down.

He's hot on my heels, and I can't stop the smile that graces my lips. Yes, we are going to the Sanguine Empire, not something that I have a good feeling about… but with Kian by my side, we have got this.

I shriek in alarm when he suddenly catches up, grabbing the reins of my horse and pulling it to a stop. I hold on as my horse neighs, rearing on its hind legs. He smirks in victory, grabbing my elbow and flipping me onto his horse. I cling to him like a ridiculous damsel in distress, my heart pounding at his wild move. Yet… the moment those lips of his meet mine, I forget everything else because, in his arms, I'm a mess, losing myself in his perfect kiss…

It takes us two nights to reach the Sanguine Empire and infiltrate the border patrol, making our way through to the palace undetected. I know all the ins and outs of this place, it's not been hard at all.

We are now in my old bedroom. To my surprise, it's well dusted and kept clean, yet there was no one using it, nor have my things been removed…

"It's strange," I whisper, looking around my room. The nostalgic memories of me spending time in this room return strongly. Oh, how it felt like decades ago…

"What is?" Kian asks, staring at my wall of weapons. "This wall is impressive."

"Thanks. I selected that dagger to kill you with from here," I smirk, my smile fading when I realise it had been placed back on the wall where it belonged. Weird…

My brother had wanted me gone, I'm surprised he didn't burn everything I ever owned. So why is this room kept like this?

My heart skips a beat when I realise who must have kept it. Uncle.

"What's strange, my beautiful blood rose?" Kian murmurs, wrapping his arms around me from behind. I press myself against him, feeling his package against my ass. Is it wrong that I want him all over again? His lips meet my neck, and I shiver in pleasure.

"That this room is exactly like I left it," I say softly, sighing at his touch. Kian's hand runs up my waist, his fingers brushing my breast, and my stomach flutters, sending that throbbing need to my core.

"Perhaps someone here cares. Your uncle tried to plead for your life after all back then…"

"Hmm… that's true…" I moan as his hand travels down my stomach and massages me between my legs. Despite the fact that I'm wearing pants, I still feel myself ache in need of him. "Fuck, Kian…" He chuckles sexily, moving away.

"As much as I want to fuck you… we need to get moving," he says, smirking slightly. I cock a brow, looking him over.

"I expect you to make this up to me… or I'm sure Thanatos will do it for you," I say, although I don't think I can handle Thanatos until after the war. He's exhausting in a very good way. I achieve what I wanted, seeing Kian frown, much to my satisfaction. "Love you, Thanatos," I say in a sing-song voice. Kian's eyes flash as he struggles to come out, but Kian wins this round, pushing him back as his eyes return to hazel.

"I'll be the one to make it up to you," he growls, yanking me roughly into his arms, just the way I like it. My chest hits his, and my breathing becomes heavy as I bite my lip.

"Good," I say, running my finger over his lips. He bites onto it, sucking it gently, and I feel him throb against me.

"You're a tease," he growls.

"I am, yet you love it." I reach down and cup his package, satisfied when he bites back a groan.

"That I fucking do," he says before he moves back forcefully. "I'll stay hidden. You go, pretend you came alone… get a scope of what's going through his mind and then we shall see what to do next… but are you sure you want to go alone?"

"I'm sure. It's better this way. I know Azrael, he'll just get aggressive if you come in like this," I say, kissing his lips before I walk to my door. Time to face him…

Kian won't be mentioned at all. If things go as planned, no one will even know he was here in the palace. That might just trigger this war even more…

I stay hidden, making my way towards Azrael's office. He's usually there at this time. I just hope he's not entertaining another random woman. I wrinkle my nose, remembering his lewd behaviour, and glance at the man who is standing guard at his door. I quickly hide behind a pillar as two servant ladies walk by.

"The little prince is so cute."

"He is… what a fine young king he will be…"

Their voices fade away, leaving my heart feeling a little excited. A prince? Anastasia gave birth! I'm an aunt! The urge to forget everything and go see the baby almost takes over, but I pout and look back towards the office door. I have to do this first… stupid Azrael. I don't want to see his ugly face, I'd rather see my nephew's…

He really does have too much confidence in his security, but I know the exact locations of the guards… I guess that's why it is so easy to get past them. Focusing on a gold-jewelled vase that stands down the hall, I raise my hand and push it over with a blast of power, sending it toppling to the ground with a loud crash. I flinch at how loud it is.

As predicted, the guard outside Azrael's office door rushes to check, and I quickly rush to the door, slipping inside and shutting the door ever so silently behind me. I let out a small breath of relief silently, turning and looking around the huge office. I can hear Azrael muttering to himself, and it's clear he is alone. No women, perfect.

I walk silently through the large arch and towards where I can hear him. The familiar sight of my brother's frowning face comes into view. His hair is slightly longer, his displeasure clear as day as he paces in front of his desk, running his fingers through his hair, which is surprisingly missing the crown that he wears so proudly.

The tables are covered with maps, and so is the floor… I frown. Why does he look almost concerned?

"That… fool…" he grumbles, pouring himself a glass of blood and splashing it over the maps. Smiling slyly, I sneak up on him, leaning in towards his ear.

"Boo," I whisper.

"Aaah!" He screams, dropping his glass as he jumps away from me, raising his hand to attack. I burst out laughing, stepping away from his reach.

"Missed me, dear brother?" I ask mockingly, staring at Azrael, who looks like he has just seen a ghost. He places a hand on his heart, looking me over.

"Morgana… is it really you?" He asks, narrowing his eyes as he steps closer and, to my surprise, cups my face with one hand. "You're real…" He lets go of me as if I am dirt and wipes his hand on his pants. I, in turn, wipe my cheek. God knows where his hands have been.

"Of course I am real. Yet you're acting weird," I say, stepping back.

"Obviously… I mean… how, how are you here?" He asks suspiciously.

"I have my ways, but care to tell me why you broke the peace treaty? When you yourself gave me away for the sake of it?" I counter, frowning coldly. He scoffs,

"Me? It is they who turned their back on me. Clearly, you gave him such a hard time that he didn't think it was worth holding up the bargain! Couldn't you have done that much for your people and spread your legs for him like the good little whore that you are?" There's the idiot I know. I cross my arms, glaring at him venomously.

"I am no whore... are you really blaming me for your own faults? Ki-Alpha Kian sent you a treaty to even consider trade with this kingdom, but - "

"And you believed him? He did nothing of the sort," Azrael replies with contempt. "I'm still concerned about how you got in here. Was it Uncle who allowed you in?"

"I snuck in; your security is not absolute," I spit.

"Well, you are no longer welcome here. You could not even protect your people, and now you come back for shelter? So, did the king no longer want you? Did he grow bored, perhaps? Did he kick you out? Whatever the reason, you are no longer part of this kingdom!" He turns his back to me.

"Do not turn your back on me, Azrael! I have come to offer you the hand of friendship with Clair De Lune one final time. For your people, consider it and withhold from this war." He scoffs resentfully, turning his head towards me.

"And what are you? The Alpha King's little messenger?" He spits, looking at me as if I'm lower than the dirt beneath his feet. I raise my eyebrow, grabbing hold of the collar of my cloak and shirt and pulling it down.

"No, I am the Alpha King's fated mate and the Queen of Clair De Lune," I inform him, my voice strong and powerful. My eyes blaze as I stare him down, baring my neck to him to allow Azrael to see the mark of the Alpha King upon my neck. "You are speaking to a queen, so if I were you, I'd show some respect."

# SOMETHING AT PLAY

MORGANA

ZRAEL'S EYES WIDEN, AND he stares at me in shock before the familiar suspicion and anger replace it.

"Mated to one of those beasts… how Father is probably turning in his grave," he says with disgust.

I close my eyes, trying to calm down. I have to, for our people and for Kian, who s doing this for me… for *my* kind.

"I am here to warn you to pick the right side. Countless men will fall if you continue on this path. Azrael, if not for me, do it for Father, whom we both loved." *Or so I hope…*

Focusing my mind on penetrating his, the familiar shrill sound fills my head before I manage to hear a glimpse of his thoughts.

*Father… I wish he were here… he would have known what to do…*

I frown and continue, "For our people and for your son… make this kingdom something he can be proud of. If you join hands with us, we are willing to give this kingdom the food and supplies it needs," I say softly.

"Then why refuse all my mail? I have sent several letters! I let my pride go and pleaded with that monster to uphold his words!" Anger blazes in his eyes, and yet I can't ignore his insulting Kian.

"He is far from a monster, Azrael. He is a king, one that you can only hope to be." I say coldly, "As for your messages, we received one with your seal saying you refused the offer we sent and that you have joined hands with the Fae!"

"That's not even possible! Only I have access to - "

The door opens, and Uncle Malachi stands there, his eyes wide.

"Morgana!" He calls, his face softening and concern flooding his features as he runs over to me, pulling me into his arms tightly. "Thank the gods you are okay!"

"Uncle…" I smile, wrapping my arms around him tightly. His heart is pounding, and he kisses the top of my head several times. "I heard from the guards that the old western small gate lock was tampered with, and there's only one person I know that used and fiddled with that exit!" My eyes widen. Uncle knew I used to sneak out? I'm surprised, but I'm glad he never mentioned it to anyone.

"So you knew I used to sneak out?" I ask, smiling up at him. He smiles warmly and nods, cupping my face.

"I knew you were safe, so I saw no harm in it," he says, stroking my hair. "How have you been, child? I'm so sorry I didn't come after you…"

"There was nothing you could have done if you had," I say quietly.

He sighs, "Well, I'm glad you are here. Is everything okay? With the war going on, I am glad you are back home and safe. Have you drunk something? Rested?"

"You two are a waste of my time. Leave," Azrael orders with irritation. I ignore him and smile at Uncle Malachi.

"Yes, I have had a drink,"

"Then sleep, it's late," Uncle says lovingly.

I can't argue right now, even if I want to discuss this more. I think I need to tell Kian about the letters…

"I will head to bed, but we need to talk tomorrow." I say, "It's very important." Uncle nods.

"Of course," he says, kissing my head. "Your room is as you have left it, Anastasia's orders." Azrael frowns.

"She just hoped you'd return someday."

"Well, my sister-in-law is far more useful than you are," I state, making a mental note to thank her.

Uncle walks me to my room. I'm about to tell him about Kian, wanting him to meet him, but, remembering what Kian had said, I don't. *Trust no one and stick to the plan.* The man is far too careful, but the walls have ears, too. We need to be cautious, I guess.

Bidding Uncle farewell, I lock my bedroom door after me, looking around the room in search of Kian.

"Kian?" I whisper.

I turn, seeing him step out of the bathroom area. I walk over to him, wrapping my arms around his neck as we kiss deeply.

"So, anything?" He asks, not letting go of me.

I quickly fill him in with everything that had occurred with Azrael. He doesn't speak, listening with a frown on his handsome face. Now, letting go of me and crossing his muscular arms over that firm chest of his, his face holds that calculating look that means he's thinking of something.

"Wait, say that again?"

"Hmm? That uncle is the sweetest?"

"No, how he knew that we snuck in…"

"Oh, he knew my old antics. He's happy I'm back. I actually want you to meet him, officially. He is the kindest soul, and that's saying something for us vampires," I say, amused, but Kian doesn't seem to find it as warming as I did.

"Your uncle, what's his story?" He asks.

"Story?"

"No children? Wife? Woman? Anything?" I frown thoughtfully.

"I… he never got married… never found his beloved," I answer sadly.

"So, someone as nice as him never settled for anyone. Is he a player then?" I raise an eyebrow.

"No…"

"Seems odd."

"Kian… are you actually thinking my uncle may not be what he seems?"

"I don't know. The fact he knew that you snuck in… okay… but why did he rush to the office? How did he know you were there? Wouldn't he have searched everywhere for you or even come to your room first? No one came here. Why was he alerted about a break-in? Why not Azrael?"

He has a point, but…

"Things and regulations may have changed, my love. It must be to help Azrael with everything that's going on. Uncle cares dearly for us. Even with Azrael being the jerk he is, Uncle loves him."

"Yet he didn't ask you anything about your life there? Just wanted you out of the room and away from Azrael?" Kian asks. I frown, feeling my irritation grow.

"Kian, Malachi Araton is not whom you're implying, and I'd appreciate it if you'd stop," I say, not wanting to get angry at him.

"Morgana, I won't sugar-coat it. I don't trust him. Something about him is fucking off, and I am a very good judge of character."

"As am I! I am far older than you, Kian. I have known my uncle for decades, he is not a bad man!"

"Calm the fuck down. Don't get defensive, just give me an answer then. Doesn't it seem a tad too fucking weird?"

"Aren't you a tad too suspicious?" I shoot back, glaring at him.

His eyes flicker as he closes the gap between us. In a flash, he has me slammed up against the wall. I gasp at the impact, glaring into my man's eyes. Even when I'm angry, that desire for him courses through me.

"Do you want to be punished for being so disobedient, love?" He growls.

"Depends on the punishment…" I whisper.

A sense of Deja-Vu flashes in my mind as I stare into his eyes.

"It might be a good one… if you calm the fuck down and see my point…" he says, pressing his body against mine, his hands still pinning mine between our chests. I struggle, but he refuses to let go. "You may be older than me, Morgana, but I assure you I have been playing this game far longer…. When it comes to the game of power, lies, and deceit… I know how the mind works. I wouldn't trust your uncle, not until you penetrate that mind of his and see what's going on in there. If you find nothing, I will admit that I was wrong, but until then, I would advise that you withhold your judgment of him and proceed with caution."

His husky voice sends shivers of pleasure through me. He is being reasonable, but he's wrong about Uncle Malachi.

"Very well… and if you are wrong, then I will punish you," I say, a devious smile crossing my lips as an idea comes to my head.

"Something tells me your idea of punishing me is going to be fucking crap," he replies coldly.

"Not at all… it's rather fun, actually. You will let me do makeup on you. Red lipstick, glitter, and all." I giggle, imagining it. He frowns, clearly displeased.

"The only red lipstick I like on me is when it comes directly off these lips," he says, taking hold of my chin and rubbing his thumb along my plump lips. I wrap my mouth around his thumb, sucking on it sensually and making him growl quietly before I let go of it, my stomach fluttering.

"So… either way, do we have a deal?"

He is silent for a moment before he tilts his head.

"Fine… but if you're wrong… then be prepared for your punishment," he says, smirking as he lets go of me and takes his shirt off. Something tells me it will not be the usual spanks… my core knots. Is it wrong that I wouldn't mind losing to him all the time if I get to be punished?

"Won't you share what the punishment is?" I ask as I turn to undress for bed, too.

He steps closer to me, running his fingers between my ass cheeks, tugging on my thong slightly and making me bite down on my bottom lip. My breasts graze his bare chest. His lips meet my neck before he whispers in my ear.

"I'm going to fuck this ass," he says huskily, making my eyes widen and heat rush to my core, igniting that forbidden desire deep within me…

The following day, Kian once again lays low whilst I leave to talk to my brother. Blood had been sent to my room, but there's only one type I drink now, and that is my mate's, the handsome, god-like man who is everything a girl could dream of and more.

I pull on a sleeveless maroon, high-neck, crushed velvet dress which falls to the floor with slits down each side, paired with a small tiara and heels. I had decided I would visit my brother's quarters because I really want to see my nephew! With Azrael, he surely wouldn't even let me look at him. I look down at the pouch in my hand. It isn't much… but it's the first time that I'm meeting my nephew, so I won't come empty-handed.

The guards that flank the doors of the king's quarters don't look surprised to see me. It seems word has gotten around that I'm back. They bow to me, and I smile faintly.

"Let the queen know that I'm here," I state.

One of them nods and opens the door, telling the servant standing inside to pass the message. I wait patiently, and a few minutes later, I'm told to enter and follow the lady-in-waiting. I walk through the luxurious halls, picking up on the scent of my nephew instantly. It's strange, but since Kian had marked me, my sense of smell is a lot stronger, something I didn't even notice; it had just come to me.

"Morgana!" Anastasia's voice comes rushing out of the archway that leads to their personal lounge.

"Anastasia."

We weren't exactly close. After all, Azrael and I clashed a lot, and I was kept at a distance from his personal life. No doubt he didn't trust that I wouldn't tell Anastasia what a sleazebag he is.

I now hug my sister-in-law. She looks the same as ever; her hair is pinned into an elegant bun with a small crown upon her head, and she wears a deep plum-coloured dress.

"And she comes to cast her negativity upon my son." Azrael's voice follows.

Anastasia says nothing, giving me a small apologetic smile, but it isn't him I'm here for.

"Oh, he has enough negativity from you. I dare not add to that. What is his name?" I ask, walking beside Anastasia into the lounge.

"Remiel," Anastasia answers as I spot the child in my brother's hands.

My heart skips a beat. I make my way towards them, staring down at my gorgeous little nephew. He's beautiful. Emotions surge through me, and I reach out for him, not even reacting to the fact that Azrael is allowing me to hold him. He's so light! His deep red eyes stare up at me with curiosity.

"Remiel… he's beautiful," I whisper, taking a seat as I cradle the child to my chest, inhaling his full head of black hair. He's at least a few weeks old…

"Thank you," Anastasia says.

*I pray that you are not like your father and grow to be a king that your grandfather would be proud of.*

"Why did you come here unannounced?" Azrael asks after a while. I'm glad he allowed me a few moments with Remiel, who is currently holding my finger.

"I wanted to see him," I answer, easing my hand out of his grip and opening the pouch that I had been holding tightly in my other hand.

Instantly, Azrael takes Remiel from my hold, his hand closing around my neck. Anastasia gasps, but I simply look at Azrael. Never have I felt so disappointed... he really doesn't know me. Does he really think I'd hurt my nephew?

"It's a gift for the future king," I tell him, masking the pain that has wrapped around my heart.

He is about to snatch the pouch from my hand, but Anastasia's hand is enclosed around his, giving him a small nod. He looks at us both with disgust but retracts his hand.

"What gift can you give him?" He spits.

I look down at the pouch in my hand, slowly opening it and doing my best to mask the fact that I feel hurt from them. He will not get to me. I retract my hand, drawing out the pendant that had belonged to Kian, one that he'd had with him and had been in our luggage. I had asked if I could have it this morning after rummaging in our small selection of supplies to see what I could give to my nephew. The chain is made of platinum gold; in looks, it appears silver and is one of the most used and expensive materials for jewellery in Clair De Lune. The chain is long with a rectangular tag at the end. The front has the image of the moon and, below it, the symbol of Clair De Lune. Behind it are the words, 'A true king bends his knee for his people'.

"From the King and Queen of Clair De Lune," I say quietly, placing the chain on top of Remial's blanket. "You may hate him, but... please don't throw the gift out." I turn to Anastasia as I say this, and she gives a slight nod, taking her son from her husband.

"Thank you," she says. I stand up, kissing the baby on his soft cheek before she takes him away. I look at my brother, who looks disgusted.

"Shall we talk?" I ask coldly.

"Yes, let's. However, it is rather early, is it not? You know I am only at my office at nine."

"War does not wait for anyone."

"Yes, and I hate thinking about it," he grumbles, entering his office and sitting in his chair as if he owns the place.

Well, he does.

"Yet you willingly signed up for war."

"Don't pin this on me," he growls.

"I know, you say that you sent letters..."

"Yes, I did! Yet you all just attacked my men on the borders! Killed our messengers! I have the letter from the Alpha King himself. Maybe that will shut you up!" He growls.

My heart thumps. A letter from Kian? He opens his desk drawer and begins looking inside. A frown crosses his face, and his movements become more irritated.

"What the…"

I infiltrate his mind, flinching as the shrill sounds scream in my head before they vanish.

*…right here! Where the fuck is it! Did she take it?*

"What is it?" I ask.

So, he had indeed gotten a letter. Someone is playing us, and it has to be someone close to Azrael to get in here. He has guards outside the door constantly… Kian's words fill my mind once more, and I really hope he's wrong.

"It's not here! Did you take it?"

"Oh, for God's sake, Azrael! How could I have taken it? I'm sure you had your guards watching my room!" I hiss. He glares at me, but I know I was right. I need to get through to him, and for that, I need to control my anger. "Azrael, listen to me. We received a letter from you, you received one from us… don't you think there's something far too suspicious about that?"

"Oh, please, the only reason you want to be allies now is because you know the Fae and us combined can take you out."

"We can still win, don't underestimate us… but for the sake of our men who will ride to battle, think calmly. Someone is pulling the strings, and we are playing right into their hands by arguing. You don't want a war, right?"

He glares at me, but it's clear he is at least paying attention.

"Azrael… Kian or the werewolves did not kill Father - "

"Oh, please! Of course, you will say that since he marked you!" He spits, jumping to his feet. I glare back at him.

"No! I read his mind!" I shout. His eyes widen, and he looks confused. "What?"

"I have the ability to. Are my eyes not enough to tell you that? I have the gift of reading one's mind, and I assure you that Kian is not behind this. I feel… I mean, I even thought it was you at one point…"

"You…" He bursts into mocking laughter. "Oh, please, you are crazy."

"Shall I prove it?" I hiss through gritted teeth. Getting this fool to listen is trying my patience.

"Go on, what am I thinking?" He asks haughtily, pouring himself a glass of blood. Dickhead…

I hone in, past the barrier, speaking every word that he is thinking as he thinks them.

*She's a fool to even think that I'd believe this joke. What the... wait... how, how is she doing that? Can you really read my mind?*

"Yes, I can," I answer, making him collapse into his seat, looking stunned.

"So, you really have more Araton blood running within your veins than I..."

"You know that the second line has higher chances of having these abilities. The firstborn becomes king... the second becomes their strength." My words fade away as I realise what I had just said...

Kian's words rang in my head like an alarm bell. *"Eyes as dark as yours..."*

Fuck...

Just then, the door opens, and I know who had entered without even turning.

Uncle Malachi...

# HIS REAL FACE

MORGANA

"Ah, you two are here already, earlier than I thought. Now, what are we discussing?" He asks, coming over to the desk and smiling warmly.

"Morgana here - "

"I was saying how we should try to stop this war. Shall we have a drink first?" I interrupt, grabbing two more glasses and a fresh bottle of blood from Azrael's blood bar.

"Oh, I have had breakfast," Uncle says, smiling.

I do my best to keep my heart steady. A theory… our eyes are lighter the less we drink. What if someone wanted to keep their abilities a secret and, to do so, drank far less than they needed? My stomach flutters as I pour three glasses, making sure to fill Azrael's, too. He seems rather displeased that I had cut him off, but… if Uncle is the culprit, I do not need him to know of my abilities.

"You may have had your breakfast, but it's my first day back here, Uncle. Will you not drink for me?" I ask, looking into his eyes. He holds my gaze before simply smiling and nodding slowly. I pick up two glasses, handing him one, and look at Azrael, who is grumbling away.

"I don't have time to drink with you! I have things to attend to, we are moving for war soon enough!" He says, standing up. He downs the glass, giving me a glare with his eyes that don't change colour. Typical Azrael would never starve himself. In fact, I know if he had special abilities, he would make sure the entire kingdom had known of it. "You can tell Uncle all your crazy theories!"

"I will!" I retort, trying to act as normal as possible as Azrael storms from his office.

I smile at my uncle as we clink our glasses, both of us downing it in one go. It tastes nothing like Kian's. He has even ruined blood for me.

"That was pleasant," Uncle says, placing his glass down. My gaze stays trained on him, waiting for him to lift his head.

"It was," I agree, placing my glass down as well.

"So… when did you figure it out?" Uncle asks softly.

My heart races when he turns towards me. I stare into his eyes which are now a deep, dark red, mirroring my own.

"It hasn't been long," I admit, strangely calm as I stare at him. "You knowing I was here might have been the first alarm bell…"

Although that was something Kian pointed out, I was far too adamant that my uncle could never be so… it almost feels as if I am seeing him for the first time. How had I never noticed this before?

The screaming truth that's blaring in my head, telling me that he was responsible for my father's death, makes my heart clench. How could he? And then pretending to care for us, for me? I remember how loving and caring he always acted throughout our lives…

He smiles and nods, pouring himself another glass and picking it up. Although something tells me not to let him get his strength up… I don't move. I need to hear the truth from him.

"Why did you do it?" I ask quietly. "Father loved you." He smiles faintly, raising an eyebrow.

"You seem to have all the answers, Morgana. I'm sure you know."

Yes, I do; for power. The greed for the crown and the title of king.

"For power… but then… I'm surprised that Azrael is alive, considering you want the throne for yourself," I say calmly. Right now, I wish I had the ability to mind-link Kian. I just hope he can feel what I'm feeling through the bond because I might need him…

"Well… I didn't want an all-out war. Things have to be planned. With him as king, he will have to ride out to war, which will leave the throne clear for me to take."

"Wrong, you are third in line after Azrael!" I growl, my eyes flashing and my heart thundering at the very thought that my nephew may be targeted.

"You really are so innocent." Reaching over, he caresses my cheek. I smack his hand away, glaring at him.

"Don't touch me with those hands that murdered my family!" I hiss. How dare he kill both Kian's and my father! He will not get away with this.

"These hands have held yours, caressed your hair and cheeks for years... the hands of your uncle's have always been the same," he mocks.

"How could you?" I ask, disgusted. "Did you feel happy knowing that you took your own brother's life?"

"He never saw it coming. He was a lot like you, actually." Uncle smiles, sending a chill down my spine. "Impulsive, proud, full of love and compassion, yet so stupid that he was blinded by a few acts of kindness... I wouldn't have killed him if his stupid advisor hadn't started to get so suspicious of me... well, not that soon anyway."

The enchanter who had kept my truth masked... he was so powerful, though. How Uncle had even got the upper hand on him, I had no idea.

"How do you think I felt the moment he died? The little bastard princess had eyes as dark as my own? It angered me, looking into that wretched face of yours," he hisses, now looking at me with unmasked resentment. "I first thought you would make a good partner... someone who would side with me and trust in me, but you seemed to have a strong will to do the right thing. So, what better way than to target the fool Azrael and pit him against you?" My stomach churns at his words. He really did that?

"What exactly did you tell him?" I ask, focusing my abilities to look into his mind. I hit a blank wall, but at the same time, he doesn't seem to realise anything. My heart thunders, but I remain passive. Do his abilities give him the power to block his mind? Does he have the same ability as mine, or is it different? He knows more about my abilities than I do of his.

"Just fuelled his thoughts on how you were more loved, how your father only saw you, and how he was a failure... subtly, of course, but he drank it all up, thinking of you as someone who wants his throne. Poisoning the mind of someone who already feels threatened is a lot easier than one would think." He smiles at me, that same smile I grew up seeing. But now, all I can see is his reality, which still feels too hard to digest.

"So, I'm presuming you're the reason he hated my mother?" I ask quietly.

"Perhaps. Killing her was not hard either."

I feel as if I have been slapped across the face. He did that. He *did* that. My heart is thundering, and I feel as if my head is squeezing with the revelation.

"Why?" I whisper.

"She was far too smart for my liking and influenced your father a lot. He often took matters of state to her and listened to her. Now, we couldn't have that happening, could we?" My anger flares inside of me, and I clench my jaw. I need to hear it all.

"And the Alpha King?"

"Araqiel? He wanted to join ties with this kingdom, and my brother was a fool to agree. So… I decided to nip that in the bud before they threw water on my plans," he says icily. "What's wrong, Morgana? Does it hurt to know that your entire life was a lie?" He paces around me, yet I make sure to keep my eyes on him, turning as he does.

"No, just disgusted at what your aim is. It is clear you intercepted and manipulated the letter that Kian sent."

"Kian. So you are on a first-name basis…"

"Yes, perhaps," I say coldly. "You don't need to know." I'm glad I'm wearing a high-collared dress to hide my mark. If he wanted to hurt Kian, he could instantly kill me and end Kian, too. I can't risk that.

"So, you killed both the previous kings… instigated everything… made Azrael join the Fae…" I murmur. "You will pay for your crimes, Uncle."

His eyes flash dangerously, and I instantly raise my arm, raising a shield. I blink, realising he had disappeared. I spin around, sensing him behind me. What the- how?

I send a blast of power, spinning around, ready to deliver a kick, but he is gone once again. My leg connects with the ground. I turn as something hits the back of my head, and I manage to connect with his hip, sending him staggering back, but, once again, he vanishes. Teleportation? My heart is thundering as I look around the room.

Do I stay or find Kian?

Kian.

I run towards the door, only for Uncle to appear before me. A cruel smile takes hold of his face as he kicks me in the chest, sending me to the ground. I roll over, jump to my feet, and run at him, sending a blast of power at him. Once again, he vanishes before it reaches him, and suddenly I feel the coldness of a blade pressed to my neck. I freeze, knowing one wrong move and my head is gone.

Our hearts are pounding, and we are both breathing heavily as he leans in towards my ear. His breath in my ear makes me shudder inwardly.

"See? The abilities we have are far too different... I am and always will be superior."

I feel the power around me, and, in the last moment, I send a blast of power towards Azrael's collection of bottles, sending them shattering to the ground and praying someone hears. My eyes are trained on the door, yet the moment I see it open, everything shifts, and I am somewhere dark and cold. The blade slices into my neck, and I am thrown to the floor roughly.

I spin around. Nothing...

All I can see are the stone walls of a cavern with no entrance.

"No one will ever find you here..."

Those are the last words Uncle speaks before he vanishes, leaving me alone in a tomb where not even the rats can reach me...

# ᑕOR ᑕWO ᛕINGS

KIAN

$S$OMETHING IS WRONG. THE moment I feel her storm of emotions through the bond, I leave the room, grabbing some poison, antidotes, and a long sword from her collection. I follow her scent as my emotions fill me like a storm, not caring about the guards who start shouting and chasing me.

"I need to find Morgana!" I growl, ripping them off me as I let my nose lead me, trying to calm the worry and fear that grip me for her safety.

**Mate is in danger!** Thanatos thunders and I can feel him trying to come to the front.

I rush through the doors where her scent is strong, and several guards are gathered, clearly looking for something. Morgana's scent is strong here, as well as the overpowering smell of blood. I take in the scene before me; the entire floor is practically covered in blood mixed with shattered glass, and several guards are searching the room.

"What the… who are you?" One of them asks.

I raise the sword I had taken from Morgana's room, a silent warning to the ones who are trying to approach to stop in their tracks.

"I wouldn't come any fucking further if I were you," I growl. "I'm Kian Araqiel, and I want my mate."

"Mate?"

"Morgana! Her scent led me here. I felt something wasn't right. Where the fuck is your king?" I snap, my eyes blazing. Actually, I have no fucking time to waste. I'll find him myself! I run from the room, remembering the fucking asshole's scent.

"Alpha... she was in that room. We heard a crash, and she's gone... we don't know how they left," one of the dickheads following me explains. That's why I'm finding her fucking brother or uncle.

"What are you doing here?" The Vampire King's fucking irritating voice asks, and I stop in my tracks, grabbing him by his neck and slamming him against the wall, letting my aura surge around me.

*Where is she?* I growl.

"Who?"

"Morgana!" I hiss, feeling several knives at my back.

"She... she's with our uncle in the study! Now let me down!" Azrael hisses. I drop him, spinning around and knocking the weapons away.

"I went to the study. There's no one there. Something happened to her," I growl.

"Your Majesty, we heard the sound of crashing, but when we opened the door, both their highnesses, Malachi and Princess Morgana, were missing." Azrael seems to realise something as he presses his lips together.

"Speak nothing of what happened here to anyone. Tell the rest of the men not to spread the news of our... guest," he says, staring at me. "Guard your queen and prince with your life and allow no one, and I mean no one, to see them. Dismissed!" Once the men bow and walk off, he looks at me. "So... then... is it possible that Malachi is..." Well, at least he didn't see as much good in him as Morgana did.

"Yeah. As you know... we did not want war.... but it's clear your uncle had plans." I turn away. "I need to find her."

"To send me to my death..." Azrael murmurs, almost in shock, before the irritation settles in. "I will assist you in finding them!" His eyes are filled with anger. I glance at him, not bothering to wait for him as I let my senses and the pull of the mate bond guide me...

Twenty minutes have passed, and I am growing restless. Morgana's scent had just vanished, so we had switched to tracing Malachi's instead. It's futile; he is nowhere in fucking sight.

"Is there any place he may have gone?" I ask Azrael, who hadn't been of any fucking help.

"I don't even know how they left my study…" he admits.

"Just think of where they'd go, not fucking how," I say, feeling my restlessness growing. He frowns thoughtfully before he snaps his fingers.

"The tombs."

"The tombs?"

"We have some underground tombs… I was told by one of my pairs of 'eyes' that Uncle headed to the tombs at times…" Eyes? So he is a suspicious man. Guess he isn't a complete fool.

"Lead the way there," I order coldly. "So, you never trusted him?"

"I trust no one," he replies, leading the way deeper into the palace.

I don't trust him, either. He could be leading me to my death for all I know… yet… I have nothing else to hold on to but the fact that I should never have allowed Morgana to go out there alone. If anything happened to her, I'll never forgive myself.

My heart skips a beat, and the sudden feeling that she is close fills me. Thanatos begins pacing in my head. I'm trying to remain calm, but I can't deny the worry and fear that fill every inch of my mind that is threatening to explode.

"Why can't I smell you?" Azrael asks suddenly, his red eyes glinting suspiciously.

"I'm using a cloaking spray," I explain, frowning. "I think she's close…"

"How?"

"I can sense it."

"Mates…" he says with disdain.

We are heading lower, deep beneath the castle; it's getting colder, darker, and narrower. The damp and cold bite into my skin, reminding me of the icy temperatures outside. Azrael slows down when we reach a dead-end. I look at him sharply, yet he is observing the wall.

"I don't actually know the way in," he admits.

**Fucking stupid.**

I agree with Thanatos. I frown, stepping forward and staring at the wall…

"The old tongue…" I murmur, stepping back and staring at the cracks in the walls. "It's etched in the walls."

"I don't understand our ancient tongue, nor do I speak it," he replies.

"I do… I learned each of the seven tongues…" I murmur.

"The seven tongues? Do you mean you even understand the elven tongue and the languages of the dying race of dragons?" He asks, shocked.

"I may not be as old as you, but I assure you, I put my time to use."

"Hmph," he scoffs, clearly irritated.

"Slice your hand and smear it on the wall…" I say after a moment. I pray she is here…

He frowns, taking out a dagger and slicing his hand before rubbing his hands along the rocks. Nothing.

"What a waste! Clearly, you know - "

We feel the ground tremble slightly before a gold hue rushes through the cracks in the stone, and his blood spreads across it.

"What the…?"

"These tombs can only be opened by a royal," I explain, glancing at Azrael. How this man is related to Morgana is beyond me.

"Ah…" he says as we now stare down a dark corridor.

I don't wait, my heart thundering and Thanatos' encouragement that Morgana is near fuelling me as I rush ahead. However, we hit another wall, and once again, Azrael unlocks it. The moment the wall opens up, we are looking into a huge cavern. The smell of blood is mixed in with Morgana's intoxicating scent and the faintly familiar smell of her uncle.

"Kian?"

I see her get to her feet, my heart thundering as I close the gap between us and pull her into my arms. Sparks rush through us like electricity, and our hearts beat as one, fast, relieved, and fucking happy that we are united once again.

"Kian! Thank god!" She whispers, her arms tight around my neck.

"What happened?" I ask, kissing every part of her neck, shoulder, and face I can reach.

She takes a shaky breath, her eyes closed as she lets me kiss her, her grip on me tight before our lips meet in a desperate kiss that fuels my raw emotions. Fear… I had felt it, and now that she is here in my arms, I can breathe again.

"Finally, you found someone who can tame you," Azrael's remark makes her pull away slowly as the entrance behind him closes with a grating rumble.

"Yes, I have," she says softly, looking surprised to see him here. "You're here… Uncle... he killed both the kings of our kingdoms and my mother! He poisoned you against me!" Her heart is thumping as she looks around as if he may just appear. "He can teleport, he has an ability… I saw his eyes, Kian. They were like mine."

I frown, taking in what she said, when Azrael steps forward, anger clear on his face, but at the same time, I can tell he is putting all the pieces together.

"He truly wants me dead then. Teleportation… wait, my family!"

"He doesn't know Kian's here. If he returns, and he will, we can get him. Then he won't do anything to Anastasia or Remiel…" Morgana says. Her heart is thudding, and I know she, too, is worried about her brother's family.

"We move fast. I have a poison that will work well on vampires. The moment he comes close, Morgana… if you can inject him… I'm sure it will stop him from teleporting, and then I'll move in," I say, caressing her waist, glad she's fucking okay.

"We move in," Azrael corrects, his voice laced with fury and hatred.

I don't argue, knowing we can use all the fucking help we can get, especially if he can teleport. I just hope he doesn't realise we got here…

"How did you know your uncle came down here if he was teleporting in?" I ask, letting go of Morgana and looking at her brother as we both move away into the shadows.

"He would often come from the lower floors. Maybe that's why the rock looked so unused. I doubt he was using his blood to get in…"

"So it could be possible he can only teleport short distances?" I question.

"No fucking idea," Azrael says.

Morgana looks at me, and I know that this is our only chance. Our eyes meet, and I silently tell her it's going to be okay. To know that our fathers were killed by the same man… we were never enemies but one and the same, suffering due to the same man…

Tonight, Malachi Araton will die.

Time seems to pass slowly, although it is probably not even an hour before I see the man materialise in the centre of the room. He grabs Morgana, who had been sitting on the floor, yanking her up. My eyes flash; I know he'll sense us immediately, and hope that Morgana manages to inject him.

When it comes to her, it's fucking weird. I can rely on her, like I know she is my fucking equal, that we're a team, despite the strong urge to protect her…

A piercing roar of rage echoes in the tomb as Malachi stumbles to his knees. Perfect.

"What did you do?" He hisses as Morgana wrenches free.

Both Azrael and I move forward in a flash. Act fast. With the way he is… I don't trust that he'd try to teleport.

"No… what!" He sees us both, and anger fills his eyes. "You two…."

It's as if he isn't seeing us at all. His body begins to tremble as he frowns, and I know he is trying to teleport.

"You killed Father and tried to have me killed?" Azrael hisses.

"No, no… it's lies!" Malachi hisses as he gets to his feet, drawing a dagger and lunging at me. "They are here to kill you, Azrael!"

"Oh? So, you just happened to forget to mention your special abilities?"

Azrael deflects his hit, but Malachi is faster, kicking him away. Instantly I move in, bringing Morgana's sword up. I block his attacks, aiming a roundhouse kick at him. He stumbles back, and I spin around, punching him in the face. The sickening crack makes him hiss as I strike him with the sword down his chest.

"This is for every innocent soul you took, for every ounce of fucking pain you caused, my mate, and for the two kings who wanted peace," I hiss, plunging the sword straight into his chest. Blood splatters over me, but it causes me nothing but satisfaction. I wish I could torture him, but with the likes of him, ending it fast is best.

"And for our people," Morgana adds, quietly approaching us just as Malachi manages to push the sword from his chest, blood dripping from his hands from the blade. I give her the smallest nod, and she drives her hand into his back, ripping out his heart. His eyes widen in shock. No, he hadn't seen that coming.

"Mor…" He falls forward dead. I step back as the body hits the ground, kicking his face off my foot.

"Give me his heart," Azrael says, snatching it from Morgana's hand.

I raise an eyebrow as he bites into it, feeling a tad fucking disgusted. I know that tradition of the vampires; eating the hearts of their enemies is a sign of victory, not that he was the one to kill him… but I'd rather Morgana didn't eat it.

**Yes, let's keep Mate's mouth full with our tongue instead. The vampire can keep the heart,** Thanatos mutters.

For once, I fucking agree with him one hundred percent. Although I don't think he realises we literally rip people to shreds with our teeth… yeah, let's just fucking forget that fucking part. I look at Morgana. Even with splashes of blood across her hands and face, she still looks fucking beautiful.

We did it. Together.

I pull her into my arms, making her gasp, those sparks rushing through me as I claim her luscious lips in a deep kiss, one that she returns with equal passion…

# THE BEGINNING

MORGANA

NIGHT HAS FALLEN, AND Kian and I are seated with Azrael and Anastasia having dinner, although it is only Kian who has food considering how scarce it is in the kingdom. Kian looks at his plate of rabbit meat with some vegetables; compared to the food in the Clair De Lune kingdom, the three-course meal is very small. He doesn't comment on it and simply eats. I appreciate it. He already knows the situation of our people, and I know he would be willing to open trade negotiations.

We have, in fact, been discussing everything since Uncle's death. The truth is out, and luckily, both kings want peace despite their clear dislike of one another.

"You need to call this off. Tell the Fae you will not ride into battle," I say, very aware of Kian's strong arm brushing against my bare one and resisting the urge to shiver in pleasure.

"They aren't so easy to simply say no to, not when we have already made an agreement… one that Uncle kept advising me was the right thing, even when I asked him if he was concerned that you were in Clair De Lune."

"Anything to refuse to go to war, correct?" I ask haughtily.

"Yes, sister. I'm a king, made to sit upon my throne, not go to war and risk my neck," he snaps back, glaring at me. Kian's eyes flash as he glares at Azrael.

"Respect my queen," he says coldly, his power exuding from him despite his voice remaining low. Azrael simply frowns.

"If we pull out, they are far too powerful still... in fact, I fear they may turn on us..."

"Then join us. We aren't alone, even if you think we might be," Kian says. "We can win if it comes to that."

I watch Azrael frown thoughtfully, Anastasia silently watching him with concern clear on her face.

"The Onis Kingdom offers us nothing in supplies, yet... Clair De Lune does," she adds softly. Azrael simply looks at her with a displeased glare on his face. He isn't one who likes women to talk about matters of state, one of the reasons he never liked me.

"My men are already gone. They have joined the Fae's ranks already." His words send my heart into worry.

"Since when?" I ask sharply.

"Three nights ago." I exchange looks with Kian, who frowns thoughtfully.

"Then what will you do?" He asks Azrael. My brother sighs.

"I will ride with my battalion, and I will pull back my troops. I will not join in. That is all I can promise you," he says after a few moments, with finality in his voice. It isn't the best, but Azrael's cowardly behaviour is not one that will change. His pulling out is the best we could hope for. Kian nods as he drinks his wine.

"Very well, that is enough."

"How long will you be gone?" Anastasia asks Azrael.

"Not long, but I will return to you and Remiel. This kingdom will prosper," he promises confidently, drinking his glass of blood. I hope so because the people of the Sanguine Empire need it, and although he just expects things to fall into place, I hope he realises he needs to put work in, too...

"When are they planning to attack?" Kian asks.

"Oh, in three days' time. I was to set out soon."

"We ride at dawn," Kian says, his eyes shimmering gold as he stares ahead, his brow furrowed.

"We will win this."

I place my hand on top of his. This war is not going to be easy... but we shall come out of it victorious.

Two days have passed, and Kian and I have headed back, ready to meet our army and defend our kingdom. Word was sent ahead, and despite the coronation being delayed, everyone already sees me as queen.

We are now at camp, near our chosen location just beyond the borders, awaiting the Fae army. I know their scouts probably know we are at the Arch of Olen already, and our own men are ready for any movement or oddity.

Orrian has also arrived with his men and, to our surprise, is accompanied by an extra ten thousand men given by his father. The captains of the elven army, along with our own Beta and Deltas, spend most of the afternoon planning and setting up backup plans, going over everything repeatedly to make sure things are in place. In the late afternoon, we turn in to get some rest. I'm not able to sleep; I simply spoon against Kian's chest, knowing that even he is not asleep.

Night has now fallen, and I am in our tent. The flickering candles light the tent and cast shadows upon the walls. I look at my black tunic with gold trim and my chainmail made of the finest lightweight gold of Clair De Lune. The roaring wolf on the corner of the tunic makes my heart skip a beat. This is it.

Taking a deep breath, I braid my hair, tying it with a black hair tie before I slip on my black leather pants and shirt. I'm about to pick up my chainmail when I hear Kian enter the tent. He approaches me, wrapping his arms around me from behind.

"Are you sure you want to do this?" He asks as I close my eyes, leaning into him for a moment.

"We are one. Where you go, I follow," I state, picking up my arm guards.

"I know… surprisingly, it fucking shocks even me that I know you are fucking capable of this and that I'm fucking agreeing," he says, kissing my neck. I smile faintly.

"We both know I don't listen."

"That's true," he agrees softly before moving away and taking the arm guards from me, slipping them on for me and strapping them shut.

"This armour you got made for me is beautiful," I say softly.

"Well, unlike us wolves, you will be in human form." He quietly adjusts them and picks up my chain mail before putting it on over my head.

"It's beautiful," I repeat as he helps me put my tunic on. I look at the helmet; it is fully covered around the head and frames the face. A black fabric veil will cover my face, leaving only my eyes unmasked. "Will you be in wolf form, too?"

"Not to start with," he says, cupping my face. "I love you. If things get rough, I want you to promise me that you will fall back."

"It's war, my love. Things will get rough… but I know my carelessness can cost you your life, too, and for you, I will be careful," I promise softly.

He nods. I look down at him in his black tunic, similar to mine, and pants. His sword hangs at his belt and reaches his boots. He looks as handsome as ever, like the king he is. His head is raised in pride, power, and a strong belief in protecting his people. My king.

The sound of a howling wolf fills the air, and Kian's eyes flash.

"They're here," he said, making my stomach flutter.

I nod as he pulls me into his arms, cupping my face as he kisses me hard. His heart is beating fast, my own thumping as I kiss him back, trying to commit the feel of his lips to memory. He breaks away, brushing his thumb over my lips. It feels too short…

"I won't let anything happen to you," he says quietly, picking up my helmet and slipping it on.

"Be safe for me too…" I grip his shirt.

"I will be," he promises quietly, giving my hand a gentle squeeze.

"I love you, Kian," I whisper. Never have I felt so strongly for anyone. It's… immeasurable.

"I love you, too, sunshine."

He kisses my hands before he leads me out. A black stallion is waiting for me, and he helps me onto it. I am one of the rare ones who will be riding on horses from our kingdom.

The time has come. Kian and I exchange a final look before we make our way to the front of our army…

The wait for the first attack feels like forever, but it comes, just not in the form we expected. The Fae control the elements, and with the snow around us, the water elemental Fae take the front, manipulating it, yet we are ready.

The moment the first attack hits, Kian gives the signal motion for the first round of elven archers to shoot. The moment they fire and the first line of defence rushes forth to fight, chaos ensues. The sky is ablaze with different coloured surges of power. The narrow entrance makes it easier to cut the Fae down as they come, yet they make a blizzard roar to life, blasting us back. We hold our flanks.

I send blast after blast of my own force field at certain attackers, creating a shield where needed. Everyone has become split, although Reuban and three others of Kian's men flank me the best they can. I cut a Fae down, seeing Azrael in his red and black talking to a man in deep forest green just beyond the pass.

"What is the meaning of this?" The Fae's icy hissing voice comes in the distance. I frown. Is he the leader? I can't be sure…

I hone in, despite being so far, trying to hear what they are saying above the shouts, howls, and roaring of the blizzard.

"We will not be taking part in this battle…" Azrael says curtly.

"Do you think you can do that at the last moment?" The man hisses.

I block an attacking Fae, sending a rush of my power at them as their flames erupt in mid-air.

"I can't risk my men when they have the elves with them!" Azrael retorts, "You never said they had allies!"

"So, you wish to change sides?"

I slam a Fae aside, pulling at my reins and barely missing a ball of flames.

"Not at all. We will simply not be involved," Azrael says. "Move out!"

I glance at the man, feeling his rage as Azrael begins to call back his army. Without the vampires, the Faewill be weaker, and I am sure it will mess up their plans.

"We will remember this, King Azrael," the man hisses.

"As will I if you cause more problems," Azrael shoots back.

I block another two Fae, running one through with one of my two swords, swords that are laced with poison to weaken and target the Fae. I can't hear them anymore, but I hope that the Faewill do nothing to him because, right now, the vampires are among the Fae army. Attacking him would cause an internal battle on the other side of the arch. If Azrael wanted, they could do severe damage to the Fae army, yet it would cost them many lives, too. Azrael wouldn't risk that.

"Look out!" I hear Reuban shout just as my head snaps upwards to see Olen's Arch being targeted by the Fae. That was our plan… but looking around, I realise we are the ones closer to the arch. Shit!

My eyes fly open as I turn my horse to avoid it coming crashing down upon us. The Fae are using it against us. I watch as the blocks of ice come rushing towards us, crushing our people beneath it. I raise my hands at the last moment, trying to protect as many of our men as I can that are fighting below it…

Pain shoots up through my body, and I flinch, almost dropping my sword. What the…

My stomach twists as realisation strikes.

"Kian!" I gasp, trying to focus through the pain…

# Blood Ties

AZRAEL

*I*'M TURNING AWAY WHEN I hear Morgana shout. I look back sharply as I sit upon my horse, staring through Olen's Arch.

I know Morgana, no matter what she wears or if her face is covered. She always holds the grace and power of an Araton royal; the way she holds her swords, the way she fights, and the way she strikes down her enemies. She is one of the finest swordsmen of our kind.

She is doubled over, gripping her waist as she fights off a Fae. Jaylen, the dick I was talking to and one of the four Fae princes, raises his hand, motioning for them to storm through the arch that no longer stands where it once did.

Morgana…

"Your Majesty, we need to go!" One of my men calls out to me.

I hesitate, staring back through the arch. I turn away, my heart racing as a memory from long ago flashes in my mind.

*"Brother! Brother, look what I caught!"*

*I glared down at my little sister. She was almost ten now, and although she was still just a fledgling, her talents were beginning to show through.*

*"What is it, Morgana?" I asked, irritated.*

*I hated how everyone always compared her to me at that age. It was irritating.*

She smiled brightly, a smile far too innocent for this world, as she held up the butterfly she had caught.

"Useless. Go make more use of your time!" I scolded, walking away. She didn't reply, unphased, as she ran alongside me, letting the butterfly free.

"Brother, weren't you happy I caught a butterfly?" She asked, her large eyes full of sadness.

"No! It's stupid and useless! If you want to impress me, then go and learn to bear arms!" I stormed away, hating her irritating behaviour, but her vexing reply followed me,

"Oka,y brother! I'll become the best bearer of arms in the kingdom and make you proud!"

I pull at the reins of my horse as I break into a trot, putting distance between the Fae and me, but with each passing moment, my stomach knots uncomfortably, and my hesitation grows.

She may have forgotten it, but the child in her always strived to please me. She had once looked up to me… yet…

"Your Majesty, what is it?"

She had surpassed me without even realising it, and slowly, she stopped looking for approval from me. What approval was I to give when she was more admired in the court than I?

"Your Majesty?"

I frown, realising I have stopped moving. All my life, I've taken the easy way out… I knew I would never be known as the greatest king of our time… I never did anything to be remembered for… by anyone.

My brows knit together, and I stare at my gauntleted hands.

Then perhaps my sister may remember me…

"We turn!" I announce suddenly, looking up through the blizzard of snow that whips around us. My men stop, looking surprised, but to my utter shock, several of them smile and nod.

"We fight alongside our allies, Clair De Lune. You fight for your king, for your people, and for your princess, the queen of Clair De Lune! To war!"

As one, we all turn, raising our swords and galloping back down the hill, meeting the Fae army with a clash. I race through, slaying Fae as I go. My aim is not to reach the Fae but to reach Morgana.

She looks up, and her eyes showing through her veil are wide with shock. I smirk as I pull on my reins, bringing my horse to an abrupt stop in front of her.

"You really are too foolish, sister!" I scoff, "Can't even hold your own in battle."

MORGANA

My heart is hammering as the pain fades away. Kian had gotten injured, but Reuban told me he is okay.

I return to focusing on the throng of Fae attacking as I move west. The thickest of the Fae army is attacking the centre flank, which is led by Kian. I glance off into the distance, watching wolves fighting Fae. I can see Kian, the biggest of them all, his dark grey fur standing out as he tears through the army.

I cut down another Fae, glancing around my area. The Fae are still strong, and thanks to them bringing down Olen's Arch, the barrier between us is gone. I realise Reuban is the only one not shifting; I know it's to keep me in the loop since I don't have the mind link like the rest.

The most shocking thing is when Azrael comes galloping towards me, his army right behind him as they fight the Fae.

"You really are too foolish, sister! Can't even hold your own in battle," he mocks as he slices two Faes' heads off in one go, his black hair flicking in his eyes and the jewels in his crown-like helmet glittering.

My heart thrums as I stare at him, an influx of emotions hitting me, unable to comprehend what is happening. I simply smile. This is a miracle of the gods, yet I won't complain. With the vampire army on our side, we will surely win this.

The ground trembles, and my horse neighs in panic as large cracks begin tearing through the earth.

"Earth Fae! Abandon your horses!" Azrael shouts.

I jump off my horse, watching the animal fall into the bottomless pit. Unlike us, they aren't as lithe.

Blood. Screams. Loss.

In every direction, it's all I see; Fae clashing against vampire, elf and werewolf… there are no longer any flanks. The trembling earth beneath us is causing havoc and disruption. Everyone is fighting for their own survival.

"Luna, fall back, Alpha's orders!" Reuban shouts from somewhere far off.

"Okay!" I shout in return.

I'm about to turn when I feel a powerful aura behind me. My heart skips a beat, and I raise my hand just in time as the man I had seen Azrael talking to earlier sends a storm of ice shards at me. They hit my force field with such impact that I am thrown back, gasping as I fall and roll into the thick of the Fae. My back hits something hard, and pain lashes through it. Fuck...

"*Luna!*"

"I'm fine!" I shout. I don't need Kian to worry. I...

The trickle of blood down my back tells me my armour has been pierced. I groan as I roll onto all fours, realising I had fallen on some sort of axe that had been upended in the snow.

"The queen..." the Fae man murmurs, his platinum blond hair falling into his dangerous yet beautiful face. Shit... he knows who I am. "Kill the queen... kill the king," he says quietly. A small smile creeps across his face...

Fuck...

I get to my feet, but the pain in my back isn't helping. I can feel Kian's emotions, his panic and fear. I try to calm myself down, hoping he thinks I'm okay.

"Why do you hate us so much? What is your purpose behind this war?" I ask, readying myself and scanning the ground. I had dropped my swords somewhere, and I can't see them.

"The world is ours," he says, and with that, he sends a strong blast of shards of ice at me. I raise a force field, but his powers are far too strong. Fuck!

I'm forced back, and another Fae attacks from my left. I lose concentration, stumbling back just as my vision blurs slightly.

*Clair De Lune, the kingdom at the heart... the one with the most prosperity... claim it, and the world is yours...* I remember those words from long ago. So, it's all greed for more power....

I grab a discarded sword from a fallen Fae, blocking another attack as their leader advances.

"Long may his reign last," he whispers, mockingly raising a sword that looks as if it is made of pure ice.

"Jaylen!" Azrael shouts.

I take the moment to swing a kick at his ankles. I struggle to my feet as he jumps back. The Fae's eyes darken, the energy around him growing as he faces off with Azrael. I raise my sword, blocking another Fae who is trying to attack Azrael from behind. I glance around. I can see a few wolves, the odd elf, and one or two vampires, but we are a little too in the thick of the Fae, and the ground is far too unstable.

I spin around, turning my back towards Azrael's. Back to back... who would have thought that one day my childhood dream of fighting alongside him would come true? A dream I long gave up on as I grew up and our relationship changed so much. Unlike my fantasy of the glamour of war, the reality is different. There's nothing magical about it, survival and victory are all that is on my mind. We fight in sync despite never ever doing this before, but... he is the first man that I ever watched. I used to hide behind the pillars or up on the balcony watching him train... back when he was the brother I so admired. I had forgotten...

A smile graces my lips as I plunge my sword into a Fae, but he grabs the blade, yanking me forward. Tendrils of fire surge up the sword, wrapping around my arms and making me gasp as the flames burn my skin.

"Morgana!" Azrael shouts as I try to rip free futilely. Another Fae takes the chance to attack; I block with a blast of my power, but there are far too many...

"She will die, and, with her, the Alpha King!" Jaylen hisses, raising his hands as he sends another wave of thick, sharp ice shards towards me.

Kian... no! I...

I close my eyes, struggling to get out of the way, but it's pointless...

I flinch when the sound of the shards impaling flesh fills in my ears. But...

My eyes fly open as I stare at Azrael's back, five of them piercing through his body. He protected me...

"I may not be an ideal king, but I am still one of the finest swordsmen!" Azrael grunts, raising his sword as he plunges it straight into Jaylen's chest before pulling his sword free and killing the Fae. My heart is ringing in my ears as Azrael falls to his knees.

"Azrael!" I cry, dragging free and slicing off another Fae's head as I catch my brother before the shards go right through him. "You... why?"

"I don't know, myself," comes his haughty reply, making my heart clench.

"You cannot do this!" I shout, my voice breaking. "You hate me... so, why?" A broken sob leaves my lips as I slap his shoulder lightly. My hands tremble as I clutch his head. I half kneel, tears stinging my eyes.

"I know," he grunts, his breath heavy. He can't die unless... his heart has to be okay! I stare at the stake of ice that is embedded straight into his heart. My stomach twists.

"You..." Our eyes meet, and he reaches up, tugging my veil off. Sadness and regret are clear in his eyes.

"I was never a good brother, nor a good king or husband... tell Anastasia that I love her, and... raise my son to be a fine king, that at least the world knows the son of Azrael was a worthy man."

"Azrael, don't... I..."

I hate this. No, don't die. I don't like you, but you're still my brother. I still love you.

"You are strong, sister... and the world needs Morgana Araton more than Azrael Araton... I love you... as much as I hate you.... I do...."

His eyes flutter shut, and I don't even realise that the scream that pierces the sky is mine as I clutch his head to my chest. *Not like this, please not like this...*

He's gone. The passing of another of my family members... gone...

I close my eyes, and for a moment, everything is quiet. He died for me...

Anger surges inside of me, and I feel a wave of power flare inside. I slowly place his head down on the ground, picking up his sword.

"For our king," I hiss, knowing that every vampire here will follow me.

Those who are close turn, realising the loss of their king and looking to me, ready to fight and to die. I turn, my eyes blazing and my heart thumping with rage and sorrow as I raise my sword, ready to kill.

# RIVERS OF BLOOD

KIAN

**B**LOODSHED. IN EVERY DIRECTION, people are fighting. Bond after bond snaps as I lose men, knowing that with it, their mates will soon die, too.

I rip through a Fae. We are winning, but… we need to defeat the commanders, the four Fae princes, because we are still losing far too many. I'm battling one of them right now, growling as I rip his arm off before my claws sink into his body, tearing him to pieces. The sun is beginning to rise in the sky, and morning is close.

Pain suddenly shoots through my back, and my heart pounds.

**Morgana! Where is she? She's hurt!** I shout through the link to Reuban, trying to control the fear that fills me.

**I'm getting to her! Her brother's joined the battle, Alpha! He killed one of the four commanders! The Ice Prince!**

I'm shocked that he actually did… for Azrael to turn around, that is no small feat.

**I'm trying to get to her! She's back up! Her brother is -**
**Reuban? Reuban? Fuck! What is it!?**

**The Vampire King's dead, Alpha. He died shielding the Luna.** He sounds shocked. My stomach lurches.

Morgana. If her brother hadn't protected her… would I have lost her?

**Get her to me!** I growl. I had placed her at the arch, thinking the enemy was slightly thinner through there, but clearly, they had been able to break through in masses.

**Yes, Alpha!** Reuban replies just as I see Luca being thrown to the ground in his wolf form.

**Luca! Behind you!** I shout, but he isn't moving. Worry for my closest friend consumes me. I leap over the bodies of Fae, werewolves, and elves all mixed together. Dawn is approaching, yet the rivers of blood are still flowing.

I'm so close to Luca when a Fae drives their sword through him just as he shifts back. A vicious growl of rage leaves my mouth as I rip the Fae's head off, feeling another link snap within me…

Luca…

I shift back myself, looking down at the body of someone who has been important to me. Fuck… no! I drop to my knees, my heart thundering, feeling another few bonds snap away. Maybe it wasn't him, maybe -

**He's gone, Kian,** Thanatos says quietly as I stare at the lifeless body before me. No heartbeat…

"No… fuck…"

I take a deep breath, exhaling slowly as I stare into the eyes of someone I've considered my best friend. One who will never speak to me again…

I close his eyes, knowing I'll never see them again. There was no good-bye… fuck…

I get up, my eyes blazing as I assess the situation. Orrian had killed one of the princes, as had Azrael and I. Then there is one left. Where is he? I scan the area, my men keeping the Fae away as I realise that he may be in the back flanks. The fire Fae is the strongest of the four… the future king of the Fae…

I'm about to shift back into my wolf form, frowning as my attention is drawn to one of my men, who is fighting clumsily. Is he injured? He hasn't shifted at all, and unlike most of my warriors, he has remained in human form. From his build, it's clear he is young. Who the fuck is he? I can't pick up a scent. The smell of blood, dirt, and charred skin is strong in my nose.

"Fall back!" I growl. He's just going to die at this rate.

He doesn't respond, and I realise that through the battle, this boy has remained by my side. I frown, trying to focus on his scent, but… nothing.

From the corner of my eyes, I see another Fae rush towards me, and I turn, tearing them to pieces. Another four run towards me; I manage to kill two, grabbing another, but the fourth... I try to turn, sensing him coming from behind, when I hear a strangled gasp from behind me. I kill the Fae in my hold and spin around before his body even hits the ground.

That voice... I glance towards the boy in shock, seeing him stagger back, a stake of wood buried in his chest. In a flash, I tear the Fae's head off, turning to the warrior, who falls back and hits the floor. I bend down, pulling their helmet off, my heart thrumming as I look down at the full head of brown hair.

"Sage..."

Her eyes flutter open, tears trickling out of the corners of them.

"Kian," she whispers. I look down at the stake, wrapping my hand around it, but I know if I pull it out... she will still die...

"Sage... what the fuck are you doing here?" I ask, my heart thudding as guilt and worry fill me.

"I wanted to be by your side," she whispers, coughing up blood. Fuck. I'm the reason she's here...

"You aren't a warrior!" I growl. There's nothing I can do for her. She smiles weakly, tears streaming down her cheeks.

"If I was to die... I wanted it to be for you... I love you, Kian... I really do."

She gasps, her eyes widening and her body stiffening before she becomes limp, the light fading from her hazel eyes. I close my eyes, feeling the pain of her loss rip through me. I had promised her a life of happiness... and then took it away, making her give up her mate and, ultimately, her life...

I close her eyes and stand up, staring down at the woman before me. One more death...

I turn away, shift, and run towards the Fae. I need to find the fire prince. He is said to be the strongest of his brothers, the most powerful...

I keep going, knowing many of my men are following, and it's then that I see him. He is dressed in dark maroon that looks almost black, his arms crossed, and his flaming red hair in a high ponytail. His dark orange eyes meet my own, and a smirk crosses his lips.

"The Alpha King himself comes to me," he whispers, and without him even moving, a ball of flames rush towards me. I duck, rushing past and leaping over the other Fae. With a menacing growl, I try to reach him, but another blast of fire throws me back. "The werewolf race will fall," he says, advancing as he unsheathes the huge sword from his back.

I don't think so. I snarl in rage, expressing my opinion as I pad towards him, letting my aura roll off me. Our eyes lock as I lunge at him, blocking his hits. I try to rip his head off, but he's fast, moving with an agility that even his brother, whom I had killed, did not have. He's at another level. His eyes are fixed on me as we seem to dance around any proper attack. I'm fast enough to avoid his fire, yet his sword is dangerous, and the long length of it doesn't help.

He manages to throw me back. It frustrates me that I'm not able to get to him. The entire ground around us is burning with flames, burning the bodies of our dead as it spreads. I hiss when his sword slices into my left flank, wanting to wipe that smirk off his face. I jump, grabbing his sword in my teeth. As he summons his firepower, I feel a light foot on my back. Someone I recognise uses me as leverage, flipping above me just as I'm thrown back. My eyes widen as I see none other than Morgana spin in the air, a long sword in hand that she now raises, throwing it down at the Fae prince in the exact manner she had attacked me long ago. I feel the surge of power she put behind it, making sure it reaches her target in a flash.

It's almost as if it's in slow motion… watching the Fae prince smirk as I hit the floor, clearly not having noticed the figure above him. The large ball of flame comes blasting towards me just as Morgana's sword impales his neck, only seconds before she lands. Grabbing the hilt of her sword, she spins around, slicing his head off in one clean sweep. Her helmet is gone, her hair open, her face covered in blood, and those eyes of hers blazing as she turns to stare at me. The flames rise high around her, and the rising sun illuminates her from behind, making her look beyond beautiful. A true warrior queen…

My queen.

Our eyes meet, and she smiles victoriously.

We won.

# FOR WHOM WE LOVED

MORGANA

*W*E'VE WON!
A trumpet sounds, along with the howling of wolves ringing in the air. I know for miles around it will be heard, resounding our victory. The Fae seems to realise what has happened and begin to fall back.

Kian shifts back, motioning for our men who are chasing the Fae to stop, yet his eyes don't leave mine. My heart thumps seeing him completely fine… alive… we made it.

I know he's probably angry at the reckless move I pulled, but when Reuban had pulled me from the thick of the battle, I had shouted at him that I needed to go back. That was until I saw Kian's wolf in the midst of the fire. I rode on his back until I came to where Kian was fighting the final of the four commanders. The idea had come suddenly to me, and seeing the opportunity, I had gone for it.

"That was fucking crazy," he growls, his eyes flashing as my stomach flutters. "But…" I blush faintly, realising he is completely naked as he pulls me into his arms.

"But…?" I ask, my heart pounding as I hold on to him tightly.

"But fucking incredible. Just don't fucking do that again," he says huskily before his lips crash against mine, sending rivets of pleasure coursing through me.

I lock my arms around his neck, not caring that we are both covered in dirt and blood. The pain that I know are both feeling at the loss of our friends, family, and people remains, but right now, all I need is his touch to tell me it is all okay…

"We have won," he whispers against my lips. I smile softly, moving back as I stare into his eyes.

"We have."

He pulls away, looking around at our people. Vampires, elves, and werewolves are gathering. I see the two captains of the vampire armies, Orrian, Ajax, and Reuban. Where is Luca? I look at Kian questioningly as one of his men gives him some pants, and he shakes his head. My heart clenches. We lost him…

"As one… we defeated this enemy. In the process, we lost a king… a Beta… and many more. Each loss was not without cause. From this day forth, I promise that our kingdoms will always unite with yours. The Kingdom of Elandorr and the Sanguine Empire will always have Clair De Lune by their side. In hardship and when in need, we will be there for you. Today, victory was ours, yet it cost us greatly. Bury our dead, and burn the enemy!" He says. I turn to the sun that is now in the sky, putting the burning fire around us to shame.

We had done it.

Two weeks have passed since that day. We had lost many, including Luca, Corbin, and, to my surprise, even Sage. I know Kian will always feel guilty for her end, and I understand that. She truly loved him… and she had died for him…

And Azrael? I had gone to break the news to Anastasia… I will never forget the way she fell to her knees, crying for the loss of her beloved. I remained there by her side for two nights, promising to take care of my nephew, and to always be there for him. Azrael had died to save me. Despite his wrongs in life and his attitude, in the end, he had somewhat redeemed himself and did what was right. I will make sure Remiel becomes a king that both his father and mine will be proud of. Anastasia will remain queen and run the kingdom alongside the royal advisors until Remiel is old enough. I make sure to let Anastasia know that I will always be there for them when they need me.

When I had returned to Clair De Lune, we had my coronation with only the vital members of the council as witnesses, and I took my oath as Luna and queen. A celebration will take place, but not until things are settled and the mourning period is over.

I now look at Liana, who sits on her bed, her face pale. She looks lifeless. My heart clenches for her, for I know that she won't last long. It broke me to learn that she is pregnant. Kian's words from earlier ring in my ear. *"She won't last long after the baby is born."*

"How are you feeling, Liana?" Kian asks, sitting on the edge of her bed as he takes her limp hand in his own.

"Dead," her hollow reply answers as she stares past us out towards the window, unseeing.

"I know…" Kian says quietly. "The doctor said the baby is doing well…"

"An orphan," Liana whispers, now turning her gaze to Kian as I sit next to her pillow, wrapping my arms around her shoulders.

I know Luca's death has affected Kian, no matter how strong he acts. I can only imagine what Liana is going through. Just thinking of losing Kian makes my chest squeeze painfully.

Kian sighs, "It won't be an orphan; I will raise Luca's child as my own. I promise you that." He says quietly, "Your child will always have the love of parents." Tears start streaming down her cheeks, and she nods.

"Thank you…"

She knows she'll die soon. I, too, promise silently to always take care of this child.

Kian's gaze turns to mine, and I give him a small, sad smile as our eyes meet. Time doesn't heal everything, but it does make things easier…

KIAN

The aftermath is worse than the battle. Knowing how many we lost, how many more we will lose as they follow their mates… how many children will become orphans?

There is never enough strength to handle it all. Nothing is ever as planned. Even the battalions I had organised in hopes Morgana was at the safest point had thrown me fucking off, a mistake on my part, knowing that in war, anything can happen. The worry I had felt for her when I couldn't get to her had made me sick. Watching Luca die… everything…

Time… time would make it easier.

We have already begun trade with the Sanguine Empire. The food is so shockingly scarce there that I'm surprised they were even surviving, but it's clear Malachi Araton wanted to destroy their kingdom from the inside first before pretending to raise them to great heights.

It's evening now, and I'm heading to the cells to visit Cain. He had requested a meeting with me and so, I agreed. As for his mate, I have given her and their children a home. Cain will pay for his crimes, but his family is not part of that. I give the guards curt nods before walking through the cold halls until I reach his cell. He's sitting on the stone floor, but the moment he sees me, he stands up, grabbing the bars and rattling them before letting go as the silver burns him.

"Let me out!" He hisses.

"You wanted to see me. I hope you had a reason because this is the last time I'm going to bother to ever come here," I say coldly.

"You can't keep me here forever, Kian! I will not let this slide!" My eyes flash, and Thanatos' growl echoes in the cell as he fights to take over.

"You will respect your Alpha!" I growl, our voices overlaying one another's. Cain looks away, and I know, despite being an Alpha, Thanatos has an effect on him, even if it isn't absolute.

"You are here because of your mate and children. Otherwise, I would have killed you," I say coldly. "You will never be free, Cain. You will remain here until your last fucking day."

"No! *No!*" He shouts.

"We are done."

I don't care. If he has nothing to say, then I'm done. With those words, I turn and walk away. His shouting of promises to kill me and to ruin me follow, but that's all he can do. The weakest always bark the loudest…

I returned to my quarters feeling exhausted. The last two weeks have been hard. The few days Morgana had gone to the Sanguine Empire had been the worst. I vowed to never let her go anywhere without me ever again.

I enter my bedroom to see her in a black silk nightdress with criss-cross string back detailing. It reveals her smooth, creamy skin and those jutting shoulder blades as she sits on her vanity stool, braiding her hair, something I want to see her do every night… to return home every night to her.

She turns, a smile crossing her face as she looks at me. Her eyes instantly soften with concern as she approaches me, her hips swaying, and, fuck it, like always, she captures my attention. I shut the door, pulling my shirt off, too tired to do anything but simply want to hold my woman and sleep. She cups my face.

"Want to talk about it?" She asks softly. I snake my arms around her waist, pressing my forehead to hers and relishing the sparks that course through me.

"Can I just hold you?" I ask quietly. For once, Thanatos remains quiet, probably understanding how fucking drained I feel.

"When has my sexy hot chocolate ever asked?" She whispers seductively, making me fucking twitch.

"Good fucking point," I reply huskily.

I have no fucking idea how she can get me turned on, even with one fucking sentence, but she does. I groan, tangling my hand through her hair, not caring that I'm ruining the braid she had just done as I claim her lips in a passionate kiss.

She guides us to the bed, breaking away to move the blanket back. She pulls me down, resting her head on the cushions, and tugs me down until my head is resting on her arm. I slip my hand under the arch of her waist, curling my arms around her as I pull her flush against me until my head is buried in her breasts. She strokes my hair.

"Sleep, my love, it's been a tiring few weeks for you," she whispers softly.

"Hmm… I love you… you fucking know that, right?"

"I do," she replies softly. Leaning over, she turns the lamps off, plunging us into darkness as I inhale her scent, enjoying the closeness to her. "Kian… your journals, can I read them?"

My journals? My thoughts… scraps of paintings I've done… if anyone asked me a year ago if I'd ever let anyone read them. I would have scoffed, but Morgana? The answer is clear.

"Of course."

"Really?"

"They are spelled though. Only the keys around my neck can open them, and only if I give these keys to someone willingly," I reply.

"Damn, so even though I once wanted to read them… I wouldn't have been able to. You really are careful." I can hear the amusement in her voice. I raise an eyebrow and stare up at her.

"Care to fucking share?" I ask.

"Let's just say I've wanted to see what secrets you were hiding in those journals for a long time," she replies, kissing the top of my head.

"Yeah, well, if they were that easy to get into, they wouldn't just be lying around…" I murmur, raising an eyebrow before reaching up and tugging her down.

"I guess that's true," she frowns slightly, her gaze dipping to my lips as I smirk.

"Exactly."

I kiss her once more.

# HEAVEN & HELL

KIAN

THE FOLLOWING MORNING, I leave Morgana with my journals. Not something I want to do, but... she's mine, and if she wants to know my past, she has the fucking right to. I just don't want to be around before she discovers all my fucking secrets, especially my doubts and doodles.

I'm trying to remember everything I'd written when I freeze. Wait... I'm sure there are some passages about Sage. Fuck! Before I can even get up from my office chair, there is a knock on the door, and Kai steps inside.

"You called for me, Kian?" He asks.

I run my hand down my face, massaging my jaw. The chances she'd read those chapters are minimal... right? There are several journals. I better make this fucking quick.

"I did. Take a seat." I motion with a jerk of my head towards the seats opposite. "I know things have changed between us with time. Our priorities and decisions shaped our future, and it, in turn, made us take different paths... but you are a good person, Kai. Let's work on our bonds before it's too late." Kai nods.

"Thank you, Kian... I'm just grateful to get to be around. What you did for Cain's family speaks highly of the king you are, one that our parents would have been so proud of," he says with a smile.

"Tell me, Kai. What should a good king be? Feared, loved, just, or respected?" He seems uncertain about my question before he becomes thoughtful.

"A good king is loved and respected, a fair king is just and feared, but the best of kings is the one who puts his people before everything, the one willing to let go of everything as long as it means their safety. You should go to the capital city, Kian. People are singing praises of yours and Lady Morgana's deeds, your venture to Elandorr and the Sanguine Empire. You are not a good king, nor are you a fair king, but you are the greatest king we've ever had, and I'm proud of you," he says with a smile on his face. He is too innocent for this life, but his words still move something inside.

"Have you heard of that saying, behind every successful man is a great woman?"

"Yeah, like you and your Luna," Kai says. I shake my head, thinking of my little she-devil's smile.

**She's fucking gorgeous,** Thanatos adds.

I agree.

"No, not like Morgana and me because she isn't behind me. She is always right beside me. We are one and fucking equal," I say with pride. Kai grins.

"Damn, the sexist, arrogant Kian treating a woman as an equal. I'm surprised but proud," he says before realising what he had just said. "Sorry, that was uncalled for - "

"It's fine. In fact, you're not wrong. She changed me. We were like heaven and hell, clashing over everything. I hated her for who she is, not knowing it was what she is that I needed," I explain quietly. "Anyway, enough about me. The reason I called you here is because I've decided to make you my Beta." His eyes fly open, and he looks at me in complete shock.

"Me as Beta? But…"

"I trust you, Kai. I believe you can be the Beta my pack needs, this kingdom needs. Let's forget the past and start afresh," I offer quietly. He looks at me, hesitating for a moment before determination settles into his eyes, and he nods.

"I won't let you down."

"You won't, or I'll fucking have your head," I smirk as I stand up. He grins.

"I wouldn't have it any other way."

"We'll have a small initiation soon." I say, "Now I need to go do something."

He nods, and I leave my office, wondering how much Morgana has read…

**Serves you fucking right if she gets angry at you. I just hope she doesn't get angry at me, too, for your deeds!** Thanatos growls. **But I can take over if she's angry, and you can be on time out. Mate would like that.**

**You can carry on fucking wishing for that.**

MORGANA

I had spent the morning reading Kian's journals. It felt like an entirely new world. He paints! He paints, and I didn't even know how good he is until now. He has small pages slid in between his journal of things he's made. God, he is so talented. I can't deny he is good with those hands, whatever he does with them.

The recent one talked a lot about the worries he had for the kingdom, and there were several entries about me; the night he first saw me… it made me blush because, despite him not being much of a talker, he sure knows how to pen down a beautiful paragraph…

*… wanting to bend before her and treat her like the goddess she is. Her creamy, flawless skin was almost begging for me to leave my mark on every inch of her…*

The last entry is about him fearing his falling for me and how no other woman appealed to him any longer, that he needed and wanted me, and me alone. I love that I can really see his emotions in his words.

I open an older diary, beginning to skim through it. Ten minutes later, I'm annoyed. Some parts really piss me off.

*Another great night with Sage. I think she'll make a fine Luna. She keeps me satisfied and she isn't up in my face unless I want her to be. She's the type of woman I can picture as my queen.*

And then this,

*That Omega was fucking fine. Those breasts were fucking perfect, I think I'll add her to my favourites -*

My eyes blaze with irritation just as the door opens, and Kian stands there.

"I hate you!" I yell, throwing the journal at him. He ducks, and it narrowly misses him.

"Yeah, worst fucking mistake to give those to you," he admits as I jump off the bed and glare at him.

"Oh, yeah? That's your worst mistake? Not everything written in that? Well, you should go find your Omega with those perfect breasts, I don't want to see you." I frown, crossing my arms. He raises an eyebrow, picking up the journal.

"This is a few years old… and I'm sure we've made it clear that no one is on par with you," he says.

"Yeah, but reading that really pissed me off!" I snap, jealousy flaring inside of me. "You talking about having the perfect night with your ex isn't pleasant to read!"

"I wasn't talking about it… it was written, remember?"

He yanks me into his arms, and I hit his chest, struggling to free myself, but he refuses to let go, the sparks at his touch coursing through me.

"Let go of me, Kian!"

"Not until you calm the fuck down. It's my past, I'll get rid of that shit. You're the one who wanted to read them," he reminds me, looking around for something. I glare at him.

"Still irritating to read." I say, "I want to burn it all."

"Then go the fuck ahead. You are all I fucking want," he growls, his eyes flashing as he tilts my head up, crashing his lips against mine.

I gasp the moment his tongue assaults my mouth as his rough lips dominate the kiss. I pull away, despite the pleasure that consumes me. He walks over to the shelf, taking something off of it.

"What is that?" I ask as he holds something out to me. Matches.

"What does it look like? Burn it. It'll probably calm you the fuck down." I glare at him.

"I assure you I will burn it," I say, feeling extremely possessive of him. He's mine, and if there is one person he should call perfect, it's me, even if I'm not perfect!

"Go ahead," he repeats.

I frown as he kicks away the rug on the floor, leaving a large section free with only the journal that had pissed me off in the middle. I pout. Why do I feel like this is a trick?

"I'll do it," I threaten. He smirks.

"Do it then. I'm getting bored of this hesitation, sunshine. If you want to destroy it, get a fucking move on," his arrogant voice answers.

Frowning, I bend down, lifting the diary from the corner. I light a match, lighting the corner of the book and watching the flames eat the paper with speed. I glance up to watch Kian challengingly as he stands there, arms crossed. Unbothered. I drop it to the ground, staring at him. He smirks as I raise the match to my lips. I stick my tongue out and lick the flaming match, putting it out with a fizzle.

"Done," I say seductively, despite the challenge in my voice. I toss the match to the floor where the fire burns bright.

Kian's eyes are blazing gold as he closes the gap between us, pulling me close and slamming me up against the wall as his lips crash against mine. Pure carnal hunger rages through him, and I can feel it through the bond, mixing with my own desire to unleash my anger and lust in the way we both know best.

"You're fucking lethal, my beautiful little she-devil," he rasps, his voice mixed with Thanatos' as his lips press against mine roughly again.

I moan, loving the way he dominates me completely, his hands pinning my wrists against the wall, his hard-on pressing against my stomach. He breaks away from my lips, assaulting my neck with bruising, delicious kisses. His hands let go of my wrist, ripping my clothes off, not caring about the burning pile on the floor or the ash that floats in the air. I know even if we burn the entire room down, we wouldn't care. His hands squeeze my breasts, twisting and pinching the nipples.

"Kian…" I gasp the moment his fingers slam into my pussy.

"I owe you a punishment," he growls as I rip his shirt off, scraping my nails down his chest.

"Oh, fuck!" I moan, feeling pleasure rock my body as he curls his fingers inside of me.

"Like that, baby?" He asks huskily, his thumb rubbing my clit.

"Fuck, yes! Kian, that's it…" I whimper, my mind consumed by how good this feels. I twist my fingers into his tight curls, knowing it would hurt a little. But what's love and sex without a little pain?

"Fuck," he growls, delivering a sharp tap to my pussy. "Look at that pussy, all wet for me…"

I rip his pants off him completely, licking my lips at the sight of his cock that is standing to attention. Oh, fuck... I love everything about him. I bite my lip.

"Punish me then," I whisper, parting my legs, cupping my naked breasts, and sticking my tongue out before I lick my upper lip seductively.

His eyes blaze, his free hand wrapping around my neck and his lips crashing against mine in a mind-blowing kiss. I can feel my orgasm building, that knot inside me growing as the pleasure builds.

"Fuck, Kian... oh, baby, that's it!" I whimper loudly.

He speeds up, and I gasp. His fingers fuck me hard and fast. I scream out, feeling intense pleasure grow inside of me as my juice squirts everywhere, making him growl in approval as I drench his hand.

"That's my girl, fuck!"

I let out a loud moan as my orgasm rips through me and my entire body sizzles with euphoric pleasure, trembling from the jarring release. He doesn't give me time to recover. His lips are on my breathless ones for a moment before he pulls me towards the bed, one hand still massaging my pussy. He pushes me down onto the bed, his eyes on my breasts as they bounce. He pushes my legs apart and goes down on me.

"Kian, I…" I moan when his tongue begins licking up my juices. I feel extra sensitive, but it's perfect… fuck…

I throb, feeling my orgasm building once again, but this time, he pulls away from my clit, sucking on the corners of my inner thighs and making me gasp at the sting of pain and pleasure, knowing he has left a few hickeys.

"Now… time for that punishment," he murmurs. For a moment, I don't realise what he means until he walks off to his drawer, taking out a sealed tube of lube. "Ready for me to fuck that ass of yours, love?"

My eyes widen in shock as I look at that dangerously sexy smirk on his face. My eyes dip to his massive cock. Well, what's a punishment without fear? As much as I know this will hurt, even if he uses an entire bottle of lube, I also want it, the anticipation within me growing.

"Ready as can be," I murmur, rolling onto my stomach and wiggling my hips before squeezing my ass. "Fuck me hard, Alpha."

A growl rips from his throat, and I hear him flip the lid, squeezing some of the gel onto his hands.

"On your knees."

I oblige and I feel his finger rub between my ass cheeks, one hand parting them as his finger slowly penetrates me. I bite my lip, feeling the sharp pain. It isn't the first time he has used his fingers; he's definitely stretching me out and getting me ready for him.

"That's it, relax," he murmurs.

Despite how much I know he wants me, he is still taking it steady. Squeezing another dose of lube onto his fingers, he squeezes another finger into me, making me whimper.

"Fuck, that's it," I whisper, pleasure coursing through me.

His fingers move inside of me, relaxing me. It feels so good… I moan, as he works on readying me for him. Two fingers and his cock are two different things, and when he puts some more lube onto his dick, I bite my lip, relaxing my body for him.

"If you need me to stop, let me know," he growls, but I think we both know I'm not going to. I can take it. He was made for me, in every way.

The moment his mushroom tip presses against my entrance, I bite my lip, feeling the intense pleasure as he slowly rubs against my back entrance, pressing himself into me bit by bit.

"That's it, fuck, Kian…" I breathe, gripping the sheets tightly. It's intense. He's stretching me out, and I have to remember to breathe as he squeezes in.

"That's it. Look at this ass taking me so fucking good."

"Fuck, baby," I whimper as he slowly begins to move inside of me. *Breathe…*

His hands massage my ass as he slowly begins to fuck me, each thrust pushing into me a little bit more.

"Fuck, Kian! Oh, that's it," I whimper, gasping as he speeds up. "A little faster."

He listens, and I am soon moaning in pure pleasure mixed with the pain. The intensity of having him in my ass is so fucking strong and, although I know this is going to hurt afterwards, I don't care. I begin to meet his thrusts with my own, making him growl in approval.

He spanks my ass, making me throb harder. His groans of pleasure mixing with my own moans are so perfect. The smell of fire, ash, and sex in the air is all mingled. His hold on my hips is bruising as he fights to keep from ramming into me completely, despite me taking a good amount of him.

"Oh, fuck, I'm coming!"

I gasp, my eyes stinging with tears of pure ecstatic pleasure as my orgasm rips through my body, making me scream out. Dots appear in my vision as my entire body trembles. Kian lets out an animalistic growl as he shoots his load into me, making me moan as I collapse onto the bed on my stomach.

His body comes down on top of me, and I feel his dick slowly slide out of me as he rolls onto the bed next to me.

"You're bleeding," he murmurs, massaging my ass slowly.

"I'll heal," I say, turning over as I pull him against me and claim his lips in a deep kiss. "I love you."

"I love you more, Morgana," he says quietly, my name rolling off his tongue so perfectly as if it were made for him.

Actually, it was because I was made for him.

# Under the Stars

MORGANA

"Is it to your liking, my lady?" The Omega asks as I stare into the mirror at my reflection.

Tonight is the night of our official celebration. It has been two months since the war ended and things have changed for the better. Life is finally returning back to normal.

I'm dressed in a luxurious, rich, satin maroon-coloured dress. It's strapless with the bodice being sheer and lace work on the breast area. The satin skirt is fitted to the knees before it flares out with a trail. A thick lace embroidered border trims the entire trail, and around the hips is a wrapped, pleated layer of satin that trails the ground as an additional layer. My make-up is smoky on the eyes, and my skin is glowing with a soft shimmer that covers my entire body. My lips are coloured a deep matte maroon, and my nails are glittering gold. I wear a large diamond necklace and earring set. On my wrists, I have diamond bracelets on both arms and a few rings. My hair is volumized and styled into an extravagant, regal hairdo, ready for my crown to be set upon it.

"I love it," I say, smiling at her before admiring myself in the mirror. I look breathtaking.

The moment the heavy crown is placed upon my head, glittering under the lights, the Omega spritzes some fragrance on me before bowing her head to me. I stand to my full height, and two Omegas fix my skirt as I walk out of my room. Reuban, Ajax, and Kai stand there waiting to accompany me downstairs. They both look me over before Reuban lowers his head.

"You look breathtaking, My Queen."

"Thank you... is it okay if we stop somewhere before heading to the hall?" I ask hesitantly. Reuban raises his eyebrows curiously. "To the kitchens," I explain.

"My lady, I don't - "

"It's my choice," I say, waving my hand. Kai chuckles as Ajax mutters something along the lines of 'She won't listen.' I won't, indeed!

I glance at Kai, Kian's younger brother, the one who had apparently warned Kian about not trusting me.

"How is being Beta suiting you?" I ask.

"I'm doing my best," he says politely. I raise an eyebrow.

"You do know that Kian told me that you warned him about trusting me?" I ask, making the younger man gulp.

"Uh… I was only looking out for him; I do apologise for - " I smile.

"You really are different from your brother, so adorable!" I tease, patting his cheek, making him frown slightly. "I'm glad you did because it shows you cared. I've heard you're one of the best when it comes to training and have a good head on your shoulders. Perfect for the second in command. Just don't be scared to voice your opinion."

"Got it," he says, smiling. "You're a great queen, and perfect not only for Kian but for the kingdom."

"Thank you," I say quietly as we make our way down the stairs, my entourage following. I hope I am because even if I am a vampire, I love my people, the people of this pack and kingdom. This is my home, my kingdom.

"Do we really need to go to the kitchens?" Ajax asks. I cock a brow.

"Ye, because I want to see Andrei. He was the first one to be nice to me when I came here," I retort.

That seems to surprise him, but he nods, and we head towards the kitchens. Approaching it, I smile. The smell of cooking and the hustle and bustle reaches me before Kai even opens the door, reminding me of long ago when I was sent to work down here… oh, how long that was.

The kitchen falls silent as all eyes turn towards us. We are probably quite a sight, three big men flanking me and four Omegas fussing with my dress.

"Your Majesty! You shouldn't be here; the smell of the food will get onto your dress!" Andrei exclaims.

"It doesn't matter," I assure him as he hurries over.

"My, you look beautiful, Luna! How can I help you?" I look at him, smiling faintly, and reach out to take his hands in my own, much to his surprise.

"I wanted to say thank you. When I first came here, you were the first one who treated me well."

"You have already thanked me, my lady," he says, looking as emotional as I feel.

"I know... but this time, it's your queen thanking you. I won't ever forget that moment. You were the first one to teach me that werewolves are not beasts, and that there are those from within you who do have compassion. Thank you. " I swallow as I try to blink back my tears.

"My lady…" I step closer, hugging him tightly, much to his surprise.

"Thank you," I whisper as he pats my back, unsure of what to do.

"You are most welcome, but I don't want the king to kill me."

"He won't." I laugh. Our eyes meet, and we smile at each other. Exhaling sharply, I turn and look at the men who are watching us. Each one's face holds a mix of emotions, and Ajax is doing his best at hiding it. "Are we going to the hall, or are we planning on staying here all night?" I ask, leading the way.

"The king's already getting irritated that we haven't arrived," Reuban murmurs.

"Well, that's nothing new," I say as Kai chuckles.

It has been hours since I saw him, and I really want to see him, too. We reach the hall, and I take a deep breath as Kai steps ahead, and the Omegas slip away after I thank them.

"Here we go," Kai murmurs, pushing open the doors. The laughter, and the hustle and bustle instantly die down. The music is turned low as all attention goes to Kai. "Presenting Her Royal Majesty, Morgana Araqiel, Queen Luna of Clair De Lune!"

A low, dreamy song begins to play, and I steps into the light. A thousand lights from the glittering chandeliers above shine down upon me, and all eyes are on me as I slowly make my way down the steps, my eyes seeking out my king. My heart skips a beat when I see him standing there looking extremely handsome in a black tux. For the first time, I see a crown on his head, and it suits him well. My stomach knots as our eyes meet, and everyone else seems to fade away in that glamorous hall. My heart and his are the only sounds that I can hear. His scent stands out from all the expensive perfumes that fill the room.

His eyes slowly trail over me, glittering yellow seeping over his hazel ones, eyes that darken with desire and lust. He doesn't need to say anything to tell me what he thinks of how I look. I can feel it through the bond, my stomach fluttering at how intense his emotions are.

He is mine. My man, my love, my mate, and my king.

He holds his hand out to me, and I place my own in his. Sparks weave up my arm, rippling through my body, and my breath hitches as he raises my hand to his lips, kissing my knuckles softly as everyone in the room bows down to their king and queen…

The night has been magical. Not once does Kian leave my side; his hands constantly touching me, caressing my waist, brushing his knuckles down my bare arms and back, or resting on my behind. He kisses my shoulder, back, neck, and lips. His compliments don't fail, his eyes on me and me alone. Even when other single females approach to 'congratulate' us, it's clear their eyes are on *my* mate, but even then, Kian only bothers with me, and I know some of them may have been women he had slept with, but it's in the past. He's mine now.

The room is decorated in gold and red with the Clair De Lune roaring wolf on the black and gold banners hanging above. The large chandeliers glitter brightly, whilst candles and flowers decorate the entire hall. Food has been served in a luxurious seven-course meal, and alongside it, there is a bottle of blood that I know was from Kian the moment I taste it.

A few Vampires are in attendance, and a few elves, but Orrian did not come. I know that, although he said he is busy, seeing us together is hard for him. I understand that, but we were the past. Anastasia has come, along with my beautiful nephew. Everyone has been very welcoming of them, and blood had been served to them, too.

"I don't know how the fuck you managed to dance in that thing," Kian says when he leads me off the dance floor, his hand on my waist as I tilt my head.

"With ease, as you saw, my king," I tease. It's what I have called him all night. With that crown on that I know he doesn't like wearing, it's fun to tease him. I've adjusted it on purpose several times. He didn't complain, getting an eyeful of my breasts each time.

"Yeah, you're pretty incredible when it comes to moving, regardless of the way," he remarks, his eyes running over my body. "Remind me again why the fuck we're still here?"

"Because,e Alpha King Kian, we all wish to meet our beautiful quee,n too."

I turn, looking at one of the elder vampires who had accompanied Anastasia and Remiel, also, the royal advisor that was appointed to guide Anastasia. Azrael had fired him from his spot as co-advisor when he had become king, and I wondered if it was Uncle Malachi's doing or Azrael's own. Either way, we had decided he would be the ideal choice for royal advisor. Anastasia left a lot of decisions to me, and I did what I thought was best.

"Lord Mikael." I hold my hand out to him, and he kisses it.

"You look beautiful. I just want to say we are grateful for the remarkable hospitality you have shown us, Alpha Kian," Mikael says, smiling at us both.

"It's a pleasure to host our neighbours, and Morgana's home kingdom. You are always welcome here. I'm sure our treaty will be profitable for both of our kingdoms to flourish and grow," Kian says, his voice as strong and cold as ever, yet I can see beyond that to the man that my king is.

"Thank you, Your Majesty. We are already shocked at the level of produce that has been sent to our kingdom, without ever asking for payment…" He seems hesitant as he says this, clearly shocked as to why.

"I never gave any dowry, or anything in return for taking the most prized possession of the Sanguine Empire. Consider it a late wedding gift." He looks at me, and I smile slightly.

"Ah, but we all know our princess was always meant to be the Alpha King's possession," Mikael replies with a nod and a small smile.

"I would say she is far more than that, but yes… it all started there…" Kian says, taking hold of my chin. "No matter what you do, a queen will never be anything less than her birthright and destiny. She would even rise from the ashes of the very fire that tries to destroy her."

I raise an eyebrow, smiling faintly at the compliment that makes my stomach flutter. Once Mikael moves away, I nudge Kian.

"I couldn't agree more. I am Morgana Araqiel, Queen and Luna of Clair De Lune, and I would settle for nothing less," I tease, making Kian chuckle and pulling me against his hard, firm chest. I gasp, my heart skipping a beat thanks to his sexy chuckle that even makes a few who stand around us stare in our direction. I don't blame them; our king never laughs. Well, in public anyway.

"I never get bored of that line… although I like it a lot more now," he murmurs. I raise an eyebrow.

"Oh? Since perhaps, I don't know, my name changed?" I ask.

"Yes, obviously that," he says, making me think back to my Luna ceremony, which is like a marriage. We had signed our marriage papers that night.

"I agree… I love it, too," I whisper, placing my head on his shoulder. His arms tighten around me, and I close my eyes, inhaling his seductive scent. This is where I belong, where my home was, right here in his arms…

The party is finally dying down. The number of people I have greeted and talked to is countless. By the end of the night, it is all a big blur. Now, we are full of drinks and food, feeling giddy and light. The warmth of the inside of the venue had been a lot, and so Kian, Kai, Ajax, Reuban, and Oliver, both of whom have their mates by their sides, step outside. They are both nice; although they are still rather wary of me, they stay cordial and polite. I'm sure with time they'll open up.

Liana remains in her room, although I make the effort to visit her daily. She is but a shell, and has stopped talking or noticing anyone who comes in. It hurt knowing Luca and Corbin are gone from our little group, but perhaps one day we will reunite in the afterlife…

"Ah, I think I drank too much," Oliver says, patting his stomach.

"You did, baby," his mate whispers, stroking his abs.

"It's been a good night," Ajax remarks.

"I couldn't agree more," Reuban says, staring up at the starry sky. The full moon shines down upon us, the sky clear of any clouds.

"The weather is beautiful tonight," I whisper, my hand in Kian's as we walk side by side.

"It is, but nothing compared to you."

He quietly removes his crown as we come to an open area in one of the gardens. Two water fountains are gushing soothingly, and Kian is the first to drop onto the grass, tugging me onto his lap. I curl into him, my huge dress splayed around me as I lock my arms around his neck, kissing him. The rest sit down, too, some of them laying back as they stare at the sky.

Kian takes his jacket off, tossing it down next to his crown before unbuttoning his shirt cuffs, pushing his sleeves up, taking his bow tie off, and loosening his shirt buttons.

"I fucking hate smart wear," Kian growls.

"It looks good on you," Kai adds.

"I agree, you looked incredibly handsome," I say, biting my lip.

"Yeah? Well, I'm glad it's fucking over," Kian adds, kissing my neck. A comfortable silence falls over us as we enjoy the pleasant night.

"I've never felt so at peace," Oliver murmurs.

"I couldn't agree more. Clair De Lune is saf,.» Kian says with barely masked pride and happiness in his voice as he lays back on the grass, tugging me down on top of him.

The smell of fresh earth and flowers fills my nose as Kian snakes his arms tightly around my waist and begins peppering kisses over my collarbones and breast. My heart thrums, very aware that we aren't alone, yet it's clear no one cares. He freezes mid-kiss and moves back, frowning.

"What is it? Are you okay?" I ask, concerned. He nods, sitting up before pulling me up onto my knees. To my surprise, he places his face next to my stomach. "Kian…" He suddenly jerks back, his heart thudding as he stares up at me in shock. "You're scaring me…" I say, my own heart pounding, knowing that all eyes are on me.

"You're pregnant," he says, sounding awed and confused at the same time.

My heart seems to jump into my throat. I can't speak, my heart pounding wildly and my stomach fluttering nervously as I stare at Kian whose hands are stuck on my hips. His words resonate in my head.

Pregnant.

*God, am I pregnant?*

"Fuck…." he murmurs. "You're pregnant…"

"A pup, really?" Ajax asks, shocked.

"I don't get it, we were safe…" Kian says, staring at my stomach clearly, seeming not to care that we have an audience. I roll my eyes, laughing breathlessly. It doesn't feel real.

"Seriously? Since when has pulling out been one hundred percent effective?" I joke. The rest chuckle, and I smile at Kian, but I need to see his reaction. "Ready to become a father then?" I ask softly, staring into those hazel eyes of his. His heart is racing, as is my own.

"Congrats, guys, happy for you…" someone murmurs before I vaguely see them all slowly get up and leave, but I'm far too concerned about Kian's reaction. He runs his fingers over his head, slowly looking up into my eyes.

"Ready as I'll ever be… are you happy?" He asks quietly. I smile, taking his hand and placing it on my stomach before nodding.

"As happy as I'll ever be," I whisper.

"Then I'm fucking glad," he says, his heart thudding as our eyes meet, his hand still on my stomach. I lean down, claiming his lips in a passionate kiss before he wraps his arms around my waist and pulls me down on top of him as he lets his back hit the ground.

"That thing won't fucking fall off, will it?" He asks, glancing up at my crown.

"No, it's pinned in place." I laugh, staring into his eyes.

"Good, I don't need it poking a fucking eye out," he says as he rolls us so I lay on the grass and he is above me, bracing his weight on his hands.

"You really aren't a crown person."

"Definitely not… do you think it'll be a girl or boy?"

"I don't know… I don't care either way, as long as it's healthy," I say, my heart fluttering at the thought of our baby.

"I fucking agree with that… but… I don't know. I'd love a little Morgana," he says it so quietly that I almost didn't hear him. Smiling, I tug him down and claim his lips in another passionate kiss. This is my life, one I love with every ounce of my being…

That night, we lay under the stars, staring up at the beauty of the night and allowing sleep to overcome us, Kian's hand never leaving my stomach, promising me that we will always be there for one another, and I know we will be because although we are from two different kingdoms, two different races, and two very different individuals, we are one.

# &PILOGUE

## JUST OVER TEN YEARS LATER

KIAN

"Xendaya!" NIKO CALLS TO his younger sister. His hazel eyes are full of irritation as he glares at his sister. At ten, he is already a big strong boy. He has patience when it comes to his sisters, but Xen tests it often.

I turn, hearing her mischievous laughter. She is eight now, but she is her mother's replica. Despite Xendaya having hazel eyes and hair that falls in waves, she has the very same mischievous smile that her mother has, and she is always up to no good.

"I didn't take it!" She denies.

Lie.

"Daddy, Xenie did!" Morwenna states softly, blowing her hair out of her face. My little six-year-old petal, with her doe red eyes and soft black curls, she's the only one who is definitely a vampire, needing blood from birth, whilst the other two seem more wolf, but until their shift, we won't know.

"Xen, what did you take?" I ask, frowning as I put down my paintbrush.

"My dagger that King Orrian sent for me on my tenth birthday!" Niko almost growls. I raise an eyebrow.

"Well, if you don't have proof that I took it, then I don't have it," Xendaya says, shrugging dramatically.

"Oh?" Morgana's sensual voice comes, and I turn to look at her as she steps out into the sun. Dressed in a slinky deep pink top and black pants, she looks as gorgeous as the first fucking time I saw her… "Xendaya, return his dagger."

My fiery little angel, if you could call her one. She furrows her brow. I think we all fucking know not to mess with Morgana… but like myself, she loves to challenge her mother. I smirk, picking up my paintbrush and beginning to put Morgana into my picture, leaving the mother-daughter duo to deal with it.

Morwenna had wanted me to paint, and although she is supposed to be painting with me, she had gotten distracted by a squirrel. Pups…

**Our pups are perfect!** Thanatos says, growling in approval.

**Yeah,** I agree, glancing at Xendaya as Morgana talks to her, her scent reaching my nose as Xendaya glares at the ground.

**I made that one,** Thanatos says proudly. I raise an eyebrow. is he for fucking real?

**Carry on wishing. It was my dick that did the fucking job, and you can't even fucking be sure of that.** He always fucking annoys me.

**Yeah, but I use mini-Kian better.**

I block him off. Seriously?

I watch Xendaya hold out Niko's elven blade that she had hidden under her top before glaring at both Niko and Morgana, then stomping off to the far end of the garden. Morgana shakes her head, placing a soft kiss on Niko's forehead as he runs off inside and she approaches me. I push my chair back, pulling her into my lap and tugging her head down as I kiss those plush lips of hers. The familiar rush of sparks course through me as she slides her hand around my neck, deepening the kiss. Fuck, this is life, but she moves back far more quickly than I want, sliding out of my lap and into the chair that is slightly in the shade.

"I don't know how Xen stays in the sun for so long."

"She's a hybrid, I'm sure," I say, returning to my picture.

"What are you making?" Morgana asks, leaning over and giving me a view of those perfect breasts of hers, breasts that were wrapped around my dick just last night. I look away smoothly, trying to ignore the twitch in my pants at the memory of our hot night, and look at the painting.

"Just this scenery. The little petal wanted it, but she's run off," I explain, raising an eyebrow as I glance at her crouching beside the flower bed. Morgana smiles.

"I love it…" she says, looking at the image of the gardens, the kids, and the beginning of Morgana standing on those steps. "Where are you?"

"Right behind you," I say, making a stroke as I begin to paint myself behind her. She smiles softly, admiring my work.

More than a decade has passed since I met her, yet she has not aged a day. I can see the slight change in myself, but her, she's ageless, beautiful as ever and carved so perfectly that even the fucking gods would be jealous of her beauty. In fact, with each passing day, I think I am falling more and more in love with her, even when I think it isn't possible to love any deeper.

"I love it... you're so good at this," she says softly, her hand lingering on my thigh.

Painting, something I used to do long ago when I needed to get my mind off things. Something she made me bring out into the open. So what if I'm an Alpha or a king? I can have a hobby.

Well, there are plenty of painting sessions that I really, truly love, which consists of me painting her nude, although it often takes a few long sessions before a painting is complete. Seeing her with her legs spread apart as she touches herself is enough to make me cross the room and fuck her brains out. My fucking perfect muse.

A decade. That's how long it has been since the war. A lot has changed since then. We get enough water from the dam, and we are trading crops with the Sanguine Empire, making our kingdom grow wealthier. The Fae kingdom retreated. It's rumoured that the fire prince's son will take the throne when he comes of age, but apart from that, they raised their walls and once again keep to themselves. Since then, they have not caused any issues, although I often wonder if they are just biding their time, yet going against the three united kingdoms would be dangerous and suicide. Apart from that, there are rumours about a dragon king rising in the east, but we aren't sure how true those rumours are. After all, that race died out a long time ago.

Kai has found his mate, but surprisingly Ajax hasn't, to a point that we told him to take a chosen mate, but he refused. A life without your mate isn't a life worth living; it's empty, full of temporary emotions and pleasure that do nothing to fill the hole within your heart. The choice is his, though.

Cain remains in the cells to this day, yet he hasn't broken. His arrogance and threats come as strong as ever. His family stopped coming to see him, apart from his mate who visits him every week.

"Uncle."

I look up to see Lycus, Luca's son, come over. Liana had passed exactly seven minutes after the birth of her son. She hadn't even chosen a name yet; it was Morgana who named him and kept him by her side from the start. He calls her mother, despite addressing me as uncle. I treat him just how I treat Niko, and I love him just as much. Sometimes it is hard to see him, knowing with each passing year he resembles his father more and more.

"What is it?" I ask.

"Is it alright if Niko and I go to watch the warriors' sparring match?"

"Sure, just make sure you're back before evening. We are going out for dinner," I say. He smiles and nods, glancing at Morgana, who gives him a smile.

"See you later!" He quickly runs off. "*Niko*!"

"How time flies, they've grown so much. Tell me, Kian, where exactly are we going tonight?"

"Out for dinner, the six of us. I'm sure we can agree that we need a break."

"Definitely, I agree. Besides, the children will enjoy it. So, what restaurant?" Morgana ask. Her love of trying out different dishes is something that hasn't faded. Despite being a vampire, she sure loves to eat.

"You can choose, just… make sure you wear black," I say, my gaze running over her body.

"Under or on top?" She asks seductively.

"One layer. I expect you to wear nothing underneath," I say, ever so quietly, making her eyes darken as she presses those perfect thighs together.

"Daddy!" We both turn to see Morwenna come running over, holding a handful of flowers. "Look what I made for Mommy!"

"Nice, where's mine?" I ask. She pouts, ignoring me, and quickly hurries to Morgana.

"Those are beautiful, Mori," Morgana says, lifting her into her lap and kissing her head. Morwenna giggles and gives her bouquet to her mother.

"For you!"

"Thank you, baby," Morgana says, kissing her. Xendaya comes over and sits next to her mother, placing her head on her shoulder.

"So, can we go to that grill place near the river?" She asks her mom. So, she has her ears over here, as usual.

"Oh, I like that one!" Morgana agrees.

I sit back watching them, thinking not only had Morgana become a great queen, but she is also the best mother and mate one could ever hope for, and I'm fucking lucky that she's mine.

"Daddy, can we go to the grill house then?" Xendaya persists.

"Sure." I reach over and plant a kiss on her forehead.

My perfect family.

THE END

# Author's Note

Hello everyone, if you enjoyed this book, please feel free to check out my other books and if you can kindly leave a review on Amazon for me, it would mean a lot. Morgana and Kian were a fun couple to write and I am equally excited to write about their daughter Xendaya in the second book in the trilogy, which will be titled: The Dragon King's Seduction.

# MOONLIGHT MUSE'S WORKS

**THE RUTHLESS KINGS TRILOGY**
Book 1 – The Alpha King's Possession
Book 2 – The Dragon King's Seduction (Coming soon)

**THE ALPHA SERIES (AVAILABLE ON KINDLE& PRINT)**
Book 1 – Her Forbidden Alpha
Book 2 – Her Cold-Hearted Alpha
Book 3 – Her Destined Alpha
Book 4 – Caged between the Beta & Alpha
Book 5 – King Alejandro: The Return of Her Cold-Hearted Alpha

**THE ROSSI LEGACIES (SPIN-OFF SERIES TO THE ALPHA SERIES)**
Book 1 – Alpha Leo and the Heart of Fire (Coming to Kindle soon)
Book 2 - Leo Rossi: The Rise of a True Alpha (Coming to Kindle soon)
Book 3 – The Lycan Princess and the Temptation of Sin (GoodNovel App)
Book 4 – Skyla Rossi: A Game of Deception and Lies (Goodnovel App)

**THE UNTOLD TALES OF THE ALPHA AND LEGACIES SERIES**
*A collection of short novellas.*
Book 1 – Beautiful Bond (Coming to Kindle soon)
Book 2 – Precious Bond (Coming to Kindle soon)

**MAGIC OF KAELADIA SERIES**
Book 1 – My Alpha's Betrayal: Burning in the Flames of his Vengeance
(Available on Kindleb & Print)
Book 2 – My Alpha's Retribution: Rising from the Ashes of his Vengeance
(Available on Kindle & Print)

**STANDALONES**
His Caged Princess (Available on Kindle & Print)
Mr. CEO, Please Marry My Mommy (Available on Goodnovel App)

## SOCIAL MEDIA PLATFORMS

| | |
|---|---|
| **Amazon Page** | https://www.amazon.com/stores/ Moonlight-Muse/author/BOBICKZFHQ |
| **Website** | https://authormoonlightmuse.com/ |
| **Linktree** | https://linktr.ee/Author.Muse |
| **Instagram** | https://www.instagram.com/author.muse/ |
| **Facebook** | https://www.facebook.com/author.moonlight.muse |

# SUPPORTING OTHER AUTHORS:

### JESSICA HALL
*Fated to the Alpha Series* (Kindle & Print)
Along with this bestselling series, Jessica Hall has a large collection of incredible books! Many which are available on Kindle.

### CASSANDRA M
*He's My Alpha* (Print)
Cassandra has several other intriguing novels on Goodnovel App, definitely check them out!